The
Beauty Queen
of Jerusalem

The
Beauty Queen
of Jerusalem

SARIT YISHAI-LEVI

Translated from the Hebrew by Anthony Berris

THOMAS DUNNE BOOKS   ST. MARTIN'S PRESS   NEW YORK

THOMAS DUNNE BOOKS.

An imprint of St. Martin's Press.

THE BEAUTY QUEEN OF JERUSALEM. Original text copyright © 2013 by Sarit Yishai- Levi and Modan Publishing House Ltd. English translation copyright © 2016 by Anthony Berris. All rights re-served. For information, address St. Martin's Press, 175 Fifth Avenue, New York, N.Y. 10010.

Published by arrangement with the Institute for the Translation of Hebrew Literature.

www.thomasdunnebooks.com
www.stmartins.com

Designed by Steven Seighman

The Library of Congress Cataloging-in-Publication Data is available upon request.

ISBN 978-1-250-07816-2 (hardcover)
ISBN 978-1-4668-9050-3 (e-book)

Our books may be purchased in bulk for promotional, educational, or business use. Please contact your local bookseller or the Macmillan Corporate and Premium Sales Department at 1-800-221-7945, extension 5442, or by e-mail at MacmillanSpecialMarkets@macmillan.com.

Originaly published in Israel in 2013 by Modan Publishing House Ltd.

First U.S. Edition: April 2016

P1

To my parents

The
Beauty Queen
of Jerusalem

1

My mother Luna passed away shortly before my eighteenth birthday. A year earlier, while the whole family was sitting around the table for lunch as usual, and she was serving her famous sofrito with peas and white rice, she sat down on her chair and said, *"Dio santo,* I can't feel my leg."

Father ignored her and went on reading the paper and eating. My little brother Ronny laughed and shook Mother's leg under the table. "Mother's got a leg like a doll's!"

"It's not funny," my mother said angrily. "I can't feel my foot on the floor."

Father and I continued eating.

"Por Dio, David, I can't stand on my leg," she repeated. "It's not doing what I tell it."

Now she was on the verge of hysteria. Father finally stopped eating and took his head out of the paper.

"Try and stand up," he said. Mother was unsteady on her feet and held on to the corner of the table.

"We should get you to the doctor's," Father said.

But the minute they walked out the door, Mother's leg did as it was told, and she could feel it again as if nothing had happened.

"See? It's nothing," said Father. "You're being dramatic as usual."

"Yes, right. *I'm* dramatic," Mother replied. "If it had happened to you, people would have heard the ambulance siren from here to Katamon."

The episode passed as if it had never happened. Mother would recount it over and over to Rachelika and Becky and anyone else who was prepared to listen, and Father would lose his temper and say, "Enough! How many times do we have to hear the story about your marionette leg?"

Then the second incident occurred. Mother came home from the grocery, and just as she was about to walk inside, she fell and lost consciousness. This time an ambulance was called and Mother was rushed to Bikur Holim Hospital. She couldn't stand or walk and was diagnosed with cancer. That was when Mother began to stop talking, especially to Father. He'd try to engage her and she just wouldn't answer. Her sisters, Rachelika and Becky, neglected their families so they could sit with her almost around the clock. Despite their pleading, she refused to leave the house, ashamed that people would see her, Luna, the woman who had the most beautiful legs in Jerusalem, in a wheelchair.

As much as I hardened my heart at the time, it was distressing to see Rachelika peeling an orange for Mother, begging her to eat her favorite fruit, and Becky gently painting Mother's nails with red polish, for even then, when she was so sick and weak, she was still meticulous about her manicure and pedicure. Rachelika and Becky both did their utmost to behave naturally, as if nothing terrible was happening, and chattered away, "yackety-yak like a couple of hens," as my grandmother Nona Rosa used to say. Only Luna, the biggest chatterbox of all, remained silent.

At night one of them would stay over to sleep with Mother, who now occupied the living room sofa's pullout bed, encircled with dining chairs to prevent her from falling off. All of Father's pleas that she sleep in their bedroom and he in the living room fell on deaf ears.

"She says she can't breathe in the bedroom," Rachelika told Father. "At least *you* can get a proper night's sleep so you'll have the strength to look after the children."

But my little brother Ronny and I didn't need Father to look after us. We both took advantage of the fact that everyone was preoccupied with Mother and gave ourselves the freedom to roam. Ronny preferred the company of boys his age and spent whole days in their houses, and many nights as well, while I spent my time with Amnon, my boyfriend. Amnon's parents had a bookshop at the center of town and his sister was married, so their big house on Hamaalot Street was ours for the taking. Had my father known what we were up to, he would have beaten Amnon to a pulp and sent me to live on a kibbutz.

After her diagnosis, Mother no longer called me a "street girl" or threatened to tell my father when I got home late. She wouldn't even look at me, but just sat in her wheelchair staring into space or whispering with one of her sisters. Father would make dinner, and he too wouldn't ask me any questions or show interest in what I was doing. It seemed they all preferred that I spend as little time as possible at home so I wouldn't annoy Mother, God forbid, who even when in her wheelchair didn't get good behavior from me.

One afternoon when I was about to leave the house to meet Amnon, Rachelika stopped me.

"I have to stop home," she said, "so stay with your mother until Becky gets here."

"But I have a test! I have to go to my friend's to study."

"Ask your friend to come here."

"No!" My mother's voice, hardly ever heard in those days, made us jump. "You're not asking anyone to come here. If you want to go, go. I don't need you to stay here and look after me."

"Luna," said Rachelika, "you can't stay here on your own."

"I don't need Gabriela to hold my hand. I don't need her to look after me or you to look after me or Becky to look after me or the devil to look after me. I don't need anything, just leave me be!"

"Don't get angry, Luna. It's been two days since I saw Moise and the children. I have to go check in."

"Go wherever you want," my mother replied and withdrew into herself again.

"God forgive us," Rachelika said, wringing her hands. I'd never seen my aunt in such despair, but she quickly regained her composure. "You're staying here with your mother!" she ordered me. "I'm going home for a few minutes and I'll be right back. And don't you dare leave her for one second."

She turned and went, leaving me alone with my mother. You could have cut the air with a knife. My mother sitting in her wheelchair, her face sour and angry, and me standing in the middle of the living room like an idiot. At that moment I would have done anything just not to be alone with her.

"I'm going to my room to study," I said. "I'll leave the door open. Call me if you need anything."

"Sit down," my mother said.

I paused, caught off guard by her request.

"I want to ask you for something."

I tensed. My mother never asked me for anything. She only ever told me what to do.

"I want to ask you not to bring your friends here. I don't want any strangers in the house until I die."

"Until you die?" I was so alarmed that the only way I could deflect what she'd said was to respond with words that even I couldn't believe. "You'll bury us all."

"Don't worry, Gabriela. It will be you who buries me," she said quietly.

The room felt too small for the both of us.

"Mother, you should be thanking God. There are people who get cancer and die right away. God loves you. You can talk, you can see, you're alive."

"You call this living?" My mother snorted. "My enemies should live like this. It's a living death."

"You're the one who's choosing to live like this," I retorted. "If you wanted to, you could get dressed, put on makeup, and go out."

"Yes, right," she said. "Go out in a wheelchair."

"Your friend the redhead, the one who was in the hospital with you during the war, he was in a wheelchair, and I don't remember him not leaving the house, and I remember he was always smiling."

My mother looked at me incredulously. "You remember him?" she asked softly.

"Of course I do. He used to sit me on his knee and spin us in his wheelchair like the bumper cars at the Luna Park."

"The Luna Park," Mother murmured. "The ghost train." She suddenly burst into tears and with her hand signaled that I should go.

I took to my heels. The almost intimate conversation we'd had was too much for me to take. It was the closest we'd come to having a mother-daughter talk, and it too ended in tears.

My mother wept in waves that rose and fell, and in my room I shut my ears with my hands. I couldn't bear the sound of her despair. Years later I'd regret that moment. Instead of my heart opening, it closed up tight. Instead of taking her in my arms and comforting her, I lay on the cold floor of my room, hands over my ears, and uttered a silent cry to God: Shut her up, God. Please shut her up.

And God foolishly heard me and shut her up. That night the ambulance siren wailed and its brakes screeched outside our house. Four brawny men climbed the fifty-four stairs to the top floor of our apartment building, laid my mother on a stretcher, and rushed her to the hospital. On the operating table the surgeons discovered to their horror that my mother's body was completely ravaged inside.

"It's all over," my father told me. "There's nothing the doctors can do. Your mother's going to die."

Many years after her death, when I found room in my heart for my mother, my Aunt Rachelika told me the secret of her suffering, the never-receding pain. But by then it was already too late to fix what had been broken between us.

I'm a woman of autumn, of yellowed falling leaves. I was born at its back door, two steps before winter.

As a child I'd eagerly await the first rain and the blossoming of the squills. I'd run to the fields, roll in the damp grass, press my face to the soil, and inhale the smell of rain. I'd collect tortoises and stroke their hard shells with my slender fingers, save wagtails' nests that had fallen from trees, pick autumn saffron and crocuses, and follow the snails that populated the fields.

I'd disappear for hours, and Mother, who was sure I was at Nono and Nona's, never came looking for me. When I'd get home with damp soil stuck to my clothes and a frightened tortoise in my hands, she'd glare at me with her green eyes and say in a whisper that felt as harsh as a slap, "So different from everyone else. How? How did I have a child like you?"

I too didn't know how she'd had a child like me. She was so thin and fragile, always dressed in well-cut suits that showed off her slim waist, with high heels like those in the magazines at the seamstress, who'd make all my mother's clothes according to Hollywood fashion.

There was a time when Mother would sew identical dresses for herself and me, from the same cloth and in the same cut. She'd dress me, warn me over and over not to get dirty, tie a matching ribbon in my red curls, clean my patent leather shoes with spit, and hand in hand we'd go to Café Atara near our house on Ben-Yehuda Street. But after I dirtied the dresses time after time, didn't show them the proper respect, she stopped.

"What kind of a girl are you? A *horani*, a primitive. You'll never be a lady. Sometimes I think you were born in the Kurdish neighborhood!" she'd say, and that was the most terrible thing she could have said, because my mother despised the Kurds.

I could never understand why Mother hated the Kurds. Even Nona Rosa didn't hate them, certainly not in the way she hated the English. I never heard her say, "May the name of the Kurds be erased." But whenever there was mention of the English who were in Israel before I was born, she'd always add, "May the name of the Ingelish be erased." It was well known that Nona Rosa hated the English from the time of the Mandate, ever since her little brother Ephraim disappeared and went in hiding for years as a member of the Lehi underground organization. My mother, on the other hand, had nothing against the English. On the contrary, on numerous occasions I heard her say it was a pity they'd left the country: "If the English had stayed, then maybe the Kurds wouldn't have come."

I actually liked the Kurds a lot, especially the Barazani family who lived in the other half of Nono and Nona's house after our family's financial situation forced my grandparents to move into the Kurd neighborhood. The two yards were separated only by a thin fence, and once a week Mrs. Barazani would light a fire in the yard and bake a tasty pastry with bubbling cheese inside it. And before the day my mother, with threats of a beating, forbade me to go anywhere near the Barazanis' side, I'd wait for the moment when "the Kurdia," as Nona called her, invited me to sit on the floor by the tabun and enjoy the heavenly pastry.

Mr. Barazani would wear a big dress—"like the Arabs in the Old City," my mother would say—and a rolled-up kerchief on his head, sitting me on his knee as he laughed with his toothless mouth and talked to me in a language I didn't understand.

"*Papukata*, where did your mother buy you, the Mahane Yehuda Market?" Mrs. Barazani would laugh. "Because it's impossible that you and she are related."

It was only years later that my Aunt Becky told me that our family had a long score to settle with the Kurds.

My Aunt Becky was Nono and Nona Ermosa's youngest daughter, and she loved me as if I were her little sister. She looked after me and spent far more time with me than my mother did. I was also her alibi when she went to meet her boyfriend, Handsome Eli Cohen, who was as good-looking as Alain Delon. Every afternoon Handsome Eli Cohen would pull up on his shiny black motorbike and whistle. Aunt Becky would go out into the yard, dragging me after her, and shout to Nona Rosa, "I'm taking Gabriela to the playground." And before Nona had a chance to answer, we'd already be on the bike, me pressed between Becky and Handsome Eli Cohen. We'd drive along Agrippas

Street to King George Street, and as we passed the modest building opposite the Tzilla perfumery, where my mother bought perfume and lipstick, Becky would always say, "There's our Knesset." Once we even saw Ben-Gurion leave our Knesset and walk toward Hillel Street, and Handsome Eli Cohen drove after him on his motorbike until we saw him enter the Eden Hotel. "There," Becky told me, "is where he sleeps when he's in our Knesset, in our Jerusalem."

At the city park, they'd send me off to play on the swings or slide and they'd kiss until it was almost dark. Only then, when the park emptied of children and mothers and I was the only one left in the sandbox, Handsome Eli Cohen would drive us back to Nono and Nona Ermosa's. Mother, who'd come to collect me, would yell at Aunt Becky, "Where the hell have you been with the child? I've been looking for you all over Jerusalem!" And Becky would reply, "If you'd take her to the playground yourself instead of sitting in Café Atara all day, then maybe I'd be able to study for the exam I have tomorrow, so you're welcome!"

My mother would smooth her sleek skirt, pass a hand over her perfect hairdo, examine her red-polished nails, and murmur, "Go to hell," through clenched lips before taking my hand and leading me home.

Eventually Aunt Becky got engaged to Handsome Eli Cohen at Café Armon. It was a lovely party with tables of food and a singer who sang Yisrael Yitzhaki songs. Aunt Becky looked as beautiful as Gina Lollobrigida. When the family had our photograph taken with the engaged couple, Nono Gabriel sat in the middle surrounded by the whole family, and I sat perched on my father's shoulders and looked down at everyone. That was the last photograph taken of Nono Gabriel, because five days later he died.

Only after he died, during the shiva, the seven-day mourning period, when my mother fainted all the time from crying so much and they had to pour water over her so she'd wake up, and Nona Rosa kept saying, "*Basta*, Luna! Pull yourself together so we don't have another tragedy in the family!" and Tia Allegra, Nono Gabriel's sister, said, "May he rest in peace, Gabriel. Not only isn't she crying for him, she won't even let her daughter faint over him"—it was just then that Becky found the right time to announce her wedding date. They all congratulated her but said she had to wait a year out of respect for Nono Gabriel, and Becky said there was no way she'd wait that long, because by then she'd be too old to have children. And Tia Allegra said, "Gabriel, God forgive your sins. What kind of girls did you raise that they won't even give you the respect of a year?"

My mother, who had come around from her faint, whispered, "Thank God she's finally getting married. I was worried she might die an old maid." A fight broke out and Aunt Becky ran after my mother with her *sapatos*, her slippers, and threatened to murder her if she ever dared call her an old maid again, and my mother told her, "What's to be done, *querida*. It's a fact. At your age I was already a mother." At that Aunt Becky darted out of the house and I after her down the steps of Agrippas Street until we reached the Wallach hospital grave-yard. She sat down on the wall and sat me next to her and suddenly burst into tears.

"Oy, Papo, Papo, why have you gone, why have you left us, Papo? What will we do without you?" Eventually she stopped crying, hugged me tight, and said, "You know, Gabriela, they all say that Nono Gabriel loved your mother Luna more than any of us, but I never felt that he loved me less. Nono Gabriel had a heart of gold and that's why everybody took advantage of him. And you, my lovely, never let anyone take advantage of you, you hear? You'll find your-self a boy like my Eli and marry him and be happy. Isn't that right, my good girl? Don't search right or left. When you meet a boy like Eli, you'll feel the love here." She took my hand and laid it between her breasts. "Right here, Ga-briela, between your belly and your breasts, you'll feel the love, and when you feel it you'll know you've found your Eli and you'll marry him. Now let's go back home before Nono Gabriel gets angry with me for running away from his shiva."

In the end Aunt Becky waited a year until the mourning period was over and only then married Handsome Eli Cohen at Café Armon, where they'd gotten engaged. I wore a white dress and walked in front of the bride, throw-ing sweets with my cousin Boaz, Aunt Rachelika's eldest son, who was stuffed into a suit and bow tie. Mother and her middle sister Rachelika had picked out my and Boaz's outfits together. They did everything together. When Rachelika wasn't in her house on Ussishkin Street, she was with my mother, and when my mother wasn't in our house on Ben-Yehuda Street, she was at my aunt's.

After Nono died, my grandmother remained in her and Nono's house, and every now and then she'd stop by ours for a visit. She'd always come with chocolate and bamblik licorice sweets, and fascinating stories about the time she'd worked in the homes of the English.

"Enough of those stories already!" my mother would say, annoyed. "Clean-ing the toilets of the English isn't exactly a great honor."

And Nona would muster up strength and say, "It's also nothing to be ashamed of! I wasn't born a princess like you, with a silver spoon in my mouth. I had to feed my brother Ephraim, and besides, I learned a lot from the Ingelish."

"What? What did you learn from the In . . . ge . . . lish?" my mother would reply mockingly, drawing out the word *Ingelish* for as long as she could. "And anyway, how many times do I have to tell you, it's English. English."

Nona would ignore Mother's taunts and reply quietly, "I learned to lay a table. I learned Ingelish. I speak Ingelish better than you who learned it in the Ingelish school, and to this day your Ingelish is like my troubles."

"Me? I don't know English?" My mother would become angry. "I read magazines in English. I don't even read the subtitles at the cinema, I understand everything!"

"Right, right, we've heard all about you. You understand everything except for one thing, the most important thing, respect and manners. *That* you don't understand, beauty queen of Jerusalem."

And Mother would storm out of the kitchen and leave me with Nona Rosa, who'd sit me on her knee and tell me, "Remember, Gabriela, there is no work that is beneath a person, and if ever, God forbid, you find yourself in a situation, *tfu-tfu-tfu,* where you have no choice, there's no shame in cleaning toilets for the Ingelish."

I liked spending time with Nona Rosa. She was a marvelous storyteller and I was an excellent listener.

"Before you were born, a long, long time before you were born, Gabriela *querida,*" she would tell me, "our Jerusalem was like abroad. In Café Europa on Zion Square an orchestra played and people danced the tango, and at five o'clock on the terrace of the King David Hotel there was tea and a pianist, and they'd drink from delicate porcelain cups, and the Arab waiters, may they be cursed, wore tuxedoes and bow ties. And the cakes they served there, with chocolate and cream and strawberries . . . And the gentlemen would come in white suits and straw hats, and the ladies in hats and dresses like they wore at their horse races in Ingeland."

But my grandmother, so I learned years later, had never been to Café Europa or the King David. She told me what she'd heard from the people whose houses she cleaned. She told me her dreams, some of which would come true years later, when her wealthy brother Nick, who Nona called Nissim, would come visit from America and the whole family would gather on the King David terrace, and he would order coffee and cake for everybody. And as the pianist played, I'd steal a glance at my nona, dressed in her best clothes, and I'd see a rare glint of pleasure in her eyes.

Nona Rosa had a hard life. She lived with a man who respected her but didn't love her the way a man loves a woman. She never knew true love, but she never complained and she never cried. Even during Nono Gabriel's shiva, when rivers of tears flowed from my mother's and aunts' eyes, threatening to flood all of Jerusalem, not a single tear trickled from hers. Nona Rosa would never hug. She didn't like touching and didn't like being touched. But I'd sit in her lap, wrap my little arms around her neck, and plant kisses on her withered cheek. "Enough, stop it, Gabriela, *basta*, you're annoying me," she'd chide me and try to shake me off, but I'd ignore her, taking her rough hands and putting them around my body, forcing her to hug me.

Once Nono died, Nona stopped inviting the family over for Shabbat, and we'd hold it elsewhere. After the heavy Shabbat meal I'd walk with Nona to her house and stay there until Mother or Father came to get me. What I loved about her house were the glass-fronted cabinets in which porcelain and crystal tableware stood in perfect order, and the wedding photographs of Mother, Rachelika, and Becky in their silver frames. I loved the big picture of Nono and Nona on the wall: Nono, a handsome young man in a black suit, white shirt, and tie, a white handkerchief peeping from his jacket pocket, sits upright on a wooden chair, his elbow on a table and a rolled-up newspaper in his hand. Nona stands beside him in a black dress buttoned to the neck, the hem reaching to her ankles, with a gold pendant relaxing against her breastbone. She isn't touching my nono but her hand is on the back of his chair. Nono's face is finely chiseled, the nose, the eyes, the lips almost perfect. Nona's is broad, her black hair styled as if stuck to her skull, her eyes wide. They are not smiling, just looking at the camera with serious expressions.

There was the heavy dining table with its lace cloth and center bowl that was always filled with fruit and the upholstered chairs around it, the wide, deep-red couch with cushions that Nona herself had embroidered. My favorite of all was the wooden wardrobe that stood in Nona's bedroom, which was separate from Nono's. Lions had been carved into the top, and I would stand for hours in front of its mirrored doors, pretending I was Sandra Dee kissing Troy Donahue and we were living happily ever after.

Their yard, partly protected by the tiled roof, was surrounded by an iron fence entwined with purple bougainvillea and lined with geraniums in white-painted cans. There were stools in the yard, and the chair with the upholstered cushion in which Nono Gabriel loved to sit as evening fell, and next to it a wooden table on which Nona sometimes served dinner. After Nono died, his chair became a monument to his memory and nobody sat in it.

The yard was my kingdom. I'd sit on a stool, gaze at the sky, and wait for a rainbow, because I'd once asked Nona Rosa what God was and she'd told me God was the rainbow in the sky. When I wasn't searching the sky, I'd imagine I was one of the Hollywood actresses my mother so admired. After all, it was in our Jerusalem that they shot *Exodus,* and the star, Paul Newman, who my mother said was even better looking than Handsome Eli Cohen, stayed at the King David. Every afternoon during filming my mother would take me by the hand and we'd walk to the entrance of the hotel in the hope of catching a glimpse of him. After a few days of failing to see him, we crossed the road to the YMCA tower, bought tickets for five grush, and climbed to the top, the highest point in Jerusalem. "From here," she said, "nobody can hide Paul Newman from me."

But from there we couldn't see him either because each time he arrived at the King David the black car took him right to the hotel's revolving glass door, and he slipped through without even a glance back at the crowd that had formed to see him. Eventually Mother managed to see Paul Newman as an extra in the scene where the establishment of the state is announced. She brought the binoculars that Father had bought her for bird-watching on our walks in the Jerusalem hills, and though she had finally gotten to see Paul Newman with the binoculars, my mother was disappointed.

"I saw him, but he, *nada,* he didn't see me. Well, how could he from a mile away?" My mother was convinced that if only Paul Newman could have seen her up close, he wouldn't have been able to resist her. Nobody could resist my mother. Somebody just had to mention to Paul Newman that my mother was the beauty queen of Jerusalem. But nobody told him, and Mother made do with going to see *Exodus* every day when it was showing at Orion Cinema. Alberto, the usher who had lain wounded in the hospital with Mother during the war, got us in for free.

My mother very much admired movie stars, first and foremost Paul Newman and Joanne Woodward, Doris Day and Rock Hudson. I dreamed that one day I'd go to Hollywood, even though I didn't know where Hollywood was, and come back as a famous film actress, and then Mother would stop calling me "primitive" and stop saying that I was different from everyone else and asking how, how had she had a daughter like me. And so I would practice until I made it to Hollywood.

At every chance I got, when Nono and Nona's yard was empty, I acted like I was living in a movie. I was named Natalie, like Natalie Wood, and I'd dance for hours in James Dean's arms, and when James and I finished dancing I'd bow to an imaginary audience. One time after I finished dancing I heard loud applause and shouts of "Bravo! Bravo!" I froze and saw the whole neighborhood standing by the fence. Embarrassed to my core, I ran into the house and directly to Nono's room, lying on his bed and burying my head in the pillow, my eyes filled with tears of shame. Nona Rosa, who witnessed the whole scene, didn't come after me. A long time later, when I came out of the room, she sat in her armchair in the living room, looked at me, and said, "Gabriela *querida,* why are you embarrassed? You dance so beautifully. You should tell your mother and father to enroll you in ballet lessons with Rina Nikova."

Of all our family I was closest to Nona Rosa. While Nono Gabriel was alive his and Nona's house was the center of the family. We gathered there on Friday evenings for Shabbat, and on Saturday mornings for huevos haminados that we'd eat with cheese-filled borekitas and sweet sütlaç rice pudding, on which Nona would draw a Star of David with cinnamon.

After Shabbat breakfast we'd play in the yard, Mother, Rachelika, and Becky would chat, and Father, Rachelika's Moise, and Becky's Handsome Eli Cohen would talk about soccer. There was always shouting because Father was a Hapoel Jerusalem fan and Eli and Moise were Beitar fans. That's how the time passed until lunch when we'd eat macaroni hamin. After the hamin Nono would take his afternoon nap, and we children were sent for a nap too so we wouldn't disturb him. Mother, Rachelika, and Becky would carry on chatting, and Father, Moise, and Eli Cohen would go to my father's sister's house. Aunt Clara and her husband Yaakov lived on Lincoln Street opposite the YMCA stadium, where every Shabbat afternoon there was a Beitar Jerusalem soccer game. "Watching a game from Clara and Yaakov's balcony is better than sitting in the reserved seats," Uncle Moise would say.

My little brother Ronny and I nicknamed Uncle Yaakov "Jakotel" after we saw *Jack the Giant Killer,* which translated to Jack Kotel Haanakim in Hebrew, at the Orna Cinema maybe a hundred times, because the usher there too had been in the hospital with Mother during the war. "It's lucky that Mother almost died in the War of Independence," Ronny would say. "Otherwise how would we get to see movies for free?"

After Nono died and Nona stopped cooking, the Shabbat lunch macaroni hamin tradition moved to our house, and instead of napping after the meal we'd all go to watch the Beitar game. From below, I felt that at any moment Aunt Clara and Jakotel's balcony would collapse together with the millions of family members on it, so I'd make sure not to pass under the balcony and instead walked on the crowded side of the street next to the stadium.

Left with no choice, every Saturday Father was forced to watch the Beitar Jerusalem team with us from the balcony, even though he always cursed "the sons of bitches" and prayed they'd lose. Everyone would yell, "Damn you, David. Is this what you came for? To put the evil eye on the team?"

Nona Rosa never came with us to see a Beitar game and would go back to her house after lunch. Sometimes I'd walk with her, and while she took her afternoon nap I'd rifle through all her drawers looking for hidden treasure, and when she woke up she'd lose her temper with me and say, "How many times have I told you that you mustn't put your hands into places that aren't yours? You know what happened to the cat that put its paw into a drawer that wasn't his? His paw got trapped and his fingers were cut off. Do you want a hand with no fingers?" And I'd be so frightened that I buried my hands deep in my pockets and swore I'd never ever put my hands into places that weren't mine, but I never kept my promise.

Every now and again in the afternoon, when Mother went out to Café Atara or someplace else, Nona would come and look after me and Ronny. I'd beg her to tell me stories about the old times before I was born, about the time of the Ingelish and Nono Gabriel's shop in the Mahane Yehuda Market and his black car in which they'd drive to the Dead Sea and Tel Aviv. And about the time when they lived in a house with an elevator on King George Street, and how the whole family came to see the bath with the two faucets, one for hot water and the other for cold, a bath like my nona had seen only in the homes she'd cleaned.

I asked lots of questions, and my nona would say that I must have swallowed a radio and I was giving her a headache, but you could see that she enjoyed telling me what she'd perhaps never shared with anyone before.

One day Nona sat down on Nono's chair for the first time since he'd died and said to me, "Gabriela *querida*, your nona's an old woman who's seen a lot in life. I've had a hard life. My father and mother died in the cholera epidemic in our Jerusalem and we became orphans. I was ten years old, Gabriela, like you are today, and Ephraim, may he rest in peace, was five and the only one

I had left. My brother Nissim had run off to America, and the damned Turks hanged our brother Rachamim at Damascus Gate because he didn't want to join their army. We had nothing to eat and nothing to wear, and every day I'd go to Mahane Yehuda after it closed to collect what was left on the ground, tomatoes, cucumbers, sometimes a bit of bread. I had to take care of Ephraim and started doing housework for the Ingelish, and there the lady would feed me and I'd eat half and save the other half for Ephraim.

"And then, when I was sixteen, Nona Mercada married me to her son, your Nono Gabriel, may he rest in peace, and all of a sudden I had a good life. Gabriel was very rich and handsome. All the girls in Jerusalem wanted him, and out of them all, Mercada chose me. Why she chose me, the poor orphan, I only found out after muchos anos, many years, but back then I didn't ask questions. I knew Gabriel from the shop in the market. Every Friday I'd go to get cheese and olives that he and his father, Senor Raphael, may he rest in peace, would distribute to the poor. Who could have dreamed he would end up my husband? That I would be the mother of his daughters? What chance did I, an orphan from the Shama neighborhood with no family and no pedigree, have of even coming close to the Ermosa family? And then, out of the blue, of all the girls in Jerusalem she chose me for her son. *Dio santo,* I thought I was dreaming, and although she told me I could take some time to think about it, I told her yes right away and my life changed completely. Suddenly I had a house, suddenly I had clothes, I had food, I had a family. That's not to say that everything was rosy. A lot of things were bad because of my sins, but that didn't matter to me. The main thing was that I no longer had to clean houses for the Ingelish, and I knew that Ephraim would now grow up with clothes and food. Instead of the family I'd lost, I'd have a new one: a husband, children, a mother-in-law I hoped would be like a mother to me, sisters-in-law I hoped would be like sisters, and brothers-in-law I hoped would be like brothers.

"Gabriela, mi alma, I'm an old woman and soon I'll die, and after I die, you will be the only one to miss me. My daughters, may they be healthy, will cry a bit and get on with their lives. That's the nature of people. Time heals, people forget. But you, querida, you don't forget, not like your mother, who has the memory of a bird. I noticed it when you were still a baby. You never shut your mouth, *avlastina de la Palestina,* asking questions all the time as if you wanted to inhale the whole world. Now, querida mia, I'm going to tell you about your Nona Rosa and Nono Gabriel and our family and how, from being very wealthy and living in a house with an elevator and a bath, and having the loveliest shop in Mahane Yehuda, we became horanis, poor primitives, with barely enough money to buy wine for Friday Kiddush.

"Everything I know was told to me by your Nono Gabriel, who related the family history as he'd heard it from his father Raphael, may he rest in peace. After Raphael died, Gabriel promised to continue telling the family story, from the day they arrived from Toledo after King Ferdinand and Queen Isabella, may their souls burn in hell, expelled the Jews from Spain to Palestine. And because Gabriel and I, for my sins, had no sons, he would tell the story over and over to Luna, Rachelika, and Becky, and make them swear to tell it to their children. But I don't trust your mother to tell you because her head's in the clouds and her memory, *wai de mi sola*, so it's best she keeps quiet. So come, mi alma, come, bonica, sit here on your old nona's knee and listen to Nono Gabriel's story."

I did as she asked. I climbed onto her knee, burrowed into her bosom, and closed my eyes, inhaling her warm familiar scent that had the sweetness of sütlaç and rosewater. My nona toyed with my curls, rolling them around her thin finger, sighing deeply and pausing the way you do before saying something very important. Then she continued with her story as if she were telling it to herself and not to me.

"After they expelled the Jews from Toledo, the head of the family, Senor Avraham, and his parents, brothers, and sisters traveled all the way from Toledo to the port of Saloniki and boarded a ship that brought them directly to the port of Jaffa."

"And your family, Nona?"

"My family, mi alma, also came from Toledo to Saloniki and stayed there for many years until my great-grandfather, may he rest in peace, came to Palestine. But I won't tell you about my family, Gabriela, because from the day I married your grandfather and became part of the Ermosa family, the story of his family became the story of my family too.

"Now listen and don't interrupt again, because if you do, I won't remember where I stopped and won't know where to continue."

I nodded and promised not to interrupt anymore.

"From Jaffa, Senor Avraham traveled for maybe three days, three nights until he reached Jerusalem. His dream was to kiss the stones of the Western Wall. In Jerusalem he met other Spaniols who took him to the synagogue and gave him somewhere to sleep. At the time small merchants, shopkeepers, artisans, and also goldsmiths and silversmiths who traded with the Arabs lived in the Jewish Quarter in the Old City. There was respect and good relations with the Ishmaelites, and the Spaniols wore dresses like theirs. They even spoke Arabic, and some of the Arabs even spoke Ladino.

"Life was hard in this country back then—Dio santo. A woman had eight children one after the other, and they all died at birth or when they were babies.

"I also had five children with your Nono Gabriel, but only my three daughters, may they have a long life, *pishcado y limon*, lived. The boys lived less than a month, and after Becky was born my womb closed up.

"I did everything I needed to do to give Gabriel a son. Between the engagement and the wedding I and my future husband, your nono, were invited to a relative's circumcision. During the ceremony they let me hold the baby and then hand him to my future husband, who passed him on to others, which was the custom for ensuring that a young couple would have sons.

"And truly, blessed be His name, not many days passed after the wedding and I had conceived. How I loved being pregnant. Even my mother-in-law Mercada, who never made life easy for me, was good to me. She and all the women in the family pampered me with honey sweets to make sure I wouldn't have a daughter, God forbid, and that with God's help a son would be born.

"Now you shouldn't speak ill of the dead, Gabriela, but whenever she could, my mother-in-law Mercada, may she rest in peace, would stick a knife in my back and through my heart too, but during that first pregnancy she made sure that everyone showered me with love.

"And when the time came, Gabriel rushed to the synagogue with the other men in the family to pray for my well-being and the well-being of the baby. I stayed with the midwife and the women in the family, and my shouting that night was heard from our house in the Old City as far away as Nahalat Shiva in the New City, and I pushed and pushed, *dala dala dala,* until my soul almost left my body, and it was only when I was sure that the Almighty was taking me to Him that a male child was born. Mercada opened the door and shouted, '*Bien nacido,* it's a boy!' and all the family standing outside the door responded, '*Sano que'ste,* may he be healthy.' The midwife took the baby, washed it, wrapped it in a white cotton cloth, and laid it on my bosom. But before I could even kiss his red hair Mercada took him from me and ordered the children to run to the synagogue and fetch Gabriel.

"When Gabriel came, he took the baby from Mercada and held it to his heart as if it were precious crystal. Only after he gave thanks to the Almighty did he turn to me, lying between the sheets like a muerta, and for the first time in our lives he kissed me on the forehead.

"What can I tell you, querida mia, that was one of the happiest moments of my life. For the first time since the wedding I felt a little love from Gabriel. Even Mercada, with her face as sour as a lemon, who never smiled at me and always spoke to me curtly and never asked how I was, said to me, '*Como 'stas, Rosa? Quieres una cosa?* How are you, Rosa? Do you need anything?' And before I could reply, she ordered her daughter Allegra to fetch me some leche con dvash, milk and honey.

"I was happy, Gabriela. I felt that for the first time since I'd become an Ermosa, Mercada and Gabriel were pleased with me. I'd given Mercada a grandson and Gabriel his first son. I felt a warmth in my heart, pride. I felt that now perhaps I belonged. Now perhaps I was part of the family.

"The baby was named Raphael after your great-grandfather, who had died a short time before I'd married Gabriel.

"How I loved Raphael, the apple of my eye. As tired as I was after the labor, I cleaned the room we lived in until it gleamed so the baby wouldn't catch an illness, God forbid, and die, God forbid, like the babies of the Yemenites in Silwan who dropped like flies just from all the dirt. Raphael's cradle stood under the window, and over it I hung a tara, an oil lamp that Gabriel brought from the synagogue, and every day after evening prayers Torah scholars would come and recite from the Book of Zohar in honor of baby Raphael.

"But the baby, as much as we pampered him and loved him and prayed for him, he cried all the time, in his cradle, when I carried him whispering words of love: 'Querido mio, hijo mio, mi alma, what's hurting you, Raphuli? What's hurting?' I didn't know what to do. I was a child myself, sixteen, maybe seventeen. The baby cried on and on, and then I cried until I ran out of tears, but he never did. He cried without even a break to breathe. Mercada said maybe I didn't have enough milk, maybe we should bring in a wet nurse, but I didn't want my baby to feed from another woman, didn't want strange hands clasping that little body to strange breasts. To increase my milk, Mercada forced me to eat garlic even though I hated it, telling me over and over that only garlic would make baby Raphael feed properly, and then he'd be happy and stop crying.

"Most of all I was frightened of the evil eye and evil spirits. I'd even dress Raphael in girls' clothes to deceive Lilith, the worst spirit of all, who we knew especially liked to harm baby boys. According to our belief, Gabriela, to appease the evil spirit we had to 'sell' the child to somebody else. Gabriel's mother had been sold when she was a baby, and that's why she was called Mercada, which means bought.

"When the time came to sell little Raphael, I went to my good neighbor Victoria Siton and informed her, 'I have a slave for sale,' which was the code for selling the child. Victoria agreed to 'buy the slave' and as payment gave me a gold bracelet. The next day our two families got together and slaughtered a goat for absolution and changed Raphael's name to Mercado—bought."

"Is Victoria my other nona?" I asked, interrupting Nona Rosa.

"Back then we didn't know that Victoria's son, your father David, would marry Luna and we'd become related, but at the time Victoria Siton was our neighbor in Ohel Moshe, and it was custom to sell your child to a neighbor. Victoria Siton kept baby Raphael in her house for three days, and then we held a new sale ceremony and bought him back from her. But nothing helped, Gabriela, not the girls' clothes I dressed him in or selling him to Victoria Siton. The damned evil spirits outsmarted us, and when Raphael was almost a month old and we hadn't yet held the redemption of the firstborn ceremony to celebrate that he'd been bought back, he turned blue like the eye hanging over his cradle to protect him, and by the time Gabriel and Mercada arrived, he was already dead. Mercada lifted Raphael's blanket over his body and looked Gabriel in the eye and told him it was God's punishment. At the time I didn't yet grasp why your grandfather deserved such a punishment from God, and it was only after muchos anos that I understood what that sour old woman meant.

"On the night little Raphael died, I died too. I didn't die when the accursed Turks hanged my brother Rachamim at Damascus Gate, I didn't die when my father and then my mother died in the cholera epidemic and I remained alone in the world, a ten-year-old orphan girl with a five-year-old brother. I didn't die when I realized that my husband didn't love me and perhaps never would and that the only thing that seemed to interest my mother-in-law was making my life miserable. But when my child Raphael died, I died too, and your grandfather Gabriel died as well, and it was only after your mother Luna was born that he began to live again.

"After Luna was born, we had another son, and he died even before we were able to have him circumcised and give him a name. But for me, even after Luna was born, joy did not come back into my heart, and it didn't after Rachelika and Becky were born either. Do you know who restored joy to your nona?"

"Who?" I asked, looking wide-eyed at her.

"You, mi alma," Nona Rosa replied, and although she didn't like kissing, she kissed my head and I felt as if my heart might burst.

"You brought happiness back to me. My daughters, may they be healthy, have never loved me the way you do, hija mia, and perhaps I didn't love them the way a mother loves a child. My heart was filled with pain and longing for baby Raphael, and there was no room left for them. But you, querida mia, you, mi vida, my life, I love you a lot. The moment you were born my heart opened again, and into it you brought happiness I'd forgotten could exist in this world."

"I love you, Nona, I love you best in the whole world," I said, tightening my arms around my grandmother's broad waist.

"Love." Nona Rosa laughed. "In our family, Gabriela, love is a word we never spoke. I never heard words like *love* from my mother, may she rest in peace. Her whole life was spent in poverty until she died from the epidemic that almost killed the whole of Jerusalem, and Gabriel, of blessed memory, I never once heard him tell me 'I love you.' And anyway, what is love? Who knows? Before they got married, my daughters said 'I love David,' 'I love Moise,' 'I love Eli,' and I said, 'Love? The time of the Messiah has come.' It's luck, luck from heaven above that we only had girls, because in our family the men marry women they don't love. The men of the Ermosa family, Gabriela, don't let the word *love* out of their mouths, not even when no one is there to hear. But stories about love that broke hearts, Gabriela, stories about love in which there was no love, that's something we have in the family. That, praise God, He didn't keep from us."

She sighed. "Well, get up. That's enough for today. I've already said more than I wanted. Get up. Your mother will be here soon to take you home and she'll be annoyed that you haven't had dinner. Come, querida, help me cut vegetables for the salad."

The following Saturday after we ate the macaroni hamin and everyone went to watch the Beitar game from Clara and Jakotel's balcony, I went to Nona's again. Once more she sat me on her knee and continued the story of the Ermosa family.

"Your great-grandfather Raphael was a very pious man, a scholar who studied the Kabbalah and even made the journey all the way from Jerusalem to Safed to pray with the Holy Ari, Rabbi Isaac Luria. They say that Raphael had decided never to stand under the wedding canopy, that he almost vowed never to have children and instead devote his whole life to Torah study."

"So how was Nono Gabriel born if his father wasn't married?"

"Paciencia, querida, all in good time. Listen to me and don't interrupt, because if you interrupt again I'll forget what I wanted to tell you and you won't know anything. Dio santo, why do all the girls in the Ermosa family have no patience?"

Nona took her time before going on with the story, lowering her voice as if whispering a secret. "They say that one day Raphael's righteous father came to Safed and informed him that he'd found a bride for him—Rivka Mercada, the fifteen-year-old daughter of Rabbi Yochanan Toledo, a pious Jew and rich merchant. Raphael couldn't disobey his father, but he demanded, and was granted, permission to remain in Safed for three more months, when the wedding would take place. From that moment he dove even deeper into a modest, ascetic way of life.

"The three months passed slowly, and as the wedding date approached, Raphael became even more pious and spent days fasting. And then, Gabriela, then something happened that changed Raphael's life forever.

"You're still a little girl, Gabriela, but you should know, mi alma: Love is not only blind, it also blinds. Love can bring great happiness, but it can also bring great tragedy. Your grandmother, Gabriela, didn't know what the emotion of love was. Your grandfather never loved me the way a man should love a woman, and perhaps I too didn't love him in the way the Song of Songs says. I was just by his side and gave him daughters, *sanos qui 'sten*, may they be healthy. I took care of him and the girls and did my best for us to have a good life, no more and no less. But every night before I fell asleep I'd think about what love was, and I couldn't get this story I'd heard about your great-grandfather Raphael out of my head.

"One day, so I heard, Raphael was walking down one of the alleys in Safed toward the Yosef Caro Synagogue, immersed in himself and murmuring a prayer. His eyes half closed, he accidentally bumped into a young girl. Raphael was startled, and when he raised his head, his eyes met hers, blue as the sea and deep as a well. Her hair was pulled into two golden braids and her skin was white as snow. Raphael, who felt as if he'd seen the beauty of the Divine Presence, quickly covered his eyes with his hand and hurried on his way. But in all the days and nights that followed, he couldn't clear the girl's image from his mind. It came to him in the morning when he said the morning prayer, and at night when he said the evening prayer. It came to him in the mikvah ritual bath, and it came to him when he lay down to sleep. He didn't understand what he was feeling. He only knew that her blue eyes had hit him like a bolt of lightning. Dio santo, he thought to himself. It's a sin, what I'm feeling for this strange woman, a sin.

"He decided to fast even more and swore he would keep away from places where women were permitted, for he knew that his betrothed was waiting for him in Jerusalem. But the image of the Ishkenazi girl in the alley haunted him like an evil spirit and allowed him no peace. No matter what he did, he could not drive the girl from his thoughts, and he soon found himself lying in wait for her at the top of the alley where he had first bumped into her. He saw her leave one of the houses and followed her, but when she turned and transfixed him with her blue eyes, he again fled for dear life.

"That same day Raphael decided he'd return to Jerusalem earlier than planned to rid himself, once and for all, of the dybbuk with the blue eyes. He couldn't even imagine speaking to the girl who came from the Ishkenazi community, for he knew that things like that were forbidden, a sin. Do you understand, Gabriela? A sin!"

I didn't really understand what the Ishkenazi community was, and certainly not what sin meant, but Nona didn't notice. She carried on telling the story as if possessed by a dybbuk herself, absent-mindedly rocking me on her knee as if she forgot I was there, and probably went on talking even after I fell asleep.

When I woke up, it was quiet and only the murmur of praying and calls of the congregation from the nearby synagogue could be heard. I found Nona sitting pensively in Nono's chair. "Good morning, querida mia," she called to me even though it was already evening and dinner was on the table in the yard. Every now and then when I slept over at Nona's, she'd bake borekitas especially for me and make me sütlaç with the Star of David just the way I liked it.

"And not a word to your mother, Gabriela, so she doesn't get used to it!" she said. "Let her go on making borekas for you and not ask me to do it."

Like the rest of the family, Nona didn't know that Mother bought ready-made borekas from Kadosh, and believed that she baked them herself. My mother had made me swear never to tell anybody, and I kept quiet.

Nona carefully peeled a hard-boiled egg and split it into four. "Eat, eat, good girl. You need to grow." Then she sat back down in Nono's chair and continued the story from where I'd fallen asleep a few hours earlier.

"Do you understand what happened, Gabriela? Raphael, may he rest in peace, fell in love with the Ishkenazi girl from Safed, and it was absolutely forbidden for Spaniols to marry Ishkenazim. It was the time of the Turks, when there were maybe six thousand Jews in Palestine and almost all of them lived in Jerusalem. At the time there were not only Spaniol Jews in the country but also Jews from the Ishkenazi countries. *Wai wai,* how hard it was for the Ishkenazim. Miskenicos, poor souls, they didn't know Arabic and they didn't know Ladino and they just didn't have a clue. Well, the Ishkenazim were Jews too, right? So the Spaniols opened their doors, let them pray in their synagogues, and the Ishkenazim did everything like the Spaniols, even started speaking Arabic and wearing dresses like the Spaniols, who dressed like the Arabs. They did everything they could to blend in with the Spaniols, because after all, we were all Jews and we should help one another. But marry? Heaven forbid! Because the Spaniols wanted to keep themselves for themselves and only marry one another, so as not to mix, God help us, with Ishkenazim and have half-and-half children.

"*Wai de mi,* Gabriela, what scandal and shame an Ishkenazi bride could bring down on a family. Like Sarah, the daughter of Yehuda Yehezkel, who married Yehoshua Yellin the Ishkenazi. And though Yehuda Yehezkel reminded everyone over and over that the groom's father was an esteemed Torah scholar, it didn't matter. Nothing helped, what shame. The Sephardim were so opposed to marriage with Ishkenazim that Sir Moses Montefiore himself offered a prize of a hundred gold napoleons to anyone entering into a mixed marriage. And do you know how much a hundred gold napoleons is, Gabriela? Something like a thousand lirot, maybe ten thousand lirot, and despite the poverty in Jerusalem and even though a hundred gold napoleons was a sum that most people could only dream of, nobody jumped at the offer.

"Raphael, may he rest in peace, couldn't stop thinking about the Ishkenazi girl. Her blue eyes followed him wherever he went. You understand, Gabriela, mi alma, even though he'd just caught a glimpse of her she'd plunged deep into his heart and stayed there, and instead of studying Torah day and night he thought about the Ishkenazi girl. As I said, he walked the alleys of Safed moonstruck, looking for her—in the morning after morning prayers, in the afternoon when the hot sun forced people to stay inside their cool stone houses, and in the evening after prayers when his friends gathered at the synagogue. Late at night too, when even the moon and stars went to sleep, he would wander through the alleys, peeking into windows, opening yard gates, hoping he'd see her. But it seemed that the Ishkenazi girl had vanished. He never saw her again, and although she was still in his heart, deep inside he felt relief and saw it as an omen from heaven.

"A few weeks before the wedding he went with his father to the home of the bride's family to meet her for the first time. The whole way there Raphael was silent and didn't ask his father even one question about the bride. And the bride, poor thing, locked herself in one of the rooms in the house and refused to come out and meet her groom. For the three days and three nights prior, so they said, she had been so frightened she didn't stop crying, and all her mother's words of kindness and love didn't help. The more her mother told her about her role as a wife and the more she gave her precise instructions on how she must behave with her husband on their wedding night, the more she wept.

"Raphael and his father sat in the family's living room for a long time, waiting for the bride-to-be to come out. When her father's patience expired, he excused himself, went into the room where his daughter was crying her heart out, and threatened her with a thousand deaths if she didn't stop shaming him.

"Rivka Mercada finally left the room, hiding behind her mother, and peeped at the groom with the red beard, not daring to look him in his eyes, which anyway were fixed on the floor. The meeting was short and Raphael was glad that on their way home his father didn't ask his opinion of her.

"On the morning of the wedding the groom's mother, the bride's mother, and relatives from both sides gathered in the bride's house, and together with her close friends they escorted her to the bagno, the bathhouse, singing and dancing and throwing sweets at her. After the ritual bath Raphael's mother took the cake she had brought from home, sliced it above the bride's head, and gave the slices to her virgin friends and blessed them, saying she hoped that they too would find a groom swiftly in their time, amen. Then each of the women went to their own houses, and Raphael's mother had a talk with her son, giving him specific instructions for how to treat his bride on their wedding night.

"'Querido mio,' she said, 'today I am putting you into the hands of another woman. From today you are hers, but don't forget, I am your mother and I will always be more important than your wife. And when you have a child, with God's help, and he marries, your wife, his mother, will be more important than his wife. That's how it is with us. The mother always comes before the wife. The mother is the first senora. Your wife, mi alma, is one of us, a good woman. Your father and I chose her after we met with many girls. Her father and mother have spoiled her, and that's why you must put her in her place right from the start so she knows who the master of the house is! Don't pamper her the way her father has. She has to make sure you have a clean house, cook for you, and do your washing, and with God's help give you healthy sons, but you have to care for her too, provide for her, respect her, and treat her like a princess. On the night of the wedding, mi alma, treat her as a man should a girl, but be gentle with her, do not force her, and if it doesn't work the first time, then try again, and if it doesn't work the second time, then try a third time. Very slowly, gently, and with God's help, in nine months' time we'll celebrate a circumcision.'

"Raphael was embarrassed and lowered his head, trying not to hear what his mother was telling him. But she talked and talked, and only when he raised his eyes and gave her a piercing stare did she stop.

"'Just one more thing, querido,' she said before he lost patience with her. 'Just before you stomp on the wineglass, put your foot on the bride's foot for a moment to make sure that you will be the senor of your house, the master, the king.'

"When the time of the wedding arrived, with good fortune Raphael dressed in his best clothes and strode at the head of a big procession to the Yochanan ben Zakai Synagogue. After the marriage was sanctified, after he swore, 'If I forget thee, O Jerusalem, may my right hand lose its cunning,' and after his mother whispered in his ear not to forget the matter of the foot and he did as she asked, he stomped on the wineglass and everyone shouted, 'Mazal tov!' Then he found himself alone in the yichud room with his bride, both of them standing embarrassed and not knowing what to do. Raphael felt that something had broken inside him, and from that moment he lost the fervor of faith. On the spot he decided to give up fasting and Torah study. And when he lifted his new bride's blushing face and forced her to look into his eyes, he swore that he would make his wife a happy woman and would do anything for her and their future children.

"On the wedding night he treated her with gentleness, and she submitted to his touch and let his body enter hers. But in the act of love on that first night and the nights that followed, he did not kiss her even once. And Rivka Mercada, whose mother had never spoken one word about kissing, didn't feel that Raphael was keeping something from her, and she lay silent until he got up, went to his own bed, and left her to sleep in peace.

"Aaach . . . God forgive my sins." Nona Rosa sighed. "That's how it all began."

"What began?" I asked, not understanding what my grandmother meant.

"The whole business of the men in the Ermosa family wanting other women and not their own wives," she replied in such a low whisper that I hardly heard her. "It began with Mercada and Raphael. He wanted another woman and was married to Mercada. He came to her at night but not out of love, and she didn't suspect he was keeping something from her. And I too never enjoyed the act of love. I just lay on my back and waited for my husband to finish. You're still young and don't know about making love. When you grow up, I pray for your sake that the curse passes you over. Don't look at me like that, mi alma, you don't understand what I'm saying now, but when you grow up and meet your betrothed, promise me you'll do everything you can to feel love. Don't lose the opportunity like I did. Promise me, Gabriela, never marry a man who you feel doesn't love you more than you love him, so that life doesn't pass you by and you become a dried-up old woman like me. Love, Gabriela, fills a person, and anyone whose body does not flow with love, withers. Remember, Gabriela, remember what your grandmother's telling you."

My Nona Rosa never spoke to me again about love or the men in our family who loved other women and not their wives. Never again did I sit on her knee in Nono's chair. Mother no longer dropped me off to sleep over at Nona's, and Nona didn't come to our house to babysit Ronny and me when my parents went to the cinema or dancing at the Menorah Club. Instead Father picked up Nona every Saturday in the white Lark and brought her to our house, and when I'd run to her and encircle her body with my arms, kissing her wrinkled cheeks, she wouldn't shake me off with a laugh as she used to and say, "Basta, basta, Gabriela, you're hurting me." She wouldn't say anything. She'd just look at me like I wasn't there. She also forgot how to speak Hebrew and spoke only Ladino, which I didn't know, and when I'd tell her, "Nona, I don't understand. Tell me in Hebrew," my mother would lose her temper and say, "That's all I need right now, for you to start nagging. Leave Nona alone and stop bothering her." And my father would say, "What do you want from the child, she doesn't understand what's happened to Rosa." My mother would reply, "And you do? Who understands what's happened to her? Old people get sick, but she's as healthy as a horse. She just forgets. My mother's different from other people."

Now my nona too, not only me, was different from other people. Perhaps that's why I'd felt as if she and I had shared a covenant, and the more she shut herself up in her world, the more I wanted to enter it. But from day to day my beloved nona moved further away, and her face that I loved so much turned blank, and her eyes dimmed, and her big soft body turned stiff, and when I put my arms around it I felt like I was hugging a wall.

Nona also started doing strange things. One Saturday when Father brought her to our house and sat her at the table where we were all eating macaroni hamin, she took off her dress and sat there in her petticoat. Ronny started laughing, and I realized that something awful had happened because Mother got hysterical, and Father quickly covered Nona with her dress. For the first time in my life I wasn't forced to eat everything on my plate, and in the middle of the macaroni hamin we children were sent to play downstairs. My parents stayed in the living room with Rachelika and Moise and Becky and Handsome Eli Cohen, and they talked and talked until it got dark. They forgot to call us back upstairs, so we went up without being called, and as I peeked into the small living room, I saw that Aunt Becky was crying and Rachelika was crying and my mother was standing at the window smoking a cigarette, and my father and Moise and Handsome Eli Cohen were talking together. And in the middle of it all Nona Rosa was sitting completely detached from the commotion around her. I heard Rachelika say that Nona mustn't be left alone, that she should sleep at our house that night. Mother said, "But where can she sleep? With me and David?" And Father replied, "I'll sleep on the couch in the living room and she can sleep with you." And Mother said, "Don't talk nonsense, David. How can I sleep in the same bed as my mother?"

Then I came into the room and said, "I'll sleep with Nona Rosa in my bed," and Mother said, "That's a good idea. Gabriela can sleep at my mother's and look after her." Father lost his temper. "Are you out of your mind? A ten-year-old girl, what kind of 'look after her' do you have in mind?" And Mother said, "All right, she'll sleep here on the living room couch, but only tonight. Tomorrow we'll have to think about an arrangement. It can't go on like this."

That night they put my nona to bed on the couch and covered her with a blanket, and when everybody else had gone to bed I got up in the dark and saw her sleeping with her eyes open and whispered, "Nona," but she didn't reply, so I stroked her cheek and kissed her and hugged her tight until I fell asleep.

In the morning Father found me on the couch, but Nona wasn't there or anywhere else in the house. She went missing for a whole day. Nona had gotten lost.

They found her only late at night in the Mahane Yehuda Market, sitting in the doorway of the shop that had been Nono's. Another time she was found wandering in the Abu Tor neighborhood, trying to cross the border and get to the Shama neighborhood, where she was born and which since the War of Independence had been in Jordanian hands. My Aunt Rachelika decided to move Nona into her own house and look after her. "Because if I don't take her in, she'll be taken to the Talbieh asylum," she'd said.

Nona Rosa died in her sleep on the eve of Yom Kippur.

There was no way that Mother would allow me to attend the funeral.

"A cemetery is no place for children," she said, and for the first time Father didn't take my side and argue with her. Ronny and I stayed at home on our own, and Ronny, who could feel that I was sadder than usual, didn't tease me as he normally would. On the sideboard in my parents' living room, in a beautifully worked copper frame, was a photograph of my Nono Gabriel, my Nona Rosa, and their three daughters: Luna, Rachelika, and Becky. I brought it to my lips and kissed my nona, and the tears that fell from my eyes threatened to drown me. I missed her so much and was incapable of accepting that I would never see her again and that she would never again tell me about our family, whose men married women they didn't love.

For many months after Nona Rosa's death I'd walk from our house on Ben-Yehuda Street to hers, stand by the locked gate, and wait for her. Perhaps Nona wasn't really dead. Perhaps this time too she had just gotten lost and would soon find her way home: She'd walk in her measured gait down the five steps to the narrow alley, across the cobblestones, taking care not to catch her foot on a stone so she wouldn't fall, Heaven forbid, and crack her skull as she'd warned me so many times, her large frame swaying from side to side "like a drunkard," my mother would say irritably, and talking to herself as she did before she died, "like una loca," my mother would say in Ladino so we children wouldn't understand.

Nono's chair still stood in its place in the yard, and beside it the table at which I'd eaten sütlaç with a cinnamon Star of David so many times. I approached the small stone house, put my face to the window, and peered in. Everything was in order as it was when Nono and Nona were both alive. No one had touched the house since Nona had passed on, as my father used to say. I pressed my nose to the window as hard as I could, doing my best to see the photograph of Nono and Nona that hung on the wall, but I couldn't see it.

A hand touched my shoulder. "*Chaytaluch*, what are you doing here, Gabriela?"

I turned and facing me was Mrs. Barazani, the neighbor my mother hated, in her big floral housedress and a rolled-up kerchief on her head. She clasped me to her warm body that surprisingly felt like my nona's.

"*Ma guzt akeh?* Where's your mother? How long have you been standing here? Your mother must have gone to the police by now." She took my hand and led me to her house, sat me in a chair, and sent one of her boys to run and call my mother.

I curled up in the chair, watching my nona's neighbor running here and there, explaining in Kurdish and broken Hebrew to the other neighbors who'd followed us in that she'd found me in the yard, "trying to get into the house, *papukata*, poor thing," she told them. "How she misses her grandmother." And in the same breath she said to me, "Soon your mother will be here to take you home. Meanwhile, eat," and she placed before me a plate of kubbeh swimming in yellow gravy. But I wasn't hungry. I just missed my nona terribly and still hoped that in another moment the door would open and she'd come in and hug me and take me to their side of the yard and sit me on her knee and tell me stories. But instead of my nona it was my mother who came through the door like a gale force wind, and before she even said "Shalom," she slapped my face twice.

"What kind of a girl are you?" she hissed. "Who gave you permission to go to the Kurdish neighborhood on your own?"

I was so shocked that she'd slapped me in front of Mrs. Barazani and her neighbors that I didn't answer, didn't even cry. I just put my hand on my tingling cheek and stared hard at her.

"A street girl!" she went on, whispering so as not to embarrass herself in front of Mrs. Barazani any more than she already had. "Just wait and see what Father does to you. My slap was nothing. Just get your little bottom ready."

"This child has given me a heart attack," she said apologetically to Mrs. Barazani.

"Sit down, sit. You've probably been running around with worry," Mrs. Barazani replied.

My mother released a deep sigh, swallowed her pride, and sat in the chair offered to her, straightening her posture as much as she could and smoothing her skirt that had ridden above her knees.

"Here, drink, drink," Mrs. Barazani urged as she gave her a glass of water. I wondered how my mother could refuse to see what a good woman Mrs. Barazani was, how even though my mother detested her, even though my mother hadn't said a word to her for years, she was concerned for her and gave her a glass of water.

My mother didn't touch the glass of water. She shifted uneasily in the chair, and I could sense that she wanted to get out of the Kurdia's house as quickly as possible, but on the other hand, she didn't want to be rude. Despite the terrible pain in my cheek I smiled inwardly, pleased by my mother's discomfort. I didn't understand why my mother didn't like Mrs. Barazani, and why because some Kurd had screwed my grandfather a million years ago all the Kurds in the world were to blame.

Then Mother quickly rose, grabbed my hand, and roughly pulled me up from where I was sitting. She grasped my hand so tightly that I wanted to scream in pain, but I held it in as she dragged me toward the door, and for the first time since she had stormed in, turned and said reluctantly, "Thank you for looking after her and for sending your son to call me." She didn't wait for a reply and pushed me outside, closing the door behind her. By the time we got to my father waiting in the white Lark, she had already managed to yell at me like a madwoman. "You do this to spite me, don't you? It's because you know I can't stand them, isn't it?"

"But I didn't go to the Kurds," I said, trying to get a word in.

"You didn't go? I'll show you 'didn't go,'" she said and shoved me into the backseat of the car. "She's driving me out of my mind, your daughter. She's killing me," she told my father as she dramatically threw her hand across her forehead as if she was passing out.

My father didn't say a word. Every now and then I saw him glance in the mirror to check on me in the backseat.

"She's an embarrassment to me," my mother went on. "What's she looking for in the Kurdish neighborhood? And to put me in a position where I have to say thank you to the Kurdia, where I have to stand there like a fool, and in front of who yet?" My mother carried on talking about me as if I wasn't sitting there, curled up with my nose pressed to the window.

"Why did we take out a loan and move to Ben-Yehuda? Why did I send her to the Rehavia school? Why did I send her to school with David Benvenisti in Beit Hakerem?"

Yes, why? I asked myself. Why do I have to take a bus to Beit Hakerem when all the children in the neighborhood go to school in Arlosoroff, a few yards from their house? But I didn't dare say out loud what I was thinking and only scrunched up in my seat even more.

"Just you wait and see what Father does to you when we get home," she went on, threatening me. "Tell her, David. Tell her you're going to beat her until her bottom's as red as a monkey's in the Biblical Zoo."

"Stop putting words in my mouth," my father said, getting angry for the first time. My mother tried to go on, but he shot her one of his looks that always shut her up, and she straightened in her seat and patted down her hairdo. She took a red lipstick from her purse, twisted the mirror, and carefully applied the lipstick, even though her lips were already red, whispering Ladino words I didn't understand through clenched teeth.

When we got home she sent me to my room. I sat on my bed and waited. Father came in a short while later carrying the belt with the painful buckle, but instead of hitting me on the bottom like my mother had promised, he asked me quietly, "What were you looking for with the Kurds? You know your mother doesn't permit it."

"I didn't go to the Kurds," I whispered.

"So where *did* you go?" my father asked, not understanding.

"I went to Nona Rosa," I replied and burst into tears.

"My darling," my father said, dropping the belt, kneeling, and taking me in his arms. "My sweetie, you know that Nona Rosa won't be going back to her house anymore. She's living at Har Hamenuchot now."

"I thought she'd gotten lost again and that she'd soon find her way back," I wept. "But she didn't come. She didn't come." My father kissed me and tried to pacify me, but the spring of my tears welled uncontrollably.

"Dio santo, David, I asked you to give her a little slap, not kill her," my mother said from the doorway, looking astounded at the sight of her weeping daughter clasped in her husband's arms.

"She was missing Rosa," my father said. "She went looking for her at her house."

My mother looked at me as if she couldn't believe her ears, her stare morphing into an expression I hadn't seen before. Perhaps there was even some tenderness in it. But instead of hugging me like I wanted so much, instead of consoling me as my father had, she simply walked out of the room and closed the door behind her.

Then came the day when the family decided it was time to remove the furniture and belongings from Nona Rosa's house and return it to its owners, the Barazani family. Mother said we should sell it all to the junkman, because we'd already sold everything of value when we'd needed the money and everything leftover was worthless.

"Nothing's worth anything for you!" Becky exclaimed. "The dinner set is worthless? The Shabbat candlesticks? The chandelier? It's all worthless?"

"So you take them, but we'll sell the rest to the junkman."

"Calm down, Luna," said Rachelika, who was the most reasonable of the three sisters. "The cabinet's worth a lot. It has crystal mirrors and a marble surface."

"So you take it. I'm not bringing junk into my house. I have enough garbage as it is."

"All right," Rachelika said, "I'll take the sideboard and the cabinet."

"And I'll take the dinner set," said Becky.

"No, actually I want the dinner set," my mother blurted.

"You just said it's all junk," Becky said, annoyed.

"No, the dinner set is from Father and Mother's wedding. It was a gift from Nona Mercada."

"So why should you get it?" said Becky, not giving in.

"Because I'm the eldest, that's why. I've got rights."

"Just listen to her. I'm going to explode!" Becky stood up and started shouting. "Just a moment ago it was all junk, and just when I said I wanted the dinner set, she suddenly wants it for herself. If Rachelika's taking the sideboard and you're taking the dinner set, what's left for me?" She was on the verge of tears.

"Whatever you want," my mother said. "As far as I'm concerned you can take it all: the armchairs, the couch, the table, the pictures, everything."

"I want the wardrobe with the mirrors and the lions," I said.

The three of them looked over at me, astonished.

"What did you say?" my mother asked.

"I want the wardrobe with the mirrors and the lions on the top that was in Nona's room."

"Don't talk nonsense," my mother said.

"I want it," I said, stomping my foot.

"And where are you going to put the wardrobe with the lions? On my head?"

"In my room."

"All right, you've been heard, Gabriela. Don't interfere in grown-up matters. Go outside and play."

"I want the wardrobe with the lions!" I persisted.

"And I want a Cadillac convertible," my mother replied. "Go downstairs and stop getting in the way." She turned her back on me and continued dividing up Nona's things as if I wasn't there.

"All right, we're in agreement," she told her sisters. "Rachelika's taking the cabinet, I'm taking the dinner set, and Becky, you take whatever you want of what's left."

"I want the wardrobe with the mirrors and the lions!" I repeated.

"You can want all you like!"

"What is it with you and that wardrobe?" Rachelika asked gently.

"I want a memento of Nona," I said, weeping.

"But sweetie," Rachelika said, "it's huge. Who's going to carry it up five flights to your apartment? Your mother's right. You don't have room for it. I'll take you to Nono and Nona's house and you can choose whatever you want."

"But the wardrobe," I wailed, "I want the wardrobe with the lions."

"Enough, ignore her. Why are you even talking to her?" my mother said to Rachelika irritably.

"Luna, basta! Can't you see the child's sad? It's not the wardrobe. It's the sentimental value, isn't it, dolly?"

I nodded. I wished Rachelika were my mother. If only I could swap so that my mother would be Boaz's mother and Rachelika would be mine. My mother loved Boaz more than me anyway.

Rachelika held me to her and kissed me on the forehead. I sank into her arms. The softness of her belly and big chest enveloped me, and for a moment I felt I was being hugged by Nona Rosa. Feeling warm and safe surrounded by my aunt's big body, I finally calmed down.

They sold the wardrobe with the lions to the junkman as well as the chandelier, the couch, the table, the chairs, the armchairs, and the tapestries. Mother took the dinner set but gave in to Becky on the candlesticks and the rest of the porcelain crockery. Rachelika took the glass-fronted cabinet and the big grandfather clock that nobody else wanted.

As I stood in Nono and Nona's yard for the last time and watched the junkmen load their precious and cherished possessions onto a cart harnessed to a tired old horse, the tears flowed from my eyes. Rachelika wiped them away and showed me a bunch of items wrapped in an old tablecloth that in a moment would be heaved onto the cart. "Pick whatever you want," she said, and I chose a big oil painting of a river encircled by mountains with snow-covered peaks that reached into a clear blue sky. I had never really paid the painting any attention before, but it was all I had left, and I clutched it close to my heart.

And when the junkmen finished emptying the house and it was time to load the wardrobe with the mirrors and the lions, I stood to the side as they struggled to get it through the door. It was as if the wardrobe was resisting, and they were left with no choice but to remove its doors. I couldn't stand the sight of the doors separated from one another, and as I ran toward the cart, my mother shouted to Becky, "Catch her! Why did we have to bring her here with us?"

Every day at two o'clock on the dot Father would come home from the bank. While he was still downstairs he would whistle to the tune of "Shoshana, Shoshana, Shoshana" so we'd know he'd arrived, and I'd run to the landing and look down over the railing. He always carried the rolled-up copy of *Yedioth Ahronoth* that he'd pick up on the way. Once he walked through the door, he'd go and wash his hands and then take off his jacket and carefully hang it over the back of a chair so it wouldn't crease. Father always took great care with his appearance when he went to the bank. Even in the summer when everybody was wearing short-sleeved shirts and sandals, Father kept his jacket on and wore shoes that he took extra care to polish. "A person should respect his place of work," he'd say, "so that his place of work will respect him."

After he'd take off his jacket he'd loosen his tie, and only then would he sit down at the table for lunch. One day, when Mother served macaroni with kiftikas con queso, cheese croquettes in tomato sauce, Father topped his macaroni with a respectable portion of kiftikas con queso and sauce, mixed it up, and ate it all together.

My mother lost her temper. "Why are you eating like a primitive, David? You should eat each thing separately, first the kiftikas and then the macaroni, and put the tomato and salted cheese sauce on the macaroni."

"Don't tell me how to eat," my father said. "I learned to eat macaroni long before you even knew what macaroni was. The Italians eat macaroni exactly like this, only they have kiftikas with meat and they sprinkle cheese over it."

"I want mine like Father's," I said.

"Of course you want it like Father's," my mother hissed. "Great, David. Now your daughter will become uncivilized like you."

Father ignored her and continued eating. "Not enough salt," he said.

"That's because I'm not in love," she replied. But I didn't understand what she meant.

"And pepper too," my father went on. "You cook like my troubles, without flavor and without aroma."

"If you don't like it, then go eat at Taraboulos."

Ronny and I tried to ignore the daggers flying across the table. For a long time now our parents' relationship had been tense. Through the wall that separated our room from theirs I'd hear them arguing at night, my mother crying, my father threatening he'd leave if she went on nagging, the door slamming, words of hatred shouted in a whisper so that we children wouldn't hear. I'd cover my ears with my little hands and pray to God that Ronny was asleep and couldn't hear what I did.

One afternoon, when Rachelika came over with her children and they sent us off to play while they whispered together in the kitchen, I heard my mother tell her, "If it weren't for the children I'd have sent him to hell a long time ago." And Rachelika replied, "Paciencia, hermanita. It's just a bump in the road, and it'll pass," to which my mother said, "It'll never pass. It's how he is, always looking at other women. Only now he's looking at the same one all the time and I have to live with it."

Rachelika said, "I thought you didn't care what he did," and my mother replied, "Of course I don't care about him, but he's my husband and he humiliates me and I get so upset I could kill him. And worst of all, he lies. I know he has someone on the side, and he lies about it."

And Rachelika said, "Enough, Luna, you have to get hold of yourself so that nothing happens to you. You must think of the children. Don't break up your family, God forbid."

"What frightens me," said my mother, "is that if anyone breaks up the family, it'll be him, and what will I do if he gets tired not only of me but of the children as well? How can I raise two children on my own? That woman, may she burn in hell, I'd tear her clothes off and throw her naked onto Jaffa Road."

Then they started talking so quietly that no matter how hard I pressed my ear to the wall I couldn't hear, and the more I tried to understand who the woman was my mother wanted to throw naked onto Jaffa Road, the less I understood. And most of all I didn't understand how it could be that my mother didn't care about my father, and why my mother was frightened that Father would break up the family, and what breaking up a family meant. Was it like tearing down a building, like they did with Ezra's grocery in Nahalat Shiva, and putting up a new building in its place?

After lunch my father rose from the table and went straight into the bedroom without helping my mother clear the table. Unusual for her, my mother didn't say a word about it. She cleared the plates and put them in the sink, cleaned the tomato sauce from Ronny's face, and took off his stained shirt.

"You're a primitive too," she scolded him, and after she changed his shirt and sent me to my room to do homework, she washed the dishes and lay down on the living room couch, warning us to be quiet and not wake her. And it occurred to me then that my mother hadn't been going to nap in the bedroom with Father for a long time.

When I saw that Mother had closed her eyes, I slipped into their bedroom. Father was asleep on his side in his undershirt and underpants and hadn't bothered to cover himself. I went over to him quietly and waved my hand over his eyes to make sure he was really asleep and wouldn't, God forbid, suddenly wake up and surprise me. Peeping from the pocket of his pants that were folded neatly over the back of the chair by the bed was his brown leather wallet. I carefully removed it, took out a five-lira note, and put the wallet back.

I hid the five lirot deep inside my backpack, and the next day, after getting off the Number 12 bus at the last stop on my way home from school, I stopped at Schwartz's store and bought myself a new pencil box with colored crayons, and even had enough money left over for a pack of yellow Alma gum and a chocolate-banana ice cream. And when my father didn't say a word about five lirot missing from his wallet, I continued taking from it, a different sum each time but never more than five lirot.

As time went by, I got bolder. I started stealing money from the teachers' purses at school and stuff from the children's backpacks in class: erasers, pencil boxes, stickers, and the allowance their parents had given them. One time I stole so much money that I had enough to take Ronny to the Luna Park and go on all the rides and buy us both a falafel and soda.

Mother and Father were so busy fighting that they didn't notice. Even when Ronny, despite my warning, told Mother that I'd taken him to the park, she said, "That's nice," and didn't ask questions. The fights taking place behind Father and Mother's bedroom wall became more frequent. My mother's crying tore through the silence of the night as my father tried to hush her. Sometimes he'd leave the house, slamming the door, and I couldn't fall asleep until I heard him come back hours later. One night when they couldn't control their volume and even my fingers couldn't drown out the noise, Ronny crawled into my bed, hugged me tightly, and cried. I held him close, stroked his head, and rested my lips on his forehead until he fell asleep. When I woke up in the morning I was soaked to the skin. Ronny had wet my bed. Mother came in and when she saw the soaking bed asked me, astonished, "What's all this? Did you do peepee in bed?" and I wanted to tell her it wasn't me, but my little brother's sad eyes stopped me and I stayed quiet.

"That's all I need right now," she said. "You should be ashamed of yourself! A big girl like you doing peepee in bed."

That day after morning recess I was called to the principal's office, and I knew the game was up—I'd been caught.

My legs were trembling as I knocked on the principal's door. He was sitting at his big desk, and behind him hung a large picture of Prime Minister David Ben-Gurion, and beside it, one of the president of the State of Israel, Yitzhak Ben-Zvi. Without speaking the principal signaled me to sit in the chair across from him. As soon as I sat down, my homeroom teacher Penina Cohen got up from the chair next to mine and stood beside the principal, who pointed to my backpack situated on his desk.

"Is this your bag?" asked Penina Cohen.

"Yes," I nodded.

"Yes what?" she asked harshly.

"Yes, miss."

And then without a word the teacher emptied its contents onto the desk. Pens, erasers, crayons, pencil boxes, and piles of coins and bills fell from it together with my textbooks and homework books. The principal looked at me and said, "Gabriela Siton, can you explain this?"

I couldn't and didn't want to explain. I just wanted the ground to open up and swallow me so I could disappear from that room, from the school, from the world, forever.

Everything that took place in the principal's office next has been erased from my memory. It was only at home afterward that I heard the story from my father. When teachers' complaints about missing items increased, they realized that a thief was active in the school. No one suspected the students until students began reporting missing erasers and pencils and pencil boxes and money. And when my teacher noticed that I was her only student who hadn't complained about theft, and when the children began telling about my after-school spending sprees, the suspicion immediately arose that the thief was

Gabriela Siton. And just to make sure it was me, they took me out of the class-room and then searched my backpack without me knowing.

That day I was sent home early. My parents were summoned to the princi-pal's office, and after they got home, my father beat me with the belt with the painful buckle, but this time he didn't pretend to pacify my mother. He really thrashed me. Ronny cried and threw himself onto the floor. My father was in a rage and hit me again and again until even my mother came to my defense: "Enough, David, you'll kill the girl." He stopped only when I was writhing in pain on the bathroom floor. But that was nothing compared with my real pun-ishment: facing my friends in class the following day.

From then on my status changed. The other kids in school bullied me. Years later whenever I couldn't sleep, instead of counting sheep I'd recount the nicknames of the children who were with me in school. I remembered them by the order in which they sat in class: Ita Pita, who was bullied because she was fat, Fay the Lay, who, so rumor had it, let boys feel her tits after school, London Bridge, who'd immigrated from London just as we started to learn English, and me, the girl who until then had been class queen, I was called Ganefriela, a play on the Hebrew word for thief.

My father walked around like a caged tiger, trying to hold back his anger. "I'm a bank employee," he said, "as straight as a die, but my daughter's a thief!" He couldn't forgive himself for his terrible failure in my upbringing, and he refused to forgive me. But he certainly made no attempt to understand why a girl who had "ev-ery-thing," as my mother repeatedly said, had to steal.

My mother didn't give a thought to it. She didn't know about the hell I went through every day at school, the insults I suffered, the bullying, and even if she had, I doubt she or my father would have done anything to stop it. They surely would have thought it a fitting punishment for somebody who'd brought such shame on the family. So I didn't say a word.

They never mentioned my thievery again. My father and mother carried on with their petty, sad life, and as time went by their quarreling was gradually replaced with tense silences.

When I outright refused to continue with my classmates to Leyada, the Hebrew University Secondary School, they disapproved but didn't force me. When I went to enroll in a school considered far inferior, they didn't even bother to come with me to a meeting with the principal, and I handled the entire process myself. And when, at age sixteen, I went to a party at Beit Hacha-yal, the soldiers' club, came home with a handsome boy in a white navy uni-form, and stood in the doorway to our apartment building kissing him like there was no tomorrow, my father came downstairs, pulled me roughly out of the boy's arms, beat me, locked me in the bathroom, and gave me a strict pun-ishment: to come straight home after school, not meet my girlfriends, not listen to Radio Ramallah, not go to the cinema. To go into my room each day and not come out until it was time for school the next morning.

That was the day that the unspoken alliance between me and Father was finally broken, an alliance that had saved me from my mother's anger more than once, an alliance that until then had made my father my safe haven, a place where I was welcome and loved unconditionally. When Nona Rosa died my father had become my only refuge. But no longer. The seeds of the rift had been slowly sown during my adolescent years, and my father was un-able to accept the fact that I had become a young woman with needs of her own.

On the third day of my sentence, instead of going to school and coming home directly after, I walked to the central bus station, boarded a bus to Tel Aviv, and then headed to Rothschild Boulevard, where Tia Allegra, my mother's elderly aunt, lived.

I knew the boulevard well, after all the pleasant vacations I'd spent there. I stood outside Tia Allegra's house and took in the beautiful Bauhaus building she'd lived in for years, the rounded balcony, the tall trees and shrubs in the entrance garden. I drew in a deep breath, the air of freedom that spread throughout my body every time I came to Tel Aviv, pushed open the wooden door, and slid my hand over the banister as I climbed the marble stairs to Tia Allegra's apartment on the second floor and rang the bell.

"Who is it?" my mother's aunt asked.

"It's me, Gabriela," I replied. Through the locked door I could hear the old lady hobbling along with her cane.

Tia Allegra opened the door. "Dio santo, Gabriela, what are you doing here, querida? Don't tell me it's Sukkoth today and I didn't know!"

I fell into my old aunt's arms and started to cry.

"What's happened, querida mia? What's the matter, hija? Why are you crying?"

"I'm tired," I told my old aunt. "I want to sleep."

She led me into one of the rooms and said, "Lie down, querida, and when you wake up you can tell me why you're here. But rest now, and I'll make some habas con arroz because you'll probably be hungry when you wake up."

I don't know how long I slept, but when I woke up it was already dark and Tia Allegra was sitting in her deep armchair by the balcony door. Next to her was her usual trolley with a cup of tea and a plate of biscuits.

She smiled at me. "Did you sleep well?"

"Yes." I nodded. "I was very tired."

"Go into the kitchen," she instructed. "I've made you something to eat. Warm it up. My legs won't take me anywhere these days, and they hurt from standing over the stove."

I entered the kitchen, loaded a plate with white rice and beans in tomato sauce, mixed it, and went back to the living room to eat it beside my aunt.

"How's the habas con arroz?" she asked. "I've lost my sense of taste recently and my children are always complaining that there's not enough salt in it."

"It's delicious," I said, enjoying the comfort of food I'd known since the day I was born.

"I called your father at the bank," she said. "He told me that I should put you right back on a bus to Jerusalem. I told him it would be better if you stayed the night. In the morning my son-in-law Shmulik will take you to Jerusalem in his car so we're sure you make it home and don't run away to God knows where."

I remained silent. At least I'd bought myself one night of freedom.

"What's happened, querida?" Tia Allegra asked gently. "Why have you run away from home again?"

"My father beat me and punished me. I can't leave the house for ten days."

"Why, what did you do?"

"I was kissing a boy from the navy who'd brought me home from a party at Beit Hachayal." I was too ashamed to tell her that my father and I no longer got along.

My mother's old aunt laughed. "*Wai de mi sola*, your father beat you for that? What, he's already forgotten that he himself was young once?"

"Do you remember when you were young?" I asked her.

"I remember what happened when I was young far better than I remember what happened yesterday." She sighed. "I remember what I lost long ago and I'm still losing things today."

I recalled how Nona Rosa had once told me that nothing ever got lost because there was a land for all the lost things and there, so Nona Rosa told me, lived all the lost memories, the lost moments, the lost loves. And when I asked Nona where the Land of Lost Things was, she replied, "Do you remember, querida, that once you asked me what God was and I told you that it's the rainbow? Well, there in the land where God is, the Land of the Rainbow, are all the lost things too."

"But how do you get to the Land of the Rainbow?" I asked my lovely nona.

"The Land of the Rainbow, mi alma, is very, very far away. You need lots of patience and you must go far to reach it."

"But where's the road to it?" I persisted.

"*Corazon,* to reach the Land of the Rainbow you have to walk to the end of our neighborhood and from there to the fields of Sheikh Badr, where the new Knesset is being built. And after you walk through the fields for a long, long time, you come to a little river, and by the river there's a long, long path that goes through the mountains and the valleys. And after days, maybe nights, the path melts into the sea in Tel Aviv, and there the path crosses the sea and goes on and on until it comes to the end of the sea. And there, at the end of the sea, where the sun meets the sky, is the Land of the Rainbow, and in the Land of the Rainbow is the Land of Lost Things."

I told Tia Allegra about Nona Rosa's Land of Lost Things and she laughed and said, "Your nona, God rest her soul, I didn't know she knew how to tell stories."

"She told me lots of stories," I said proudly. "She told me stories about our family and about the men in the family who don't love their wives."

"God forgive my sins, is that what Rosa told you, may she rest in peace? El Dio que me salva, is that any way to speak to a little girl?"

"She told me that Great-grandfather Raphael didn't love Nona Mercada and that Nono Gabriel didn't love her, and I know that my father doesn't love my mother either."

"*Pishcado y limon,* hija, what are you saying? Where does this nonsense that your father doesn't love your mother come from?"

"Is it true?" I asked my aunt, who seemed to have shrunk into her chair and now looked smaller than ever. "Is it true that the men in our family don't love their wives? And that Nono Gabriel didn't love Nona Rosa?"

"Gabriela Siton, stop talking nonsense," she scolded me. "You probably misunderstood your nona. She probably said that Gabriel *did* love her."

"No!" I insisted. "She said he didn't love her. She told me about Great-grandfather Raphael who loved an Ashkenazia but married Mercada, and she told me that of all the young girls in Jerusalem, Mercada chose her, the poor orphan, to marry Nono Gabriel, and when she was ready to tell me why Mercada chose her, she died."

"May she rest in peace. I can't understand why she'd tell you such nonsense."

Tia Allegra, who if Nona Rosa hadn't died would have been the same age as her or perhaps even a bit older, was very different from my nona. Tia Allegra was wearing wide pants, a white blouse, a buttoned cardigan, and round glasses, while Nona Rosa, even when she couldn't see very well, had refused to wear glasses. And unlike Nona Rosa, Tia Allegra knew how to read and write, and on her tea trolley there was always a copy of *Davar,* to which she had a subscription. "Tel Aviv turned her into an Ishkenazia," Nona Rosa used to say.

I finished eating, took my plate and spoon into the kitchen, washed them, laid them on the dish rack to dry, and went back into the living room. My mother's old aunt was sitting deep in thought. I looked at her and wondered what people did when they got old, when their legs became heavy and they couldn't go downstairs to the boulevard and feed the birds, and when they did go down, it was hard for them to climb back up. What did old people do when evening fell and the street noises were replaced by silence, and even the birds stopped their twittering? It was then that I realized I was easing Tia Allegra's loneliness. For years she had taken care of Nona Mercada, who'd lived with her until she passed away. She, I knew, could continue our family story from where Nona Rosa had left off. I couldn't let the moment pass and become another lost moment in the Land of Lost Things, so I asked her to tell me what my nona hadn't had time to relate.

"Why is it so important for you to know all this?" Tia Allegra said. "Why waken the dead from their sleep? Why talk about things that time can't change?"

"I want to understand," I told her. "I want to know about our family and the men who didn't love their wives."

Tia Allegra sighed deeply and seemed to sink into contemplation. She remained silent for a long time, and I studied her lovely face that so reminded me of Nono Gabriel's: the same high cheekbones that even in old age gave her a noble appearance, the same slanted green eyes, the same chiseled straight nose. In the light of the lamp I could imagine her as a young woman, as proud as my grandfather, a young woman who admired her elder brother.

Tense, I sat on the edge of my chair, afraid of losing the opportunity. I wanted Tia Allegra to tell me why Nona Mercada had forced my handsome grandfather to marry my poor, orphaned grandmother from the Shama neighborhood. I needed Tia Allegra to remove the veil concealing the curse of the Ermosa women, a curse that maybe I carried with me, even though back then I couldn't yet have known.

And then, when I was sure that the old lady would entrench herself in her silence and that there would be nobody to continue my grandmother's story, she suddenly spoke in a quiet voice. "Our family, querida, the Ermosa family, is a good family, a fine family. But something happened, and since then our family has not been the same. It affected all the women and all the men in our family. I'll tell you about my mother Mercada, who was—how did my sister-in-law Rosa put it?—a sour old woman. But to tell you about Mercada I have to begin with my father Raphael and the time he went to Safed. Listen well, Gabriela, to what I'm telling you, because I'll say it only once, and I'm still not even sure I'm doing the right thing by sharing it with you."

The soft light of the lamp illuminated Tia Allegra's lined features. It's going to be a long night, I thought and made myself comfortable on the couch. As I gazed at the old woman, I missed my nona terribly. Tia Allegra didn't resemble her: not in her build, which compared with Rosa's was slim; not in the gray hair gathered into a bun at the back of her neck, compared with Nona's braid that she wore coiled around her head. Not in the soft jumper that covered her small breasts or her slim feet in their orthopedic shoes, compared with my nona's swollen ankles that were always in her sapatos. Not even in her body language. But in one thing she reminded me of her very much: her speech, which combined broken and proper Hebrew and Ladino, whose literal meaning I couldn't understand but whose essence I could.

"I'm listening," I told Tia Allegra like a disciplined child. "I'm all ears."

"Where should we begin?" Tia Allegra asked herself.

"From where Raphael met the Ashkenazia in Safed and fell in love with her," I replied.

"Dio santo, did your grandmother tell you that as well? What else did she tell you?"

"That she entered him like a dybbuk and that he hurried back to Jerusalem to marry Nona Mercada."

"May God forgive my sins, what are you getting me into, chicitica? I truly hope that your grandmother, may she rest in peace, doesn't haunt me in my sleep."

"She'll come to you in a dream and tell you you're doing the right thing," I said. "She'll tell you that if she hadn't passed away she would have carried on telling me our family story herself."

"All right." Tia Allegra sighed. "May God forgive me if I'm making a mistake."

2

"FROM THE DAY HE MARRIED Mercada, my father Raphael Ermosa, may he rest in peace, became a hardworking man in a class of his own. He'd get up early every morning, bless the Creator for restoring his soul, put on his phylacteries, hurry to morning prayers at the synagogue, and afterward, while the other worshippers chatted, Raphael would already be on his way to his father-in-law's shop at Souk al-Attarin, the perfume market. His father-in-law had brought him into the business right after the wedding. Senor Yochanan Toledo was a big merchant who imported spices and other goods from Lebanon and Syria. As well as turmeric and cinnamon, cardamom, curry, and cloves, he sold medicinal herbs for relieving pain and warding off the evil eye, and he traded with Jews and Arabs alike. There was a big demand for medicinal herbs in those days because many people in Jerusalem were sick.

"Raphael Ermosa fell in love with the market's vibrant atmosphere. He loved the long lines of fellahs, the Arab farmers from the villages around Jerusalem who brought their produce to market every morning. He looked on amazed as the Arab women carried their wicker baskets filled with fruit and vegetables on their heads.

"There were a thousand smells in the market, the intoxicating fragrance of flavors from all over the world: the smell of burnt chickpea clusters that were sold in the market's alleys by vendors calling '*Hamla malana, hamla malana!*'; the smell of pita bread baking in the tabun; the sweet smell of tamarind juice; the stink of the dung dropped by donkeys loaded with sacks and jugs that passed through the narrow alleys; the smell of the people, Arabs and Jews, who shouted, jostled, shoved, and together with all the other scents and flavors formed a colorful throng.

"When Raphael's firstborn son, your grandfather Gabriel, reached the age of twelve months, he went to Souk al-Khawajat and ordered a gold bracelet for Mercada. He'd kept the vow he'd made on his wedding day to make his wife the happiest of women and treated her like a princess.

"And Mercada, the weeping girl who had been scared to death of the moment she would have to leave her father's house and marry, became an industrious, assertive woman, a balabusta, as the Ashkenazim say, who took good care of her husband and children. She ran her family with an iron fist and her home was held in high esteem by neighbors and relatives. And the more strength, influence, and power she gained, the more she treated her husband like a king. She was an inquisitive woman who didn't stop at cooking, cleaning, and raising her children. As the years went by, Mercada became a well-known healer who was in great demand by the residents of the Jewish Quarter. Her expertise was in livianos, curing anxiety and fears.

"And yet Raphael still searched among the Ashkenazi women in the market for the girl from Safed. Even though he'd done everything in his power to expel her from his heart, more than once he found himself thinking of her. Sometimes his feet would carry him to the Mea Shearim quarter, where the very religious Ashkenazim lived, and he'd wander between the closely packed houses and through the alleys, surreptitiously glancing at the women. Even if she were covered from head to toe, as was the custom with pious women, he would have recognized her by her blue eyes. But he'd never see her.

"In the early years of their life, Raphael and Mercada lived in a house next to the Eliyahu Hanavi Synagogue in the Jewish Quarter of the Old City, not far from her parents' house. After her father's death, when Raphael sold his father-in-law's shop and bought a shop in the Mahane Yehuda market in the New City, outside the walls, they moved to the Ohel Moshe neighborhood, where houses were arranged in rows around a central yard with a cistern that provided water for residents.

"Their house in Ohel Moshe became a magnet for the Jews of their neighborhood and the surrounding ones too. Neighbors would come to Raphael for donations and to Mercada for treatment. The house was always spotless and the yard around it was enchanting, flooded with light and big clay pots of herbs and geraniums. And so life progressed smoothly. Senor Raphael Ermosa met success in business and traveled once in a while to bring fresh goods from Lebanon and Syria. When his son Gabriel turned ten, Raphael took him along, training him in commerce so he'd be ready to take over the business when the time came. When they weren't traveling, Gabriel attended a Talmud Torah school in the morning and worked in the shop in the afternoon. He so excelled at the shop that it wasn't long before Raphael put him in charge of running it, while he himself spent more and more of his time sitting idly on his wooden throne in the shop's doorway.

"During the First World War, the Turks started recruiting young men into their army, forcing them to join against their will. To save Gabriel from a fate faced by many Jewish boys, Raphael decided to smuggle him out to America. And so that he wouldn't have to make the long journey alone, he decided that Moshe, the oldest son of his shop assistant Leon, would join Gabriel at Raphael's expense. So the two boys sailed from Jaffa to the Port of New York and settled in Manhattan, where Gabriel found a job as a butcher's apprentice and Moshe as a tailor's apprentice. For almost two years there was no contact between Gabriel and his parents. Raphael almost lost his mind with worry, but Mercada kept her composure and strengthened him: 'Que no manqui, we should not lack anything, amen! Trust in Senor del mundo. He is watching over the boy, and when the accursed Turks go back to their own country, he will come back to us, sano que 'ste, well and in good health,' she'd say.

"Time went by and the Turks, may their name be erased, left Palestine and in their place came the English, may their name be erased too, and one day, without warning, Gabriel showed up at his parents' door. Mercada, who had been watering the plants, almost dropped her watering can, and Raphael almost fainted with excitement, so before Mercada could fall into the arms of her beloved son who had returned from America, she had to quickly pour water over her husband and pick strong-smelling herbs to bring him around.

"Mercada could barely recognize her son. He had left Jerusalem a sixteen-year-old youth with a hint of stubble, short and as skinny as a beanpole, and had come back a handsome, tall, and well-built eighteen-year-old man. They gathered all the family and neighbors, and Mercada made cold lemonade with mint, brought up the watermelons from the cistern, and crumbled goat's cheese over them. She sat Gabriel in the middle of the yard, and everybody around him urged, 'Tell, tell us como es America, what America's like.'

"Gabriel told them of a place with buildings that touched the sky and automobiles that drove like locos, and his work on the Lower East Side with the butcher Isaac who only spoke Yiddish and didn't know a word of English, and about the first words he learned, and how today he could pull the wool over the eyes of any Ashkenazi in the market with his Yiddish. And about Moshe who decided to stay in New York and not come back to Jerusalem. When his father Leon heard this, he burst into tears, and Gabriel consoled him: '*No llores*, don't cry, Senor Leon. Moshe will be successful. He's already found a bride, one of ours, and he's going to get married and one day he'll bring you to America too.'"

"Uncle Moshe?" I interrupted Tia Allegra. "Our rich uncle from America?"

"The very same, querida. In the years they lived together in New York, he and Gabriel were like brothers, and they forged a bond they nurtured all their lives. Moshe became very wealthy and came to own women's clothing factories and shops all over America."

"He sent us packages from America!" Again I interrupted Tia Allegra. "Thanks to him I was the first girl in school to have real jeans."

I knew the story of the rich uncle from America very well, the uncle who, a short time after Nono Gabriel's return to Jerusalem, had married, had children, and established a fine family in New York. I'd heard many times how, as the years passed, Uncle Moshe's dream had come true and he'd become a millionaire. The packages from America arrived every three months in big boxes, and Father and Mother even saved a particularly pretty green one and used it to store bed linen.

One time, a long silk and lace bridal gown arrived with a photograph of the bride Reina, Uncle Moshe's youngest daughter, pinned to it.

"Tronchos de Tveria, cabbageheads from Tiberias," Mother said, "they've made a Purim costume out of it? Isn't it a pity, such an expensive dress?"

"Purim costume?" Becky said. "They've sent it for Gabriela."

"*Pishcado y limon,*" said Nona Rosa. "No time soon."

"If it's for Gabriela, then I'm taking it," Mother said, and nobody opposed her because nobody had any need for a bridal gown.

That night, when everyone was asleep, I got up quietly and crept into the living room. The bridal gown lay on the couch, shining in the darkness. Awestruck, I moved over to it and started stroking the soft silk and the pearl buttons that adorned the front. I lifted it gently and undid the buttons one at a time. It took a while because there were so many of them. Then I wiggled my little body into the dress, very slowly, so, God forbid, I didn't rip this dress that was so huge I drowned in it. When I eventually managed to get my arms into the sleeves, I tried to stand up so I could button it, but then my feet got tangled in the hem and I fell onto the floor, and at the last minute I grabbed at the low side table on which sat a vase of flowers. The table rocked, the vase smashed into pieces, and the dress and I found ourselves drenched with water and covered in shards of glass. Soon enough my mother was standing over me, screaming, "What the hell do you think you're doing!" And before checking to see if I was hurt, she ran her hands over me to see if the dress was damaged, and then stood me up and smacked my bottom.

"Destructive child! What are you doing in the living room at twelve o'clock at night? And who gave you permission to touch the dress? Go straight back to bed!"

Her yelling woke up Father and Ronny. Right away Father started yelling at Mother. "Why are you waking the whole neighborhood!" He picked me up as I cried and took me to the bathroom, washed my face, and changed my pajamas while he murmured, "It's okay, good girl. Everything will be okay." Then he put me into bed and covered me and sang right into my ear, "Sleep, sleep, my little one," and the moment before I closed my eyes I heard my mother whispering angrily, "She ruins everything, the ruffian."

The next day Mother took the bridal gown to her seamstress and had a dress made for the army veterans ball at the Menorah Club, where she and Father had been married. This time she didn't have a matching dress made for me. The dress was a dizzying success, and Mother, so Aunt Rachelika told me, was the belle of the ball. But that was nothing new. My mother was always considered the most beautiful of the Jerusalem girls. Every time Ronny and I walked down Jaffa Road with her, people would turn and look, and Mother would hold her head high, grasp Ronny's hand with one hand and mine with the other, and ignore the stares.

Mother loved buying shoes. Before Rosh Hashanah and Passover she would always take Ronny and me to the Freiman & Bein shoe store in the Pillars Building, and sometimes we even went when it wasn't a holiday. While she'd try on shoes surrounded by a flock of assistants who complimented her on her ankles, Ronny and I would get giddy and play on the carousel and train slide they had in the store. But Mother didn't always buy shoes. Sometimes she'd just try on all the shoes in the store and then decide she didn't like any of them. The assistants never got angry with her. On the contrary, they'd compete over who'd climb higher up the ladder to grab her more shoe boxes. My mother would giggle with them, saying, "Shalom, thank you, and good-bye," and we'd all leave the store with heads held high and walk to the taxi stand on Lunz Street, where Mother would stop and chat with the driver "uncles," who'd been at Hadassah Hospital with her during the war. Sometimes she'd say, "Wait here for a few minutes with the uncles, I'll be right back," and then she'd disappear and return after what seemed like an eternity. In the meantime we'd sit on little chairs on the sidewalk and wait for her. Once when it took her especially long to return, Ronny started crying, and when she came running back, she begged a thousand pardons and told us for the thousandth time, "You know who the driver uncles are? They're hero uncles, they defended our Jerusalem for us during the War of Independence, so every time we meet the hero uncles you behave yourselves properly and be patient, and you, Gabriela," scowling at me and wagging a finger, "not a word to Father. If you tell Father I'll never take you to the carousel in Freiman & Bein ever again."

One day Mother left Ronny with Nona Rosa and took just me to the store. On the way there rather than the way back we passed the taxi stand. All the driver uncles stood by their vehicles, and they stopped talking when my mother approached. My mother, who always wore rouge on her cheeks, went as pale as a ghost, and her hand holding mine trembled. One of the drivers came over and hugged her tightly. It seemed strange to me that someone who wasn't my father was hugging her. He whispered something in her ear, and she let go of my hand and gave a stifled cry.

Someone brought her a chair and she sat down, took her handkerchief from her purse, and started sobbing. I stood there not knowing what to do. My mother was sitting on the side of the street by the taxi stand and crying, and I didn't know why. Was she crying because of me? Had I behaved badly and upset her again? I stood there helpless for a long time while the driver uncles consoled her. Eventually one of them noticed me. "Here, little one, have a sweet," he said and offered me a toffee. "Come on, don't be frightened. Your mother will take you home soon."

I popped the toffee into my mouth and then the uncle lifted me up and said, "Do you know why your mother's crying?"

"No," I said, shaking my head.

"Because Uncle Ginger has passed on," he said.

I was confused. On the one hand I didn't know what "passed on" meant, but I could sense that something bad must have happened to the uncle who had red hair and laughing eyes and who would always sit me on his knee and twirl us around in his wheelchair. "Hold tight," he'd say and put my arms around his neck and then roll the wheelchair fast along the sidewalk. I'd be helpless with laughter, and Mother would shout, "Stop, put her down, she's heavy. You shouldn't be carrying her like that!"

"He's passed on," the driver said. "He was badly wounded in the War of Independence when he was defending our Jerusalem, and his wound never healed, and now he's dead." I sat with the driver uncle for a long time until my mother took my hand once again and we walked home.

That evening Mother was quiet, hardly exchanging a word with Father, hardly speaking to Ronny and me. In the middle of the night I was awakened by the sound of her crying. My father wasn't able to calm her and left their bedroom. When he saw me and Ronny standing in the hallway he said, "Go to bed. I'll be right back," and left the house.

He returned a short while later with Aunt Rachelika, who hurried into Father and Mother's bedroom. As soon as Mother saw her, she burst into more tears and sank into her arms. Father came into my and Ronny's bedroom and lay down on my bed beside me. "More over a bit," he whispered. "Make room for your father." And for many nights after, he'd sleep like that, with me in my bed.

My mother didn't stop crying all night and all the days that followed. Why did she cry so much? Why was she sad? Why did she go from being a woman who spent all day out "measuring the streets," as my father used to say, to being a woman who locked herself up in the house? Why did she shut herself up with Aunt Rachelika? And why only after months did she return to routine was something I would not understand until many years later.

The day I ran away to Tia Allegra in Tel Aviv, I didn't yet know the answers. But I needed to. It was stronger than me, this thirst for the story of the women in my family, for the secrets that would help me understand. I knew I might discover things I'd regret knowing afterward, but since my nona had opened this Pandora's box, I had to know so I could move forward with my life.

"On condition you don't stop me again," Tia Allegra warned me, "because it's already late and soon my memories will get tired together with me."

I swore that from then on I'd keep silent and lay back on the cushions, closed my eyes, and listened.

"The Turks finally left Palestine and the English came in their place. A short time later your Nono Gabriel returned from America and started work in Great-grandfather Raphael's shop. He was handsome, as tall as a cypress tree, a young man of eighteen at the peak of his physical strength. He worked in the shop in the Mahane Yehuda Market from morning till night. While the other merchants had not yet opened their eyes to say the morning Shema prayer, he would already be carrying sacks out of the shop, arranging goods in their tins, and waiting for the first customer to arrive. Gabriel was the most industrious young man, and he had a great many ideas for expanding his father's business, enlarging the shop, and bringing in merchandise that would attract Ashkenazi customers. He persuaded our mother to prepare large quantities of olives and pickled cucumbers in big jars, and soon her pickled cucumbers were famous, and people began coming from all over Jerusalem for Mercada's pickles.

"To make it harder to resist, he'd take the salty cheese they bought from the Arab women out of its tin and lay it on the counter so the customers could 'taste it with their eyes,' as he'd describe it. He'd arrange the dried fruit in their sacks outside the shop, placing the best, biggest fruit on top and the more wrinkled ones further down. Later he added colored candies, row after row of anis-flavored bamblik sweets, pink and white sugared almonds they threw in synagogue at a groom or bar mitzvah boy, and the pistachios that came directly from Aleppo in Syria. It was a sight for sore eyes. And so the family shop became famous all over Jerusalem, and every Friday there was a long line of housewives that ran from the shop door on Etz Ha'Haim Street as far as Eliyahu Banai's fruit and vegetable shop on HaAgas Street.

"One day the widower Leon asked to speak privately with Senor Raphael. He told him he was thinking of marrying an Ashkenazia widow who had two children.

"'An Ashkenazia?' Senor Raphael asked, aghast. 'Why not find a good widow who is one of our own?'

"'I've looked,' Leon replied. 'But no widow of ours is prepared to marry a poor market assistant with a young son to feed, another son to marry, and a third one in America whose best years are behind him. The Ashkenazia widow doesn't mind that I'm no longer a young man and have sons. I need a wife to cook, wash, care for my young son, and I ask for your blessing.'

"When Raphael realized that Leon was determined to marry the Ashkenazia, he gave him his blessing and a handsome sum as a wedding gift.

"The Ashkenazia widow easily got along with the Sephardi women in Ohel Moshe and learned their customs, but she didn't give up her own. For her husband she cooked both Spaniol and Ashkenazi dishes. Her specialty was fruit-flavored custards. They were so tasty that Gabriel offered Leon a special counter in the shop where he could sell his Ashkenazia wife's wonderful custards on Fridays for Shabbat. Its success was immediate, and Gabriel, Leon, and the Ashkenazia had more work than they could handle, so Great-grandfather Raphael decided to bring in his younger brother Eliyahu, who everyone called Leito, to work in the shop as well.

"From the moment Leito started, he was put in charge of the cash register. Leon helped refill the sacks, metal barrels, and jars with fresh supplies, and Gabriel mingled with the customers and persuaded them to buy more than they'd intended.

"'*Pishcado y limon*,' Great-grandfather Raphael would say to Nona Mercada at the end of the day, 'your son, may he be healthy, could sell rocks and say they're salty cheese.'

"Mercada would sigh with pleasure. 'That boy is a gift from heaven, God loves him. He'll make us truly rich.'

"'We don't need to be richer than we already are,' Raphael would grumble. 'We have everything we need. We have a home, we have food, we're in good health and so are the children. We shouldn't be greedy and we don't need people to be jealous of us. We should thank Senor del mundo for everything He has given us and be satisfied with what we have. And now basta, enough of this chatter, make me a cup of tea.'

"And Mercada would fall silent and hurry to the yard to pick sage leaves to infuse for her husband's tea, and in her heart she'd give a prayer that her son Gabriel, may he be healthy, be successful in all his endeavors. Her husband was right, they should be modest, for after all there were many in Jerusalem who had nothing to eat, and they, thank God, had everything a person needed and even more. And to fend off the evil eye she increased the family's donation to the poor, and although they gave handsomely, she knew that there were always people who had something to say and there were always people with big eyes, so she put up several hamsas in the shop and on the house walls, may His name be blessed and may He protect her son and her family from the evil eye, *tfu-tfu-tfu*.

"Like everyone else in Jerusalem, Mercada believed in the evil eye and was afraid of evil spirits. When she came home from the market at dusk, staggering along with her baskets on the cobblestones of the Ohel Moshe neighborhood, she could swear she heard the sound of footsteps following her, and convinced that at any moment she would encounter an evil spirit, she would walk faster and murmur, '*Pishcado y limon.*' Like all the other Spaniols she too believed that the combination of the two words *fish* and *lemon* would fend off the spirits.

"Mercada was so afraid of evil spirits and the evil eye that she didn't dare speak their name and called them *los de avashos,* those from below. Like human beings, the spirits were divided into male and female, and they were headed by the male spirit Ashmedai and the female Lilith. Lilith, belief had it, was frightened by red, so Mercada tied a red thread around her children's wrists, her husband's, and her own to keep her away. When Gabriel told his mother he felt like a woman with the thread around his wrist, she grabbed the hem of his coat and ordered him, 'Hide the thread under your sleeve, but God forbid that you take it off. Querido, there is an eye on us.'

"All she wanted was to keep the evil spirits away from her family and her home. It was because of this belief that she increased her activity in livianos, the healing ritual used to drive out evil spirits. The more she drove out the fears of others, she believed, the more she'd drive out her own.

"Mercada and her livianos became well known throughout Jerusalem, and people came to her house for help. She would seat the person seeking a cure on a low stool in the yard and drape a white sheet over their head, preventing them from seeing what was going on around them. Then she'd take lead pellets and melt them over a fire she set in the yard, whisper a prayer, and pour the molten lead into a bowl of water held over the head of the person. The water would give off a dense, mysterious smoke, and when the smoke dispersed, Mercada would take the lead out of the water and interpret the strange shapes it had formed. If she saw the shape of a dog, she'd ask the person if he or she had been bitten by a dog. When it had the form of an evil spirit, she'd ask if a spirit had appeared to him or her in a dream. And if she saw a human shape, she'd try and understand who it was. The shapes told her the person's fears, and she'd talk to the person about them and provide herbs and instructions on how to behave to drive out the spirit. People were so satisfied with the treatment that although Mercada stressed her services were free, there was a charity box overflowing in the doorway of the house, and once a week Mercada would donate the money to the Eliyahu Hanavi Synagogue. But the longer she treated people with livianos, the more she insisted on curing serious and trivial complaints alike, the more she donated her money to charity—the more her own fears increased, and the feeling that a catastrophe was about to befall her house would not leave her.

"Since she couldn't treat herself, Mercada decided to go and see Jilda la Vieja—Old Jilda—in the Jewish Quarter of the Old City. Jilda was ancient, perhaps a hundred years old, maybe more, and was thought to be a wise woman with whom even Ashkenazim consulted.

"One morning after Raphael and Gabriel left for the market and the rest of the family had gone off about their business, Mercada took her basket and walked down Agrippas Street to Jaffa Road, and from there until she saw the walls of the Old City and Jaffa Gate. When she reached Jilda la Vieja's yard, there were dozens of people who had been sitting on stools for hours, waiting their turn to see the old healer. There wasn't a single free stool, so she sat down on the stone steps in the entranceway and waited.

"*Wai de mi sola*, she thought. It'll be hours before it's my turn to see the old woman and I'll have no choice but to go back home empty handed. She opened the Book of Psalms she carried with her and began reading. At times like these, she was glad that unlike many of her relatives and neighbors, she could read and write. When they were young, her husband had taught her the Hebrew letters, and it was revealed that she possessed a brilliant mind. Whenever he brought home the *HaZvi* newspaper, she was able to read the news and discuss it with her husband. Once she even attempted to gossip with him about Ben-Yehuda's son Itamar's love affair with Leah, the beautiful daughter of Senor Abu Shadid, that all of Jerusalem was talking about, but he had silenced her with a gesture.

"He, of course, concealed from her the fact that the love story between the Ashkenazi and Leah the Sephardia was giving him sleepless nights. Times are changing, he thought to himself. Now Senor Abu Shadid has no choice and his daughter is marrying an Ashkenazi. Who knows, perhaps if I'd told my father about the blue-eyed Ashkenazia . . . And then he'd banish the notion, knowing that for all the money in the world his father would not have broken the agreement with Mercada's father to marry their children. Not only that, he would never have consented to a marriage between his son and an Ashkenazia. And though whenever he shared Mercada's bed he never experienced the feeling that had shot through him when he was struck by the Ashkenazia's blue eyes, and even during all the years of their marriage he had never felt excitement when his body touched his wife's, Raphael knew that all in all, fortune had smiled on him and that the good Lord had given him a wonderful wife and mother.

"As Mercada studiously read the Book of Psalms, her body swaying back and forth as she brought the pages to her lips and kissed them, something disturbed her concentration. On a stone wall nearby, a young girl was sitting, swinging her legs. The sound of her heels hitting the wall was driving Mercada crazy.

"'Could you stop banging your feet?' she asked the girl. When the girl raised her head and stared at Mercada, Mercada saw the bluest eyes she'd seen in her life, set in a face that was a perfect oval with blond hair in a flawless braid. Wide-eyed on seeing the breathtaking beauty of the girl, who looked back at her as if seeing right through her, Mercada felt uneasy. The girl's stare bewildered her. She got up from the steps and sat down again, confused, unable to remember why she'd spoken to her in the first place. And then it hit her: This girl isn't a girl at all. She's an evil spirit! This girl is Lilith, the one that makes Ashmedai, king of the demons, seem a guiltless saint. She immediately picked up her basket, hurried out of Jilda la Vieja's yard, and spat three times, *tfu-tfu-tfu,* her feet quickly carrying her out of the Old City. All she wanted was to get home as fast as possible. Nine times, so her mother had told her, you must repeat the Song of Ascents nine times so that your wish comes true. She had never prayed more fervently, never been more convinced that she had just encountered the evil eye in person, Lilith, may her name and memory be erased, Lilith, who was biding her time to harm her loved ones. The red thread she had tied around her loved ones' wrists had not driven Lilith away, hija de un mamzer!

"She resolved to expel the evil eye, and the next day went to see the Kabbalist Rabbi Shmuel of the Eliyahu Hanavi Synagogue in the Old City. The Kabbalist prayed and read the Talmud deep into the night, and Mercada brought him and his disciples steaming hot tea and her home-baked bizcocho.

"'Rabbi Shmuel,' she said, 'I have come to you to exorcise the evil eye that is on me and my family, and because of which I know no peace.'

"The rabbi took Mercada into the yard, lit a fire, and ordered her to stand over the flames with her feet apart and say her name, her mother's name, and her grandmother's name. He closed his eyes and said a prayer, and then all at once the embers glowed and sparks shot in all directions. Rabbi Shmuel opened his eyes, looked deep into hers, and told her to repeat the words of the prayer and supplication after him. When he finished, the embers stopped spitting sparks and the fire went out, and the rabbi said, 'You were right, Senora Ermosa, there was a big evil eye on you. But now it is all over, it has flown with the wind, we have exorcised it completely, and with God's help you are clean. Go back to your husband and children, and may you be healthy.'

"Mercada was filled with a sense of purity. The glowing embers, the sparks, the crackle of the wood as it was consumed by the flames, the kindly eyes of the Kabbalist rabbi, and the sight of Mount Moriah from his yard all made her feel that she had been cleansed. She thanked the rabbi and left a substantial sum of money in the box in his doorway. Before returning home, she stopped at the bagno, immersed herself in the ritual mikvah, and offered up a prayer of thanksgiving to Senor del mundo. When she got home she felt as pure and white as a bride on her wedding day."

"As the Ermosa family business flourished, the shop became too small to hold all the goods as well as the customers that frequented it, so when two adjoining shops became vacant after their owners passed on one after the other, Raphael purchased them, and Gabriel broke down the dividing walls.

"Raphael handed over the reins to Gabriel and stopped working in the shop almost completely. Instead he would sit in his wooden chair in the doorway leaning on his cane, twisting the curls of his beard that was now white, playing with his worry beads, and looking on satisfied at the growing number of customers, and at his son, who managed the shop so well.

"One day Gabriel came to the shop with white aprons, tied one around his waist, and told Leon and Leito to do the same. 'Like in America,' he explained to his father, who looked at him in astonishment. 'Now,' said Gabriel, 'now we have to give the shop a name, like in America.' And the next morning a big sign was put up over the shop: Raphael Ermosa & Sons, Delicatessen.

"The shop continued to thrive and the family's financial situation significantly improved. The family's other children also found their way in life: Clara was married and expecting her first child, Avraham and Matzliach opened a carpentry shop, Shmuel was still studying in a Talmud Torah school, and I, Allegra, who had gotten married while Gabriel was still in America, moved to Tel Aviv with my husband Elazar and gave Mercada and Raphael two grandchildren, may they be healthy, without the evil eye.

"That was when Mercada told Raphael, 'It's time we found a bride for Gabriel. The boy is twenty already and until he's married his little brothers won't get married either.' Raphael gave his approval and Mercada considered the list of possible young women. It wasn't difficult. After all, the Spaniols lived in a tight-knit community and knew one another well, and they sometimes even married distant relatives. She thought that Estherika, the daughter of Shlomo Molcho, a relative three times removed, might be a suitable match. The community's rabbis encouraged marriage within the family on condition that the couple were not blood relatives, so that defective children wouldn't be born, God forbid. Over the years, as the Spaniol community had dwindled, they feared that their sons and daughters would marry spouses from other communities, heaven help us.

"'Before you start thinking about a bride, sit down and talk to your son,' Raphael ordered Mercada.

"'What's to talk about?' she replied. 'His time to marry has come, and I'll find him the best bride of all the young girls in Jerusalem.'

"But still, she took her son aside for a talk. He was her dear son, her pride and joy. She had raised all her children wonderfully. 'They were born one after the other,' she liked to say, 'without a break, the way God wished it.'

"She didn't speak of the four children who had died at birth or before they were a year old. I've already told you, Gabriela querida, that the death of babies in those days was nothing out of the ordinary. Your nono Gabriel had been named after the Angel Gabriel so he would protect him and ensure that he not die, God forbid, before the redemption of the firstborn ceremony. Even after the other children were born, Mercada treated him as if he were her only son. When he went to America, she missed him so, and no one was happier than she when he returned. She felt sorry for Leon, whose son had chosen to stay in America. 'I'm like Mother Goose,' she said. 'I like my young under my wing.' Now she was resolved to find the most suitable bride for Gabriel.

"'Hijo querido,' she told him, 'it's time we made a wedding for you.'

"He didn't resist and didn't argue. He knew his time had come, but of all the girls he knew, there wasn't one he liked. While friends and relatives his own age had married one after the other, and Moshe, his friend who was like a brother, had married in America, and Clara and I, who were both younger than him, were also married, Gabriel remained a bachelor. He gave his consent to our mother, and right away she started on the task of finding his bride.

"'In two months we'll have a wedding,' she told her husband. 'All the girls in

Jerusalem are standing in line for your son.' She knew her son was a desirable groom. He came from a respected family whose financial situation was far better than that of most families in Ohel Moshe, Mazkeret Moshe, Nahalat Shiva, Sukkat Shalom, and the Old City together. He was good-looking, educated, and he'd lived in America. She took her time and visited the homes of many young girls. Girls of sixteen and seventeen from wealthy and respectable homes were first on the list, and afterward she narrowed them down based on their appearance. A girl who was too thin was immediately disqualified; one who dared to raise her head and look her straight in the eye was considered too forward; an educated girl was also frowned upon. They, she told herself, are not sufficiently obedient and certainly won't submit to my authority. She also judged the prospective brides by the refreshments served in their homes. Those who served tea and bizcocho were disqualified, but if they set a full table for her and the prospective bride's mother kept on filling it with delicacies, and both mother and daughter urged her to taste this and taste that until she was sated, the candidate would immediately be advanced on the list.

"'I'll find the best bride, the most beautiful of all the Jerusalem girls,' she told Raphael when she came home exhausted from another round of visits. 'I shall choose the girl who is to be the mother of my grandchildren, and I'll scrutinize her until I deem her worthy of joining the Ermosa family.'"

"Raphael was sitting in his usual place in the shop doorway. After many days of rain the sun had finally come out and its warm rays caressed his face. The strong fragrance of freshly picked oranges from the coastal groves mixed with the aroma of spices and the smell of fresh vegetables, fish, and meat. The familiar scent of the market filled his nostrils, and as Raphael drank them in, he felt happiness spread through him.

"Then he saw them approaching: an older woman dressed in black from head to toe, limping and clasping the hand of a younger one, whose blond hair was twisted in two braids around her head. Something about them drew his attention, and his eyes followed them until they stopped in front of the shop. When the older woman's eyes caught his, his heart skipped a beat. *Dio que me mate*, may God strike me dead. He felt the blood pounding in his temples and gripped the arms of his chair. He recognized her with certainty. The woman's body was slightly hunched and thin, her face wrinkled, but her eyes, even though they were somewhat dulled, were the same blue eyes that had first bewitched him twenty years earlier. He inhaled deeply. Upon meeting his stare, the woman had immediately looked away, grabbing the girl's hand and urging her to quicken her pace, but by the time Raphael was back to breathing normally, the two women were again in front of the shop, arguing in Yiddish. The young girl wanted to go in, but the older woman was hesitant. Suddenly the girl raised her eyes and stood as if transfixed. Raphael followed her gaze to see what had caught her attention, and then, fearful, he saw that it was Gabriel.

"From behind the counter, Gabriel's eyes locked onto the girl's and his jaw dropped. The knife that he had been using a moment earlier to slice cheese seemed suspended in midair. Raphael looked back at the girl, and to his amazement she didn't avert her eyes from Gabriel's gaze as she should have. Dio santo, she's bewitching him, the awful thought flashed through his mind. The way her mother bewitched me. It all happened in a second. Soon enough the mother was dragging her daughter out of the shop, but the girl turned her head as she was pulled away, not taking her eyes off Gabriel, who was standing as if paralyzed. Gabriel immediately regained his composure and started after them, but he was stopped by Raphael's thunderous voice. 'Donde vas? Where are you going?' Gabriel didn't answer and went back to his place behind the counter. They didn't speak about what had transpired, about the woman and her daughter. And for the first time since he had married her, Raphael didn't share what had happened in the shop that day with Mercada.

"That night Raphael was beside himself and didn't sleep a wink. The image of the dybbuk from Safed remained before his eyes. Despite the oaths he had sworn, he found himself thinking about her again and again. She had come here with her daughter, hija de una putana, to haunt him and his son. He would not let that happen. He'd drive her out of the market if he had to. Anyway, maybe it was all just in his head. Maybe he was only suspicious of his son because of what he himself had felt all those years ago. He sighed and asked himself what he would tell Mercada if his restlessness woke her up. But she was sound asleep, never imagining that this was the last night she would sleep peacefully."

"That hadn't been the first time Rochel had spotted Gabriel in the market. But since they never went into Raphael Ermosa & Sons, Delicatessen—they could only afford the basics—Rochel had otherwise only seen him from a distance.

If her father found out she'd been looking at a man, and a Sephardi one at that, he'd cut off her braids and lock her up in the house until she died.

"Rochel was considered to be a strange girl. Unlike her sisters, she disobeyed her mother and refused to help with the housework or look after her little brothers. For most of the day she'd sit on the steps and stare dazedly at the children playing in the yard or at the women hanging their washing on the line.

"'Rochel, kim aher,' her mother would call, but she'd pretend not to hear, and her mother's words would be lost to the sounds of the students' praying in the nearby yeshiva and the hubbub of the yard.

"'Rochel, kim aher,' the children would mimic her mother and pull her braids. What hadn't her parents done to drive out the evil spirit that possessed her! Her father brought a Kabbalist from Safed to exorcise the dybbuk, but she'd resisted, stomping her foot and screaming like a lunatic until they were forced to tie her to her bed. With her parents' consent, her big brother beat her, but that hadn't helped either. In the end, Rochel realized that she would do well to cooperate with her parents and agreed to go to the strange old Spaniol woman in the Old City for livianos treatment.

"Rochel hadn't been able to stop thinking about the man in the market, his broad, white smile, the dimples creasing his cheeks. She could feel her heart pounding when she thought about him, the blood climbing through her veins and flushing her face. And she, who always preferred sitting on the steps and staring at the sky, she, who refused to help her mother with the washing, cleaning, and taking care of her little brothers, now she jumped to carry her mother's basket to the market for the Shabbat shopping each week.

"One day, when her mother stopped at the Arab woman who sold oranges, she sneaked away and stood outside the shop as if examining the sacks of dried fruit, every now and then glancing at the handsome man behind the counter. She blushed when she saw him smile at customers and the two dimples on his cheeks deepen. Before she even heard her mother calling, she moved to slip away so he wouldn't notice her. But he *did* notice her, and their eyes met. She saw how his brow furrowed as he unashamedly studied her. And she, instead of averting her eyes, stared back at him! If her father or brothers had seen her, they would have beaten her half to death. If her mother had understood what was happening in her wildly beating heart, she would have sheared off her braids, shaved her head, and sent her to the Ratisbonne Monastery to live with the nuns, as she'd threatened so many times in the past.

"And now that Rochel had caught his eye, she was determined to go back.

The following day, while her mother was busy in the kitchen and her sisters were looking after their little brothers, she crossed Mea Shearim Street, hugging the walls and praying she wouldn't run into her father or big brother or, God forbid, a relative or friend, and walked to the Mahane Yehuda Market.

"The shop was full of customers, so nobody noticed Rochel standing by the counter waiting her turn. Not even Gabriel, who was busy attending to shoppers. And then, when her turn came, he looked at her and almost fainted at the sight of those blue eyes boring straight into his. He was beside himself. He was dumbstruck.

"'How may I help you?' he asked nervously.

"She didn't reply but continued staring at him, not taking her eyes from his for a second.

"'Olives, cheese, pickled herring?'

She shook her head to decline.

"'Heideh, girl, I don't have all day,' said the woman behind her.

"Gabriel took a handful of pink sugared almonds and put them into her hand, and his touch sent a shiver down her spine. She quickly closed her fist around the sweets, and without a word of thanks and without paying, she left the shop.

"She sat for a long time on the steps of the nearby Alliance School. She wasn't tired, hungry, or thirsty. She wasn't thinking about her parents, who were probably going out of their mind with worry and searching for her all over Mea Shearim, or about the beating she'd get from her brother when she got home. In the afternoon she witnessed the old man arrive and sit in the wooden chair in the shop doorway, rolling amber worry beads between finger and thumb the way the Arabs did. A few hours later she saw how, after drinking several cups of tea and chatting with passersby and his son, who came to the door every now and then, the old man got up and, leaning on his cane, went on his way. She waited as toward evening the other workers took the sacks and barrels inside, removed their aprons, and then left.

"The market emptied of shoppers, the stallholders and shopkeepers locked up their merchandise, the Arab peddlers went back to their villages, and then, when the red ball of the sun lingered in the west, he finally came out of the shop, bolted the heavy wooden doors, and headed away. She emerged from her hiding place and followed him.

"When Gabriel heard footsteps behind him, he turned his head, and their eyes met. The last of the sun's rays kissed her face, and he recalled how, long ago, he'd had asked his mother what God looked like, and she replied, 'Like golden light.'

"She quickly turned around and started walking away. He didn't know what roused him from his daze, but he followed the blue-eyed girl until they reached the Alliance School yard, his feet moving of their own volition. His heart thumped as she sat down on the steps and looked up at him. Gabriel was a man who controlled his urges, but what he felt at that moment was unlike anything he had felt in his life.

"On more than one occasion he'd had sinful thoughts, but he had never been carried away by them. He remembered how, as he and Moshe were strolling down Fifth Avenue on a spring Shabbat in New York, his eyes had fixed on the slim ankles of a young woman in a light, airy dress and sheer silk stockings. He felt such a rush of desire it gave him goose bumps, and he was unable to take his eyes off the ankles until his friend nudged him and said, 'Try not to trample the young lady.' He noticed the beauty of women and wondered more than once about what their dresses concealed, imagining their curvaceous bodies under the flowing fabric, lightly grazing their intimate parts. But he held back.

"Moshe, on the other hand, had the courage to speak directly to women. One evening, when each of them came back from work to their miserable room, Moshe suggested they go to the public bathhouse.

"'What's the occasion?' Gabriel asked him. 'It's not Shabbat eve.'

"'It's a special night,' Moshe replied. 'Tonight we're going to the bathhouse and then to the bordello.'

"Gabriel stopped what he was doing and looked at Moshe in astonishment. Not that he hadn't toyed with the idea of visiting the bordello, the single-story building in the Bowery whose heavy drapes hid what went on inside, allowing only the sound of voices and music to escape. Sometimes when they passed it on their way to the bathhouse he'd see inebriated men leaving, accompanied by full-bosomed, heavily made-up women with plunging necklines. But the distance between thought and action was great.

"'Go and enjoy yourself,' he told Moshe. 'I'm going to bed.'

"Moshe laughed. He loved his friend like a brother. When would the troncho notice that women wanted him even more than he desired them? When would he realize that it was time to free his lust and that it was not a sin, despite what their teachers at the Talmud Torah school had told them over and over again? But he knew Gabriel wouldn't be tempted, so he didn't try to persuade him.

"Moshe became a regular customer of the bordello. Gabriel, despite his curiosity and Moshe's repeated urging, chose to hold his lust in check. Even nowadays, when he stood behind the counter in the market and women made eyes at him, he would avert his own. Not that he didn't notice them. He saw them enter the shop, some thickly fleshed and clumsy, some thin, others with thighs as round as the hills that adorned Jerusalem. The girl now seated on the Alliance School steps was unlike any of them. Her body was slim with not an ounce of surplus flesh, her hands were long and slender, and her small breasts were like a child's. She was wearing a long-sleeved black dress and black stockings that hid her legs. Only her slender neck, her angelic face, and her golden braids were exposed, but he could imagine the pure white skin beneath her clothing. As he sat there in the dark with this blue-eyed girl, he knew his mother, father, and brothers were surely worried and that he must say goodbye and go home right away. But it was as if someone had nailed his feet to the ground, and he stood there, drowning in her eyes. The sun had long since set, and the Jerusalem sky was sown with stars. He would not be saying the evening prayer in the synagogue this night. Time seemed to stand still until she suddenly started, her whole body trembling.

"'Oy vey iz mir,' she said. 'My father will kill me.' And before he could process what was happening, she was gone.

"He was paralyzed, breathless, unsure of what had transpired from the time he had closed the shop and met the girl's eyes until now. He brushed off his clothes, straightened his cap, and turned toward Ohel Moshe.

"His mother was the first to see him. 'Querido mio, where have you been? What happened to you? I sent Leito to the shop to look for you, I ran to your sister Clara, and you, nada, not a trace!'

"He didn't reply and remained as silent as the Sphinx. He had never lied to his mother, and anyway, what could he tell her? That he'd followed the blue eyes of an Ashkenazia girl?

"'May He forgive my sins, hijo,' she said, wringing her hand, 'what's the matter with you? Has the cat got your tongue? Why don't you say something? Have you been robbed? He's been robbed! They've stolen all the shop's takings! The cursed Arabs from Sheikh Badr have robbed him!'

"'Nobody's robbed me,' he said quickly, and that, at least, was the truth.

"At that moment Raphael came in, his gray beard disheveled, his face chalk white. He leaned against the table and said to his son in a poisonous whisper, 'I didn't go to the synagogue, I haven't said the evening prayer, I haven't eaten supper. Wash your hands and sit at the table.'

"Raphael had not the slightest doubt about where his son had spent the last few hours. He knew that his worst fears had come to pass. He didn't tell a soul, and certainly not Mercada, but from the moment he'd seen the dybbuk from Safed in his shop doorway, he'd had no peace. He could barely breathe during the day and hardly slept at night. Her image once again haunted him, but his thoughts now, unlike those in the past, were shaded with anxiety and fear.

"When Mercada sensed that her husband hadn't been his usual self, she asked him, '*Que pasa,* mi querido, is everything all right?' and he replied impatiently with some flimsy excuse or other.

"Raphael increased his donations to charity and prayed with intensified devotion in the synagogue, begging the Almighty, blessed be He, for the Ashkenazia to go back to where she'd come from, that no harm should come to his family because of the daughter of the strange woman, that life should return to how it was before she and her daughter had shown up from heaven knows where and disturbed his days and nights.

"And as if in answer to his prayer, for the next few days the Ashkenazia and her daughter were nowhere to be seen. He gave thanks to the Almighty, blessed be He. Instead of rekindling his passion, the encounter with the dybbuk from Safed had done exactly the opposite: It was as if the flame had been dwindling and all that remained were the dry twigs, slowly being consumed until the fire would be completely extinguished. Again he gave thanks to his father, may he rest in peace, for marrying him to a fine woman like Mercada, and he even seized the opportunity to go to her bed after a long period of abstinence. And she, for whom anything to do with men's behavior could not surprise her, again closed her eyes and prayed for him to finish what he was doing and leave her alone. But to her shock, for the first time since they'd been married, he didn't get up immediately afterward and go to his own bed. He stayed between her sheets, lay his head on the pillow, and said, 'You must get Gabriel married quickly.'

"Surprised, she replied, 'What's the rush? I still haven't checked out all the possible brides.'

"'We must hurry. Tell Shlomo Molcho that we'll call on them with Gabriel on Saturday evening after Havdalah to agree on terms.'

"'Raphael, querido, haste is devil-sent. Why this insistence?'

" 'Don't argue with me, woman! The devil can make as much haste as he likes, and you'll curse the day you didn't listen to me and get to Estherika in time.'

"Mercada was seized by fear. What was her husband hinting at? Was her biggest nightmare about to come true, God forbid? Was the bad feeling she'd had for months not just her imagination? Despite the purification she'd undergone with the Kabbalist rabbi, had the evil eye not been removed from her family, and was Lilith still lying in wait?

"She said nothing more, and after dinner the following night, she knocked on Shlomo Molcho's door and told him to ready the house. On Saturday evening she and her husband would be coming with Gabriel to ask for his daughter's hand."

"Just as Raphael felt tranquility would reign in his life once more, he saw the girl. He had been sitting in the shop doorway, rolling his amber worry beads, and felt as if his heart had stopped. Her gaze was fixed on Gabriel, and Gabriel was not taking his eyes off her. But when Raphael turned back to look at the girl, she was no longer there. 'A demon,' he whispered to himself and spat three times. 'A true demon. One minute she's there and the next she's not!'

"May God forgive my sins, he thought. If Mercada finds out about the girl she'll set the whole of Jerusalem alight with rituals! She'll go to all the rabbis in Jerusalem to exorcise her, and she won't sleep at night. Her life will become a living nightmare. He decided he still couldn't tell her. Anyway, the girl would soon disappear from their lives. He would make sure of it. If he had to, he'd take her to her father, who would beat her to within an inch of her life, shave her head, and declare her a loca, a madwoman. He didn't care. If she wouldn't go willingly, he'd make sure she went to *jahannam, Allah yahdi inshallah,* he found himself cursing in Arabic.

"That day, when Gabriel was late from the market, and after Leito arrived and told them that the shop was closed and that he didn't find Gabriel at Clara's or at the synagogue or with the backgammon players in the porters' market, Raphael knew: His son had been possessed. It was a sign from heaven. He had been bewitched by her mother's eyes and now his son had been bewitched by her daughter's. If this was the decree of fate, then he would disobey it! His son, *ras bin eini,* his pride and joy, would have nothing to do with the Ashkenazia girl, no matter the cost.

"The next morning when they went to the shop, Raphael noticed that Gabriel wasn't his usual self. Again and again his eyes roamed to the door, and he didn't go home for his break in the afternoon. When Mercada came with a pan of sofrito she'd made for his lunch, he'd told her he'd been too busy to come home.

"Raphael also noticed that Gabriel was in no hurry to lock up the shop that day.

" 'You go home, Papo,' he told Raphael. 'I've still got some work to do. I'll be home soon.'

" 'Not soon and not later!' Raphael said forcefully. 'Either you come now or I wait until you lock up and we go home together.'

"Leito and Leon had already brought the barrels and sacks inside and headed home. The Arab women had gone back to their villages, the stallholders had shut up their stalls, the market had emptied of shoppers and sellers, and she still hadn't come. Even if she did, Gabriel thought to himself, how could I follow her with my father waiting?

"Raphael saw his son was on edge. He'll become a four-eyes, God forbid, if he keeps on squinting at the door like that. I must talk to him. I must warn him, he decided. I'll find the right time.

"When Gabriel finally locked up, the two men started toward Ohel Moshe. Gabriel supported his father as they walked in silence. He was deep in thought about Rochel. What if she never came looking for him at the shop again? What if he never saw her again? He would not let that happen. If she didn't come, then he'd go looking for her! And then, just before they crossed Agrippas Street and were about to go through the stone gateway to Ohel Moshe, he spotted her flitting between the alleys like a shadow.

"Lilith, the thought rushed through Raphael's mind when he too saw her.

"Gabriel's eyes sought the girl. 'Rochel!' he shouted, forgetting his father beside him.

"Raphael was alarmed. Rochel, may God forgive my sins, he knows her name. And as he tried to see what was happening, Gabriel took his hand from his father's elbow and started running after the girl.

"Raphael brandished his cane and shouted, 'Rebellious boy! Come back here this instant! Stop, I tell you. Stop!'

"Gabriel hesitated—after all, he had never disobeyed his father—but the fear that Rochel would disappear and he would never see her again was stronger, and he went on running after her through the market's alleys, leaving his old father standing in the darkness, waving his cane and shouting to the heavens with no one to hear. Gabriel continued after Rochel like a madman until she stopped and fell into his arms. He gathered her to his chest and brought his lips to hers. He had never felt such a powerful feeling, as if their bodies had been drawn together. She encircled his neck with her slender arms, standing on tiptoe, and he grasped her waist, drawing her body to his, feeling her small breasts through the coarse material of her dress. Then he held her away from him and she looked into his eyes and said in Yiddish, '*Ich hob dich lieb*, I love you.'

"At that moment the world around them ceased to exist. They didn't stop kissing, holding onto each other for dear life, her small body enfolded in his, his mouth whispering words that had never before escaped his lips, and she drinking in each one. Even though she didn't understand every word, she understood his breath on her face, the touch of his lips on her cheek, his heart pounding against hers.

"He'd completely forgotten his old father and didn't think at all about the price he'd pay, for there was no price for what he felt for the girl, who had now taken his hand and inserted it into her dress. He touched her bare skin and shuddered, quickly removing his hand.

" 'No, Rochel. It's forbidden.'

"She didn't reply but continued leading his hand to the lower curve of her belly. He stopped her. 'No, Rochel,' he said, fighting himself, 'no.' But his hands started moving over her body, caressing her small, soft breasts. He felt he was struggling to breathe, that in another moment his soul would leave his body, and before he realized the words had come out of his mouth, he said, 'We mustn't until we get married. We mustn't.'

"Rochel was very quiet, very brave. If her father or brother heard that she'd let a man's hands touch her body, they'd kill her, throw her body into the street, and nobody in Mea Shearim would condemn them for it. She wanted to stay with Gabriel on the filthy sidewalk in the Mahane Yehuda Market and not go back home. She knew what awaited her there. She could feel her father's rage and the blows of her brother's belt. She knew he would tie her to the bed and starve her of food and water for days until blood oozed from her arms. But she was prepared to suffer a thousand deaths for a few minutes in Gabriel's arms."

"The scandal that erupted in the weeks that followed threatened to tear Jerusalem apart. The extraordinary love story of Rochel Weinstein, the Ashkenazia from Mea Shearim, and Gabriel Ermosa, the Spaniol from Ohel Moshe, was the talk of the town. Not only had Gabriel fallen in love with an Ashkenazia, and a pious Ashkenazia from Mea Shearim to boot, but they were seen holding hands by the Alliance School steps in broad daylight. Raphael went berserk. Mercada fainted. The shouting, the weeping, the rending of garments were to no avail. The oaths and the livianos ceremonies and the exorcisms didn't help either. Gabriel was resolute in his love for Rochel and informed his parents that if they didn't give him their blessing, he would marry her anyway.

" 'It will not happen!' Raphael roared. 'My son will not marry an Ashkenazia!'

" 'Adio Senor del mundo, how have I sinned,' Mercada wailed and recalled the terrible day she had first seen Rochel and realized she was the devil's daughter, Lilith.

"Rochel was thrown out of her father's house in shame.

" '*Ich hob nisht mir eine tochter,* I don't have a daughter any longer,' her father cried. He stood up, tore the lapel off his wife's blouse, off his eldest son's shirt, and then his own.

" '*Mir sitzen shiva noch Rochel,* we're in mourning,' he told his wife and children. 'Tell everyone in Mea Shearim that we are sitting shiva. Rochel is dead.'

"Since being thrown out of her parents' house Rochel had slept in a different place every night, which Gabriel arranged for her. One night she stayed at Leon's house. His Ashkenazia wife took pity on her, and despite the protests of her husband, who feared going against the will of Mercada and Raphael, she agreed to let her sleep together with her children.

" 'But just for tonight,' she told Gabriel. 'Leon won't agree to any longer.'

"Rochel also spent a few nights in the home for the aged opposite the Wallach hospital. She paid by changing the residents' beds and emptying their chamber pots, but she couldn't stand the terrible stench, the feeling of nausea that rose in her throat, and she told Gabriel that she would rather sleep in the graveyard across the street. Gabriel swore to her that he would move up the date of their wedding and find them a house. He begged her to remain in the home for a few more days until he could come up with a solution. Rochel agreed, on condition that she'd work the night shift, when most of the residents were sleeping. And except for the deafening screams of one old man who had nightmares, the nights passed relatively quietly and she was able to sleep on the hard bed they'd given her. In the morning, she'd hold her nose as she emptied the chamber pots, and as soon as she'd finished she would hurry out, returning only that night for her next shift.

"In the daytime, Rochel would go to the Western Wall and pray for hours, pleading with God to get her father to forgive her, for Gabriel's father and mother to accept her so that they would be able to start a family. One time, even though she couldn't read or write, she left a note in a crevice in the wall in which she wrapped the few coins she had. Her tears, so she believed, would reach the Almighty faster than her words.

"Afterward she'd wander for hours through the streets, stopping at Yemin Moshe to watch the windmill turn in the breeze. 'Go wherever you want,' Gabriel had told her, 'but don't come to the market. We mustn't rub salt in my father's wounds and anger him. Let me bring him around slowly, and with God's help he will eventually welcome you into the family.'

"She also avoided the alleys of Mea Shearim, but she did so willingly. Almost from the day she was born, she had felt that the stone walls of the houses, the winding alleys, the yards abutting each other, the laundry hanging on clotheslines, all closed in on her. Her soul yearned for freedom, to venture out into the world. She was an inquisitive child, stubborn and rebellious, always seeking the forbidden, always asking questions, and her parents hadn't known how to deal with her. All they knew to do was beat her or tie her to the bed.

"One evening when the market emptied and she met Gabriel at their usual place on the steps of the Alliance School, he wrapped her in his coat and she snuggled into his arms. 'Stay with me tonight,' she begged.

"'It's forbidden, querida mia, it's blasphemy. We can't be together before we're husband and wife by Jewish law.'

"'I can't be in that home for one more night. I can't stand the smell of death, the people's shouts at night. It scares me even more than my big brother's beatings.'

"'If you really can't bear it, I'll speak to Leon and ask him if you can sleep there again, my love. Another few nights and everything will work out. A few more days and we will be man and wife and we'll have our own house. Paciencia, my precious, paciencia. Everything will be fine. You'll see.'

"She didn't want to go back to Leon's house. He'd scowl at her in hatred and shout at his wife and threaten that if she didn't get rid of the Ashkenazia, he'd get rid of *her*. Her body shook and she started crying. Gabriel stroked her head. 'I want to stay with you. I don't want to sleep in the aged person's home or at Leon's house.'

"Rochel was radiant in the moonlight, her golden hair shining and her blue eyes welling with tears. Gabriel dried them and took her hand, and she let him lead her without asking where they were going."

It was very late and it seemed that Tia Allegra was tired from telling her story. She closed her eyes as if she were about to fall asleep and sighed. "Basta, querida," she said. "I've told you enough. I'm tired. Perhaps we'll carry on another time."

"Please, Tia, please," I begged. "You've already gotten this far. I need to know where Nono Gabriel took the Ashkenazia. You must tell me what happened with their love story."

"What happened with their story, querida mia, I heard from my sister Clara. I was in Tel Aviv by then, sound asleep beside my Elazar, may he rest in peace. I didn't know that while I was dreaming, my darling brother's life was being turned upside down. I didn't know that when I got up in the morning, the Ermosa family wouldn't be the same Ermosa family it'd been when I'd gone to bed."

Tia Allegra sighed again and closed her eyes. Another moment, I feared, and she'd be fast asleep. I scooted my chair closer to hers, shook her arm, and urged her on. "What happened to Gabriel and Rochel? Please, Tia, where did he take her? Who agreed to put her up?"

"Stubborn girl," Tia Allegra scolded me. "You're as stubborn as my mother Mercada, as stubborn as your mother Luna. You all have the seed of stubbornness. When you want something, you bang your head against the wall. You sink your teeth into your prey and don't give up till you get what you want."

I didn't like the comparison with my mother and sour old Mercada, as Nona Rosa had always called her, but this wasn't the time to argue about it. I so much wanted Tia Allegra to go on with her story that I nodded in agreement.

"It was late by the time Gabriel knocked on the green wooden door of Clara's house," Tia Allegra said. "Clara, her husband Yaakov, and their children had been fast asleep. Yaakov, bleary-eyed and alarmed, opened the door.

"'Get my sister,' Gabriel ordered him.

"'Now? At this hour? *Que pasa?*' Yaakov asked, shooting frightened glances from him to Rochel.

"'Don't ask questions, Yaakov. Just get my sister.'

"Clara rushed up to them in her nightgown, her hair disheveled. 'Qualo quieres, what do you want?' she asked Gabriel, looking suspiciously at Rochel, who was standing meekly in the doorway.

"'She's sleeping here,' Gabriel replied.

"'Father will kill me if he finds out I let the Ashkenazia into the house,' she said, disturbed.

"'And I'll kill you if you don't,' Gabriel told her.

"Clara was shocked by her brother's forceful behavior.

"'She has nowhere to sleep, and starting tomorrow she'll be your sister-in-law, a family member, so let her in!'

"Clara's jaw dropped, but she opened the door without another word.

"Ignoring his sister, Gabriel held Rochel's face in his hands, kissed her eyelids, and said, 'Don't worry, mi alma. Tomorrow we'll have a home.'

"After leaving Rochel with his sister, he set out toward his parents' house. As silently as a burglar he opened the door and went inside. His parents were in bed, but he knew they weren't asleep. He had fully expected his mother to get out of bed and start cursing Rochel again: hija de un perro, daughter of a dog, hija de una putana, whore's daughter, el Dio que la mate, may God strike her down. But his mother didn't say a word and his father didn't raise his voice. He only said tiredly, 'You've come home again from the Ashkenazia putana? When will you get it into your head that we don't marry Ashkenazias?'

"Gabriel went to his room, covered himself with a blanket, and before closing his eyes saw Rochel's blue ones. If somebody had told him that he would defy his parents' wishes and marry an Ashkenazia without his family present, he would either have laughed in his face or beaten him half to death. But now he was about to marry Rochel. He hoped his parents would relent once they were married and had children, that they'd accept her once they witnessed the love they shared. But he couldn't deny his feelings. It was bigger than him. It was fated. He closed his eyes and sank into a deep, dreamless sleep.

"Deafening shouts roused the household. 'Dio mio! Si murien! Raphael el tsaddik si murien!'

"Gabriel woke up in a fright. 'He's dead! He's dead!' he heard his mother screaming. He came out of his room. The house was full of people, his brother, his sister, the neighbors, relatives. He had slept deeply and nobody had thought to wake him. As soon as she saw him, his mother went at him with her fists. 'You've killed him! You've killed your father, you and your Ashkenazia putana. You've killed your father!'

"The stunned Gabriel didn't understand what was happening. *'De que 'stas havlanda?* What are you talking about?'

"'Your father, your father Raphael, the righteous, sainted man, your father is dead. *Si li rompien el corazon,* his heart broke. You broke his heart, you! You!'

"Gabriel went to his father's bedside, and the relatives made way for him. Raphael was on his back, as pale as a ghost, his eyes wide open. Gabriel brought his face close to his father's and placed a hand under his nose, hoping that his mother was being hysterical for no reason and her fears were mistaken, that his father would start breathing and everything would return to normal. But there was no sign of life. His father was dead. Gabriel collapsed over his father's body and wept uncontrollably. *'Perdoname, perdoname,* Papo. Dio mio, forgive me, forgive me, Father. God in heaven, Father. What have I done to you, Father?'

"Mercada couldn't believe her eyes: Her strong son was weeping like a woman. Although beside herself with grief and pain, she realized that this was an opportune moment to set things right. Without hesitation she went to her son, laid a hand on his shoulder, raised him up from his father's body, and in a voice as cold as steel said, 'You've killed your father. You've made me a widow and bereaved your brothers and sisters. If you don't want to kill me too, swear to me on your father lying here dead because of you, swear to me that you will not marry the Ashkenazia and that you will never see her again.'

"Gabriel fell into her arms and wailed, 'I swear, Mother, I swear. I beg your forgiveness. I'm so sorry.'

"'What do you swear on?' Mercada demanded.

"'I swear on my father.'

"'You swear what?' Mercada persisted. 'Say it so your brothers can hear. So your sister Clara can hear. So your sister Allegra all the way in Tel Aviv can hear. Say it so the whole of Ohel Moshe and all Jerusalem can hear. So your father lying here dead can hear. What do you swear?'

"'I swear that I will not marry the Ashkenazia and that I will never see her again,' Gabriel sobbed.

"Mercada moved away from him. 'Here,' she said, giving him a handkerchief, 'dry your eyes. Stop crying. Be a man! We must take your father to the Mount of Olives.'

"From that day on your Nono Gabriel didn't see Rochel even once," Tia Allegra said with a sigh. "He didn't say good-bye to her and didn't inform her of his decision not to marry her. He simply behaved as if she had never existed in his life. And Mercada, she never mentioned her name again and neither did we. Only the gossipmongers in Ohel Moshe clicked their tongues and in hushed voices related the story of Gabriel's grand love for the Ashkenazia from Mea Shearim that broke the heart of that saintly man, Senor Raphael Ermosa, and ultimately killed him."

"And Rochel?" I asked Tia Allegra. "What happened to her?"

"Ah, that, querida, I don't know, and to tell you the truth, I was never interested. All I know is that in the middle of the night, after they came to inform my sister Clara of our father's death, may he rest in peace, she threw Rochel out into the street, cursing her and calling her a murderer, and the girl vanished into thin air. No one ever saw her again.

"And your Nono Gabriel, a year after our father Raphael died, our mother married him to Rosa, *una buena boda*, a wedding I wouldn't wish on my worst enemies, a wedding without guests, without family, without refreshments, without joy. Just a minyan, a quorum of ten men. None of us knew the bride, not her or her family. All we knew was that she was an orphan from the Shama neighborhood who worked cleaning houses for the English."

Pale gray light came through the window of Tia Allegra's apartment as dawn broke and night was replaced by day. Although I'd been awake all night, I was far from tired. I thought about my grandfather and his unfulfilled love for the Ashkenazia, a love that filled his heart and left no room for Nona Rosa. I thought about Mercada, who despicably used Raphael's death to force Gabriel into swearing the terrible oath never to see the love of his life again. I thought about the hasty marriage forced upon him and poor Nona Rosa, who didn't have the faintest idea that Mercada, coldly and calculatingly, was using her as a pawn in the game she was playing against her son.

And I thought about the most terrible thing of all: How could it be that my family carried such a dark secret and lived with it in peace? How was it that nobody had ever let it slip, nobody had blurted a word that might give the secret away? How could it have happened that in all the years she had lived with him, my grandmother had been tormented by her unrequited love without understanding why her husband hadn't loved her as she loved him? And how was it possible that in all the years that had passed, nobody knew what had become of my grandfather's pitiful beloved, thrown into the street from his sister's house that night, and what's more, nobody cared?

I had lots of questions, and I wanted answers. I wanted Tia Allegra to continue the story, but she was tired, very tired.

"Heideh," she said quietly, "I've talked enough for a hundred years. Help me up and to my bedroom."

I helped her up from her chair, and with her cane she started hobbling toward her bedroom.

"God help me, Gabriela," she said before closing her bedroom door, "I can't remember why you came here from Jerusalem, but I remember the tiniest things that happened forty years ago. That's how it is with old age. There are things you miss."

3

THE MARRIAGE BETWEEN NONO GABRIEL and Nona Rosa was my great-grandmother Mercada's way of exacting revenge on her beloved son. She married him to a woman with no family, no pedigree, no money, and no looks. But Gabriel didn't open his mouth in protest.

It was, so they say, *una boda sin cantadores*, a wedding without singers, the way the poor get married, not the Ermosa family. And it was only when he stomped on the wineglass and said, "If I forget thee, O Jerusalem, may my right hand lose its cunning," and they became man and wife, that he realized he had no idea what color his new wife's eyes were.

Despite her plainness and poverty, sixteen-year-old Rosa was an industrious woman. Immediately after the wedding she stopped work as a cleaner in the homes of English people and began helping in the shop at her husband's side. Her husband did his duty as a provider and fulfilled all her basic needs, but no more than that. Ever since his father's death he'd withdrawn into himself.

Sometimes when Mercada looked at her daughter-in-law, the thought flashed through her mind that maybe marrying her handsome son to the thick orphan had been too severe a punishment, but she'd quickly brush it aside and remind herself that grace is deceitful and beauty is vain. Just look at what that cursed Ashkenazia's beauty brought down on us!

Nine months after the wedding, Nona Rosa gave birth to their first child, Raphael, but he died before he was a month old. My mother Luna was born exactly eighteen months later. She liked to say that when she was born, all the birds in Jerusalem sang and all the church bells rang and could even be heard in the Misgav Ladach hospital where she was born. When I asked Nona Rosa about it, she said, "That one, who's got the memory of a bird, remembers how the birds sang when she was born? I don't remember it, so how can she?"

But Nona Rosa clearly remembered what happened when Nono Gabriel held my mother in his arms for the first time. As he hugged her close to his chest, she held his pinkie finger and opened her eyes. His heart missed a beat, and for the second time in his life he saw beams of golden light, this time illuminating his daughter's face.

"Preciosa," he whispered, "preciosa mia, my precious, my beautiful one." Then a miracle happened, and Nono Gabriel, who hadn't smiled since Great-grandfather Raphael died because of him and the Ashkenazia, and hadn't laughed even once since he married the orphan Rosa, laughed joyfully. He lifted his little daughter over his head and started dancing with her around the maternity ward. A full moon flooded the ward with bright light, and my grandfather looked at my mother, lifted her up to the window, and said, "Look, preciosa mia. Look at the moon shining like you, Luna mia." And that's how my mother was named Luna after the moon, which on the day of her birth lit up my grandfather's life anew.

Every day after work Gabriel would hurry home to little Luna. "Bring her to the shop," he'd say to Rosa. "Bring her at least twice or three times a day. This child is a blessing. She brings me luck."

Rosa would diaper Luna in cotton cloth, dress her in pants and a pink tunic with pompons, and put white socks on her tiny feet and a white hat on her head, all of which she'd knitted while she was pregnant. Despite Rosa's half-hearted protests, Mercada had insisted that she get rid of the clothes she'd made for baby Raphael, may he rest in peace, right after they buried him, so that the dead baby's clothes wouldn't bring, *pishcado y limon*, bad luck. They were given to babies at the Sephardi orphanage together with the boy's cradle, and Rosa sobbed her heart out. Her mother-in-law had let her weep and told her daughters not to bother her. "It will pass by the time she has another baby in her belly," she had said. Gabriel, who hadn't known how to cope with his young wife's pain, threw himself into his work in the shop. When Rosa had gotten pregnant a second time, they'd all made life easy for her. She shouldn't overdo it, lift things, bend. Her sister-in-law Allegra would come once or twice a week to sweep the floor, and following Mercada's orders, the cousins switched off cleaning the house. Mercada even forbade Rosa to cook, so the neighbors took turns bringing over food—kiftikas, sofrito, habas con arroz—and Mercada herself made the Shabbat macaroni hamin with haminados and the borekitas and the sütlaç.

After dressing Luna, Rosa would put her into a white wooden pram and cover her with a thick patchwork quilt. Rosa was very proud of the splendid pram, which very few could have afforded. Gabriel had gone specially to Tel Aviv to buy it. When she reached the Mahane Yehuda Market Rosa felt like the queen of England. All the market dealers, stallholders, and shop owners would greet her and call out, "Mazal tov, Senora Ermosa, *que estes sanas tu y tu nina*, may you and your daughter be healthy," and Rosa would smile from ear to ear. This was her finest hour. The women would come over to the pram, click their tongues, and fawn over the gorgeous baby. And Rosa, who had long since forgotten the days when she and her brother barely had enough to eat, would smile and thank them all. Nobody, not even her husband, knew that when she was alone at home with the baby, she lacked patience. The baby's crying drove her crazy, and she'd lift her out of the cradle roughly, take out a breast, and stick the nipple into her mouth to shut her up. Nobody knew that when she was alone at home and the shutters were closed, she'd sit on the bed staring into the distance, waiting for the sun to rise so she could again go for a walk with the baby in the pram.

Rosa saw how Gabriel's eyes lit up every time he looked at Luna, how he took her in his arms with infinite gentleness, kissed her eyes, raised her in the air and exalted her as if she were a work of art. But she, she didn't have room in her heart yet. She hadn't finished mourning for baby Raphael, may he rest in peace, and now this one had come too soon.

Deep down, she was also jealous of the special attention that Gabriel lavished on their daughter. To Rosa, he was distant and spoke only about the baby and the house. He never honored her with words or gestures of love. He always simply did his duty. He had come to her bed only a few times since they were married, and not once since Luna was born. Even when he did come to her bed, he did only what he needed and then got up and went back to his own bed at the other side of the room. Rosa never complained, as life with Gabriel was far better than her previous life. She had food and clothing and was able to provide for her young brother. She was very fortunate to have been married into the wealthy and respected Ermosa family. Who would have believed she could be so lucky?

Although she blessed her good fortune, in her heart she hoped that her husband would eventually treat her lovingly and perhaps, just perhaps, touch her once the way she wanted to touch him, with pleasure, tenderness. Perhaps just once when he came to her at night, he would kiss her on the lips. He'd never kissed her, not even under the wedding canopy. She knew she'd disappointed him when baby Raphael died. He hadn't uttered a word of consolation, laid a hand on her shoulder. He'd never said a word to her about it at all.

Mercada had daily conversations with Raphael. After Luna was born, she lifted her face to the heavens and told him, "Luckily the child came out looking like Gabriel. God help us if she'd looked like Rosa."

The insult she'd felt when Gabriel had not shown her the proper respect by naming the baby after her, as was customary, she didn't reveal to anyone, and certainly not to the baby's parents. Mercada had no doubt: This was Gabriel's way of expressing his displeasure that she had forced him to marry Rosa. If it makes him feel better, so be it. I don't need any favors, she thought, and she never raised the subject. And when her daughter Clara tried to comment, she cut her off and said, "Thank God, a healthy, sound child was born, and that's what's important. And you, *sera la boca,* shut your mouth, not another word about it, not to your brother and not to anyone else!"

Mercada understood her son's anger. In the evening, when all the women neighbors sat around the well on low stools and gossiped, Mercada would cast her eyes over them, noticing they all seemed worthier than Rosa. She also found herself visiting the homes of her other children more and more, especially Clara's. "God forgive me," she said to her daughter. "I thought I was punishing Gabriel, but I punished myself. I can't stand his wife. I can't stand her smell. I can't breathe with her in the same house. I'm coming to live with you!"

"With pleasure, Mama querida," Clara replied. "But don't forget that I, Yaakov, and the children live in the same room, so where will you sleep?"

"I don't care. If necessary I'll sleep on the floor, but I'm not living in the same house as that *gorda,* that fat one."

The next day she packed a few belongings and moved into Clara's house without informing Gabriel or Rosa. When Gabriel came home from work, he asked where his mother was. Rosa shook her head and said she hadn't seen her since the morning, when Rosa had taken the baby for a walk in the pram.

Gabriel didn't pay further attention to his mother's absence. He went to Luna and lifted her up. She was his consolation, the reason he loved coming home each night. He would take her out to the yard and chat with the neighborhood women as if he were one of them, admiring his daughter's red hair and her clear eyes with their green and brown hue, her tiny hand and its perfect fingers. Each time she held his finger, he swooned, and when she smiled at him, his face glowed, and he'd give her little kisses and laugh. The neighbors were captivated by Gabriel's great love for his daughter, *sano que 'ste*, may he be healthy.

"He's not like a man, he's like a woman," one of them said. "My husband was never like that with his children. Rosa's lucky she's got a husband like him." When they saw him diapering the child, their awe reached new heights. Whoever heard of a man diapering his child? Nothing like it had been heard of in all of Jerusalem! When one of them revealed he not only diapered the child but also bathed her—she swore on her eyes that she'd seen Gabriel bathing the baby in a tin bath as if he were a wet nurse or its mother—Gabriel's stock was never higher.

And Rosa was quite happy to share child-care duties with whoever volunteered, all the more so if the volunteer was her husband. Before the baby was born, he'd go from the shop to the bagno and come home washed and clean, but now he came right home, washed himself in the water that Rosa heated for him, and quickly changed his clothes so the smells of the market wouldn't cling to the baby, God forbid. He'd take her out of the cradle and return her only when it was time to feed her and put her down to sleep. He loved Luna with all his heart. For a moment she managed to banish the thoughts of his other love, the one he'd sworn to forget. For the first time since his father's death and Rochel's disappearance, he felt much happiness.

It was only after he'd bathed Luna, diapered her, and dressed her in her pajamas, only after he'd handed her to Rosa to nurse, and only after he'd lain her down in her cradle and sung her a lullaby in Ladino, only then did he notice his mother's continued absence.

"Where's my mother?" he asked Rosa, who suggested she'd gone to the neighbors. He went into the yard and from house to house. "*Vizina, 'onde 'ste mi madre?* Neighbor, where's my mother?"

They all said they hadn't seen Mercada all day.

"Perhaps she's gone to the Western Wall," one offered.

"Maybe she's gone to the Eliyahu Hanavi Synagogue," said another.

"Nobody came to her for livianos today," a third told him. "There wasn't a single person here in the yard."

Concern began gnawing at Gabriel. His mother didn't usually just vanish.

She was always at home or in the yard. Since Raphael's death she had stopped visiting the shop and rarely exchanged a word with him, saying only what she had to.

Although as time passed she had softened and her tremendous anger with him had dulled, Mercada hadn't let her son sense it. Even when Luna was born, she didn't lose control and fuss over the baby, though inside she was delighted when she saw how the baby had brought Gabriel joy. She had given him a lifelong punishment when she'd married him to Rosa, and had decided that was enough. She didn't need him to suffer any more than that.

And he, ravaged with guilt, had done everything he could to appease her. He married Rosa and went on managing the shop successfully. Although since his father's death and the loss of Rochel he had distanced himself from his God and become a secular Jew, he continued attending the synagogue to honor his father's memory and pray for the elevation of his soul. Gabriel was neither angry nor embittered. He named the child Luna not to punish his mother but because he truly felt that on the night she was born, the light of the moon had lit up his life anew. He had no doubt that he would name the daughter born after Luna after his mother.

Worried and anxious, Gabriel hurried to Clara's house in Sukkat Shalom and knocked on the door. When he saw his mother sitting at the table in the middle of dinner, surrounded by her grandchildren, daughter, and son-in-law, he heaved a sigh of relief.

"Thank God, I've been looking all over Jerusalem for you."

"You've found me," Mercada replied and carried on eating.

"But why didn't you tell Rosa that you were going to Clara's? Why did you worry me like this?"

"No more than you worry me," she said with a sour expression.

"Mother," he pleaded, "has something happened? Did Rosa do something?"

"She doesn't need to do anything. It's enough that she's like a bone stuck in my throat."

"But she's my wife. Where do you want her to be?"

"In her own house, and I'll be here at Clara's. From now on I'm living with your sister."

"Why with my sister? You've got a home."

"I don't have a home. It's Rosa's home now, and thanks to you, I don't have a husband either, so I'm here," she said, hitting the floor with her cane as if confirming a fact.

"Mother, por Dio! Come home with me."

"Over my dead body."

"What happened with Rosa?" he asked again. "What has she done? Did she not speak nicely to you?"

"She didn't speak to me at all. I'm not speaking to her, and that's that."

Gabriel was silent. After a long period of suppressing his feelings and adopting a sort of numbness, he felt anger begin to roil inside him. He took a deep breath to dispel the sense of suffocation that gripped his throat, gritted his teeth, and clenched his fists, and when he could no longer contain himself, he roughly seized one of his sister's children by the shoulders, hauled the child out of the chair, and sat down facing his mother.

The frightened children stopped eating, his sister and brother-in-law looked in disbelief at his gradually reddening face, and only his mother went on slurping her soup as if what was happening had nothing at all to do with her. He felt he was going to explode at any moment. He hammered the table with his fist and said in a voice he didn't recognize, "You, you're not speaking to Rosa? You can't stand Rosa? And what about me? Do I speak to her? Can I stand her? If it weren't for you, Rosa wouldn't be living in our house. It was you who was in such a hurry to marry me to the *pesgada*, the clumsiest of all the girls in Jerusalem and the whole country. It was you who turned my life into a living hell, and I accepted the punishment imposed on me by the Almighty and you. I agreed to marry a woman for whom I feel nothing, nada! A woman to whose bed I've gone no more than three times in the three years I've been married to her, and then only so you'd have grandchildren. A woman who is of no interest to me whatsoever, with whom I've nothing to talk about, and you, *you're* not speaking to her?"

Clara quickly shooed the children out of the room. She and her husband moved from the table to the couch to spectate, not believing what was happening before their very eyes: Gabriel daring to raise his voice to Mercada.

Mercada went on calmly eating her soup and asked, "Have you finished?"

"No, I haven't finished. You ruined my life and now *you're* complaining?"

She stopped eating for the first time since he'd started talking, and leaning on her cane, stood up and looked him directly in the face. "Listen to me, disobedient son that you are! If you hadn't killed your father because of the Ashkenazia, none of this would have happened. If your father hadn't died because of the catastrophe you brought down on our family, today you'd be married to a wife who's one of ours from a fine and respected home, a wife who would have brought respect to the family, not a cleaner of English people's toilets! You would have married like a king, not a pauper. Not only did you have *una boda sin cantadores,* a wedding without singers, you had *una boda sin novia,* a wedding without a bride, and it wasn't me, it was *you* who brought this curse and this bride down on yourself."

Gabriel took a deep breath, leaned over the table, looked his mother in the eye, and said quietly, "You are my mother and I've respected you all my life. You were always the most important woman in my life, even when there was another woman who was as important to me as life itself," he said, avoiding any mention of Rochel's name. "But listen and listen well: You chose the bride for me, you married me to Rosa, and she's the mother of my daughter, your granddaughter. She will bear me more children and she'll be the mother of my children. From here to eternity, until the day I or she dies, I shall care for her, provide her with food and clothing. If she dies before me, I'll say kaddish for her. If I die before her, she'll be my widow, and when her time comes, she'll have a place beside me in the Mount of Olives cemetery. From this day on, she is the woman of my house. She is the senora. You will live in her house, not she in yours. From this day on, you will treat her with respect, as if she is a queen, no less, a queen! From this day on Rosa is Senora Ermosa, wife of Gabriel Ermosa, mother of Luna Ermosa, and daughter-in-law of Mercada Ermosa, and you will treat her as a mother-in-law treats a daughter-in-law, just as I treat her as a husband treats his wife."

Mercada didn't move, and Gabriel took another deep breath. Then, in a quiet, authoritative voice, he said to his mother, "And now, por favor, get up and collect your things. You're coming home with me."

A few days later, when Rosa took Luna for their daily walk to the Mahane Yehuda Market, Mercada locked the door of the room that was hers and Raphael's. With great difficulty she dragged the heavy bed away from the wall, counted seven tiles on each side, and exactly in the middle of the room she lifted a tile and from a nook in the wall removed a pile of coins and gold she'd salted away for years. She gathered all the coins into a scarf and tied it into a bundle. Then she went to the wardrobe, took out a few dresses, kerchiefs, and her jewelry box, packed it all into a bag, kissed the mezuzah, and without a backward glance left the house and walked toward the taxi station on Jaffa Road, where she paid a driver to take her to her daughter Allegra's house in Tel Aviv.

When Gabriel got home from the market that day, he went into his mother's room and saw that the bed had been moved and that the space once hidden behind the tile was empty. Without a word he replaced the tile and dragged the bed back to its place, left the room, and from that day forth never entered it.

Gabriel couldn't go on living for another minute in the house where his father had died and in which his mother had abandoned him. But he was also unable to leave the house where he and his siblings had been raised. If only he'd had the courage, he would have looked for a house for himself and his family as far as possible from Ohel Moshe. If only he could have moved away from it all, left the shop in the Mahane Yehuda Market, and turned over a new leaf. But the burden of making a living and providing for his wife and daughter weighed heavily on his shoulders.

Gabriel had become a sad, silent man. The only one who could put a smile on his face was his daughter Luna. When the baby boy born after Luna died before he was a week old, Gabriel didn't shed a single tear and was glad that Rosa didn't either. They buried the child and went back to the routine of their life.

Once every few months he would visit his mother in Tel Aviv, but she'd still treat him like a stranger.

"Dio santo, Gabriel, why do you bother?" his sister Allegra asked him. "May God forgive me, she's my mother, but I wouldn't wish a mother like her on my worst enemy."

He shrugged, and despite Mercada's cruel and hurtful behavior, he continued his trips to Tel Aviv.

On one such visit, his brother-in-law Elazar, Allegra's husband, suggested that he open a branch of Raphael Ermosa & Sons, Delicatessen, in Tel Aviv. "There's a good location on Shabazi Street. How about opening another shop there?"

Gabriel considered the proposition: Leon and Leito can continue running the shop in Jerusalem, I'll move to Tel Aviv with my wife and daughter, and perhaps, he hoped, I'll be able to regain a place in my mother's heart.

The young family moved to Tel Aviv into a small house on Hayarkon Street, walking distance from the new shop. Almost from the start the delicatessen became a grocery store, selling basic foodstuffs, as the residents of Shabazi Street couldn't afford delicacies.

Rosa hated every moment in Tel Aviv and dreamed of returning to Jerusalem, even daring to express her feelings to her sister-in-law Allegra.

"I miss it, I miss the Jerusalem air. I can't inhale the air of Tel Aviv. Everything here is dust and sand dunes and camels, basta. I miss Jerusalem, the Mahane Yehuda Market, my neighbors in Ohel Moshe. And the sea, leshos, keep it far away. It scares me. You can go into it, but God help you if you can't get out."

Unlike Rosa, Gabriel liked the White City, and even though the shop on Shabazi Street didn't bring in the income he'd hoped, he wasn't ready to give up so easily and went on fighting for it. In order to survive, he fired his only assistant and every day cycled from Neveh Tzedek to Jaffa to buy stock from the Arabs. That was the straw that broke the camel's back, since he viewed the task as beneath his dignity. At the first opportunity he sold his share to his brother-in-law Elazar and prepared to return to Jerusalem. But then Nissim, Rosa's brother who had fled to America at the time of the Turks, returned to Palestine and made Gabriel an offer he couldn't refuse.

"The most successful thing in New York right now," he told Gabriel, "is the shoeshine parlor. You need to rent a big shop, get hold of a few shoeshine boys, sit them in the shop, and they'll shine gentlemen's shoes."

Nono Gabriel, who was both a gentleman and something of a dandy who liked his shoes shining like a mirror, enthused over the idea to the displeasure of Rosa, who thought it was terrible but didn't dare come between her brother and husband. They rented a big shop on Nahalat Binyamin Street, hired ten shoeshine boys, and waited for the first customers. But as early as the first week, it became clear that the business was doomed to fail. Unlike in New York, there weren't enough customers in Tel Aviv for whom polished shoes was so important that they'd pay twice the going rate of shoeshine boys on the street. Even the big ceiling fan that was supposed to cool customers from the scorching heat of the Tel Aviv summer didn't lure people into the shop, and the shoeshine parlor closed down after only a month. Nono Gabriel lost a lot of money, and his brother-in-law got out by the skin of his teeth and went back to America.

Gabriel's dream of finding his way back into his mother's affections didn't come true either. Throughout the time he lived in Tel Aviv with his wife and daughter, she wouldn't come to his house even once. Instead he'd visit her at his sister's and bring along his sweet little daughter, since at least Mercada didn't scowl at her and sometimes even spoiled her with candy.

Tired, depressed, and broke, Nono Gabriel and his wife and daughter returned to the house in Ohel Moshe, only to discover that the successful business of Raphael Ermosa & Sons, Delicatessen, was also on the brink of bankruptcy. Regretfully, Gabriel was forced to let Leon go and fired his brother Leito, who had proved to be a failure as a financial manager. Not only that, it was whispered that he had brazenly stolen from Gabriel.

Gabriel went back behind the counter and tried to return the shop to its good days. But it seemed that good times were a thing of the past. He barely eked out a living, and most of the time the shop was empty of customers and stock, for where could he find the cash to buy stock?

Then a miracle happened that restored the shop to its former glory and prosperity. The soldiers stationed in the British army camps in Jerusalem discovered Raphael Ermosa & Sons, Delicatessen, and they began coming to the shop to buy the various types of tea, especially the English tea that reminded them of home, which they drank with condensed milk that tasted like cream. Rosa, who had learned to cook in the English homes where she had worked, began making pies that reminded the British soldiers of home cooking, especially steak and kidney pie, which was the most popular. When Rosa began frying fish for them, the English asked Gabriel to make fried slices of potato to go with it, but he drew the line there. He didn't like the English, but business was one thing and liking was another, so thanks to "the cursed English," the finances improved and Nono Gabriel was happy again.

Luna was playing in the yard with the dolls Gabriel had bought her on his last trip to Beirut. Whenever he traveled to Lebanon or Syria on business, he came home loaded with presents for his little Luna. Occasionally he even brought a present for Rosa too.

"Bonica, basta!" the child prattled, mimicking her mother when she got angry with her. She sat on a low bench, feeding one of her dolls, sticking the spoon between its eyes instead of into its mouth. Then she took the other doll from the pram, murmuring loving words into its ear the way her father did with her.

"Dio santo, give me strength," Rosa said to her neighbor Tamar as they observed Luna. "Esta chicitica can talk to her dolls for hours, *avlastina de la Palestina*, she doesn't shut her mouth. And it doesn't help if I call her in, nada, she doesn't hear. What can I do with a child who never listens to me?"

"What do you want from the girl?" Tamar replied. "She's bored, the miskenica. It's time you gave her a brother, with God's help."

Rosa sighed. "*Sano que 'ste*, may we be healthy." For what else could she say to her neighbor? That since the baby born after Luna had died two years ago, Gabriel had not come to her bed even once? What could she tell her, that he slept on one side of the room and she on the other? How could she tell her neighbor Tamar that her husband hardly looked at her? That he hardly saw her? And that the only living creature that interested him was Luna, and she, to spite her just like her father, didn't see Rosa, didn't hear her, didn't talk to her. She laughed only with her father, kissed only her father, and her, Rosa, she rejected. Even on the rare occasions when Rosa tried to hug her, lift her up like every mother did with her child, her daughter eluded her and slipped from her arms.

"May you be healthy, you're raising the girl like a princesa," Tamar said to Rosa. "And if you don't bring her a hermano or hermanita, she'll grow up into a hoity-toity little brat."

"From your mouth to God's ears," Rosa said, and nodded. "Even now she's busy all day with her dolls, that one, and nothing else interests her. She dresses them, undresses them, feeds them for hours on end. And I, her mother, call her and nada, she acts like she's deaf. But her father only has to step one foot into the yard and she drops the dolls and runs to him and jumps into his arms. 'Papo! Papo! Papo!' She can't stop giggling."

"And her laugh, praise God," Tamar said and laughed, "you can hear it all the way from the market!"

And me, who hears *me* laugh? Rosa wondered. When was the last time *I* laughed?

For dinner that night Rosa made habas con arroz with a little sofrito, but before Gabriel ate, he put Luna on his knee and fed her. She covered her mouth on purpose, blocking it with her little fist, and he took the spoon, filled it, and brought it around in a big circle, saying, "Toot-toot-toot, where's the train?" It's unbelievable, Rosa thought. A grown man, such a serious man, making himself a troncho de Tveria, a cabbagehead, for his little girl. And when Luna opened her mouth and he pushed the rice and beans inside, he was as pleased as if he'd found a treasure trove of gold. Only when Luna finished eating, no more than a few spoonfuls—she didn't like eating, the flaca, the skinny one—did he eat his own food.

"Rosa, it's not hot," he grumbled.

"Of course it isn't hot. How can it be hot if while it was sitting ready on the table you were busy playing with your daughter?" she murmured to herself.

Gabriel was different from other men. A man only had to step through the door and expected food to be waiting on the table. Gabriel wanted his daughter first, so what could she do? On her mother's honor, may she rest in peace, she sometimes felt like throwing the food in his face and going out the door to never return! But where would she go? To clean the Ingelish's toilets again? So she took the plate, put the food back into the pot, and relit the stove. While the food was heating, Gabriel querido got up from the table and went to ready his daughter for bed, his usual routine of changing her into her nightgown, brushing her curls, and tying them with a ribbon.

As Rosa sat on the windowsill gazing at the olive tree, she could hear them laughing and chattering. What have I done that my husband doesn't love me? she asked herself. Not only doesn't he love me, he doesn't see me. He is generous and treats me with respect in company and even praises me, but when he's alone with me in the room, he hardly says a word.

How she'd hoped after Mercada went to live with Allegra in Tel Aviv, gracias el Dio, that things would be better between them, without that sour old woman interfering with her poisonous looks and comments. At least when Mercada had made her life a misery, it meant someone had taken *some* interest in her life, but now there's nothing, nada. It's as silent as death.

Rosa got up and went into her room. Unlike every other night, Gabriel was lingering on his side of the room. Not yet undressed, he stood by his bed hesitantly, and then all at once he turned to her and said, "Aren't you going to bed?"

"Soon," she replied. "I'll just do the dishes first."

"Leave them till morning," he told her. "Get into bed."

Rosa was surprised. Since when had Gabriel cared what time she went to bed? And since when had she gone to sleep before him? It was she who usually waited until she heard his deep breathing and snores before getting undressed and into her bed. And now he was telling her to get into bed before him? And how, in the name of the compassionate and merciful God, could she get undressed when there was light in the room and he was still awake? How could she change into her nightgown in front of her husband?

As if he'd heard her thoughts, Gabriel turned off the light. She undressed quickly, her arms getting tangled in her sleeves and the buttons of her dress refusing to come undone. Gabriel was standing with his back to her, but she felt as if he'd had eyes in the back of his head, and she sat down, trying to hide her body with her hands. She finally managed to take off her dress and put on her nightgown and got under the quilt. She closed her eyes and prayed for sleep to come.

Was she imagining it, or could she feel breath on her face? She opened her eyes and couldn't believe it. Gabriel's eyes were close to hers, his nose almost touching hers, his lips close to hers. His hand groped in the darkness, raising her nightgown to her waist, caressing her belly with a soft hand, and gently removing her baggy underwear.

Her heart pounded. Her face flushed. She wanted to bring her body closer to his. How she had prayed for this moment when Gabriel would come to her, but here she was, paralyzed with fear, unable to move. Gently Gabriel tried to separate her legs, but they seemed glued together and wouldn't open. He tried again. Her husband was a very gentle man, never raised his voice, never got upset. She wanted him to get angry, shout, take her by force, feel something! But he never felt. He did only what he had to. He clothed her, provided for her, and finally, God be praised, attended to her bodily needs.

Gabriel gently turned her onto her side and drew her to him, coming at her from behind like the dogs in the yard. He tried to insert his thing into hers and didn't succeed. He didn't say anything, just held her tight, close to him, one hand holding her belly and with the other trying again. She was as dry as the desert. It'd been such a long time since he came to her bed, and it hurt her, it hurt terribly, but she bit her lip and didn't make a sound. The third attempt was also unsuccessful, and the fear stole into her mind that he'd stop and go to his own bed. She needed to have intercourse with him. It was her only way of holding on to him so he wouldn't throw her out and replace her with another woman. Don't let him throw me back into the street, Dio mio. Don't let him tire of me and go back to his bed and leave me like this.

Rosa didn't know the woman who then turned to Gabriel and said to him in a voice she didn't recognize, "It's better like this," and lay on her back with her legs open and took his thing in her hands and put it between her legs.

Gabriel gripped her shoulders tightly and she felt the muscles flexing in his arms. He moved deep inside her and deeper still. In another moment he'd crush all her bones. She shut her eyes and bit her lip, stifling a cry. Don't let him think he's hurting me and pull out, she begged. He moved into her again and again and again until he uttered a muffled cry and collapsed onto her body as if he had fainted.

His body was heavy, she could hardly breathe under its weight, but she smiled. Her husband had finally come to her. Finally after almost two years they'd done what her neighbors did with their husbands every night. Finally she too could complain about her troncho who didn't let her sleep at night.

Not five minutes had passed and Gabriel was already snoring. She tried to slide from under his body, but it woke him. He got up, not even looking at her, and went to his own bed on the other side of the room.

Nine months later Rachelika was born.

When her husband told her that the baby would be named after her mother Rachel, may she rest in peace, no one was happier than Rosa. He didn't explain and she didn't ask why his second daughter too wouldn't be named after Mercada. She thanked God, blessed be He, who had given her a healthy daughter, and she thanked her husband for honoring her late mother.

As for Gabriel, he was incapable of giving the child his mother's name. On his visits to Tel Aviv his mother never once asked him how Luna was, and certainly not how the pregnant Rosa was doing. So why should he have given her name to his daughter? Even when he sent his brother Matzliach to Tel Aviv specially to inform Mercada that his second daughter had been born, she hadn't even bothered to get on the bus and come to Jerusalem and see her new granddaughter for herself.

His sister Allegra came, his brother-in-law Elazar came, his brothers and relatives, even the distant ones, came, but his mother, Her Majesty, didn't even send her congratulations with Allegra.

"Ach," Allegra said, sighing, "don't expect anything from our mother, hermano querido. She's a stubborn old woman. Don't give yourself heartache because of her stupidity."

"If that's the case," he told his sister, "I'm no less stubborn than her." And then and there he decided to name his second daughter Rachel after Rosa's late mother.

Luna was three years old when her sister was born, and much to everybody's surprise she became attached to her from the minute she arrived. All Rosa's fears that the spoiled child wouldn't want to share her father's love with another living creature were dispelled when she saw Luna's love for the baby.

"Have you seen the flaca?" she asked her neighbor Tamar. "Have you seen how much she loves her sister?"

"Yes." Tamar laughed. "Wonders will never cease, who'd have believed it? That one loves only herself."

"And her father, may he be healthy," Rosa added as she observed Luna rocking Rachelika's cradle and singing to her. "And unlike Luna, Rachelika is an easy baby. She eats and sleeps," Rosa continued. "You don't hear a peep out of her, where the flaca would cry all day, and her crying sounded like a cat yowling, and there was no day and no night, and she wanted to be picked up all the time. And Rachelika, *que no manqui,* just opens her eyes and I put a teta in her mouth and *dala,* she feeds until she falls asleep again. Praise God, that child is pure gold, una hija de oro."

Tamar nodded in agreement, remembering Luna's incessant crying and Gabriel pacing entire nights with her around the yard, disturbing the whole neighborhood's sleep.

"Dio mio," Tamar would whisper to her husband, "that child will drive us all crazy."

While Luna's features resembled Gabriel's, Rachelika was the mirror image of her mother. Like Rosa she had a broad face with a flat nose and small brown eyes, and her build was big and relatively sturdy for her age.

Luna was four when Rachelika began running after her in the yard, falling and standing up and falling all over again. The yard was filled with the girls' happy cries, Luna's rolling laugh and Rachelika's sweet squeals as she began learning words. "And what's the first word she spoke?" Rosa said to Tamar as they watched the girls. "*Nuna,* even before she said *mama,* even before she said *papo,* she said *Nuna,* that's how much she loves her sister Luna."

Since Rachelika's birth Rosa had been calmer. She now had two proofs that Gabriel came to her at night. Even though her neighbors had four, five, and even six healthy children, not counting the ones that had died in infancy or at birth, she, praise God, gave thanks to the Almighty for her two daughters, *sanos que 'sten.* In any case, the flaca was like ten children. God bless her, how much strength she needed for that child. One minute she was here and the next she was there. One minute she was in the yard and the next she was in the house, one minute on the bed and the next on the table.

"Basta! You've given me a headache!" Rosa always shouted, but she was invisible to her daughter. Only if Gabriel told her—he never shouted—"Basta, querida," only then she'd calm down a bit until she started up again.

"I don't know, adio Senor del mundo, I don't know where this girl came from," Rosa said to Tamar.

"Well, who's she like?" Tamar asked.

"Like a little devil," Rosa said. "Believe me, vizina, if they hadn't given her to me right after she was born, I would have thought they'd swapped her in Misgav Ladach."

"Go figure," her neighbor Tamar chuckled. "Perhaps they did swap her. She looks like an Ashkenazia, that one."

"They didn't swap her at all!" Rosa replied. "It's enough to see that her eyes are just like her father's, it's enough to see her red hair just like her father's, so she's my child and flesh of my flesh and she's like . . . how can I put it, may God forgive me, like a child who came into my house by accident, as if she's not mine."

"*Quieta, quieta*, shut up," Tamar cut Rosa short. "Heaven help us if you utter words like that. True, Luna gives you trouble, but she's only a child. Wait till she grows up, she'll change, she'll calm down. Paciencia, querida Rosa, paciencia. Just as you had paciencia until the Great War ended and the Turks, may their name and memory be erased, left the country, so have patience with the child. That's how it is with children. They don't always come out the way we want."

Rosa knew that Tamar was right. She needed patience, lots of patience. She hadn't gotten along with the child from the moment she'd been born, and the child hadn't gotten along with her. Perhaps she sensed her mother had no room in her heart for her. How worried she'd been that, like baby Raphael, Luna too would die before she was a month old. And like Raphael, Luna didn't stop crying. No matter what Rosa did, the crying didn't cease. The baby screamed and screamed until Rosa felt like screaming back at her. She'd cover her ears and pray to God to stop the child's crying before she went crazy.

Gabriel didn't know, but every morning after he left for the shop she'd be scared to death by the thought of remaining alone with the child. She'd close the shutters and sit in the dark, waiting for the sun to come up when she'd be able to put the beautiful child in her beautiful clothes into the beautiful pram. But her heart was hollow. Even when people complimented her on the child's beauty, she would smile politely, yet her heart was hollow. Painfully, she saw how her husband melted at the sight of the baby, and her heart was hollow.

She would burn in hell for these thoughts, but she couldn't help but envy the hugs, the kisses, the attention her husband lavished on the child. As far as the neighbors were concerned, everything was fine, thank God, she and Gabriel were lovebirds. But deep inside she was burning. She never understood where her good fortune had come from, how of all the young girls in Jerusalem, Mercada had chosen her for a quick marriage. At first she was content, but what could one do when the heart has its own ways? She hadn't planned to fall in love with Gabriel. All she'd wanted was a roof over her head, food, and a family. She hadn't thought about love, and now she loved her husband and was envious of her own daughter, the flesh of her flesh! God help her, what kind of a mother was jealous of her own daughter?

No wonder the child hated her and didn't give a damn about her. Children felt everything. You couldn't fool them. It was lucky that Rachelika had come into the world, thank God, and now she had, she finally felt they were a family.

When she'd told Gabriel that she was expecting, he had been happy and said, "With God's help, Rosa."

"With God's help, I hope we have a son," she said.

"A son, a daughter, whatever we have will be welcome," he replied. And so it was he was not disappointed when another daughter was born. He was a man among men, her husband, a mensch, as the Ashkenazim say.

When Rachelika started to stand and walk, Rosa was again with child, and that time too Gabriel came to her without her being able to prepare herself. Like the time when they conceived Rachelika, on this occasion she helped him enter her, and this time too she got pregnant right away.

I'm like a vaca, a cow, she thought. Each time I have intercourse with my husband I get pregnant. If he'd come to me more often I'd have given him twelve children by now, with God's help. How she had prayed that this time she wouldn't get pregnant, that Gabriel would go on trying and come to her again and again, and perhaps with God's help if his body was close to hers, then his heart would come closer to hers too. Nobody had ever taught her about the ways of love, so she didn't know whether the way Gabriel came to her was an act of love. Did all husbands not lay their lips on their wife's body when they were with her? And did they really not kiss her like they kiss in the cinema? She had never kissed, never been kissed, and had never complained.

And after Becky was born, may she be healthy, Gabriel never came to her again.

The three girls grew up to be beautiful and were Gabriel's pride and joy. He'd buy them the most exquisite clothes in the most expensive shops in Jerusalem and Tel Aviv, and return from his journeys to Beirut with suitcases full of gifts. He'd swell like a peacock when people complimented him on his daughters. On Shabbat morning, Rosa would take the girls to the women's section in the neighborhood Magen Zion Synagogue. When they arrived, Gabriel would raise his eyes in their direction, and no matter where he was in the service, he would always smile at them and wave. The women in the women's section would compliment Rosa on her husband who loved his family so much, but Rosa knew that the smiles were not for her. They think I have a perfect marriage, so let them think, let them look. Just don't let them put the evil eye on me!

Time flew by and reports of the charming and successful daughters spread throughout Ohel Moshe, Mazkeret Moshe, Zichron Yaakov, and the Mahane Yehuda Market: The eldest, Luna, was the beauty queen; the second, Rachelika, had her father's intelligence; and the third, Becky, had a heart of gold, she'd give you anything. Give her a chocolate, she'll take it out of her mouth and give it to her sisters.

Mercada, whose other children had each named their first daughters after her, hadn't said a word about the only one of her children who didn't grant her that honor. In bed at night, when she had her daily conversation with Raphael, she'd tell him, "He's punishing me, your son. He comes to visit me in Tel Aviv from time to time, but apart from hello and good-bye, he doesn't say a word. He comes, sits on the balcony with his sister, looks at the boulevard, and leaves, and if he does talk, he never looks me in the eye. The truth is, Raphael querido, I don't look him in the eye either. I'm an old woman, Raphael, and I don't have the strength for fighting, but in my heart I can't forgive him for you leaving me. Since you've been gone, Raphael, I have no life. I just sit here and wait to be there with you. I miss you, I miss Jerusalem, I miss my children and grandchildren who live there. I miss the life we had before Gabriel and the Ashkenazia putana ruined it. I'm in Tel Aviv, but my heart is in Jerusalem. I want to go back to my house in Ohel Moshe. I don't like Tel Aviv or Allegra's white house. Twenty-five steps, would you believe it, Raphael? You have to climb twenty-five steps to get to the door.

"I don't like the people here in Tel Aviv either. They're all new, recently arrived from Europe. And if there *are* any of ours, they've become Ashkenazim. I don't like the girls, who have no shame, walking around naked in the street. And I don't like going to the beach. It's full of English walking on the promenade with Jewish girls, God help us. I only like the boulevard. I sit on a bench, feed the pigeons, remembering how I'd sit with the vizinas under the tree in our yard in Ohel Moshe. Would you believe, Raphael, that all I do now is feed pigeons? No more livianos, no more charity, no more people coming to Mercada's house for advice. So I sit on a bench all day feeding pigeons, that's what's become of me, so how can I forgive your son? How can I forgive him for destroying our family and destroying our life and taking you from us, querido mio, when my heart is broken from missing you so much?

"Now he's named his second daughter after the mother of the *feia*, the ugly one. So be it. I sometimes think that perhaps the time has come for forgiveness and pardon, Raphael, but my pride won't allow it, and my heart, which to this day hurts remembering the day you left us, won't let me. And your son, I won't drive him away and I won't tell him to stop visiting me in Tel Aviv, but one good word he won't hear from me. Only his daughter, the one he named after the moon, the naughty one, may she be healthy, manages to make me smile. When they came in the summer, I went down to the boulevard with her and we fed the pigeons together, and all of a sudden the child climbed into my lap and hugged me tight and her smell reminded me of Gabriel's smell when he was a baby, and my heart melted. And then when I raised my head, I saw Gabriel standing on the balcony watching us and he looked sad, and I knew that his heart hurt like mine. So may he be healthy and name his second daughter after the mother of the orphan from Shama. I can live with it."

When Mercada heard that Gabriel had decided to name his third daughter Rivka after her, she sighed. What's done is done, she thought. Now that baby Rivka has arrived, it's time to lay down the swords. From now until her last day she would welcome her son and his family when they came to visit. She would be kind to her clumsy daughter-in-law, and she would love her son's precious daughters. On the day she heard about the birth of baby Rivka, she decided to visit her son and his family in Jerusalem. It'd been years since she'd visited her city, years since she'd seen her house, years since she'd been in her neighborhood. But when the day came and the hour approached and her daughter was about to take her to the bus station, Mercada told her, "*Olvidalo,* forget it. I'm not going anywhere."

"But why, Mother?" Allegra asked. "Gabriel will be waiting at the bus station on Jaffa Road, and Rosa has readied the house in your honor. The whole family will come to see you, and all the vizinas and cousins and everyone you love in Jerusalem will come to see you."

"Basta!" Mercada ordered. "Don't talk nonsense. I'm not going and that's that."

"But Mother querida, isn't it time to stop this hostility? Now the baby has been born and Gabriel gave it your name, it's a sign. Don't you understand? It's a sign that he wants to end the anger too."

"Let him end what he wants," Mercada grumbled. "I'm not going!"

And so Allegra went to Jerusalem by herself. Gabriel was waiting with Rosa and the three girls at the bus station. Luna and Rachelika were wearing their best dresses, shiny shoes, muslin stockings, and hats with pompons. The baby in the pram was an angel, her face pure, and when she opened her eyes Allegra was astonished to see her mother's eyes, those of the grandmother who hadn't wanted to come and see her, the one who couldn't find forgiveness in her heart, the one whose pride had made her look shriveled and ugly. Allegra's rage burned inside her. From day to day the old woman had become unbearably embittered and surly.

Not a muscle moved in Gabriel's face when he saw Allegra coming down the bus steps by herself.

"Gabriel querido," she said to her brother, "don't take it personally. Our mother's as stubborn as a mule." He picked up Luna and Rachelika and immediately started walking up Jaffa Road. Rosa, who seemed lost, remained behind with the pram and stared inquiringly at Allegra.

"Go, go with him," Allegra said. "I'm going back to Tel Aviv. I only came to tell you that Mother isn't coming." But before she could finish her sentence, Gabriel turned around and said, "Heideh, Allegrita, what are you waiting for? Let's go home. Rosa prepared a royal banquet. We won't throw food out just because some stubborn old woman decided to stay in Tel Aviv."

Allegra's heart lurched when they reached the family home and she saw the fine table laden with delicacies for his mother's visit. Already sitting at the table were close relatives: Mercada's children and grandchildren and the extended family and friends and neighbors and even the mukhtar, they had all come to welcome Mercada whom they hadn't seen in Jerusalem for years.

"My mother isn't coming," Gabriel told them all. "She decided that it's better for her in Tel Aviv, but we shall eat and drink and celebrate Becky's birth, so heideh. L'chaim!"

For exactly seven days he had called his third daughter Rivka. On the eighth day, the day that Mercada didn't come to Jerusalem, he called her Becky, and from then on so did everyone else.

Gabriel continued visiting his mother in Tel Aviv every few months, and every now and then he brought his wife and daughters too. He never mentioned the day she hadn't come to Jerusalem, and she didn't either. Allegra told her about the sumptuous meal, all the family and friends, how he hadn't flinched when she told him his mother wouldn't be coming, how he had deflected people's inquiries as to why Mercada wasn't there, and how he had mingled with the guests, urging them to eat, drink, and rejoice, pouring them more and more wine. "For every glass he poured, he poured one for himself," Allegra said. "And by the end of the meal he was as drunk as a lord. Standing on the table and swaying like a Sukkoth lulav, he sang, 'Rock, whose stone our life sustains,' until he collapsed and fell into the arms of the guests."

Mercada listened to her daughter's account but didn't utter a word.

Ill winds were blowing in Palestine and morale was at a low. The British, at whose arrival everyone had rejoiced, proved to be worse than the Turks.

"The Scots," Gabriel snorted with contempt every time they'd talk about the English, "don't like putting their hand in their pocket." To which Rosa would immediately add, "May their name and memory be erased."

The Jewish girls who went out with the English were the talk of the town. In almost every neighborhood there was a girl who went out with the English and brought down great shame on her family. In Ohel Moshe there were rumors that Matilda, the daughter of the Franco family, was with an English officer. "An expert in the splits," they'd say of her. "*Tfu*, she does the splits for the English, curse them."

One evening, as the neighbors sat in the yard drinking tea with bizcochos, Tamar said, "If I was in Victoria Franco's shoes I wouldn't let Matilda step out of the house."

"And what should she do, may her sins be forgiven?" Rosa asked. "Lock her in the house and tie her to the bed?"

"Those cursed goyim, catching all our good girls!" Tamar went on.

"Those girls are giving the Jews a bad name, and for what? Nylon stockings? Perfume? Coffee? Isn't it a shame for Victoria and Meir Franco? Poor things. You don't ever see them around anymore because of the shame that one's caused them," Rosa said.

"They say the Lehi group is capturing those girls and shaving their heads," Tamar added.

"God save us. It's lucky that my chiciticas are still young and we can still keep them at home."

"*Tfu,* the goyim, may their name be erased. What are you saying, Rosa? There isn't a million-to-one chance that a daughter of Gabriel Ermosa would go with the English," said Tamar, shocked.

"*Pishcado y limon,* leshos, of course there's no chance, but go figure. Matilda was a good girl too, and see what's happened to her."

More than anything else Gabriel despised the Jewish girls who went out with the British. "Whores," he'd call them, and that was the first time Rosa had heard her husband use bad language. "Perverted, rebellious girl," he'd curse Matilda and warn Rosa, "Don't let her anywhere near the girls, you hear? Not even to say hello to the whore."

"But Gabriel," Rosa tried, "how can you not say hello? We've known her since she was born. Meir and Victoria Franco are like family to us."

"Excuse me, Rosa," he replied with his usual restraint, "we were not born family. We're neighbors, and we behaved toward them like family, and now with that girl of theirs, the whore of the English, we choose not to be their family. Anything, you hear, Rosa, I'm prepared to forgive anything, but not a Jewish girl who goes out with Englishmen. That I do not forgive!"

Unlike Gabriel, Rosa did not hate the girls who went out with the English.

Unlike him, she could understand how a girl whose family suffered financial hardship would do anything to help her parents. Meir Franco, miskenico, had been out of work for a long time. He'd sit at home and there'd be no food on the table, and Matilda, she brought them coffee and biscuits and surely other goodies too, maybe even money, God help us. It wasn't Matilda's fault, it was the Ingelish, may they go to hell. They had everything you could think of in their canteen, while the children of this country were going hungry. Her and Gabriel's situation was all right, thank God. They and the girls had everything good in the world and the country, praise be, but she wasn't blind. What, she couldn't see that their neighbors had less than they did? Sometimes they didn't even have meat for Shabbat dinner.

"How happy we were when the Ingelish came," she said to Tamar. "How we wanted to get rid of the Turks. We thought the Ingelish come from Europe, they're more human than the Turcos animals, but what can you do when they're both a plague on us."

"Don't say that, Rosa," Tamar said. "Even though the English are bastardos, you still can't compare them. The Turcos, *tfu* on them, with their black mustaches like brooms, they frightened children and old people. And how they whipped people, *tach-tach-tach*. Anyone in their way would get a dose. And they'd go into Souk al-Attarin-in the Old City and overturn the fruit and vegetable stalls for no reason. And the Kishle prison, God save us. Anyone the Turks put into the Kishle wouldn't come out alive, and if they did they'd be *majnun*, mad until they died. Like miskenico Nachum Levi. One day a Turco grabbed him for no reason and put him into the Kishle. He came out after maybe six months and then he went to Ben Hinnom Valley below his mother's house in Yemin Moshe and slept in caves. He grew a beard and hair down to his waist, and every time he came up from the wadi he'd frighten the children. Abu Lele, they called him, like the demon. And when his mother saw him like that she died of grief, and it was all because of the Turks, may their name be erased."

Rosa remained silent, not telling Tamar about the night the Turks banged on the door of her parents' house, may they rest in peace. She didn't tell about how she and baby Ephraim were wakened and how the Turks turned over the whole miserable room they lived in, and how, with a whip they lashed her parents' backs, even though they were already ill with the cursed sickness and could hardly stand. How she pushed Ephraim under the bed and lay on top of him and put her hand over his mouth so he wouldn't make a sound. She almost choked him, miskenico. She didn't tell how the Turks dragged her father into the yard and warned him that if he didn't give up his sons Nissim and Rachamim to the military authorities, they'd hang him at Damascus Gate.

The Great War was at its height, and the Turks were constantly abducting Jewish children and forcing them to join their army. There wasn't a mother who saw her son after the Turks seized him. By that point, Nissim had already been in America, having escaped on a ship from Jaffa, and Rachamim had been in hiding. Rachamim, who was fifteen, was determined not to join the army even if it cost him his life. He'd sworn that even if they hanged him, he would never join the Turcos' army. Rumors of the camps set up by the Turks for Jewish deserters reached Jerusalem. It was said that there was a camp near Haifa where they worked them at hard labor like Pharaoh did with the Children of Israel in Egypt, from dawn to death. The deserters built the big railway for the cursed Turks and died from the hard labor, hunger, and disease, and mainly from the beatings.

Rosa never told a soul about that night. A month after the Turks burst into her parents' house, there was a knock on their door in the dead of night. Her parents woke up, opened the door, and then a shout was heard that tore the heavens above the Shama neighborhood. Her mother, who was already very sick, fell to the stone floor and passed out, and Rosa lifted the frightened Ephraim in her arms, trying to figure out what was happening. At daybreak, when the sun began to rise over the mountains, the whole family and all their neighbors made their way in a silent procession from the Shama neighborhood in Ben Hinnom Valley to Damascus Gate in the Old City. In the square by the gate she saw her brother. She would never forget that scene: Rachamim hanging from the gallows, his head on his chest; his curly hair she so loved was matted, his beautiful eyes were closed, his tall, thin body a marionette on strings. No, she could never forget that scene. It was etched in her memory forever. The next day, the picture appeared in the newspaper, and although she couldn't read or write, she stood near Jaffa Gate begging, and with the few coppers given to her by passersby she bought a paper and cut out the picture of the hanged Rachamim. To this day she kept it in her secret box together with her mother's pendant, a blue stone framed with gold. Someday, when Rachelika got married, she'd give her the pendant and the clipping of Rachamim. Rosa knew Rachelika would look after what was important and precious to her. Perhaps someday she'd tell about Rachamim and that night, but not now. Except for Ephraim, no one knew, and anyway, he was always so drunk he could barely remember his own name.

A short time after they hanged Rachamim, one after the other her parents died of the cursed disease and also, so she was convinced, of heartbreak. Not a week had passed after their burial that the mukhtar came and ordered her and Ephraim to leave the house. She was ten, Ephraim five, and they had nowhere to go. She put a few clothes into a bundle, took Ephraim's hand, and walked in the direction of the New City, not knowing where they would spend the night. The streets were filthy and neglected, as were the many refugees who wandered around looking for shelter. How could she, a ten-year-old girl, manage when people her parents' age, may they rest in peace, couldn't?

Night fell as they reached Nahalat Shiva, where her uncle, her mother's brother, lived with his family. She knocked on the door, and her uncle's wife opened it and rubbed her eyes at the sight of the two children standing there. "Dio santo, hijos, what are you doing here at this hour?"

"The mukhtar threw us out of the house and we have nowhere to go," Rosa replied.

"And you came here? We barely have enough room for our own children. Where can we put you, on top of the cupboard?"

"Who is it?" came their uncle's voice.

"It's me, Tio," Rosa said, "me and Ephraim. The mukhtar threw us out and we need somewhere to sleep."

Their uncle came to the door. "Why are you leaving them standing in the street? Bring them inside," he ordered his wife, who didn't even attempt to hide her displeasure.

Their five children slept crowded together on a straw mattress on the cold concrete floor, and they didn't utter a word on seeing their two cousins who had come to visit in the middle of the night. "You'll sleep with your cousins," their uncle said, and for the first time that day Rosa breathed easily.

But two days later she again found herself with Ephraim out on the street. Her uncle's wife wouldn't let them stay under any circumstances. "We've barely enough for our own children, so how can we feed two more mouths?" she'd shouted. After endless arguing her husband had given in, but although he was poverty-stricken, he snuck Rosa a little money before sending them on their way.

She managed, of course she managed. She'd always known how to stand on her own two feet. Since the day her parents had died, she'd known that the most important thing was to trust only yourself and not rely on anyone else. Until the cursed Turcos left the country, she and Ephraim lived from hand to mouth. She'd go to the market and pick up the discarded vegetables and fruit that remained on the filthy ground after the peddlers finished their day's work. She'd beg, praying that good people would take pity on her and her little brother who always sat silently at her side, never crying, never complaining, a five-year-old child who understood that even if he did cry, there'd be nobody to help him.

Then a miracle happened, and after more than four hundred years of occupation, the Turks left Palestine. The image would stay in her mind forever: oxcarts passing through the streets of Jerusalem, carrying dead and injured Turkish soldiers, the screams of the wounded pleading for help. But she hadn't pitied them. The road that led from Jaffa Road to the railway station on Bethlehem Road was crowded with carts and cars and Turkish soldiers running around like mice in a trap, doing everything they could to get onto the train and flee for their lives, throwing away their weapons, selling them to Arabs. Rosa had stood observing the chaos, keeping Ephraim close to her side.

Shells fell on the city and people fled to avoid them. The shops on Jaffa Road were ransacked, the fear of death roamed the streets, but she hadn't been afraid. She'd just calmly watched the last of the Turkish soldiers get on the train and leave for good.

And then came the English—oh, what joy! Crowds filled the streets and gave them a hero's welcome. She was so happy. She cheered the English as they entered Jerusalem, kissing the tunics of the heroic soldiers who had come to liberate them from the Turks. Such celebration! She moved toward Jaffa Gate, holding Ephraim's hand tight so they wouldn't become separated and he be trampled by the crowd. She saw General Allenby dismount from his horse and stride into the Old City as Mayor al-Husseini came to welcome him.

"God be praised," they'd said in Jerusalem. "A Hanukkah miracle." But what kind of a miracle had it been? It didn't take the English long to show their true colors. They were unable to manage the disorder that followed the Turks' departure. Apart from her and Ephraim, there were another three thousand abandoned and starving orphans in Jerusalem, and so young girls became the whores of English soldiers to put food in their mouths.

May God not hear her thoughts, but on a few occasions she too considered selling her body so that she and Ephraim could eat. Gracias el Dio for the good upbringing she was given by her father and mother, who taught her to guard her honor under any circumstances, and instead of going with Ingelish soldiers, *tfu* on them, she offered to clean the houses of the Ingelish women who had followed their husbands to Palestine.

And now, mashallah, she was Senora Ermosa. She had a spacious house in a lovely, well-tended yard in Ohel Moshe; she had three daughters, may they be healthy, and a husband, an influential husband, a big merchant, the most highly respected in the Spaniol community, *Wai de mi sola*. If anyone had seen her back then when she was cleaning the toilets of the Ingelish or going to the market at night to pick up vegetables and fruit left out for the poor, they wouldn't believe that the same young girl, the little beggar girl, had become Senora Ermosa.

Gabriel was packing a suitcase for his trip to Beirut. He always packed himself and didn't like Rosa packing for him. "I've got my own special way," he told her. And she'd give in just as she gave in to everything. The moment her neighbors' husbands got home, their wives would fill a tin bath and wash their feet.

But Gabriel had never agreed to her washing his feet. She would fill the bath and he would wash himself. He never sat in his chair like an effendi and waited for her to serve him. When he wanted coffee, he'd get up and make it himself; when he wanted mint tea he'd make it himself, and would reluctantly agree to her going into the yard to pick mint and sage from the plant pots. Shame, shame, she'd say to herself. It's enough that he runs after the girls in the yard. All I need now is for him to be seen picking mint. It sometimes seemed to Rosa that he must have felt he didn't deserve for her to serve him, because he didn't fulfill his marital duties and come to her bed at night.

Now he was putting clothes into the suitcase, and as the suitcase filled up she was emptying, her strength draining away. In his quiet way he was slowly killing her: each fold of his trousers, each fold of a shirt folded her heart. Why, *ya rabi*, O God, why? Why is he doing this to me? Why won't he let me be a wife to him? Why is he smashing me to pieces? And so courteously, quietly. She was standing tensely, waiting for him to say something. Just let him ask her and she'd jump to comply. But he didn't ask for anything and continued packing as if she wasn't there. He suddenly raised his eyes and said, "Rosa, why are you standing there? Go outside and keep an eye on the girls."

The suitcase was packed, and now, she knew, the performance would begin: As soon as Luna saw Gabriel standing in the doorway with his suitcase, she started crying. A ten-year-old girl crying like a baby. She threw herself to the ground. "Papo, Papo, don't go!" And her sisters joined her in chorus. That one screamed, the other screamed, and for a long time they didn't leave their father alone, hanging on to him, holding his legs. With one hand Luna held on to his free hand and on to the door with the other, not letting him pass. How much strength the flaca's got, Rosa thought, amazed, standing like a wall between her father and the door. Rachelika was crying and little Becky was crying but didn't know why. Her sisters were crying, so she cried too.

And Gabriel, his heart was torn. If they went on crying like this, he'd miss the train, so when Rosa finally pulled Luna away from him, he hurried out of the yard without even a good-bye to Rosa. Soon he was already on Agrippas Street, where a taxi waited to take him to the railway station on Hebron Road. From there he'd go by train to Jaffa Port, and after a short stop in Tel Aviv, he'd board the ship for Beirut.

Rosa remained standing in the yard with her sobbing daughters. Luna threw herself down onto the stone tiles, yelling like she was being murdered. Rachelika was holding on to Rosa's apron and crying, and little Becky was hanging on her legs. Rosa stood helpless in the face of the girls' behavior. The neighbors didn't interfere. They knew that in half an hour everything would calm down, and until Gabriel returned, Rosa would run the house. But they didn't know about her daily battles with Luna, the words that insolent child spat at her. Now she was lying on the tiles, kicking her feet and screaming, "Papo, Papo," as if he could hear her. He was on the train, Senor Ermosa, reading a newspaper, looking out the window at the landscape, and he'd already forgotten his daughters' weeping and screaming, and her too. What wouldn't Rosa do to change places with him? Two weeks without Luna would add years to her life. She left the screaming Luna in the yard, took the other two girls by the hands, and led them inside. Rachelika had already calmed down, but after half an hour had passed, Luna still hadn't stopped wreaking havoc in the yard.

"*Uskut!* Shut up!" Rosa heard her neighbor Attias shout at Luna. But that one, nada, what an embarrassment that girl was. After a while it was finally quiet again. Rachelika and little Becky sat at the table and she gave them dinner: a hard-boiled egg and sliced fresh vegetables, a glass of milk, and a piece of white bread with olive oil and zaatar. Rachelika ate with gusto and fed little Becky, who didn't stop chattering.

Rosa looked at her two daughters and thought, God forgive my sins, how much better my life could have been without Luna, and immediately added a *tfu-tfu-tfu,* a *pishcado y limon,* and a God forbid, I should wash my mouth out with soap like I do to Luna every time she's bad. God save me from these thoughts. What kind of a mother am I? she tortured herself. Luna still hadn't come inside, but Rosa wasn't worried. Let her stew in her own juice and then she'll come in with her tail between her legs.

The girls had finished their dinner, and Rosa filled the tin bath. She bathed Becky, and then Rachelika bathed in the same water. Gabriel hated when she did this, but he wasn't here and it was a pity to waste water, and even more so soap. Money didn't grow on trees.

When the girls were in their nightgowns and ready for bed, Rachelika asked, "Mother, where's Luna?" and only then she realized that it'd been hours since Luna's yelling had stopped and the child still hadn't come inside. She went into the yard. Empty. "Luna!" she called, but her cry was greeted by silence. "Luna! I'm coming after you with the sapatos," Rosa threatened. "*Onde 'stas,* where are you?" It was only after all the neighbors came outside that Rosa grasped that Luna had indeed disappeared.

"Dio santo, what am I going to do with that child? That's all I need now, that something should happen to her. Gabriel will kill me!" She became hysterical, and her neighbor Tamar told her, "*Calmata,* Rosa, calm yourself. She's probably someplace in the neighborhood. Where could she possibly have gone? I'll stay here with the little ones and you go and look for Luna with the men. Heideh, *no fiedras el tiempo,* don't waste time."

Rosa hurried off to search for Luna in the winding alleys of Ohel Moshe and in the garden at the center of the neighborhood. God save us, don't let her have fallen into a cistern, the fear insinuated itself into Rosa's mind. It was pitch-dark in the garden, and Senor Attias fetched a lantern and illuminated the inside of the cistern. He checked every inch of the garden and even sent his son Avramino to climb the tree. Maybe Luna was hiding in the branches. But nada, the child had vanished.

Rosa was on the verge of collapse. Adio Senor del mundo, let the child be found, don't let anything happen to her. God help us. If anything happens to her, it will be the end of my life, the end of my family. And the neighbors who saw her so worried tried to encourage her. "Don't worry, Senora Rosa, Ohel Moshe is a small place. How far could she have possibly gone? We'll find her soon."

They didn't tell her they feared that something terrible had happened to the child. These were hard times. Jews were fighting Jews and the Arabs weren't like they used to be. They kidnapped Jews and slaughtered them. And there were also sick people, *pishcado y limon,* and a girl with auburn curls and green eyes, you never know, leshos, leshos*, pishcado y limon.* They prayed that nothing had happened to the daughter of Senor Gabriel and Senora Rosa.

They searched and searched, and it was already the middle of the night and they hadn't found the girl. Rosa sat on the steps of the Ohel Moshe gate, her head in her hands as she wept. Then, from out of nowhere a British police jeep pulled up, and Matilda Franco got out, her face painted like, el Dio que me salva, the girls who sold their bodies. She was wearing a dress so tight-fitting it was like elastic, nylon stockings, and shoes with heels so high that if, God forbid, she fell off them, she'd crack her skull. Let her crack it, the putana, who cares. Rosa looked at her as if she'd seen an evil spirit, and all the neighbors stood outside the Ohel Moshe gate with their mouths agape. They'd heard about Matilda and her English officer, but they'd never seen them together. Her father Meir Franco wanted the ground to open under his feet, and her mother Victoria Franco was holding his hand so he couldn't raise it to his daughter. The surprised Matilda was standing in front of Rosa and asking what happened, and Rosa got up and fell into Matilda's arms and wept. "Luna, Luna's lost."

"How did she get lost?" Matilda asked her.

"She disappeared from the yard. The whole neighborhood has been looking for her for hours," Rosa wailed.

"You haven't found her?" asked Matilda, surpised. And Avramino, Senor Attias's son, came over and yelled, "What do you care if we find her or not, you whore of the English!" Then a fracas ensued with all of them attacking Matilda Franco, and it was only out of respect for her parents that they didn't lynch her.

Out of the corner of her eye, Rosa saw the Francos standing to the side, not coming to their daughter's defense. She saw her brothers' black eyes gleaming in the darkness, but they were standing like soldiers behind their father and mother and not moving a muscle to help their big sister. The whole neighborhood had forgotten her Luna, and all that interested them now was hitting Matilda Franco and cursing her. When a shot was fired into the air, they all fell silent. Matilda's English officer was standing by the jeep with his pistol drawn and shouting in English, "Quiet!"

"Quiet up your *culo*," Avramino Attias whispered, but then went as silent as the rest.

"What's going on here?" the Englishman asked Matilda, and in English she told him that a child had vanished.

On my life, Rosa thought. That one speaks Ingelish like in Ingeland.

The officer started asking questions and Matilda directed him to Rosa. He asked her name and Matilda translated, but Rosa didn't need translation, not for nothing did she work for years cleaning the bastards' houses. At least one good thing had come out of it, Ingelish, and so she told him in fluent English that the child disappeared from their yard three hours ago after her father left for Beirut on business.

The officer waved to the neighbors to disperse and go back home, and told Rosa to get in the jeep. She hesitated.

"Don't be afraid, Senora Rosa," Matilda whispered. "He's English, but he's a good man. He'll help you find Luna."

Rosa didn't care if he was English, Turkish, Arab, Spaniol, or Ashkenazi. All she wanted was to find her daughter.

The Englishman drove for several minutes until they reached the police station on Jaffa Road. He courteously opened the door for Rosa and helped her out. Ingelish, may his name be erased, but a gentleman, she observed. Then he helped Matilda, who despite her high heels jumped out easily. They entered the police station, and to her shock, praise God, there was Luna, sitting beside an officer. Gracias el Dio! On the one hand, her heart was overflowing with joy on seeing the girl, while on the other, she wanted to kill her. She'd almost died because of her!

"Luna," she called, and the child looked at her and started running toward her. Rosa opened her arms to pick her up, but she ignored her and leaped into Matilda's arms without even glancing at her mother. Such shame, Rosa thought. What will the Ingelish think of me? What kind of a child is she who shames her own mother? What have I done wrong in my life, adio Senor del mundo, to deserve a daughter like Luna?

Matilda's English officer sat down behind his desk and asked Rosa to sit opposite him. Matilda took a seat beside her and Luna perched on Matilda's knee, like a baby, not a ten-year-old girl. Rosa could hardly conceal her hurt.

"The child," said Matilda's English officer, "turned up at the station by herself and said that her mother had thrown her out of the house."

"She what?" shouted the stunned Rosa. "Is that what she said?"

"She said," the officer went on, "that as soon as her father left, you took her two sisters inside and left her outside."

"Excuse me, Mr. Officer," Rosa said in her fluent English, "where are you getting all this from?"

"It's all in the duty constable's report," he replied. "I'm reading word for word the statement given by the girl, who came to the station at seven this evening, three hours ago."

Dio mio, she's not a child, she's Satan, Rosa thought. How does she come up with stories like this?

"Is that true?" the officer asked.

And before she could reply, Matilda answered in her place. "Of course it isn't. The child made up a story. I know Madam Ermosa. She's a wonderful mother and a good wife."

All this time Luna was hiding her face in Matilda's shoulder, not looking in her mother's direction.

"So what did happen? Why did the child come to the station to complain about her mother?"

Rosa glanced from Matilda to Matilda's officer. "What can I say, Mr. Officer?" she replied. "The child is very close to her father, and every time he goes away on business she makes a scene. I thought I'd leave her in the yard for a while until she calmed down. I was sure that in a few minutes the chill and the dark would drive her inside. When I realized she wasn't coming in, I went out to the yard, and when I couldn't find her I turned the whole neighborhood upside down. Do I, Mr. Officer, look like a mother who'd throw her daughter out of the house?"

"Definitely not," said Matilda's officer as he got to his feet. "So that's the end of it. I'll report that there was no need for police intervention, that you came to the station looking for your daughter, and now that you've found her, you can take her home. And you"—pinching Luna's cheek—"naughty, naughty, naughty girl. Behave nicely to your mother."

Rosa clutched Luna's hand tightly. Even now, when it was clear that they must leave the police station together, she could feel the child's resistance. Nothing frightens this one, God help me. She goes to the Ingelish police to tell lies about her mother. *Wai de mi sola,* what's she going to do next?

When they got back to Ohel Moshe and passed through the gate, Rosa turned to Matilda and said, "May you be healthy, Matti. I thank you with all my heart. God will help you. You're a good girl, you don't deserve to be with Ingelish. You deserve someone better, one of ours."

Tears welled in Matilda's eyes. "Excuse me, Senora Rosa. It's getting late and I'm very tired. Have a good night," she said and walked toward her house, her skinny heels tapping on the cobblestones.

Rosa was gripping Luna's arm so tightly she was almost ripping it off.

"Ay!" Luna yelped. "Just wait till Papo comes home from Beirut. I'll tell him everything! You'll see what he'll do to you."

Rosa thought she wasn't hearing properly. The child was threatening to snitch on her to Gabriel? Her hand rose in the air and came down on Luna's cheek. "Never! Do you hear me, you bad girl, never ever dare to come between your father and me! Wait till I tell your father that you ran away from home, and of all the places in the world you went to tell lies about your mother to the Ingelish police. We'll see what your father has to say about that."

The threat apparently worked. When Gabriel returned from Beirut, Luna didn't tell him anything about what had transpired that night, and Rosa kept her mouth shut too. The secret remained between them until the day Matilda Franco was murdered.

Gabriel leaned his head against the carriage window, closed his eyes, and listened to the sound of the train's wheels clacking slowly. His forehead banged lightly against the glass, but the sensation was pleasant. He breathed deeply and for the first time in months let himself relax. An old tune started playing in his mind, a children's song his mother sang to him. He began humming it, amazed that he still remembered. After all, he hadn't heard it for almost thirty years.

He always traveled first class. Sitting in his compartment were two men wearing tailored suits and straw hats. Their behavior was foreign and distant like that of the new immigrants from the big European cities whose style flooded Gabriel with a yearning he couldn't comprehend, a yearning for something he had never experienced. He felt a sort of affection for these people who had come from Europe, the immigrants from Germany in particular. Sometimes one of these yekkes would come into his shop in the Mahane Yehuda Market by mistake and only rarely leave with a purchase. Among the abundance of goods in the shop, the yekkes never found anything that took their fancy. They didn't speak Hebrew, and unlike the immigrants from Eastern Europe, they made no effort to learn the language. They expected, in a way that awed Gabriel, that he, who was born here, should try and understand *them,* the newcomers. And yet there was something in the way they dressed, their distant politeness, that he appreciated. He would get angry when his brother Leito called them *yekke potz,* and made sure he knew it.

The two men sitting opposite him were yekkes, he suspected. They didn't exchange a word, nor did they speak to him. When he entered the compartment, they were both immersed in *The Palestine Post* and courteous enough to look up from their papers and nod a greeting, but no more.

He preferred to just lean his head against the window, even though he had a newspaper in his bag. He'd been reading *Haaretz* for years now. When he was younger he'd read *HaZvi,* which his father Raphael used to bring home. But one day his father came home angry and agitated, brandishing a copy of *HaZvi* and quoting from an article by Dov Lifschitz against the Sephardi community. "Starting today, Ben-Yehuda's newspaper will not cross the threshold of our house! We will not buy the paper and we will not mention its name!" Raphael had shouted. The Sephardic rabbis joined the boycott and forbade people to read it. There were also rumors, which were never proven, that the leaders of the community, fuming with rage over the racist article, had even informed the Turks that the paper was preaching revolt. From that day forward the Ermosa family had read *Haaretz.*

But this time, for the journey, Gabriel decided to break his habit and buy *Davar,* the newspaper of the workers of Palestine. His father wouldn't have allowed a socialist paper into the house, and he himself had once called it a "Bolshevik newspaper" and had forbidden Leito to read it in the shop. Now it was Gabriel's way of feeling freedom: first, buying a paper it's forbidden to read, then engaging in other forbidden activities before returning home to Ohel Moshe and the stifling routine of life with Rosa.

He could already envisage how he would spend his time in Beirut: how he'd take a carriage from the railway station directly to his hotel on the seafront. How he would be greeted at the reception desk: "Salaam aleikum ya hawwaja, Ermosa, it's good to have you with us again." And how the clerk would hand him the key to his favorite room, the one with a balcony overlooking the sea. He imagined opening the room door, a cool breeze blowing in and ruffling the heavy drapes, and inhaling the air from the balcony. Then he would take off his suit and put on a pair of thin trousers and a light cotton shirt, and his heavy shoes would be replaced by a pair of comfortable moccasins. After sipping the Zachlawi arak that awaited him in a clear crystal decanter in the sitting area, he would leave the hotel in his straw hat, feeling as light as a feather, as free as a bird, and hire a taxi to take him directly to Aisha in the Marfaa Quarter in Beirut Port.

Ach, *ya* Aisha. He didn't know how he could carry on living with Rosa if he didn't have Aisha. Thinking of her and what she would do to him and he to her when they met made his little bird raise its head, and he shifted uncomfortably on the seat, took the paper from his bag, and started reading. His attention was drawn to an advertisement for Ford cars. "Cut your costs! Buy a Ford!" trumpeted the advertisement, at the center of which was a picture of the car. It's time to spoil myself with a car, to fulfill an old dream, he thought.

He looked out the window again. At the foot of the Arab village of Batir, a shepherd was grazing his flock by the railway line. Alongside the line was a forest of almond trees in full bloom. Tu Bishvat, the New Year for Trees, had just passed. Business boomed at this time of year. The shop had been filled with customers buying goods for the holiday, and now the sacks of dried fruit, almonds, and raisins needed to be replenished with fresh stock. Times were good, thank God. He had turned the shop back around.

"In America, the golden country, there are twenty million people on welfare," he read in the paper. "And despite all of President Roosevelt's efforts, this is the sixth winter since the Wall Street Crash that all these millions of people will be in need of food and money, for if not they will die of hunger and cold." The land of opportunity, he thought to himself, there too people are starving.

Who knew how his good friend Moshe was? It'd been a long time since he'd had news of him or a letter. It had been very fortunate that Gabriel had been clever enough to return to Palestine. But on second thought, was he fortunate? Perhaps if he hadn't come back, he wouldn't have met Rochel, and if he hadn't met her, his father wouldn't have died, and if his father hadn't died, his mother wouldn't have married him to Rosa, and maybe today he'd be married to a woman he loved, a woman he wouldn't run away from every few months to seek love with another.

When he arrived, Tel Aviv's Jaffa Port thronged with people. Gabriel liked the atmosphere, the chaos, the acrid smells that seared his nostrils, the Arabs' exotic apparel, the voices speaking a mélange of languages—Arabic, English, Hebrew. A ship anchored outside the port, and barefoot Arab boatmen wearing sharwals rowed their big boats to the ship and ferried passengers close to the shore. From there they had to make their own way through the waves, carrying their baggage to dry land. Arab policemen vainly tried to keep order and with sweeping gestures and whistles directed the passengers to the port buildings.

Gabriel laughed. The passengers seemed stunned, their fine travel clothes becoming completely soaked. What caught his eye in particular was an older woman fighting the waves. In one hand she held an umbrella and in the other a big brown suitcase, and at the same time she was fighting to keep her wide-brimmed hat from falling into the water.

Ach, Tel Aviv, Tel Aviv. He always felt like a tourist whenever he came to the White City. Tel Aviv is like our own Sodom and Gomorrah, he thought. In Tel Aviv there isn't just one tavern, there are fifty, but not for the Jews, for the British, may their name and memory be erased. He'd read in the paper that five people had been fined for drunkenness, all of them British. The Jews don't know how to drink, it's not in our nature, he thought. He'd once read an article by an English journalist who wrote derisively that in Tel Aviv's taverns they serve whiskey and soda in a wineglass. He'd give those English kerosene to drink if he could. Not whiskey and soda, kerosene—and served in teacups.

After wandering around the port, he looked for a taxi to take him to his usual hotel, the Eshbal on Herbert Samuel Promenade, three blocks from San Remo, his favorite café. A hundred lirot a night and worth every penny. Just outside the port gates he came upon a splendid car. A stunning young blonde exited and asked if he needed a taxi.

"This is a taxi?" he asked, astonished.

The young woman indicated the green license plate, and he got in and made himself comfortable in the backseat. On the way to his hotel, the young woman told him she was a new immigrant from Berlin. She'd come with her parents who'd brought the Austin family car with them, and since she couldn't find a job, she'd been working as a taxi driver.

"What did you do in Berlin?" he asked.

"My father owned a big clothing store, and I studied accounting at the commercial high school so I could help my father manage the store. I'm a senior accountant, but here in Palestine you work at what you can get. I have no complaints."

"Good for you!" Gabriel said. She wasn't the only one. Among the new immigrants he'd already come across girls who worked at tiling floors, doctors working in factories, and lawyers working as foremen on construction sites. Once a sausage salesman had come into the shop in Mahane Yehuda and told him that he used to be a judge in Heidelberg. There's no shame in it, he thought. When he was in New York, he himself had worked as a butcher's apprentice, soiling his hands with animal blood.

The taxi driver pulled up outside the seafront hotel. He always preferred to stay in a hotel than with his sister Allegra. Being under the same roof as his mother had become unbearable. When he went to visit her with Rosa and the girls, he had no choice, but on his own he couldn't stand being with her for even a minute. Every such visit took years off his life. The anger he suppressed most of the time threatened to erupt, and his mother's lack of interest, which she didn't even attempt to conceal, didn't help either.

He went into the hotel, checked in at reception, and went up to his room. After unpacking his suitcase he started walking along the promenade, observing the suntanned people who seemed to be on permanent vacation. When did these people work? He was a Jerusalemite who loved his city, but there was something in easygoing Tel Aviv that captivated him: the women in their summery dresses that revealed alluring necks, the men in their white suits and straw hats, the young mothers pushing white prams along the promenade, the crowded cafés and the casino that actually stood in the sea. Mashallah, Tel Aviv will soon be Beirut, he thought.

Ach, Beirut, Beirut, how he loved the Lebanese capital, how he loved going to that vibrant city on the sea. He knew that he no longer needed to travel as far as Beirut to buy stock. Chaim Saragusti in Tel Aviv's Levinsky Market stocked everything he needed for his shop. Mr. Saragusti was a big merchant, much bigger than him, and he went to Beirut several times a year to buy stock that was sufficient for all the shops in the Levinsky Market and certainly for Raphael Ermosa's in the Mahane Yehuda Market too. He could buy spices at Chaim Saragusti's, sweets, Turkish delight, and arak that would last all year. But he, so long as he had the strength, would not give up going to Beirut. Only there was he able to remove the burden of life from his shoulders and felt like a young man just beginning to live. And Aisha, only she gave him the air he needed to go on pretending, to not explode. Ach, *ya* Aisha, his life had been changed since that stormy night two years ago when she'd taken him into her bed.

He had never been a ladies' man. He had only ever loved one woman, but she had been driven out of his life with unbearable cruelty. He had never needed more than one woman and one love and never sought sexual escapades. All the years he lived in New York were without a woman.

But with Aisha it was different. For the first time in his life he, a married man with three daughters, felt the way a man feels when he's with a woman. Until that night with Aisha, he'd felt like a virgin. He had loved Rochel with every fiber of his being, and although they had both wanted it, he had never been with her in the way a man is with a woman, despite sometimes feeling he could no longer hold back when she urged him. He had convinced her and himself to abstain until their wedding night that never came. He went to Rosa's bed, but he had never lost himself in the act of love. He came to her to observe the biblical precept of "be fruitful and multiply," not to feel his body shudder, not to soar on indescribably sublime pleasure, the way he'd felt that first time with Aisha.

That night would be engraved in his mind forever. A strong wind was blowing in from the sea and the heavens opened and sheets of rain lashed the streets. Gabriel returned to his hotel room from a routine day's work buying stock for the shop. Although it was early, the merchants in the Beirut market had hurried to shut down their stalls because the stormy weather deterred customers from shopping.

Normally he would bathe to wash away the day, change into light clothes, sip a glass of arak, and go down to the seafront. He'd sit in one of the cafés, smoke a narghile, and have a demitasse of the strong black coffee that only Beirutis knew how to make. He'd sometimes visit his sweetmeat merchant friend Marouane at his house in the al-Ashrafieh Quarter, and there, after dining on the splendid dishes Marouane's wife made, they'd go out onto the spacious balcony that circled the house, smoke a narghile, sip Zachlawi arak, and inhale the cool air of Beirut. On Friday evenings he'd go to the Magen Avraham Synagogue in the Jewish quarter in Wadi Abu Jamil, and if he was lucky, he'd be able to hear the bell-like sound of the synagogue's children's choir.

But it was too cold and wet to visit friends that night, and too late for the evening service at the synagogue, so he got into bed and stared at the ceiling. He was wide awake and tossed and turned restlessly. Gabriel didn't like lying idly in bed, nor did he like the thoughts stealing into his mind. He didn't want to recall Rochel. He was no longer able to bear the ache that lodged in his chest each time he thought of her. He didn't want to think about his life with Rosa. She was a good wife and the mother of his daughters, and for that he was grateful, but he couldn't feel anything for her apart from obligation. Sometimes he would notice her pleading look and he'd feel her pain, but his feet wouldn't carry him to her.

He didn't want to think about the life he might have had if he'd been able to marry his beloved, if his father hadn't died and his mother hadn't treated him as if he were a scorpion. True, he had the girls, but was being a father enough to make a man feel alive? He also had respect, the respect of the community, the market merchants, the neighbors, the mukhtar, and his family. They all gave him the utmost respect, all except his mother. His sisters and brother had long since forgiven him, but she hadn't and never would. And the truth? He didn't forgive her either. No, he didn't forgive her for burdening him with such heavy guilt. Was it really him who had killed his father? Were he and Rochel to blame for his father succumbing to a heart attack in the middle of the night? After all, Raphael, may he rest in peace, was not a young man. He was old, over fifty, and it was even inscribed on his gravestone in the Mount of Olives cemetery: "Here lies the wise old man Raphael Ermosa." And Rochel, what had become of her? He hadn't dared to ask Clara what happened the night his father died. Had Rochel returned in shame to her father's house in Mea Shearim? Had her parents married her off like his mother had married him off, in haste to a man who wasn't a groise metzieh, a bargain, as the Ashkenazim say sarcastically? Did a flawed groom who nobody wanted win the most enchanting of them all?

Ach, how much more pain could fill his heart, God help him. There was no more room in him for pain, no more room in his head for these thoughts. Gabriel got out of bed and began pacing. Through the window he saw it was raining heavily and as dark as the grave, but there, in the distance, in the Marfaa Quarter by the port, lights were flickering. There, he knew, life went on, even when the rain was coming down hard, even when chilly winds threatened the treetops, even when there wasn't a dog to be seen in the streets.

He got dressed, took his umbrella, and left the room. The hotel lobby was empty. Even the reception clerk had realized that he wouldn't have anything to do on a night like this and had gone to bed. Gabriel left the hotel, and ignoring the wind and rain, started toward the port.

The stormy night had driven the sailors on the ships anchored in the port to their cabins, and the streets were dark and deserted. Only the brothels and bars lit up the night. Gabriel had never been in this neighborhood. As he stood outside a building with a red light over its doorway, gripping his umbrella, its door suddenly opened and an invisible hand seemed to shoot out and draw him inside. "*Ya sidi,* come in, come in. Why are you standing like that in this rain? *Allah yustur,* God save us, you'll catch pneumonia."

The invisible hand was connected to a young woman in a tight-fitting red dress that hugged her bounteous curves. Her breasts threatened to burst out of her deep neckline, and reposing in her cleavage was a gleaming green stone suspended from a gold chain. Her black hair fell to her shoulders, gold earrings hung from her earlobes, and gold bracelets adorned her thick forearms as far as the elbow. Her fleshy lips bore bright red lipstick, and thick makeup covered her eyelids. Gabriel was breathless and unable to utter a sound.

The room she led him into was large, and on every wall were doors leading to other rooms. Red velvet armchairs and couches dotted the room, a chandelier hung from the ceiling, and burning candles were all around. Gabriel smelled the sweetish scent of hashish mixed with cheap perfume. Sitting on the couches were young women who paled in comparison to the one holding his hand, and there were also men in the room, some sharing a narghile with the women in their laps. The warm voice of Fairouz could be heard in the background and a wood fire blazed in the hearth. The woman removed his damp coat and hung it to dry by the fire, then sat him down in one of the armchairs.

"Salaam aleikum," he greeted the room in Arabic, and they responded with a nod and "Aleikum salaam."

The woman disappeared for a moment and came back with a glass of Zachlawi arak. "It'll warm you up," she said. He downed the liquor in one gulp and felt its warmth spread in his belly. The woman asked his name.

"I'm Aisha," she introduced herself with a seductive smile. He liked her. When he dared to look directly at her, Gabriel could see a pair of beautiful black eyes beneath the heavy makeup.

They sat there for a few more minutes, and then she took his hand and led him into one of the rooms and without much delay started undressing him. He stood there not knowing what to do, his arms too long, his body too heavy. She kneeled and started taking off his shoes, unlacing them very slowly. Soon enough he stood there in his underwear, feeling like a boy with a woman for the first time. She moved close and threw him onto the bed. She was a whore, he knew that, she was working, and he knew that too. But she was so gentle, as if she were making love to him, not simply doing what she was paid for. He was closed, completely tense, and she asked in astonishment, "Is this your first time?" He blushed like a child and shook his head. "So why are you like this, *ya habibi?*" she asked. "Why are you lying curled up like a baby still in its mother's womb?"

He was silent. What could he tell her? That he didn't exactly know what to do? That the only times he'd done it were when he'd forced his little bird into Rosa's nest, praying that it wouldn't lower its head before he'd managed to observe the biblical commandment?

Fortunately Aisha didn't ask any more questions. With tenderness she thawed out his frozen body, and he felt the heat course through him to his chest. He had never felt such pleasure, never felt his skin against a woman's skin like this. Never before had he burned the way he burned in Aisha's bed in the Beirut brothel.

For the duration of his trip, Gabriel went to Aisha at the brothel every day, extending his stay in the city to spend as much time as possible with her. Sometimes she was busy with other men, and he waited patiently for her, declining the madam's suggestion that he try a different girl. He paid generously for her services, always more than the going rate, and the extra money he didn't give to the madam, he hid between Aisha's thighs. His visits with her in Beirut every few months enabled him to function and continue with the great charade that was his life. They never met outside the brothel and never asked about each other's life. They smoked hashish together, drank arak, laughed a lot, and did with each other's body whatever they felt like doing, and he'd return to Jerusalem sated, feeling that he had been charged with a thousand horsepower.

Ach, Aisha, Aisha. He couldn't wait for the instant he set foot in the doorway of the brothel in Beirut. So many times the moment of their coming together on her canopied bed had run through his mind.

The strong rays of the summer sun in Tel Aviv beat down on him, and he awoke from his daydreaming. In Jerusalem, he thought, the sun has the color of gold. In Tel Aviv, it's the color of a consuming fire.

Gabriel continued strolling along the promenade until he reached Café San Remo and sat down at a table. A tuxedoed waiter came over, and in a thick Eastern European accent asked what he would like. He ordered a black coffee and a glass of water and rubbed his eyes at the sight of the people clad only in bathing suits passing by on their way to the beach. He'd just read an article in the paper condemning the behavior of the residents of Tel Aviv and about a new law about to be enacted that would prohibit them from walking in bathing suits on the streets by the beach. He was deep in thought about the terrible state of affairs in Palestine, about the country's declining morals, about Jewish girls going out with Englishmen, God help us, about the brothels sprouting like mushrooms after rain. Brothels in Beirut were fine for the cursed Arabs, may all their women be whores, but here, in Tel Aviv? He would never cross the threshold of a Jewish brothel. He would never do what he did with Aisha with a Jewish girl.

He looked around. The café was filled with mothers with prams, young couples, a few men reading their papers, and also British soldiers sitting with Jewish women. He hissed a curse through his mustache and gazed at the sea. And then he saw her. At first he thought he was hallucinating, seeing his own thoughts. It couldn't be her. The woman walking arm in arm with a man of British appearance seemed far older than Rochel. Rochel was a girl, a thin girl who always wore baggy, long-sleeved dresses that went down to her ankles. This woman was indeed slim but was wearing a flowing floral dress that showed off her arms and legs. Rochel always wore thick black stockings, while this woman was wearing sheer nylons and high heels, and instead of in braids, her golden hair was tied in a ponytail at her neck. He stopped breathing and looked again at the man and woman about to enter the café. He noticed her upright, confident walk. There was something rebellious in the way she clasped the arm of the man. Gabriel tried to persuade himself that he was mistaken. It was impossible that it was her! But then she turned her face toward him and he saw the eyes, the bluest eyes he had seen in all his life, Rochel's eyes.

It was Rochel without a doubt. His pure Rochel strolling like a whore with an Englishman. The blood pounded in his temples. He was breathless. His face turned red and his hand hit the glass on his table, spilling its contents over his pants. No, not Rochel, Dio santo! He laid a five-lira bill on the table and hurried out of the café. Had she seen him?

He ran for dear life. He didn't remember getting back to the hotel, he didn't remember how he got up to his room and quickly packed his suitcase, how he paid his bill and got a taxi to take him to the bus station. He didn't remember boarding the first bus back to Jerusalem.

He didn't visit his mother on Rothschild Boulevard, didn't go do business with Chaim Saragusti in the Levinsky Market, and didn't go to Beirut. Neither Aisha nor all the wonders she brought him could heal the wound that had been reopened in his heart.

4

"Always Do What You Feel, Drink Carmel Hock with Every Meal." The advertisement at the bottom of the front page of *Haaretz* roused Gabriel's ire. "To hell with them. We already have problems with drunks, and now they have to go encouraging people to drink," he mumbled under his mustache, angrily throwing the paper onto the table and striding out into the yard.

Rosa picked up the paper and searched for what had made Gabriel so angry. She stared at the printed letters, which said nothing to her until her eyes lit on a picture of a wine bottle.

"What's this? What's written here?" she asked Luna who had just come in.

"It's an advertisement for wine," she replied. "Is that the only thing in the paper that interests you?"

Insolent child, Rosa thought. But right away her mind shifted from her daughter's insolence to Ephraim. For a long time young Ephraim had been drinking himself insensible. From day to day she had seen how her poor brother was losing his human semblance, a handsome young man becoming a shadow of his former self, but she didn't have the strength to halt his decline. As much as she'd pleaded and he'd promised, he hadn't stopped drinking.

Gabriel had tried to help, taking him to work in the shop even though he wasn't able to lift a tin of salty cheese because he was all skin and bones. But the ungrateful Ephraim never got up on time for work. The troncho couldn't wake up in the morning like everybody else. Gabriel, may he be healthy, would have been in the shop since morning prayers, and Ephraim? Nada, he'd barely make it to afternoon prayers on time, and only after she'd wake him with shouts and kick him out of bed. "If he carries on like this, he can't go on living here," Gabriel had warned her. "It's not healthy for the girls to see him durmiendo all day, and when he is awake he's as drunk as a lord. You've got to do something."

What could she do? He was her little brother, he was all that was left of her family. She didn't know whether Nissim in America was alive or dead. It'd been a very long time since they'd last received a letter from him. So what remained of her family other than her little brother Ephraim, who as soon as he opened his eyes was glued to a bottle of arak and didn't stop drinking until he fell down, and didn't know the name his father and mother had given him?

Gabriel hadn't been his usual self since he'd returned from his last trip to Beirut. He'd been irritable and testy; he'd lost his famous patience. He hardly exchanged a word with Rosa, and he didn't laugh with the girls like he used to. She didn't understand what had made him come home from his trip without warning after only a day. He was usually away for at least a month.

Rosa was in the yard hanging washing on the line when he came back through the gate the day after he'd left. The moment she saw him she felt the blood drain from her head to her feet. Why is he back so soon? she silently worried. Has he heard a rumor about Luna running away from home? Has he been told that I found her at the Ingelish police station? Dio mio, how can I face him? But he passed her by and went into the house, not even stopping to say hello. The girls' happy shouts on seeing their father calmed her somewhat, such joy making her feel that nothing bad could have happened.

When she went inside they were already hanging on to his knees, waiting for him to take the presents he'd bought them from his bag, but there weren't any presents. Gabriel stroked the girls' heads and kissed them, burying his face in their necks, seeking consolation in their soft skin. Luna stole a glance at her mother, fearing that she might break her word and tell her father what she had done. Rosa's unwavering stare allayed her fears. For the first and last time in their lives, mother and daughter made an unspoken pact.

"Papo, haven't you brought anything?" asked the disappointed Luna.

"Queridas," he replied in a weary, exhausted voice, "I couldn't. I had to come back to our Jerusalem urgently, but tomorrow I'll buy you something from the toy shop on Jaffa Road. I promise."

He detached the girls, got up from the chair, changed his clothes quickly, and unusually for him, didn't unpack his suitcase. "I'm going to the shop," he told Rosa, and he was already out of the house and on the way to the Mahane Yehuda Market.

At that moment Ephraim emerged from his room. Borracho, drunk, Rosa thought to herself. All I need is for Gabriel to see him like this again. He's just opened his eyes and already he's stuck to the bottle. He can go to hell. I can't fight all these battles. He's a grown man, I've taken enough care of him. From now on it's his life. If he wants to be a drunk, he can be a drunk, but not in my house!

"Listen to me, Ephraim," Rosa said with uncharacteristic assertiveness. "If you don't stop with the bottle, you can look for someplace else to live, do you hear me? There have never been and never will be drunks in my house. So make up your mind. Either you stop drinking and carry on living with us or you go through that door and don't come back!"

Glassy-eyed, Ephraim looked at his sister and retorted derisively, "Who do you think you are, Senora Ermosa? Where do you think you came from? You've forgotten we both come from the same shit!"

"*Sera la boca!*" she ordered him in an icy voice. "Shut your mouth! Don't speak to me like that in front of the children."

"Who are you, my mother?"

Now he had really enraged her. "*Ya* Amalek, who's been like a mother to you since you were five? Who raised you? Who took food from her own mouth and gave it to you? Have you forgotten, you stupid ass, has the bottle made you forget, eh?"

"I haven't forgotten and haven't remembered. Now leave me alone," he said and left the house.

To hell with him. Let him go and not come back, Rosa thought. But when Ephraim didn't return that night and the following night too, Rosa's heart filled with concern. "Who knows where he's wandering?" she said to Gabriel. "Maybe the Ingelish have arrested him? Maybe he's lying in some pit drunk? How can we know?"

"The English haven't arrested him and he's not lying in a pit."

"How do you know?"

"I know."

"What do you know? Por Dio santo, Gabriel, tell me what you know."

"Your borracho brother is all right. I've fixed him up."

Rosa was stunned.

"I've sent him to work for my brother-in-law Elazar in Tel Aviv," Gabriel continued.

"How can he work? You know he's a drunk."

"It's better he's drunk in Elazar's grocery than with us! It's no good for the girls seeing their uncle in bed all day. And even when he's not in bed, it's better not to have to be near him with his breath stinking from arak, and the words that come out of his mouth."

"And where will he live and who'll look after him?"

"He'll live in a room over the shop and start looking after himself. Basta! He's old enough to be married."

"Gabriel querido, I beg you, he's my brother, the only one I've got. Bring him back to Jerusalem. I'll be so worried I won't sleep."

"It's all arranged!" Gabriel replied vehemently. "Ephraim's staying in Tel Aviv and that's that! He'll manage, you'll see."

Ephraim didn't come back to Jerusalem again, and neither did he make it to Elazar's grocery in Tel Aviv. Rosa didn't hear from him again until one day the British police, may their name be erased, knocked on her door. "We're looking for Ephraim Meshulam," they told her and entered the house without her inviting them in. They turned over the rooms, searched the cupboards, under the beds, in the bed linen chests. They took out all the pots and pans from the shelf under the kitchen sink, all the books from their shelves. Frightened and crying, the girls hung on to her, and only Luna escaped from the house and ran to the market to fetch Gabriel.

It didn't help when Rosa told the British policemen, "I haven't seen my brother for months. I've no idea if he's alive or dead. I haven't heard from him since my husband sent him to Tel Aviv." They didn't believe her and took her to the Russian Compound, not even letting her make an arrangement for the girls.

"Don't worry, Rosa," her dear neighbor Tamar called out, "I'll take care of the girls and Gabriel will come straight to the Russian Compound and get you out."

Within minutes of the police arriving, the whole neighborhood was outside. Rosa was taken away by the Amalekites, her girls running after her crying, the neighbors watching helplessly, not understanding what the British police wanted with Senora Rosa, Senor Ermosa's quiet, obedient wife.

They questioned her for five hours.

"But why?" she asked. "What has he done? All in all he's a good man. He's just a drunk."

"A drunk?" The interrogating officer laughed. "A drunk I can understand, but your brother's not a drunk, Mrs. Ermosa, your brother's a terrorist!"

"A terrorist, what terrorist? He sleeps all day, Mr. Officer, so excuse me, but are you sure you're talking about Ephraim Meshulam?"

"Madam," he said, taking a photograph from the file on his desk and showing it to her, "is this your brother Ephraim Meshulam?"

Rosa saw Ephraim looking at her from the photograph. His face was a little fuller than it was when he'd left, and he didn't look blank like he did when he was drunk. He looked, well, determined. He looked, thank God, like a human being.

"Is this your brother?" the British officer asked.

"Yes, sir," she replied, "that's my brother. But it's been a long time since I last saw him. I've had no contact with him since my husband arranged for him to live over my brother-in-law's grocery in Tel Aviv."

"Doesn't he visit you? Hasn't he asked you to hide him? Hasn't he asked you for help recently?"

"Why help him? Why hide him? What has he done?"

"He's caused a lot of trouble, madam," the officer said. "He's wanted for murder!"

"Murder? God forgive my sins. Ephraim wanted for murder? He's as weak as a little girl. He isn't even capable of killing a fly."

"It seems to me, madam," now the officer was angry, "that you're telling me barefaced lies! Your brother's wanted for the murder of a British policeman. He's a member of the Stern Gang, and we're going to find him and hang him and his friends too."

Rosa was shocked by what the officer had told her, but in her heart she felt great pride. Something had finally come of her little brother. He wasn't just a drunk *qui no vala nada*, worthless, as Gabriel said. He was fighting the Ingelish, damn them. Little Ephraim, may he be healthy, her dear brother, the apple of her eye, was no longer a drunk. He was a hero!

Gabriel was waiting for her outside the Russian Compound.

"The sons of bitches wouldn't let me in," he apologized.

Breathlessly she told him about Ephraim. "Can you believe that's what's become of him?"

"What are you so happy about?" he said, dampening her enthusiasm. "Being in the Stern Gang is right for him. They're all bandits, they're worse than the Arabs."

"But Gabriel," she said, "he's fighting to drive the cursed Ingelish out of Palestine!"

"We don't have to kill the English to get rid of them. We need to talk to them, negotiate. As they say in the Haganah, violence and murder are not our way. Jews do not murder for the sake of it." With that he ended the discussion and started walking.

Rosa was left not knowing what to do with herself. Only moments ago she'd been so proud of her little brother who'd stopped being a drunken oaf and become a freedom fighter, and now her husband was calling him a murderer. He can call him whatever he wants; for me he's a hero! she thought. If only she could tell him that she, his big sister, was proud of him, so he knew she was here for him! Gracias, gracias el Dio, may He be praised forever, Ephraim is a man again.

The Habima Theatre was performing *Uriel Acosta* at the Edison. At the Maccabi sports field there was a national competition between Hapoel Jerusalem and Maccabi Hashmonai Jerusalem. But Gabriel was stuck at home with Rosa, staring at the newspaper advertisements. He needed to get out of Ohel Moshe, out of Jerusalem, and escape from himself. Since the day he saw Rochel with the Englishman in Tel Aviv, he had found no peace. An awful pain had settled in his chest. Nothing made him happy, not even his daughters, not even Luna. He felt like old age had overtaken him, a man of a little more than thirty feeling like an old man of sixty.

He spoke to Rosa even less than he did before. When he'd come home from the shop he wouldn't play with the girls. He didn't have the patience. He'd lost a lot of weight and stopped shaving. Dark stubble adorned his face. The elegant, meticulously dressed man now appeared more unkempt than ever before. He started wearing a black French-style beret and spent a lot of time in his chair in the yard staring into space. He had even stopped buying *Haaretz*, the paper that once seemed glued to his hands.

For years he'd leave the shop for his afternoon break, walk to Jaffa Road, and buy the paper from Franz, the fat newspaper seller who was a lawyer in Austria, and linger for a while exchanging views with him.

"Did you hear about the tragedy in Tel Aviv?" Franz had asked in his thick German accent one afternoon before Gabriel became ill. "Tel Aviv's first grandchild, Aharon Ellman, fell from their balcony and died."

"How did he die?" Gabriel asked, momentarily coming alive.

"The mother," Franz replied, "left him in his cradle on their third-floor balcony on Hagilboa Street, the child lost his balance, fell from the balcony, and died."

Gabriel took his paper, left a half-grush coin on the counter, and went on his way.

Ill winds are blowing in the country, Gabriel thought as he walked back to the shop. The Jewish people are in danger. The death of a young child because of his mother's negligence, sad though it might be, was but a tiny grain of sand in the storm that was approaching. He felt it in the pit of his stomach. He didn't think he could endure his life any longer. Rosa, even the girls had become a burden. And Luna, she didn't give up. She nagged him, the miskenica; she wanted her papo back. But he couldn't go back to what he was, Dio mio, he couldn't go back to being her beloved papo. He didn't love himself, so how could he love her? How could he love her sisters? If only he could run. He'd join the Haganah. Perhaps if he occupied himself with the troubles of the Jewish people, he'd be less preoccupied with himself.

In Germany they're firing Jewish public transportation drivers and Jewish doctors from the hospitals. And what are we doing here in Palestine? Striking, Gabriel continued his train of thought. At such a difficult time, the teachers had decided to go on strike. They opposed teaching mornings and afternoons, so the girls were no longer going to school in the mornings, and he had Rosa going on at him. All of a sudden she'd started complaining. Up till then she hadn't had a single grievance about anything, which made it easier to tolerate her, but now, *sano que 'ste*, she had a mouth on her. First she drove him crazy with her borracho brother, that wretched drunk, making him into a national hero. Then she complained that the girls were at home all day giving her a headache. What does she want, for me to leave the shop and look after them? I still have *some* self-respect. But do I? Does anyone really have self-respect these days? We've become a people of doormats, it's disgusting! The British do as they please with us—curfews, arrests, intimidation. Just look at the big heroes in the market. All they know is talk: We'll show them, we'll do this, that, and the other to them. But each time there's a curfew they rush to close their stalls and scurry home like mice to their holes. We've got self-respect? Crates of oranges that fell off a cargo ship wash up on the beach, and the whole of Tel Aviv is there—men, women, old people, and children—looting crates that aren't theirs, foreign property, the fruit of other people's labor. *Looting the Sea,* the paper said. Is this what people do with respect?

Where have the old times gone? He longed for the pride felt in the Yishuv, the Jewish community in Palestine in 1920, after Joseph Trumpeldor, who had lost an arm in the Russo-Japanese War, fell with his comrades defending Tel Hai. Gabriel would always remember the passionate eulogy delivered by Berl Katznelson, who said, among other things, "May the People of Israel remember the valiant men and women who braved mortal danger in days of struggle."

There hadn't been much time for emotion back then. Each day brought fresh troubles as relations with the Arabs deteriorated. Gabriel, who had done business with both local Arabs and merchants from the Old City, had harbored hopes that the troubles were still caused by people from the radical fringes on both sides, as his own father, may he rest in peace, had explained to him. But when Arab hooligans ran amok in the Old City's alleys, looting shops and homes, and burst into their house and took his mother's jewelry, he began to question this belief. The sight of tens of thousands of Arabs celebrating in the city square, raising their hands to heaven and chanting, *"Idbach al Yahud!* Slaughter the Jews!"* was permanently imprinted on his memory.

When did we become enemies? Weren't we always good neighbors over the years? Gabriel wondered.

In normal times he would have taken Luna to hear the Yemenite singers Bracha Zefira and Nachum Nardi, who had come specially from Tel Aviv to perform at the Edison. He loved music, and Luna, unlike Rosa who was interested in nothing and was uneducated, Luna enjoyed culture like him. He was teaching her to enjoy the theater, the cinema, opera. When they were in Tel Aviv last year he'd taken her to the Opera House in Herbert Samuel Square to see *The Barber of Seville,* conducted by Mordechai Golinkin. Yes, he went to the opera with Luna, who was only a child, for who else could he have gone with? Which of the people in his life liked opera? His ignoramus of a wife? His sister Allegra and her fool of a husband? Perhaps his mother. If she were a normal human being and not the evil witch she'd become, she might have been a worthy companion for the opera.

Once, long ago, before the Flood, before the catastrophes befell him, when she was a mother like a mother should be, he'd learned a lot from her. "As wise as a man!" people said of Mercada. She'd explain about the celestial bodies, the Great Bear, the Little Bear, the Milky Way, the moon and stars. She'd tell him how God created the world and describe the logic of the universe. There was more depth and knowledge in her than in anyone he had ever known. Even though she had not one day of schooling, she knew more than most people.

She'd taught herself to read and write, with the help of his father Raphael, who had immense respect for her intelligence. Not one Spaniol woman of her age—neighbor, relative, or acquaintance—could read and write. Only his mother, Mercada Ermosa.

But perhaps in the end his mother wasn't all that clever. If she was, then perhaps she wouldn't have forced him to give up the love of his life, and when his father died, she wouldn't have killed him, her eldest son, whom she loved best of all her children.

For a few days now Gabriel hadn't gone to the shop. He lay in his bed like a dead man and refused to get up.

"Gabriel querido, *que pasa?*" Rosa tried to talk to him, but he didn't answer. He looked through her with glazed eyes. Those aren't Gabriel's green eyes, but the eyes of a corpse! she thought, horrified. Dio mio, who can get him out of bed? Luna, only Luna. I'll talk to the girl, beg her if necessary.

Rosa didn't have to beg. Luna was only ten, but she could sense that her father was very sick and was scared to death.

"Papo, what's hurting you, querido?" she asked him with a gentleness she had never shown to anyone else.

Gabriel wanted to speak to console her, his lovely daughter, but his voice stuck in his throat and not a sound escaped. He wanted to hug her, but he felt as if he were strapped to the bed, his arms trapped under the blankets.

Rachelika and Becky were standing next to Luna at Gabriel's bedside. Little Becky was weeping, not understanding why her father was sad, why her mother was sad, why her sisters were sad. Rachelika helped Luna rearrange the blanket and the pillows under Gabriel, who lay there unmoving like a block of wood.

"Mother, come and help us lift Papo up," Rachelika said, and as Rosa hurried over, Luna pushed her away. "There's no need, we'll manage. Go and make him some tea," she said.

The blood rose to Rosa's head. Who'd ever heard of such a thing? She won't let me anywhere near Gabriel and hardly lets Rachelika look after him. She wants him just for herself! But now wasn't the time to get angry with the flaca. She'd settle that score when Gabriel was better.

This couldn't go on. When Dr. Sabo had examined Gabriel, he'd told her, "Your husband's as healthy as an ox. He needs a little fish oil and sulfur salts to build up his strength, that's all," and wrote a prescription.

She'd fetched the medicine, but Gabriel refused to take it. He'd been behaving like a child. You'd speak to him and he'd turn over onto his other side.

In the mornings the girls went off to school and she remained at home alone with him. She was at a loss. How should she speak to him? What could she say? From where could she summon the strength to force this big man out of bed and onto his feet? He wasn't Ephraim, whom she could shout at, pull off the blankets, and kick out of bed. He was her husband, Gabriel Ermosa.

Help came from a place she'd never imagined. On a Friday, five days after Gabriel first took to his bed, five hours before Shabbat arrived, there was a knock at the door. Rosa opened it, and her heart almost dropped into her shoes at the sight of that sour old woman standing there: her mother-in-law Mercada.

"*Donde 'ste Gabriel?*" Mercada asked as she walked in without even a hello, as if it had not been years since her foot last crossed the threshold of this house that had once been hers.

As Mercada stood at Gabriel's bedside, for the first time in five days he reacted to what was going on around him. His eyes, dead and apathetic, widened at his mother standing over him and transfixing him with her gaze.

"*Como 'stas?*" his mother asked in a businesslike voice but got no answer.

Mercada didn't waste a second. She turned to Rosa and ordered, "Go outside and don't let anybody in until I open the door."

Rosa quickly went into the yard, not daring to disobey or ask questions, sat down in the chair, and waited.

When the girls came home from school, Rosa didn't let them go inside. Rachelika and Becky played hopscotch and only Luna stubbornly insisted on entering.

"Don't touch the door," Rosa told her.

"But I want to say hello to Papo."

"Soon. Nona Mercada is with him now. We'll go inside soon."

"Nona Mercada from Tel Aviv?" Luna was overjoyed and tried to turn the door handle, but Mercada had locked and bolted the door from the inside.

"Quiet, quiet," Rosa begged Luna not to disturb Mercada, Heaven forbid the sour old woman lose her temper.

It had been years since she had gone to live with Allegra in Tel Aviv, and Rosa was still as frightened of her as she had been when she first came to this house, the poor orphan from the Shama neighborhood, the frightened bride.

Luna didn't listen, the stubborn girl, and banged on the door, shouting, "Papo! Papo!"

She'll wake the dead on the Mount of Olives yet, Rosa thought. Luna didn't stop yelling and pleading with her grandmother. "Nona, Nona, open the door, let me in!"

But Nona was locked inside with her son and the door didn't open. Luna was stubborn, but Mercada was twice as stubborn!

Hours passed and the sun was already setting. It would soon be Shabbat and Mercada hadn't opened the door.

The girls lost patience. Becky started crying and Rachelika, who usually had the patience of a saint, started nagging. Luna stood with her ear to the door trying to hear and climbed up to the window trying to see inside, but the sour old woman had closed the curtains.

Soon the Ishkenazis from Mea Shearim would come past, sound a loud blast on the shofar, and call, "*Shabbes!*" and she'd still be sitting in the yard with her restless girls waiting for Mercada to open the door.

Soon she too would run out of patience. "Heideh," she told the girls, "we're going to Tio Shmuel and Tia Miriam's." By the time they reached Shmuel's house in the adjacent Sukkat Shalom neighborhood, it was almost Shabbat.

"Your mother's at our house with Gabriel," she told Shmuel.

"My mother's come from Tel Aviv?" he asked, and right away wanted to go see her.

"Don't go," Rosa said. "She told me to stay away, closed the door, and said we could only come back in when she opens it."

"How long has she been with him?"

"Almost since they closed the shops in the market for Shabbat," she replied.

While the girls played in the yard with their cousins, Rosa, Shmuel, and Miriam sat inside in a tense silence.

Miriam suddenly said, "She's probably doing livianos for him to drive out the fears that put him in bed."

As Miriam said this, Rosa's heart was suddenly quiet, calm. There isn't anyone Mercada can't save with her livianos, she thought. Before the night is over, she'll save Gabriel too, and he'll rise from his bed once more.

Rosa and the girls didn't go home that night. When the time came for Kiddush, they sat around the Shabbat table in Shmuel and Miriam's house. She and the girls hadn't bathed, so they welcomed the Sabbath in their everyday clothes, and for the first time since the girls were born, they drank the Kiddush wine at a Shabbat table that wasn't their own and with a man who wasn't their father. The girls, Rosa noticed, didn't complain, except for Luna who constantly shot angry looks at her mother and the door. After Kiddush and the Shabbat dinner, Miriam said to Rosa, "Until Mercada comes to call you home, put the girls to bed with my children. When it's time, we'll wake them up and you'll go back."

Rachelika and Becky were quite happy about having a sleepover with their cousins, but Luna stomped her foot and insisted, "I want to sleep in my own house!"

Miriam tried to pacify her, but Rosa didn't even make an effort.

"I'm going home!" Luna persisted, bolting through the door with Rosa on her heels. I'll die if I'm seen running after this girl, Rosa said to herself. I'll walk at a snail's pace so people don't think, God forbid, that I'm chasing after her, so nobody in Ohel Moshe sees how this child walks all over me. If I wasn't afraid she'd run to the Ingelish police again, I'd just let her go.

It was a ten-minute walk to their house in Ohel Moshe, ten minutes that seemed like eternity. Rosa was frightened of both Mercada and Luna. Both of them, the old woman and the girl, cast terror into her heart.

Luna stood by the door, pounding it with her fists and kicking it wildly. "Papo, Papo, Papo!" she shouted. "Open the door, Papo, I want to come in." But the door remained locked, and when Rosa arrived, the child started throwing herself to the ground, doing her usual performance. Rosa was afraid to leave her there. It hadn't been that long since the girl went to the police and told them that she'd thrown her out of the house. She remained standing beside the child, who had deafened the whole neighborhood and no doubt disturbed their Shabbat dinner. But nobody came out into the yard. Rosa was mortified. Even the neighbors had gotten used to Luna's performances.

Luna's screams and sobs shattered the Shabbat eve silence. Like a dog baying at the moon, thought Rosa, she's screaming like a lunatic! The door of the house suddenly shot open and the sour old woman was in the doorway, banging her cane on the floor as she said in an icy voice, "Basta!" All at once the sobbing stopped and the child stood agape facing her grandmother, who went back inside and slammed the door.

Rosa was petrified. Luna got up and went through the yard gate and into the alley. Rosa followed step by step, making sure she didn't go to the Ingelish police and tell them lies again. But Luna didn't go to the police. She went back to Shmuel's house.

When Rosa arrived a few minutes after her, Miriam pointed and whispered, "In there with the children." Rosa went into the little space that was separated from the living room by a curtain. The room was illuminated by the moon from outside, and she could see her girls huddled on one mattress, Rachelika in the middle. She looked at her daughters and her eyes caught Luna's. The beautiful green eyes were wide open and filled with tears.

Rosa longed to hug the child, but she was afraid of her reaction, afraid that Luna would push her away again, and she didn't think she could face any more rejection.

The door of Gabriel and Rosa's house didn't open for three days and three nights. For three days and three nights, mother and son stayed behind the locked door and closed shutters. Nobody came out and nobody went in.

"May God forgive my sins, the bread is probably stale by now and the cheese left out is soured," Rosa thought aloud. "What are they eating?"

"Each other," replied her sister-in-law, who was standing in the kitchen putting a pot on the stove. "They should stew in their own juice and put an end to this war. It's destroying the family."

"That sour old woman," Rosa said, "is probably driving the demons out of Gabriel, but who'll drive out *her* demons?"

"With God's help, her demons will go as well. Don't be frightened, querida Rosa, when her majesty our mother-in-law comes out of your door, you'll see that everything will be all right again. Gabriel was only sick because of his mother. If she forgives him, he'll forgive himself and get better. Don't worry, Rosa, only good will come of them being locked up together for so many days."

On the morning of the fourth day, just as the sun was rising, Mercada opened the door of Gabriel and Rosa's house. She came outside, walked to the bus station on Jaffa Road, and boarded a bus back to Tel Aviv.

That same morning after his mother left, Gabriel got out of bed, washed his body with soap and water, shaved his beard, dressed in fresh clothes, and headed to the market.

Matzliach, Leito, and Avramino couldn't believe their eyes when they saw him standing in the doorway. Without saying much, he took his usual place behind the counter and went back to work as if nothing had happened.

"Go to Shmuel's house, ask if they know where Rosa is, and when you find her tell her to come home with the girls," he ordered Avramino, who rushed off.

When Rosa returned home, she was surprised to find the house just as she'd left it, spick-and-span. Gabriel's bed was made, the sink empty, and the tin bath, to which a few drops of water still clung, had been hung up to dry in its usual place on a nail in the wall.

The girls took off the clothes they'd borrowed from their cousins and changed into their own.

"Heideh, hurry up," Rosa urged them. "Don't be late for school."

As they went off, she stood in the doorway. Little Becky was flanked by her two sisters, holding their hands. Rosa sighed as if a weight had been lifted from her. If Gabriel had gone back to the shop and the girls to school, perhaps her sister-in-law Miriam had been right and everything was back to normal.

But Luna didn't go to school that day. After she dropped off Becky and Rachelika, she hurried back through the school gate and ran to Gabriel's shop. When she arrived at the door breathless, her father smiled at her and she jumped into his arms, clinging to him like a baby.

"Basta, querida! You're not a baby anymore. You'll be a bride soon! What young man will want to marry you if you behave like a little girl with your father?"

He tried to get her off him and she, who was so happy to see her father smiling at her the way he used to, ignored him and continued hugging him tight, clutching his waist, sticking to him.

"I want to work in the shop with you," she finally told him.

"Basta, Luna, you're still a child. You have to go to school."

"You just said I'll be married soon and now I'm still a child? Papo, I want to help you, be here with you. I don't have to learn in school to be able to sell in the shop."

"You don't have to learn? Do you know that your grandmother and your mother didn't go to school for even one day in their lives? And you, you've got the privilege of studying and acquiring knowledge, an education . . ."

"What's an education? I can read and write. I've learned arithmetic. I don't need any more than that."

"Stop talking nonsense, Luna! Heideh, take some goodies and go to school. Heideh, there's a good girl."

"Papo, please, just today, let me stay in the shop just today."

Unable to ward off his daughter's pleas, Gabriel gave in. But her charm and beauty worried him. He would have to keep a close eye on the girl, protect her so she wouldn't become one of those modern girls who went dancing with boys at Café Europa and all the other clubs frequented by English soldiers, God help us.

Gabriel never spoke about what transpired in the three days he spent with his mother behind the locked door, and Mercada too didn't say a word. But from the moment she stepped through the doorway of his house, he began functioning as he had before. The Ermosas' life resumed as normal with one exception: Gabriel no longer went to the synagogue on weekdays and only attended on Saturdays and holidays. Rosa, who noticed this change in his behavior, as usual didn't ask questions. She had learned that the less she spoke, the better. Better to keep quiet than be answered with thunderous silence. She continued running the household, the friction with Luna lessened, and even though she didn't approve of the girl's ever-increasing coquettish appearance, she made no comment. She preferred a truce with the girl rather than the incessant bickering that exhausted her and almost always left her feeling helpless and Luna triumphant. So she raised her hands up in surrender and chose to avoid confrontation with her as much as possible.

Toward the end of the school year, the principal, Rabbi Pardess, invited the parents to a meeting about their daughters' progress. Gabriel said he would go, and Rosa, who took no special interest in her daughters' education, was quite content to stay home.

"First, I must congratulate you on Rachel's many talents," Rabbi Pardess told the proud Gabriel. "Your Rachel has a fine future before her, and I recommend sending her to the high school at the David Yellin College of Education in Beit Hakerem. Little Rivka also has good qualities. She is an industrious, diligent, and excellent pupil.

"Levana." The rabbi sighed, putting heavy emphasis on Luna's Hebrew name. "About Levana, Mr. Ermosa, I regrettably have no good news to report. I would like, sir, to bring to your attention that I take a negative view of the fact that you allow your daughter to be absent from school so frequently. I understand that you need help in your shop, but you must make up your mind: Either you want the girl to learn or you do not. If you are interested in her schooling, then I insist that she attend school every day and complete all her assignments like the rest of the pupils. If you wish to take her out of school so she can work in your shop, that is your right, but you must decide once and for all."

As he listened to the rabbi's words, a stunned Gabriel didn't know whether he should admit to Luna's lies or cover for her. His own upbringing in his parents' house had taught him never to wash dirty laundry in public, so ultimately he chose to keep quiet and not to tell the rabbi that his daughter had brazenly lied. He rose, looked the rabbi in the eye, and said, "Sir, I am very sorry. From this day on, my daughter will not be absent from school for a single day."

As Gabriel exited the schoolyard, he was boiling with rage. His daughter, flesh of his flesh, had humiliated him in front of a respected rabbi. Luna, lying so barefacedly and implicating me in her lies as well? What's happened to my daughter? Had she picked up on his vulnerability and taken advantage of it?

Although the school wasn't far from the market, he didn't go back to the shop and instead started walking down the slope of Agrippas Street toward King George. He had to calm himself before going home and confronting Luna. How he needed good advice at a time like this. For a moment he thought about getting on a bus to his mother in Tel Aviv, but the possibility of encountering Rochel again frightened him so much that he dismissed it right away.

It hadn't been that long since his mother had saved him with her livianos and exorcised the demons that possessed him. He would never forget the conversation they had just before she left his house. By the third day, he had been strong enough to get out of bed and sit at the table. His mother sat across from him, her face scored with wrinkles, yet in her eyes glinted the spark of a young woman. She was very grave as she said to him, "Adio Senor del mundo was apparently very angry with you on the day you laid eyes on the Ashkenazia. Who knows what you did for Him to punish you so severely. If it does not have God's blessing, love is cursed and brings with it the torments of hell. And your love for the Ashkenazia, hijo querido, did not have God's blessing." She sighed heavily, laid her hand on Gabriel's, and went on. "God will forgive us for the sins we have committed against each other. But if God had deemed it fit, He would have taken you a long time ago to punish you for your sins, or He would have taken me. But He didn't take either of us. He took that saintly man your father, may he rest in peace, and reprimanded both of us with a punishment worse than death. If God chose to take neither of us, it means that He wants us to remain here on earth. What is done can't be undone, hijo querido, so at least from this day on we shall behave toward each other if not like mother and son, then at least like human beings. I'm now going through that door and back to Tel Aviv. You will get up, wash yourself, and go back to your life. Try and make the life you have left as good as you can. Do your best for your daughters, for your wife, for your livelihood, and most important of all, do your best for yourself. With God's help, I have erased from your heart the woman who should never have been there in the first place. I have erased the pain and the longing, the memory, and the hope that perhaps one day you will reunite with this woman who was never for you. Now you're clean. Go and start your life from the beginning as if all this never happened."

With the help of her cane she got up and walked through the door. And he, who had been brought up on his mother's miracles and all the healing properties of the livianos, felt that she had brought him back to life.

And now the talk with Rabbi Pardess had shaken the serenity with which he had been filled since his mother had healed him. A great fear gripped his heart, a profound concern for Luna's future, and most terrible of all, doubts about her character. Did he really not know his daughter? And who knew what else she did that he didn't know about. Had he failed so badly with her upbringing? Where had the *draga de siete cavezas,* the seven-headed dragon, learned to lie?

Gabriel walked the length of King George to Terra Sancta and cut across toward Azza Street until he came to Café Rehavia, a place he'd sometimes go to escape, far away from everything familiar. He sat in the café for a long time, sipping a cup of strong black coffee, staring through the window at the passersby, trying to arrange his thoughts and feelings. Perhaps better not to tell a soul, not even his mother, about his daughter's doings. He didn't want her to be labeled a liar, a street child. He had to protect her good name, or she would never find a husband from a good family and things would get out of control. He stood up, paid the waiter, and started the long walk back to Ohel Moshe, determined to keep a close eye on Luna, to make sure he knew where she was every minute of the day. And for the first time since she was born, he decided to punish her.

When the family gathered for dinner that evening, Gabriel glanced around the table at his daughters. "Come here," he said to Rachelika, who immediately obeyed and stood beside him. He kissed her forehead and praised her for her outstanding performance at school. From the corner of his eye he saw the jealousy burning in Luna's eyes. She couldn't stand her father paying attention to anyone else, not even to her sister. Then he called upon Becky and sat her on his knee. "And you too, chicitica, are outstanding, so well done!" he said and kissed her.

After Rachelika and Becky had kissed the back of his hand in turn and returned to their places, there was a tense silence. Everyone was expecting Gabriel to ask Luna to come to him so he could praise her studies. But he said nothing. Becky, who could no longer restrain herself, asked, "And Luna? What did Rabbi Pardess say about her?" And Gabriel, ignoring Becky's question, said in a voice as cold as ice, "The food is getting cold. Rosa, put it on the table."

Without a word Rosa placed the pot of couscous on the table, and beside it, one containing peas and meat in tomato sauce. As she picked up the ladle to serve the food, Gabriel caught her wrist.

"Basta," he said, "let Luna serve it." Rosa's arm froze in midair. "Heideh, Luna, what are you waiting for? My talk with Rabbi Pardess gave me an appetite," he said without looking at his daughter.

Luna's face reddened. Her father had never spoken to her in such a tone, had never before shown her up like this. But what hurt her most was the knowledge that she had disappointed him, that she had shamed him before the school principal. She realized that Rabbi Pardess had told her father about her absences from school. How could she have thought that she would get away with it? She had implicated her father, tarnished his honor, and if there was one thing more important to her father than all else, it was honor.

Her hand shook as she ladled the couscous onto the plates. Dinner was eaten in silence except for the clink of forks on plates. Luna didn't touch her food, and unusually for him, Gabriel didn't try and persuade her to eat.

When they finished, Rosa and the girls hastened to clear the table, but Gabriel stopped them. "Leave it. Starting today, only Luna clears the table and only Luna washes the dishes. If she's not learning anything in school, she can at least learn something at home."

Every day for seven days, at every meal, Luna laid the table, served the food, cleared the table, washed the dishes, and returned them to their place in the cupboard. Rosa could barely contain her pleasure. Gabriel had chosen not to tell her about his talk with Rabbi Pardess and said only one thing to her: "Not a word about what's happening in this house with Luna gets out. You will not speak about it, not with Miriam, my brother Shmuel's wife, not with my sister Clara, not with your neighbor Tamar, not with the other neighbors, and not even with yourself." And Rosa, for whom her husband's word was law, kept silent.

For the whole week Luna seemed like a shadow of herself. She went to school in the morning, sat in class for every lesson, and didn't even go outside during recess. She was prepared to take any punishment, wash the dishes, scrub the floor, fold laundry, and even the worst punishment of all, not leave the house, but she couldn't bear her father's silence. It hurt her as if he'd beaten her with a stick. Rachelika, whose heart went out to her sister, tried to talk to her, but Luna withdrew into herself.

"What have you done for Father to punish you like this? It can't be because you're a bad student."

Luna remained silent. She was ashamed to tell even her beloved sister Rachelika why her father was punishing her.

"Luna, why are you being so stubborn? Don't be an *azno*, a mule. What have you done to make Papo so angry with you? Did you steal something?"

"Shut up, stupid! You yourself have stolen!" she said and chased after Rachelika, grabbing her by her black hair and tugging it hard.

"Ay-ay-ay!" Rachelika yelled. "Let go of my hair!"

But Luna wouldn't. She pulled her hair, almost tearing out a handful. Pulling her sister's hair made her feel powerful. Every time Luna fought with her sisters, she pulled their hair, and she did the same when she sought to show affection. Even the neighbors' children got this treatment from her. Everybody knew about her craze for pulling hair.

Rachelika's screams brought Rosa out of the kitchen. She grabbed hold of Luna's thin body and dragged her away in an effort to separate her two daughters. But Luna yelled and resisted and lost all control of herself until she fell to the ground and started crying.

For a long time Luna stayed on the floor, hugging her knees and weeping. I'll never have the strength that this child demands, Rosa thought as she covered her ears, amazed at the degree to which she had hardened herself to her daughter's suffering. She didn't know what Luna had done to make Gabriel punish her like this, what had made him bring the girl to tears, but she didn't ask him. He'd tell her if he wanted to.

Stubborn as a mule, Luna, she hasn't even asked my forgiveness, Gabriel thought as he tended to the shop. She had looked him straight in the eye without remorse at the dinner table. At least she wasn't weak like her mother. Still, he saw how she stole glances at him when he was talking to Rachelika or Becky. He saw how she bit her upper lip when he talked to Rachelika about articles in the newspaper. She couldn't hide her pain from him. Hija de un mamzer, how much character this girl has!

He had to put an end to this tension. It was killing him. But how could he, the father, humiliate himself before his daughter? Why didn't the *draga de siete cabezas* come to him and beg forgiveness? In another moment he'd break and clasp her to him and kiss her forehead, and in the end he'd ask for her pardon.

The year 1940 was almost over. For six months of the year he had been more dead than alive. The shop had certainly suffered. Gabriel was in no doubt that there had been some financial skulduggery going on while he was durmiendo. How couldn't there have been? Not that he was accusing his brother of stealing, God forbid, but Matzliach could hardly add two and two, so how could he keep the books? And even if, God forbid, his brother had his fingers in the till, he didn't want to know. He couldn't bear any more disappointment.

When he went back to the shop after his mother cured him, the stock wasn't fresh, and they were short of Turkish delight, halvah, Aleppo pistachios, and tea. The Arab women had stopped bringing cheese from the village because Matzliach hadn't paid them on time. They were short of pickled cucumbers, smoked fish, olive oil, olives. Right away Gabriel buckled down and got back into the swing of things. He didn't want to go to Tel Aviv because he feared he might see the woman who walked arm in arm with the Englishman—he couldn't even utter her name. So instead he sent Avramino to Chaim Saragusti on Levinsky Street. He made a list of everything they needed, and even though Avramino couldn't read, Gabriel knew that Chaim Saragusti could, and he trusted his old friend to fill his order and send it to Jerusalem.

Soon enough the shop, thank God, was restored to its former state and was again filled with customers. On more than one occasion the thought flashed through his mind that perhaps Luna had been right and that it wouldn't have been so bad to take her out of school so she could help him in the shop. But he'd dismiss the idea right away. The world was becoming increasingly modern, and he wasn't prepared for his daughter to be an ignoramus like her mother. She needed to have an education.

He himself regretted that he had attended only a Talmud Torah religious school. He felt that he could have been someone important, maybe a doctor at Bikur Holim Hospital or a lawyer, or perhaps—and this was his secret dream—a Haganah commander. He would have wanted to be a confidant of

Ben-Gurion, to work with Eliyahu Golomb, the leader of the Jewish defense effort. These men were the salt of the earth!

If he'd had an education, he certainly wouldn't have been a shopkeeper content to talk about mundane matters with Franz the fat newspaper seller. He would have conversed with dignitaries on matters of paramount importance, people like David Yellin, who, following the murder of his son in the riots at the beginning of the year, together with his wife Ita returned the medal of honor they had been awarded by the English bastards. How he admired Yellin, who'd said, "I consider this medal of honor to be a medal of dishonor." Ach, what people we have in this country, and here I am, stuck in the shop all day with Matzliach the troncho and Avramino the boor.

The thoughts didn't stop running through his mind, drilling away until his head was ready to burst. Gabriel took off his apron and walked through the market toward Jaffa Road. The heady smells of the market filled his nostrils, but instead of pleasing him they only intensified his headache. He arrived at the newsstand, and as he had done every day before his illness, bought a copy of *Haaretz*.

"And how are you today?" the fat newspaper seller asked his favorite customer.

"Thank God, blessed be He," the favorite customer replied as he scanned the front page.

"See what those bastards did? They wouldn't let the boat dock," Franz said, and Gabriel's eyes lit on the headline announcing that a large ship with many immigrants on board had been turned away.

"Sons of bitches," Gabriel hissed. "They're sending those poor people to Beirut. They do whatever they want, the bastards."

Gabriel returned to the shop. He despised the British more every day. He couldn't stand their haughty presence as they walked through the market in groups in their pressed uniforms, as if they were the lords of the land. Some had come to Palestine from remote villages, simple country boys who'd shoveled cow shit in their English villages, and here in Palestine they behaved as if each of them was the son of the king of England.

But how long could this situation continue? There was a war in Europe, Nazi Germany had invaded Poland, and yet in Palestine it was business as usual. How long will we go on burying our heads in the sand? he wondered. It's lucky there are people volunteering to fight the Germans, just as it's lucky there are people trying to drive the British out of Palestine.

No, he didn't mean those Stern bandits, but the good people of the Haganah. He knew that half the people in Ohel Moshe supported the Etzel and Stern's Lehi underground organizations, but there was another half, people like him, who supported the more moderate Haganah. He didn't believe in an eye for an eye, a tooth for a tooth. He believed in words.

A letter from America had finally arrived. Rosa couldn't contain herself and ran to the shop so that Gabriel could read it for her. Nissim, who went by Nick in America, wrote that he's doing very well in the "shmattes business," and thank God, because his eldest son will soon be married and his family is growing. And how is everybody in Jerusalem? he wanted to know. How is her husband Gabriel and how are her daughters? How is Ephraim and what is he up to these days? Is he working in Gabriel's shop or has he opened one of his own? And following the letter a big package will be coming by sea with clothes for her from his factory, so she'll see how well he's doing, and clothes for the girls and her husband, may he be healthy, and also for Ephraim who was a little boy when Nissim fled to America, and now he's a man and surely has a wife and children.

Rosa's heart lurched. It had been two years since the British police took her to the Russian Compound for questioning, and she hadn't heard a word from Ephraim. She didn't have anybody to talk to about him. Gabriel had only to hear his name and he'd get angry. He didn't like the Lehi. When they'd tried to kill Morton, a British CID officer, on Yael Street in Tel Aviv and instead killed Schiff, a Jewish police officer, Gabriel was so incensed that she covered her ears to protect herself from his virulent words. "They're killing Jews as well, they have no limits! They should all be thrown into Acre Jail, all of them! They're not Jews, these people. Jews don't behave like that!"

If only she could see Ephraim just once, to hear that everything's all right. There were rumors that Yitzhako, Sara Laniado's son from Sukkat Shalom, was also with Stern's people. Perhaps his mother knew something.

That afternoon she went to Senora Laniado's house and knocked on the door.

"Welcome, Senora Ermosa, welcome, come in, come in," Sara said. Rosa went inside. Three steps led from the street to the tiny room where the Laniado family lived. It was windowless, the air was stifling, and a sour smell filled her nostrils. Sara's sick husband was lying on a bed by the wall, and as she entered, he sat up to welcome her. "There's no need, Senor Laniado," she said. "Don't get up because of me. I won't be staying long."

Sara made her a cup of tea with bizcochos, and they sat at the table in silence. Rosa didn't know how to start, and Sara, who realized why Senora Ermosa had honored her with a visit, waited for her to speak first.

"So how is it in Rehavia?" Rosa asked, trying to create small talk.

"How can it be?" Sara replied. "Not even a donkey works the way my lady works me."

"*Sano que 'stas*, may you be healthy, those Ishkenazias are worse than the Ingelish women," Rosa said.

"My lady is worse than Pharaoh! Nothing pleases her. Whatever I do isn't clean enough for her. She'd make me lick the floor if she could."

"Tell me," Rosa said, realizing that the conversation was going nowhere, "what's new with you? How is everything?"

"Well, you can see that my husband's in bed and I'm the breadwinner, so what can I say?

"And the children?"

"Thank God, they're all married."

"Yitzhako too?"

"No, not Yitzhako." Sara lowered her voice to a whisper. "Yitzhako, may God protect him, is with Avraham Stern, like your brother Ephraim. They're there together."

"How do you know?" Rosa asked.

"Yitzhako told me. And not only them, our Mimo from Sukkat Shalom is there too. God be praised, we've got a fine group of them. There are maybe twenty or thirty of ours in the Stern group."

Rosa was astounded. Sara, this simple woman, knew more than she could have imagined. She decided to put propriety aside and asked Sara bluntly, "Vizina querida, I haven't heard from my brother Ephraim for two years. Perhaps your son Yitzhako has told you something about him? How he is? Is he married? Does he have children?"

"Married!" Sara laughed. "That lot marry the Land of Israel. They don't have time for a wedding with a woman."

"Tell me," Rosa pled, "has Yitzhako, may he be healthy, told you anything about Ephraim?"

"He doesn't say much," Sara said. "I only see him every now and then. He comes quietly, sleeps a while, and leaves quietly. May God protect him."

"But how, how did my brother Ephraim get to the Lehi? He was a borracho, a drunk. Why did they take him?"

"It was Mimo who took him. He met Ephraim wandering by the central bus station in Tel Aviv. And that's it, they're making life a misery for the English. Did you hear about the robbery at the Anglo-Palestine bank in Tel Aviv?"

"It was them?" Rosa was stunned.

"They steal money from the English to buy rifles and fight them."

"My husband says," Rosa said, sighing, "that they're worse than the Ingelish. He says that Jews don't behave like that."

"There are none worse than the English!" Sara asserted. "I won't tell you I'm happy that my son's a bank robber, I didn't raise him to be a thief, but the money doesn't go into his pocket. He hands it over for the Land of Israel, so even God in heaven justifies it. Every Saturday evening I listen to Stern on the radio on the Voice of Fighting Zion station. He's a good speaker, may he be healthy. Every word is the naked truth."

"May God protect my brother and your son," Rosa said before she took her leave. "If by chance Yitzhako comes to see you, tell him I ask, I beg him to tell Ephraim that I want to hear from him. I want him to show his face in my house so I can see that he's well, and if he doesn't want to come to me, tell Yitzhako, I'll go anywhere at any time. Por favor, Senora Laniado, por Dio, please do that for me."

Rosa didn't tell a soul that she was trying to make contact with Ephraim, certainly not Gabriel. She could already guess that he would tell her she was putting herself and the girls at risk. From that day on, she started keeping up with the news, asking Rachelika to read her the headlines. She learned from the paper that a reward of one thousand pounds had been put on Stern's head and that he was the most wanted man in Palestine.

On Saturday evening, when Gabriel and the girls visited Shmuel and Miriam after Havdalah, Rosa said she didn't feel well and stayed home. She turned on the Zenith radio and searched for the Voice of Fighting Zion. Stern's voice rang in her ears: "A worthy way ending in failure is unfit. An unfit way ending in victory is truly worthy." He's right, she thought to herself. To drive the cursed Ingelish out of Palestine you have to do things that aren't written in the Torah. She wondered what her Ephraim, her little brother, was doing to drive the Ingelish out of the country. If only she could tell him how proud she was, how much she supported the path he had taken. She'd tell him it didn't matter what Gabriel said, it didn't matter what the Haganah said, what most of the

Jews in Palestine were saying. There was only one way to talk to the Ingelish: Force! Only force would drive the bastards back to their Ingeland!

A year later, when a British CID officer, Thomas James Wilkin, murdered Avraham Stern in cold blood in an apartment on Mizrahi Street in Tel Aviv, Rosa would grieve bitterly. Even Gabriel, who wholeheartedly opposed the actions of Stern and his people, was shocked. "Shooting a man in the head in cold blood?" he said to Rosa who was holding on to a chair for support, her body gripped by weakness. Having listened to Stern on the Voice of Fighting Zion almost every Saturday evening, she felt as though she had lost somebody close and wept for his pregnant widow Roni.

"Whatever he did," Gabriel said, "he's still a Jew, and one Englishman isn't worth a single hair from the head of a Jew," and with that he ended the conversation. Rosa was broken by Stern's death. His voice each week had been her only connection to Ephraim. Now she could only find consolation in Sara Laniado.

"I have to see Ephraim," Rosa said one day. "I have to know he's all right. Dio mio, I can't bear the worry. My heart aches just from thinking about him. He's probably living like a dog, running from one place to another."

"That's how they are," Sara said, "living in holes in the ground, in the dark, in secret. They mustn't be seen, and that's why, Rosa, you should forget it. Now they've murdered Stern, they'll go even deeper underground. Now even my Yitzhako won't come here. Paciencia, Rosa, paciencia, the British will soon go back to their own country, and with God's help you'll see Ephraim again."

The school year ended and the summer break arrived. Each year the girls couldn't wait to visit their Aunt Allegra's house in Tel Aviv. Before the journey, Gabriel would pack a big bag of goodies from the shop and leave it in the care of Matzliach. A taxi would be waiting by the big gate to Ohel Moshe to take them to the railway station on Hebron Road. Not long ago, when they'd visit Tel Aviv, they'd walk to the central bus station on Jaffa Road with their suitcases, but the shop's renewed prosperity had vastly improved the family's finances, so this time Gabriel bought first-class train tickets.

A few months earlier, after days of stalemate, Gabriel's relations with his daughter had resumed their normal course. In the end it was she who went to him. He had just finished work one evening and was locking up the shop when she appeared by his side as if from out of nowhere. She stood there with lowered eyes, not saying a word. He understood that this was his proud daughter's way of asking his forgiveness. He stood facing her, waiting for her to make the first move, and she collapsed in his arms, weeping for his forgiveness, promising that never, never again would she lie. He hugged her and kissed her and cried with her, his heart melting and waves of love flooding him.

And yet there was one thing he still needed to know: why she had lied.

"I get bored, Papo, I can't sit on a chair for so many hours. I've got ants in my pants and I have to get up and walk. When I'm staring at the blackboard for so long, everything turns black, everything's blurred. I can't see anything and my head aches. I look at my homework book and all the letters get mixed up, and then I can't stay in the classroom any longer. So I went to the principal and told him that you need me in the shop."

"And where did you go when you left school?"

"I went to the Pillars Building with my friend Sara to look in the shop windows, to the YMCA tower to view our Jerusalem from above. We took a bus to Beit Hakerem and walked around. What pretty houses there are there, Papo, and what gardens!"

Astounded, Gabriel listened patiently to Luna. From the moment he allowed her to speak and tell him the truth, she talked and talked as if making up for lost time, a waterfall of words gushing out of her mouth. He was alarmed by the idea of his daughter roaming the streets.

"Did you go to the Old City as well?" he asked, concerned that she might be concealing some of the truth.

"I don't like the Old City, I only like the New City. I like the pretty houses in Rehavia and Beit Hakerem. I like the cleanliness and the people. They're all well dressed there. I wish we could live in Rehavia."

Why shouldn't they live in Rehavia? Gabriel thought. He could afford to move his family there, and perhaps Luna was right. Perhaps it was time for a modern neighborhood where doctors and professors from the Hebrew University lived. It wouldn't do his daughters any harm to learn a thing or two about the customs of educated people.

From the moment they entered Tel Aviv, Luna's heart opened. How she loved the boulevard where her aunt and grandmother lived, the cafés on Hayarkon Street and the promenade, the outdoor cinema at the community center. She especially loved the beach. She'd get sunburned and turn as red as a beet, and all of Rosa's warnings and Gabriel's begging were to no avail. She gave herself up to the sense of renewal and burned her skin in the sun each time anew.

There wasn't a single day in the week in Tel Aviv that Luna didn't go to the beach. Even Rachelika and Becky had enough of the sun and sand and preferred to stay in their aunt's house or window-shop on Allenby Street. But Luna always went, and when she couldn't persuade her sisters to join her, she nagged her cousins incessantly until they gave in.

"That one, may she be healthy, when she wants something she'll run through a wall," Rosa said to her sister-in-law.

"Paciencia, querida Rosa. She'll soon find a husband and then she'll be his problem."

Allegra's sons, Raphael and Yaakov, were very attached to the lovely Luna and loved going to the beach with her, taking pride in their redhaired cousin who always turned heads.

But on this occasion the vacation ended badly. Luna's white skin was burned fiery red. Her body was badly blistered and hurt like the devil. And so they were forced to cut their trip short and return to Jerusalem. Gabriel brought a jug of sour cream from the shop and ordered Rosa to spread it over Luna's body. They shut themselves in the bathroom and Rosa started spreading the cream onto Luna's back, but her mother's touch burned Luna even more than the blisters and she screamed and yelled until poor Rosa came out with tears in her eyes. On seeing his wife whom he had almost never seen shed a tear, for the first time Gabriel sympathized not with his beloved daughter but with his unfortunate wife. For years he had seen how Luna tormented Rosa, how she behaved toward her as if she was worthless, and he hadn't intervened.

With God's help Luna completed her studies at the Ohel Moshe School. Gabriel was sure that the girl would ask to work with him in the shop, and he decided that she would until she married.

But to his surprise Luna came to the shop and announced, "I want to continue studying at an English school." Gabriel was torn. Only recently he read an article condemning Jewish children learning at mission schools. "Dozens of boys and girls, Ashkenazi and Sephardi and from other communities," the article said, "come home from the mission schools in the Old City and Ratisbonne. It has become an epidemic."

Uncharacteristically, he consulted Rosa, and as usual she couldn't offer any good advice. On the one hand, she was shocked by the idea of Luna going to an Ingelish school, but on the other, maybe the Ingelish would be able to turn the hooligan in her house into a lady, and that was what she told Gabriel. But in the end the one who finally tipped the scales was Rachelika. "I've heard they've got good teachers there," she told her father. "And they teach Hebrew. And it would be better for Luna to go to a mission school than roam the streets."

Gabriel stroked his clever daughter's head. She was so different from her big sister, who was interested only in clothes and the cinema. Rachelika, with God's help, would graduate from the Ohel Moshe School and then he'd enroll her at the Beit Hakerem High School, and after four years there she'd continue her studies at the David Yellin College. Rachelika would be a teacher. And Luna? That one, with God's help, they would marry as soon as possible, and that would be that.

Every morning Luna met her good friend Sara at her house and they'd walk toward Jaffa Gate. There, opposite the Tower of David, was the English school. Luna hated the school uniform—the blue-and-green-checked skirt, the white blouse, and the blue V-neck sweater—but most of all she hated the black stockings. "It's so old-fashioned to cover the legs," she grumbled.

Each day before lessons commenced, students assembled in the yard for a ceremony in which they hoisted the English flag and blessed the English king. "And whenever the nuns talk about Jesus," Luna told Rachelika, "I put my hands on my heart to protect it from what they are saying so that Jesus won't come into my heart, God forbid."

Luna suffered. She hated the lessons, she hated the nuns, and she hated Mr. Mizrachi, the Jewish teacher who had an annoying Iraqi accent, and of all the pupils in the class always picked on her. "Quiet, Ermosa!" he'd shout, even if she hadn't been chattering, and his shouts could be heard even by the prisoners in the cellar of the Kishle next to the school.

One morning when Luna was in a particularly bad mood, she told Sara, "I've had school up to here!"

"So let's play hooky," Sara suggested. "Let's go window-shop at the Pillars Building."

"I wish," Luna replied. "But if my father catches me skipping one more time it'll be the end of me. What happened to me after I played hooky from Rabbi Pardess was bad enough."

"You don't want to, you don't have to," Sara retorted. "But I'm off!" And she was already through the school gate and walking toward Jaffa Gate.

"Wait, hold on!" Luna shouted, running after her. "I'm coming. Just pray that nobody sees us and tells my father."

Luna and Sara wandered along Jaffa Road. They passed the display windows and looked at the mannequins clothed in suits and dresses that set off the waist. Luna was mesmerized by black high-heeled shoes in the Freiman & Bein window. "Come on," Sara said, tugging her hand. "Let's go before your face gets stuck to the glass."

They moved on to the next window, the splendid Zacks & Son clothing store. Luna put her nose to the glass, never tiring of the sight of magnificent evening gowns and expensive daywear. The dresses brought her a whiff of the big world. How she'd love to drape one over her body, to feel its folds accentuating what needed to be accentuated and concealing what should be concealed.

A notice in the shop window caught her eye: Wanted. Saleslady. Her heart skipped a beat. This is it, this is what I should do! she thought. I should be a saleslady at Zacks & Son, be close to the dresses, the blouses, the skirts, the petticoats. Stroke them, fold them gently, place them on the shelves, put them on hangers. She was gripped by tremendous excitement. Her future had been revealed. Fashion, her future was fashion, not at the mission school and certainly not behind the counter of her father's shop. No, she wasn't born to sell cheeses and pickles, she was born to sell clothes. Luna pushed the door open.

"How may I help the young lady?" asked the man in the handsome suit standing behind the counter.

"I'm here about the ad," Luna replied, ignoring the stunned look on Sara's face.

"Does the young lady have any experience?"

"I don't have any experience, but I'm a fast learner. I promise you that within a week I'll be the best saleslady you've ever had," she said with confidence that surprised even her.

"I see you're still in school," said the gentleman, indicating her uniform. "So when will you be able to work?"

"Now!"

"Now?" he laughed. "Now is out of the question."

"Why? You'll see, sir, that I'll learn the work in a few hours. You won't regret it."

"I've no doubt I won't regret it, but first you'll have to get rid of those unsightly mission school clothes. Come back tomorrow in proper clothes and we'll talk about it," he told her and showed her to the door.

"Are you crazy?" Sara yelled as they headed back along the boulevard. "What do you think you're doing?"

"I've found my calling!" Luna laughed. "I'm going to work in a clothing store! Thank God for opening my eyes. All that interests me is clothes! I read the magazines from Europe and cut out dresses and shoes and stick them in a notebook. I dream about dresses at nighttime and about dresses in the daytime. Clothes are my life."

At dinner that evening, Luna helped Rosa serve the meal, cleared the table, and volunteered to wash the dishes. Rosa didn't quite understand her extraordinary behavior, but she didn't say a word.

Only Rachelika, who understood her sister as well as she understood herself, vocalized her suspicion. "What banana skin did you slip on?" she said. Luna gave her a white-toothed smile that accentuated the dimples in her cheeks and whispered, "The banana skin of my life."

"What? Tell me what!" Rachelika begged, and Luna shared her plan to leave school and work at Zacks & Son.

"In your dreams when the stars come out! Father will never agree!"

"Leave that to me."

After dinner, when Gabriel sat down in his usual chair to listen to the Voice of Jerusalem on the radio and enjoy a cigarette, Luna went over to him. "Papo, have you got a minute?"

"For you, mi alma, I've got all the time in the world."

"Papo querido, I didn't want to sadden you, but for a long time now I've been unhappy at the mission school. All the stories about Jesus and the Virgin Mary have entered my mind and I feel, God forbid, that it might influence me to become a Christian."

"Dio santo!" Gabriel said. "That's exactly what I feared, it's exactly what I was afraid of from the start. That's why I didn't want you to go to the mission school, but you insisted!"

"It was Sara who persuaded me to go to the school, and I followed her without thinking, but I can see what it's doing to me. I beg you, Papo, I beg you to take me out of there!"

"Of course, come and work for me in the shop."

"No, Papo, I don't want to work in the shop. I want to work in fashion."

"Fashion?"

"Yes! Clothes, dresses, suits."

"You're working in it already. You've got more clothes than Zacks & Son."

"Exactly!" Luna seized the opportunity. "I heard that Zacks & Son are advertising for a saleslady. I want to go and ask for the job in the morning."

"Do what you want," he said wearily. He had long since realized that Luna wasn't cut out for school, so if she didn't want to study, let her sell clothes. The main thing was that she made something of herself.

In the evening before they went to bed, he said to Rosa angrily, "You said they'll make a lady of her? They'll make a Christian of her! It's lucky the girl's clever and realized that they're taking over her soul. It's lucky she's her father's daughter."

The next morning, Luna stayed home instead of going to school. She opened the wardrobe and took out her best dress, a red-and-black floral number. She matched it with red patent leather shoes and a handbag of the same color, put red polish on her manicured nails, and applied red lipstick.

When she laid eyes on her daughter, Rosa felt she might explode. "Luna, don't you dare leave the house looking like that! You look like a girl who goes with the Ingelish. Look in the mirror, see what you look like!" She stood in the doorway, blocking her exit.

"And what do I look like?" Luna asked mockingly.

"Like a girl from the street."

"Who are you to tell me I'm a girl from the street?" Luna shouted. "We've heard about who came to my father's house from the street, who cleaned toilets for the English before she became Senora Ermosa! So don't you tell me I'm from the street!"

The vein in Rosa's neck threatened to burst. She couldn't face down Luna, who had become more insolent every day, who when Gabriel was not there spoke to her like a market woman. *Boca de jora!* A mouth like a cesspit! Only one thing could stop her: her father.

"If you go out like that with all that paint on your face, I'm going to the shop to get your father. He'll go to the Zacks & Son shop and humiliate you!"

The threat worked. "What do you want me to do?" Luna asked, deflated. "I've got to be dressed tip-top to work in fashion. I can't wear rags like you!"

"For a start take off the lipstick, that's the first thing. Then go to the shop and ask your father to go with you to Zacks & Son, so they can see you're not just any girl off the street. When they see your father, they'll treat you differently."

Luna was about to scream that she wasn't a little child and she didn't need her father to take her to her new job. But she realized that her mother had a point, and it would be better if her father accompanied her so that the esteemed Mr. Zacks would see that she came from a respected family.

The good impression that Gabriel Ermosa made on Mr. Zacks led him to take on Luna right away. And for her part she proved to be an excellent saleslady. Luna talked about clothes as if they were precious objects, each dress a diamond, every skirt a pearl. Her love for clothes infected everyone who came into the shop, and there wasn't a customer who left empty-handed.

The shop employed several seamstresses who made the clothes according to patterns that appeared in *Burda* magazine, and Luna would devour the magazine voraciously, studying it for hours on end. She spent all her wages on clothes she purchased from the shop, and was always dressed at the height of fashion, accessorized to the most minute detail. The polish on her fingernails matched that on her toenails, which matched her lipstick, which in turn matched her dress, shoes, and handbag. As she dressed, she blossomed.

Luna grew more beautiful from day to day, and her beauty was renowned throughout Jerusalem. "The beauty queen," they called her, "the beauty queen of Jerusalem." And she, who was aware of her beauty and understood the looks of the men who were unable to tear their eyes from her, shamelessly exploited it. It accorded her an advantage and power, and she felt she could conquer the world.

Suitors began knocking at her door, much to the chagrin of Gabriel, who did not appreciate his daughter's coquettishness, but none of them appealed to her. She spent her free time with a large group of young men and women made up of relatives and neighbors, dragging them to the cinema every evening. Luna loved movies so much that if she'd had the chance she would have gone to a matinee and followed it with the early showing and then the late one. Her favorite theater was Tel Or, opposite Fink's Bar, which was always packed with British officers and their Jewish girlfriends. Luna wouldn't even think of going to a place like that, and after the movie she and her friends would instead go to the Tiv Taam Restaurant under the theater. She loved dancing, and every now and again would lead everyone to Café Europa, dazzle them with her cha-cha or swing, and the boys would be lining up to dance with her. Her joie de vivre enlivened everyone around her. It was difficult not to admire the lovely Luna.

While her peers were taking an interest in the world around them—the Germans were on the verge of losing the war to the Allies, news of the death camps had begun reaching Palestine, the Jewish underground organizations intensified their attacks against the British Mandate—Luna was completely detached, living her life as if there were no world war and no struggle in Palestine. And when Gabriel and Rachelika talked about the day's events at the table, she'd ask them to stop because it spoiled her mood.

When the young Jewish Brigade soldiers returned to Jerusalem after the world war, Luna's battalion of suitors grew, but she rebuffed any attempt at courtship. "I'm waiting for my knight on a white horse or in a white car," she told Rachelika. "And until he comes along, I'm not going out with anybody!"

"And how will you know who your knight is?"

"When he comes, I'll know."

5

In the middle of the night deafening shouts roused the Ermosas from their beds. "Dio santo! What's all that noise?" Gabriel said and quickly went outside in only his nightshirt. Rosa put on a robe and followed. "Stay here and look after Becky," she ordered the girls, but Luna ignored her and headed toward the noise coming from the garden at the center of the neighborhood.

"Hija mia, hijica, they've killed her, they've killed my daughter!" Senora Franco was kneeling in the middle of the garden hitting herself in the face, her shouts piercing the night. "They've murdered my daughter, they've murdered Matilda!" she screamed. Her husband was standing beside her, his expression stoic. Matilda's body was lying on the ground, and as Rosa got closer to it, she saw that Matilda's head had been partly shaved and a large bloodstain had seeped through the chest of her white dress.

"It's the Lehi bastardos," Gabriel whispered. "They shave the heads of Jewish girls who go out with the English."

The sight of Matilda's body lying spread-eagled in the garden shocked Rosa. She hurried back to her house, pulled a blanket from one of the beds, and ran back to the garden, fighting her way through the crowd of neighbors that had formed, then knelt down to cover Matilda. At that moment Senora Franco noticed her. "You! Don't go anywhere near my daughter!" she screamed. "Take your filthy hands off my child!"

Rosa paled.

"Get away from her!" Senora Franco screamed. "It's your hermano, your brother the borracho, who killed her! It was him, I saw him with my own eyes. Why? Tell me why? What have we done to your family that the hijo de un perro, the son of a bitch, had to kill Matilda? Is this what she deserves after she found your daughter when she ran away from home? Is this what she gets?" She began hitting Rosa, who was frozen to the spot.

Gabriel took Rosa's arm and led her away from Senora Franco. "Come home," he ordered Luna, who had tears welling in her eyes. "Come home— now!" They were silent for the few minutes it took to get home, Gabriel holding Rosa's arm as she walked blindly beside him and Luna trailed behind.

Once they were inside Rosa sat on a chair at the table and burst into tears. It was the first time that Gabriel and the girls had seen her truly cry. She sobbed for a long time, and he sat beside her but did nothing to calm her. Only when she had regained her composure did he ask her quietly, "What was Senora Franco talking about? When did Matilda find the child, and which child ran away from home?" Rosa couldn't believe her ears. The flame ignited in her chest threatened to consume her.

"*El Dio que me mate,* may God kill me!" she screamed, losing control of herself. "Senora Franco says that Ephraim killed Matilda, and you're asking me which of the girls ran away from home? Ask your daughters yourself who ran away from home, who went to the Ingelish and told lies about her mother and made her mother ride in the Ingelish officer's jeep to the Ingelish police so they could question her like a criminal. Ask, ask! If you don't know, ask Becky. It couldn't be Becky mi alma who went to the Ingelish police? Maybe you, Rachelika? Didn't you, querida, tell the Ingelish that your mother threw you out of the house? Tell Papo, querida, tell him if it was you!"

Rosa's rage frightened Gabriel. He had never seen his wife so angry. Of course he'd guessed right away which of his daughters was the culprit and fixed Luna with a hard stare. She had withdrawn into herself, not daring to look at him, her eyes filled with tears. Gabriel didn't say a word. He went to the clay water jug and poured a glass for Rosa. "Drink this," he told her gently. "Drink and we'll go back to bed. Perhaps Senora Franco is mistaken. Perhaps she saw somebody who looks like Ephraim. And you," he commanded Luna, "go straight to bed. I'll deal with you in the morning."

Matilda Franco's funeral was held in the dead of night, for in Jerusalem the deceased had to be buried immediately. That same night, the British police came knocking on the Ermosas' door and searched the house. Once again Rosa was taken to the Russian Compound. This time Gabriel went with her and told the policemen that his wife hadn't seen her brother for years and that he personally opposed the Lehi thugs and wouldn't have helped his brother-in-law even if it meant leaving him in the street. Of course that wasn't true. He would have risked his life to help Ephraim. But right then he said whatever was needed to get his wife out of this mess.

Rosa sat for hours in the interrogation room. The British interrogator tried to extract details about Ephraim from her, and she repeated that since he'd left Jerusalem for Tel Aviv she'd had no contact with him.

"He's a filthy murderer, this brother of yours," the officer said, "him and his whole gang. He murdered an innocent young girl."

"But how do you know it was Ephraim who murdered Matilda?" she burst out. "It could have been anyone!"

"Mrs. Franco testified under oath that she saw him. We don't have any doubt at all that your brother's the murderer," the officer replied vehemently. "All we have to do now is find him, and when we do, I will be present in the gallows room when he's hanged."

At the first opportunity, when Gabriel went to the shop and the girls about their business the next day, Rosa hurried to Sara Laniado's house. "Dio mio, Rosa, why have you come? It's dangerous," Sara said. "You mustn't come here. We mustn't be seen together."

"Senora Sara, do you believe it was Ephraim, do you believe that Ephraim killed Matilda?"

"Yes, querida, I do. Before she was killed he and Yitzhako were here. They had something to eat and drink and sat around, may God forgive me, but I heard them talking. I heard them say that this would be the end of the putana who went with the English."

"You heard and didn't say anything?"

"What could I say? I shouldn't have listened, God forgive my sins, but how was I to know they'd kill Franco's daughter? Eliyahu and I had already gone to bed, and about ten minutes later I heard the shots and the shouting started."

"How, how has my little brother become a murderer?" Rosa was numb with pain and grief. "And why Matilda? We've known her since the day she was born."

"Rosa, you must go now," Sara said. "Go back home and don't mention Ephraim to a soul. Pray that the English don't catch him and Yitzhako, because if they do, they'll hang them. Don't come back here until it all blows over. Stay in your house with your husband and daughters, and don't tell anybody what I've told you."

"Where have you been?" Gabriel thundered when she got home.

"I went to talk to Sara Laniado. Her son's with Ephraim."

"Don't you dare go and see Sara Laniado again. Don't even leave this house. There's tension in the market and around the neighborhood. I want you to stay home and keep an eye on the girls. Keep them home from school for the next few days. And Luna shouldn't go to work either."

"But Papo, I can't miss work. Mr. Zacks will fire me."

"You!" Gabriel roared. "Don't you dare say another word. Shut your mouth and be quiet!"

"How is it," he turned to Rosa, "how is it you didn't tell me she'd run away from home and you found her at the police station?"

"It was a long time ago, Gabriel, I didn't want to bother you. It happened and it's over. She was just a little girl."

"And what is she now?" he shouted, pounding the table with his fist. "Her family's in the middle of a tragedy and all she can think about is that Mr. Zacks will fire her? Selfish child!"

"Didn't you hear what Papo said?" Rachelika said to Luna when she asked her to go and tell Mr. Zacks that she was sick. "I'm not going anywhere. I've had enough with all the shouting and Mother crying, so for once in your life behave like a normal person!"

"Rachelika, I'm begging you. I'll do anything you ask. I'll even let you wear my dresses. You've got to, you've just got to help me!"

"Who wants your fancy dresses anyway? I've had enough of you! All you do is make trouble. You go against Papo all the time, against Mother. I'm not going to any Mr. Zacks. As far as I'm concerned he can fire you!"

"In your dreams he'll fire me. If you won't go and tell him I'm not coming into work, I'll go myself."

"Go, and we'll see how Papo ties you to your bed so you can't move!"

Luna didn't dare go to Zacks & Son without her father's permission. She stayed home for three days until Mr. Zacks himself showed up at their house.

"Is Luna in?" he asked the surprised Rosa.

"Welcome, Mr. Zacks, please come in," she said politely and sent Rachelika to fetch Luna.

"Mr. Zacks? Here in our house? But I'm not dressed. I don't want him to see me looking shabby. Tell him I'll be out in a minute," Luna said to her sister and hurried to change, fix her hair, and put on some lipstick. When she appeared in the doorway Rosa's breath caught in her throat. She was lovely, the beauty queen beyond all doubt. Her dress clung to her hips and accentuated her curves, and her hair was meticulously arranged. An ear-to-ear smile was smeared over Mr. Zacks's face. He too was captivated by Luna.

"Are you sick, Luna?" he asked gently.

"No, she isn't," Rosa answered in her place. "But her father thinks she shouldn't work, she should stay at home."

"Stay at home?" asked Mr. Zacks, amazed. "Isn't that a waste? Luna loves her work. Aren't I paying her enough? Because if that's the problem, then there's no problem. I'll be happy to give her a raise of a few lirot."

"That isn't the problem, Mr. Zacks," Rosa said. "The problem is that my husband doesn't want her working for someone else. We've got our own shop, so if she wants to work she can work for us."

"I'll never, ever work in the market!" Luna burst out, opening her mouth for the first time since Mr. Zacks arrived.

Rosa was close to slapping her daughter, but she held herself back.

"Is there a problem, Mrs. Ermosa? Is there a problem with Luna working at Zacks & Son?" The man's voice shook her from her thoughts.

"With all due respect, Mr. Zacks, I don't know you," she replied coolly. "And I can't negotiate with you. If you want to talk about Luna's work, go to our shop in the Mahane Yehuda Market and speak to my husband."

"No! Don't go!" Luna said. "My father's stubborn. If you go, he'll be even more stubborn. Give me a few more days. I'll talk to him. I'll fix this. But please, Mr. Zacks, in the meantime keep my job for me."

"No problem, Luna, your job's waiting for you, but not for long. I need somebody in the shop, I can't be without a saleslady."

When Gabriel came home from the shop in the evening, he was like a bear with a sore head. He ignored the food that Rosa set on the table and went straight to the bathroom. When he came out, he sat down in his usual chair and buried his head in the newspaper.

"Aren't you eating, querido?" Rosa asked.

"The whole market's talking about your borracho brother who murdered Matilda Franco. I've lost my appetite!"

"But how do they know it was my brother? Who can swear they saw him?"

"Senora Franco saw him. Isn't that enough for you?"

"All right, so what do you want me to do, Gabriel? Am I to be responsible for my brother as well?"

"No, of course not! You're barely responsible for your daughter. You're so responsible you didn't tell me she'd gotten lost and you'd found her with the police, that's how responsible you are."

Rosa began to fume. "She didn't get lost, the street girl, and no, nobody found her. She went to the police on her own and told the Ingelish lies about her mother who leaves her alone in the yard at night and doesn't let her into the house! She drove me crazy with worry, and she was rude to me in front of the damned Ingelish. She made me a laughingstock in front of the bastardos!"

"How did she go to the police, Rosa? A ten-year-old girl goes to the police on her own?"

"Maybe a ten-year-old girl doesn't, but your dear daughter did. As soon as you left for Beirut she started making trouble. She threw herself on the floor and started shouting like una loca until all the neighbors came to their windows. I asked her to come inside but she, nada, she went on shouting and crying as if I'd killed her, and all I did was what? It was me who went to Beirut and left her? It was you, so what could I do? I took Rachelika and Becky inside, gave them something to eat, and she still hadn't come in. When I went outside to look for her, I couldn't find her and began searching with the whole neighborhood."

"And how's poor Matilda Franco connected with all this?" he asked harshly.

"She happened to come home with her Ingelish officer and saw that we were looking for Luna, so she offered for the officer to help us. She came with me in his jeep to the police station, and that's where we found your daughter talking with the Ingelish policeman, telling him I'd thrown her out of the house. Yes, husband, that's the kind of daughter you have, one who tells lies about her mother to the Ingelish!"

Gabriel made no further comment. He folded his paper, got up, and went to the bedroom. Rosa returned the food Gabriel hadn't touched to the pots, took off her apron, and went outside. It was the first time that she'd dared to raise her voice to Gabriel. She sat down on a stool in the yard, resting her back against the wall of the house, and inhaled the fresh, chilly Jerusalem air. She'd known that Gabriel wouldn't take her not telling him about Luna's misdeeds without a fight, even though it had been a long time ago. And she'd also known that Luna would continue giving her a hard time. But her worries about Luna paled in comparison with her concern for Ephraim. She couldn't bear the thought that if, God forbid, the cursed Ingelish caught him, he would be hanged. She would not let that happen. The scene of Rachamim hanging at Damascus Gate would not play out again! She had to help him, get in touch with him. She rose from the stool, walked toward Sukkat Shalom, and knocked on Sara Laniado's door.

Sara opened the door, frightened. "May you be healthy, Senora Rosa, my heart dropped into my shoes. I thought it was the English who'd come looking for Yitzhako again."

"Forgive me for startling you, but I can't sleep. I don't know what to do. I have to know what's happening with Ephraim."

"Shhh, stop talking nonsense, Senora Rosa! Now isn't the time to be looking for him. Better to leave him to hide until the English give up searching for him. If you seek him out, you'll be putting him in danger. How do you know they're not following you? I told you not to come here. You're putting us all in danger. If they think we're in contact, they might accuse Yitzhako of murdering Matilda too."

"Well, how do you know it was Ephraim and not Yitzhako who killed her?" Rosa asked assertively.

"Everybody knows! Senora Franco saw him running away. Even if Yitzhako was with him, nobody saw him. So why put him at risk for nothing? God help you, Senora Rosa . . . I beg you not to come here again. Don't endanger Yitzhako and all of us."

"But what if Ephraim needs help? What if he has nowhere to hide?"

"And if he doesn't, where could you hide him? Under your bed? Your husband will throw you and him out of the house. You'll lose your husband and your girls. You'd better go home, sit tight, and then we'll see. Be well, Senora Ermosa, go now and swear you won't come here again."

Sara hustled Rosa out the door, and with head bowed she stepped into the street. Even Jerusalem's clear air couldn't relieve the suffocation she felt, torn between her loyalty to her husband and girls and her fear for her brother.

The following few days did nothing to lighten her mood. Wherever she went, people were whispering behind her back, and she couldn't ignore it. As she went to the grocery, Matilda's two brothers turned and spat behind her. A different time Becky came home crying and told her that some children had bullied her and pulled her hair and shouted that her uncle was a murderer of

Jews. Luna and Rachelika didn't even leave the house. Rachelika helped Rosa with the housework, and Luna was very quiet and stopped complaining about losing her job.

Even her neighbor and best friend Tamar avoided her. Rosa decided to put an end to the tension and knocked on Tamar's door.

"What have I done to you that you're acting like this?" she asked Tamar.

"Look, Rosa," she replied, "I don't know what to tell you. You're like family to me, and so is Senora Franco. I'm between the two of you, and right now she needs me more. She sits on the floor all day, tearing her clothes and pulling her hair out, weeping for her daughter. I'm there with her, helping her during the shiva. What do you want me to do?"

"But how am I to blame?" Rosa said. "Even if Ephraim did kill Matilda, and I know he didn't, how am I to blame?"

"You're not, querida, but he's your brother, you're family, and when there's a murderer in the family, even the best family isn't all that good."

"You're like a sister to me," Rosa pleaded. "You can't turn your back on me now, when I need you most."

"*Ti caro mucho*, Rosa, I love you a lot, but Victoria Franco needs me now too, and if I have to choose between you and her, I have to be with her right now."

Rosa fell silent, shaken by her neighbor's response. Without a word she turned on her heel and left Tamar's house.

The three-minute walk that separated her house from Tamar's on the other side of the yard seemed to go on forever. She felt as if eyes were peering at her from every window. Everyone in Ohel Moshe, so she understood, had made their choice. Like Tamar, they too had chosen Victoria Franco.

Relations between her and Gabriel became tenser each day. He rarely spoke to her, and for a week now hadn't touched the food she put on the table. The girls became quieter than ever. Rachelika and Becky refused to go to school, and for the first time in her life Rosa decided, without consulting Gabriel, to keep them at home. They stayed in their room for most of the day and left her alone. Even Luna didn't annoy her, and it was as if she were walking around on tiptoe.

One morning, after many days of not leaving the house, Rosa went out into the yard and sat on a stool. On her knees she set a copper bowl of rice from which she picked out small stones.

The yard was very quiet. The neighbors avoided coming outside while she was there, but she was determined to stop hiding like a criminal. Even if her brother had murdered Matilda, and she believed he hadn't, she wouldn't let anybody punish her for something she hadn't done.

As she was sifting the rice, Rachelika came out and sat at her feet. "Mother, what if it's true that Tio Ephraim did kill Matilda?" she asked.

"*Sera la boca!* Don't say things like that! Ephraim hasn't killed anybody! He's being framed, and we don't say anything about Ephraim that we didn't see with our own eyes. We don't say things like that about our family."

"But Mother, everybody's saying he killed her because she went out with the English."

"So everybody's saying. Since when have we cared what everybody's saying?"

"They're saying that the Lehi kill Jewish girls only if they informed on Jews to the English, so maybe that's why he killed her?"

A powerful surge of air seemed to fill her lungs, and Rosa felt she could breathe again. That's it! If Ephraim had killed Matilda, then he had a reason. It wasn't just because she went out with an Ingelish, it was because she'd informed on Jews! The whole picture had suddenly become clear to her. In a rare display of emotion she clasped Rachelika's head in both hands and started planting kisses on it.

"Gracias, gracias, querida mia," she said to her daughter, who was unused to physical contact with her mother, never seen kissing or embracing anyone. "Gracias el Dio, now I understand everything."

When Gabriel came home that evening, Rosa broached the subject. "Do you know when the Lehi kill Jewish girls? Only when they inform. That's why they killed Matilda. She informed on Jews to the Ingelish, that's why they shaved her head. Rachelika says it's like a mark of Cain."

Gabriel felt the anger rising in his throat. "Shut your mouth!" he yelled. "Your bastard brother's got us into trouble with the whole of Ohel Moshe, Sukkat Shalom, and the Mahane Yehuda Market. I can't walk through the market. They all treat me like a leper. I'm the murderer's brother-in-law, and I—Gabriel Ermosa, a man respected by everyone—now have to walk with his head bowed and avoid people. Do you know how many years I've known the Franco family? I've known them since the day I was born! And now I can't look them in the eye. Do you know how many customers I had in the shop today, Rosa? Maybe ten. Do you know what that means? It means that our neighbors are boycotting us, and you're talking my ears off about a mark of

Cain? A mark of Cain is what your good-for-nothing borracho brother has put on my family, *that's* a mark of Cain! I don't want to hear you say one more word about Ephraim in front of the girls. I forbid you to mention his name. From now on, there's no Ephraim! You want to talk about Ephraim, then go to the Western Wall and leave a note there, speak to Senor del mundo, but in this house Ephraim does not exist!"

Gabriel truly believed that Ephraim had murdered Matilda Franco. A man of peace, he was unable to justify murder under any circumstances, whether of a Jew or an Englishman. On the day that Senora and Senor Franco, Matilda's parents and his loyal customers, came into his shop and placed a jar of almonds and raisins on the counter, he realized it was time to move his family away from Ohel Moshe.

"We want neither your honey nor your sting," Senora Franco told him. "We want nothing to do with your family, certainly not the almonds and raisins that Matilda, may she rest in peace, bought from you before your brother-in-law, may his name and memory be erased, killed her." She and her husband made a big display of exiting the shop, leaving Gabriel slack-jawed. Fortunately Avramino and Matzliach had gone to lunch and no one was there to witness his shame.

Gabriel felt weak and sat down on the chair behind the counter, his head whirling, his heart hurting. He drank some water from the clay jar under the counter and tried to put his thoughts into some kind of order. For a while now he'd thought about improving the family's standard of living and moving into a modern apartment in one of the city's better neighborhoods, but for some reason he hadn't acted on it. Now they could no longer stay in Ohel Moshe. He would move his family to the best area in Jerusalem so that his daughters could make a fresh start. Nobody in the new building would need to know that his borracho brother-in-law was a murderer.

A month later the Ermosa family moved into a spacious building with an elevator on King George Street, near the upscale Rehavia neighborhood. Rosa couldn't find herself in her roomy new home. In their old house in Ohel Moshe there were three rooms: Mercada's room, which no one had entered since she left for Tel Aviv, a room for the girls, and another that served as the living room by day and her and Gabriel's bedroom at night. In the new house she and Gabriel had a room to themselves and so did the girls, and they even had a guest room that was presently empty because Gabriel decided that they weren't moving all the "junk" from Ohel Moshe to the new place.

They didn't have enough furniture to fill the rooms. Gabriel bought new furniture for the guest room and new beds for the girls. Above each bed were small cabinets; Becky and Rachelika put schoolbooks on theirs, while Luna arranged makeup on hers. On the inside of her cabinet door Luna stuck a picture of Rita Hayworth that she had cut out of a magazine. From the Romano Brothers carpentry shop Gabriel bought a round dining table over which Rosa spread a lace tablecloth she had embroidered herself. They brought the cabinet with glass doors from the old house, a gorgeous piece that had belonged to Mercada and Raphael. The inside of the cabinet was fitted with mirrors that reflected porcelain and crystal pieces so elegant and delicate that Rosa's heart wouldn't allow her to give them away. On the cabinet's marble top rested silver-framed photographs of her and Gabriel, young and good-looking, from the time of their engagement. He is seated on a chair holding a newspaper, and she is wearing elegant black clothes of the kind she hasn't worn for years, standing beside him tense and grave. Beside their engagement picture was a family photograph of the two of them sitting on chairs, with the three girls behind them. And in Gabriel and Rosa's bedroom stood the magnificent wardrobe with mirrored doors and two lions on top.

Every day movers would unload new furniture and accessories. Gabriel picked out everything himself and didn't once ask Rosa to accompany him. Instead of the kerosene stoves and the Primus, he bought the latest trend in kitchen appliances, an electric cooker, and told her, "From now on you'll cook with electricity."

He also bought a Levitt icebox, which had a top section with room for an entire block of ice. When they lived in their old house in Ohel Moshe, the ice seller would come in his horse-drawn cart and shout, "Ice! Ice!" and ring his bell, and all the neighbors would gather on Agrippas Street and carry a quarter or half a block of ice home with special tongs. The ice cart didn't come to the new apartment; instead, a truck delivered the ice. The driver would stand on the corner of the street outside the Jewish Agency and ring his bell to announce his arrival. But Rosa never went down to buy ice, for how could she go down all those stairs and make it to the ice truck in time? And if she did, how could she carry the heavy block of ice up four flights?

"*Sano que 'stas*, Gabriel, what are we going to do about ice?" she asked him after three days without ice in the icebox and all the food going bad.

"Por Dio, Rosa, what's the problem with going down in the elevator? Don't you want to get ahead in life?"

Nothing could persuade Rosa to use the elevator. She ignored Luna's mockery and stood firm in her decision not to use the services of the monstrous machine. So Gabriel had no choice but to send Matzliach on his bicycle to fetch ice from the truck and bring it up to their fourth-floor apartment.

What am I going to do with all these modern gadgets that Gabriel's brought me? Rosa asked herself, for she didn't have a single neighbor whose advice she could seek. She didn't get used to the electric cooker either, and when Gabriel left for work she'd take out the kerosene stove and the Primus from under the sink and cook on them. Only one device in the new apartment truly amazed her: the ventilated larder, whose back wall opened onto the outside of the building and was covered with mesh, enabling a flow of air that kept the food inside fresh.

Instead of the curtains that covered the shelf under the sink in Ohel Moshe, she now had wooden cupboards; instead of the rugs she hung on the walls for decoration, she now had a carpet on the living room floor. Yet despite the modern amenities, she felt lost in the big King George Street apartment that had so many stairs and so many neighbors who rode up and down in the elevator. And despite their politeness and despite their greeting her and asking after her husband and daughters, she was unable to find anything in common with them.

"Mother, let's go to Maayan Stub," Rachelika, who sympathized with her mother, once suggested.

"What have I got to do in Maayan Stub, querida? Everything's expensive there. With what they charge for a pair of underwear, you can buy enough food for a week in the market. No, querida, better to take me to Mahane Yehuda. There's nothing for me in Maayan Stub. It's too fancy for me."

Rosa desperately missed Ohel Moshe, chatting idly in the yard with her neighbors, the shouted door-to-door conversations, sitting on stools in the afternoon with cold watermelon and salty cheese. She yearned for the warm conversations in Ladino, everyone tasting from each other's plate, the unspoken competition over who baked the best borekas and who made the tastiest sofrito. And most of all she missed her neighbor Tamar. She loved Tamar like a sister, and she remembered her fondly for all the times she had supported her without question. Now Rosa felt profoundly lonely. Not even the toilet and bathroom with its two faucets, one for cold water and the other for hot, which along with the elevator aroused the greatest excitement among the relatives who came specially to see these marvels, moved her.

One morning the Ermosa family and their neighbors in the big stone building on King George Street were awakened by a loud explosion. A bomb had gone off in the *Palestine Post* building on Hasolel Street and rocked the heart of the city. The building collapsed and adjacent buildings were badly damaged; people jumped from balconies, some to their death. The wounded were taken to the city's hospitals and the rest of the street's residents were taken with their possessions to the nearby Warshavsky and Zion hotels.

Rosa was scared to death. Afraid of being in the apartment alone, she told Gabriel, "Perhaps it would be better if the girls didn't leave the house today. It's dangerous outside. It's better if they stay here with me."

"Por Dio, Rosa," he replied angrily, "at times like this, it's dangerous every day. These aren't easy times, so what, we should shut ourselves up inside our four walls all day?"

"Querido," she pleaded, "it's dangerous outside. I don't want anything to happen to the girls, God forbid."

"Basta, Rosa!" he said. "There'll be something new all the time now. We can't stop living. Nothing's going to happen to the girls." If he recognized Rosa's fear of being in the apartment on her own, he didn't show it.

From day to day Gabriel had found it increasingly difficult to take the Hamekasher bus from King George all the way to the Mahane Yehuda Market. Very few people could afford a car, but Gabriel's success—two years earlier he had expanded his business and in partnership with Mordoch Levi had opened a halvah factory—had swelled his bank account at the Jaffa Road branch of the Anglo-Palestine Bank. He bought a used Austin 1933 from an old doctor at bargain price and enrolled in driving lessons.

On the day he received his license, Gabriel took the whole family for a drive through the streets of Jerusalem. He enjoyed driving and insisted on dropping off Becky and Rachelika at school, even though it was only a short distance from their apartment, and Luna at Zacks & Son. As he gradually gained confidence in his skills, he drove the family to visit his mother and sister in Tel Aviv, and occasionally even as far as Tiberias, where in the morning they would bathe in the Sea of Galilee and toward evening they'd go out on a fishing boat and soak up the ebbing rays of the sun that painted the lake and its surrounding mountains in hues of pink and gold. Sometimes Rachelika would jump into the water, causing Rosa's heart to skip a beat, and she'd shout at her to get back into the boat. And Luna, who saw how her sister was stealing the limelight, followed, swimming alongside with a breaststroke that kept her head out of the water so as not to spoil her hairdo.

"Like a swan," Gabriel would say, and Rosa would think to herself, like someone who doesn't know how to swim. But why would her father see it? He always sees the best in that girl. And right away she'd rebuke herself, for whenever Rachelika went into the water she'd be so worried she wouldn't take her eyes off her, but when Luna was in the water she barely glanced in her direction.

On Saturdays, Gabriel and the girls would drive to Ein Feshkha, where they'd spend the day paddling in the pools and floating in the Dead Sea. Rosa continued to observe the Sabbath and did not go along with them, but as time went by, the loneliness and sense of alienation she felt in her new home—which she would never get used to—led her to bend her principles and join in the Saturday trips. How I miss Ohel Moshe, she'd think to herself. If we lived in Ohel Moshe I'd stay at home with the neighbors and not desecrate Shabbat, but what have I got to do in this big apartment, me and the four walls, except go crazy?

But the family excursions out of Jerusalem soon ceased due to the turbulent times. One incident came hard on the heels of another. Bombings, shootings, increasing tension between Jews and Arabs, and the frequent curfews imposed by the British police all prevented travel to sparsely populated areas like Ein Feshkha. Even the road between Jerusalem and Tel Aviv was now considered dangerous, as Arab snipers lay in wait and shot at vehicles on the narrow part near the Castel landmark. That put an end to visits to Nona Mercada and Tia Allegra.

Two months after the first bombing at the *Palestine Post* building, a second one occurred. A British army vehicle blew up in the middle of Ben-Yehuda Street, two buildings were completely destroyed, and still others collapsed. When Rosa forbade Luna to go to work—she had begged Mr. Zacks for her job back once Gabriel had allowed it—and Rachelika and Becky to go to school, Gabriel was forced to agree with her. You could never know where the next bombing would happen, he thought. Better they stay home for a few days until the situation gets better.

Becky was scared to death by the explosions, and though Luna protested loudly, deep down she too was afraid of going out. But from the moment her father left for the shop, her sisters were occupied, and her mother's back was turned, Rachelika ran the short distance from their apartment to the Rehavia Gymnasium, where she and Becky attended school. She was already fifteen, and she and her friends from school had joined the Haganah, learning hand-to-hand combat, knots, and even some weapons training. On the day of the second bombing, they ran all the way to the site of the explosion on Ben-Yehuda Street. Their assignment, which they'd drilled more than once, was to form a chain and stop rubberneckers from hampering evacuation of the wounded.

Rosa and Gabriel knew nothing of Rachelika's secret life. The only one who did was Luna.

"You should join the Haganah too," Rachelika told her. "We have to push out the English so we can have a state of our own."

"Speak in a whisper. If Father hears, it'll be the end of you. You know what he thinks of Tio Ephraim."

"It's not the same," Rachelika protested. "Tio Ephraim's with the Lehi and I'm in the Haganah."

"Stop with that nonsense! Why do you need to be in the Haganah? There's a thousand boys who've just come back from the British army, and they're here, right under our noses, and we need to find a boy, you and me, and get married."

"Get married? When I finish school I'm joining the Palmach like the boys."

"What Palmach have you got in your head? Who'll let you join the Palmach? You won't be able to leave home until you get married. That's how it is in the Ermosa family. You want to leave home, go with a husband."

"I want to be part of the struggle. Why can't you understand that?"

"What's to understand? Girls don't fight. Girls wait for boys who've come back from the British army and marry them."

"Oof, Luna, I can't listen to you anymore. The ground is on fire, the entire history of the Jewish people is in the balance, and you're talking about weddings."

"*Wai de mi sola*, what words! I don't understand history, but I do understand people, and with people, a woman is a woman and a man is a man, and it doesn't matter whether it's wartime or peacetime."

"Oof!" Rachelika said, annoyed. "You, all that interests you is having a good time, pretty clothes, and lipstick. You're a foolish girl."

"I'm foolish because I like dressing well? What do you want, for me to be a shmatte like you? Dress like a primitive? You, you're like a boy. What man will fall in love with you? You carry on wearing khaki pants and a Russian shirt and you won't find a boy or anything else!"

"You're impossible. I'm telling you about my dream and you mock me. I'm not telling you anything ever again!" Rachelika said and left the apartment, slamming the door behind her.

She was determined to be part of the struggle even though she was afraid of her father. Once it was time to move up and become an instructor of Haganah Youth, Rachelika instead chose to be a leader in the Haganah's Junior Battalion, the Scouts. She knew that the Haganah Youth instructors' courses meant leaving Jerusalem, and there was no chance that her father would approve.

The first day of the Scouts course, Rachelika and her best friend Dina met in the yard outside the wooden hut, both of them dressed in their khaki uniforms. The night before, she had been so excited she hadn't slept a wink. Rachelika and Dina looked for their friends from school, but they were nowhere to be found. She approached a group of girls in the yard and asked them if they knew where the new instructors' course was being held.

One of the girls looked her up and down and replied, "There's no place in the course for Sephardi girls. Get lost!" The usually calm Rachelika was seized by a terrible rage, and without thinking twice she punched the girl in the nose. "Nobody," she told the girl's companions, "nobody throws me out of anywhere. I'm a sixth-generation Jerusalemite and this Ashkenazia just got off the boat, so tell her to show a little respect before she talks to me!"

The story about Rachelika punching the Ashkenazia took flight, and she became a legend, the outstanding cadet on the instructors' course. At the end of the course there was to be a trip to Mount Tabor, but she didn't even bother asking her father for permission to go. She knew he wouldn't allow it, so at the last minute she told the organizers that she wouldn't be able to attend because her mother was sick.

When her friends returned from the trip with their stories, she felt a twinge in her heart, and for the first time in her life she regretted not being the tiniest bit like Luna. Luna, she knew, wouldn't have given in. If she hadn't been allowed to go, she'd have taken off and gone anyway. Rachelika could not defy her father or manipulate him the way Luna did.

On completion of the instructors' course, she became the leader of the youngest Scouts, who were Becky's age. One time, as she was teaching the young-sters to tie a clove hitch, another bombing occurred. The sound came from the direction of Gan Ha'ir, close to her home, and a few minutes later the British imposed a curfew over their portable loudspeakers, and she was stuck in the hut on Hahavazelet Street with her young charges.

"I have to get home. My parents will be sick with worry," she told the scout-master.

"Nobody's leaving, there's a curfew!" he ordered. But Rachelika was very concerned about her family, so when nobody was looking, she slipped through the back gate and ran up Ben-Yehuda Street. Suddenly firing opened up around her. She found her way into a building and banged desperately on the apart-ment doors, but not one opened. She hid below the staircase on the first floor, shaking with fear. Without warning, British policemen stormed the building, and when they asked what she was doing there, she stammered that she'd been on her way home just as the curfew was implemented. "Where do you live?" one asked, but when she pointed toward Gan Ha'ir, he ordered her to stay where she was. When the police left, she waited a few more minutes before leaving the building. Taking a roundabout route, she reached Halbreich House. From a distance she could see the building surrounded by British police and realized she had no chance of getting through.

She turned around and started running toward her old neighborhood, Ohel Moshe. When a passing Arab policeman saw her, he started shooting at her, and she fled in panic, panting until she reached Tio Shmuel's house. She knocked on the door, but no one answered. Only when she shouted, "Tio Shmuel, it's me, Rachelika!" did the door swing open and Shmuel quickly pulled her inside.

"What are you doing out in a curfew?" he asked.

"I was at the Scouts when I heard the boom. It came from the direction of our apartment, and I'm worried."

"We heard about it on the radio," Tio Shmuel said. "And we're worried too. But if the English catch you, they'll put you in prison. Stay here with us until they lift the curfew."

All through the night they heard shooting and police shouting in English and Arabic, and when the curfew ended in the morning Rachelika hurried home.

"Sano que 'stes," Rosa said, taking her into her arms. "You almost killed us. You gave us a heart attack!"

Gabriel clasped her to him and told her quietly and straight to the point, "No more Scouts. At times like this you don't leave the house without us knowing where you are."

Fear at her father's reaction paralyzed Rachelika, and although she knew deep down that she'd disobey his orders, she decided not to respond. She didn't even attempt to deny that she'd been at the Scouts. She imagined that when she hadn't come home after the explosion, Luna had told her parents where she was. Her eyes scanned the room for Luna but didn't see her.

"Where's Luna?" she asked her mother.

"She's gone to Zacks & Son. That one couldn't miss a minute of work," Rosa replied.

"Well," Gabriel said, "I'm going to the shop. Come on, Becky, I'll drive you to school. And you," to Rachelika, "don't you dare leave the house, not even for school."

"But Papo, I'll miss lessons."

"You should have thought of that when you joined the Scouts without asking permission."

"I'm sorry, Papo, but I knew you wouldn't let me go and I just had to take part in the struggle. The whole school's in either the Scouts or the Haganah. You always said you were for the Haganah."

"I'm not saying that I'm not for the Haganah. I'm saying I'm not for my daughter participating in a Haganah activity without my permission, and I'm not for my daughter telling me barefaced lies!"

"But Papo, I wasn't at the Haganah. I was at the Scouts."

"It's the same thing!"

"Please, Papo, you can't keep me in the house."

"If you don't want to be shut up in the house, come and help me in the shop," he said.

Unsure whether he was being serious, she didn't move.

"Are you coming or are you staying home?" he said.

Without another word Rachelika went to the door and followed her father out.

From that day forth, she never went to the Scouts or the Rehavia Gymnasium again. She worked in the shop with Gabriel and became his right hand.

———

Total silence reigned in the big stone building between two and four, the afternoon nap time, yet since the girls had grown up and the shop was no longer close to home, nobody took naps anymore. During these hours, when the apartment was empty of the girls and Gabriel, Rosa would sit on the balcony and count the buses passing in the street below, big Hamekasher buses that would pull up at the stop across the street and let off and take on passengers. Sometimes she'd see a big black car drive through the gate of the Jewish Agency building and stop in the driveway, and people who seemed to her to be important would get out.

Rosa felt she was burning in her loneliness. On Gabriel's orders she'd stopped talking about Ephraim, but hadn't stopped thinking about him. She hadn't heard a word from him or about him since Matilda's murder. Her only source of information was Sara Laniado, Yitzhako's mother, but Sara had told her not to come again until it had all blown over. In any case, how could she get there now? How would she find her way? And what would Gabriel say if she left the house and went to Sukkat Shalom?

Once she had been close to Rachelika, but since Gabriel had forbidden her to attend school and took her to the shop, Rachelika said no more than necessary, to her or to her father. True, she went to the shop with him, worked beside him, and did everything he instructed her. But he couldn't get a smile out of her. Still, Gabriel is right, Rosa thought. On the night of the curfew when Rachelika was missing, she'd felt her end had come. It was better that she be close to her father than go to school. Who knew what dangers were waiting for her there. Anyway, she'd find a husband in another year or two, so why would she need to go to school?

And Luna, from day to day she'd become more coquettish. She looked like the girls in the magazines. Where had she gotten all her beauty from? Certainly not from her, and even her father, may he be healthy, was not as good-looking as Luna. There was nobody in his family as beautiful as Luna, nobody as beautiful as Luna in the whole of Jerusalem. God forgive my sins, only trouble will come from the beauty of that one, Rosa thought. God knows what streets she's roaming during the afternoon break each day.

One evening before Luna had gone out in heels as high as the Mount of Olives, Rosa had told her, "Be careful you don't fall off your heels and break your neck." Luna had fixed her with an icy stare and replied, "Be careful you don't turn into an armchair, sitting at home all day," and Rosa's face had paled. After all these years she was still not immune to her eldest daughter's venom.

She'd taken off her sapatos and thrown them at Luna, who'd dodged them as she'd left.

Rosa needed to get the girl out of their house! She'd speak to Gabriel and tell him to find her a husband. It was time she had her own home, where she could make trouble for her husband and leave Rosa in peace. The ring of the doorbell shook her from her thoughts. They'd been living in the apartment on King George Street for almost a year, and she still hadn't gotten used to the bell. "Just a minute," she called. To her surprise she found Gabriel standing at the door. Without even a hello he went straight into the bedroom.

Gabriel was tired and his body ached. Lately he'd felt as if his very bones had gotten heavier, and it was difficult for him to carry himself. The soles of his feet burned inside his shoes, and most of the time he felt weary and depressed. He attributed it to the situation in the country. He was worried about the unknown, the girls' safety. He had the terrible feeling that he was losing them. And he was troubled by the state of his business. The situation in the country had caused people to stop buying delicatessen, and the flow of customers was dwindling from day to day. Even the British soldiers who had been regulars had stopped coming to the Mahane Yehuda Market. Not only that, the demand for halvah was not what it had been in the past, and his stubborn partner Mordoch Levi insisted on continuing production as before.

"Don't worry, Ermosa, trust Mordoch, everything will be fine with God's help!" he'd said.

But Gabriel didn't trust Mordoch. His instincts told him that the man and plain dealing didn't go hand in hand. He didn't yet have proof, but something in Mordoch's behavior irked him. I'll have to keep an eye on the Kurd, he thought to himself before closing his eyes.

The winds of war were blowing in Palestine. A Hamekasher bus carrying children from the Old City to their school outside the wall was fired on. The windows were shattered and only by a miracle no one was hurt. A Jew named Mizrachi was murdered in the Old City while shopping in the market, Yosef Yechezkel was wounded by Jaffa Gate and lost his sight. Mr. Weingarten, chairman of the Jewish Committee in Jerusalem, went to the high commissioner's office and demanded increased protection of the city's Jewish residents, but it appeared that he could not find a sympathetic ear, and so the situation continued to deteriorate.

The winter of 1945 was a hard one. Torrential rain hammered the roofs of Jerusalem and the streets became fast-running rivers, blocking the approach roads. Gabriel's health was declining. He couldn't sleep and sweated like an animal at night. He was irritable, impatient, and quick to anger. He found it hard to get up in the morning and was already exhausted before his afternoon break. His legs didn't carry him as they used to, and he no longer walked every day to Franz the fat newspaper seller or visited the halvah factory. His movements had gradually become slower, and sometimes he lost balance.

"Go and see Dr. Sabo," Rosa told him. "Perhaps you've caught cold or eaten something bad."

But he, who had taken to a sickbed only once in his life, waved away her suggestion. "I'm just tired. I'm working too hard in the shop. It'll pass."

But it didn't pass. The girls and Rosa noticed that every time Gabriel tried to get up from his chair, he trembled slightly. Sometimes his speech became soft and slow, as if he couldn't find the words, but then he recovered.

"There's something not right with Papo," Luna said to Rachelika one day.

"I know," she replied. "Sometimes he sits in the chair in the shop and just stares as if he's not seeing anything. Sometimes his hand shakes so much he can't put a piece of cheese on the scales."

"Papo, you have to go and see Dr. Sabo," Luna appoached him later that day.

But he persisted with his story. "I'm just overworked. It'll pass."

"Papo, this has gone on for far too long," Rachelika chimed in. "Maybe Dr. Sabo will give you some medicine and then it'll pass."

Gabriel lost his temper and almost stumbled as he got up from the table. Rosa ran over and took his arm, which angered him even more. His face reddened and he swore at her and called her names, much to everyone's shock. They had never seen their father behave vulgarly.

When the situation didn't improve, Gabriel finally consulted Dr. Sabo. The good doctor listened to Gabriel's complaints, examined him, and diagnosed rheumatism. He suggested hot baths and a visit to the hot springs in Tiberias, and assured Gabriel that everything would be fine.

That evening Rosa ran a hot bath for Gabriel. It indeed relieved the pain, but when he tried to get out, he slipped and fell. The sound brought Rosa rushing into the bathroom, where to her surprise she found her husband, naked as the day he was born, sprawled on the floor. She, who in all their years of marriage had never seen her husband naked, was filled with shame and fled.

"What happened?" Luna asked on seeing her rush out of the bathroom.

"Papo's there, he's fallen on the floor," Rosa mumbled.

Luna hurried to the bathroom, grabbed a towel, and covered her father.

"Are you all right, Papo?" she asked, kneeling beside him to help him up. "Rachelika!"

Rachelika ran in and together they lifted his heavy frame. Little Becky, who had also heard the commotion, fetched Gabriel's robe from the bedroom. They helped him into it and sat him down.

"Papo querido, are you in pain?" Luna said.

Rachelika sat beside him and held his shaking hand. "Papo, what happened to you?"

He looked around and didn't reply. His soft, kind face was covered by a cloud, his eyes were glistening, and tears were falling from them. The girls couldn't believe it. Their father, this tall, handsome, strong man, was crying. Luna rubbed his back, Becky leaned her head on his shoulder, and Rachelika didn't let go of his hand. Soon all three of them were crying with him.

Rosa was standing by the door. Her heart went out to her husband, to her daughters, but her feet did not carry her to them. She was incapable of joining this demonstration of love between her husband and her daughters. She lingered by the door, as if she was about to leave at any moment, as if she didn't belong in this house, to these girls, to this family. Never before had she experienced loneliness as powerful as this.

Gabriel's condition continued to worsen. He spent more and more time in bed and hardly went to the shop. Every morning Rachelika went without him and stood in his place behind the counter. She could see how stock was running low and how Matzliach, despite all the years he had been working at Gabriel's side, had not learned a thing. Her heart aching, she saw that from day to day fewer customers were coming in. Times were hard and people were buying only the bare necessities: bread, vegetables, and a chicken for the Shabbat table. Dried fruit, halvah, sweets, and even smoked fish were too luxurious in times like these.

She decided not to tell her father.

"I don't want to worry him," she told Luna, "but I'm very worried. The situation is shit."

"So what can we do?"

"We'll wait till Papo gets better and then we'll see. In the meantime, I'm keeping an eye on that troncho Tio Matzliach. Believe me, Luna, it would be better if he wasn't around."

"We've got to take Papo to the hot springs in Tiberias," Luna said. "Dr. Sabo said it would help him feel better."

"But how can we get him to Tiberias? Papo can't drive in his condition."

"So get a license and you drive."

"Me? Papo would never let me drive the car."

"Right now Papo can't interfere," Luna replied with an assertiveness and common sense that surprised Rachelika. "Sign up at Asherov where Papo learned."

And why don't you? Rachelika thought to herself. But she knew that her beautiful coquette of a sister kept her distance from anything to do with learning, and driving you had to learn, no? Luna was very close to Papo, she'd do anything for him, but she wouldn't stop living her life. Even now that he was sick, she continued going out and having a good time, dressing up, flirting with suitors at Café Atara. But how could you get annoyed with her? How could you not be captivated by her charm, her liveliness, her desire to devour the world? Even in such hard times, with Papo sick and the country on the verge of war, for her there weren't any problems in the world. What wouldn't Rachelika give to be able to laugh like Luna.

Now that she wasn't attending school and the Scouts, Rachelika sometimes went out with her sister to Café Atara or Café Zichel, saw how all eyes were always on her, how they all hung on her every word. Luna just had to ask for a light and all ten men at the table *and* other tables would whip out their lighters. She had only to get up for a moment and they'd all stand too as if they were English gentlemen. Hah, gentlemen, more like horanis from the tin shack neighborhood. And the cigarette? The first time she saw Luna smoking she was shocked.

"Luna, are you out of your mind?" she had asked her sister as they sat in the café that evening.

"Don't you dare tell Papo."

"And why are you smoking all of a sudden? Only cheap girls smoke cigarettes."

"Really? Even Golda Meyerson smokes cigarettes. Smoking cigarettes is modern, and I'm a modern girl."

Modern. Rachelika laughed to herself. She barely finished elementary school, never reads a newspaper, and if she does read, it's only *Burda* or a film magazine. Yes, she's a real expert on that. If the Hebrew University taught fashion or Hollywood studies, Luna would have a PhD by now.

"Enough, Rachelika, don't be so old-fashioned," Luna said. "Put a smile on your face and let's go dancing."

"You have dancing in your head? I've got a thousand problems on my mind. The situation in the shop is horrible, Papo's sick, there's a shooting every day, and all you can think about is dancing!"

"Oh, come on," Luna said. "What good will sitting at home with a long face do? Will it make Papo feel better?"

"And what if he needs me?"

"Mother and Becky are there. We aren't leaving him on his own. So come on, you nudnik, what do you want? Should I get down on my knees?"

"Why not? Let's see you do it and maybe I'll come along."

That night they'd danced until midnight.

"Heideh, Cinderella," Rachelika said to Luna, "it's time to go home before Papo calls the whole British police force."

They left the café arm in arm followed by the excited gaggle of Luna's suitors, a band of young men, some of whom had recently returned from overseas after fighting with the British army's Jewish Brigade. They were young, well built, and full of life, and mainly full of stories that fired Luna's imagination.

"The world's so big and fascinating, and the farthest we've been is Tiberias," she said to Rachelika after saying good-bye to the boys who'd walked them home.

"How can you think about the world when the situation here's so horrible? When war might break out at any moment? When our Jerusalem's a mess?"

"What good will it do if I think about Jerusalem's troubles? Is there a war right now? No! We'll worry about the war when it happens. Why not dream while you can? Does it cost anything?"

"Tell me about a dream of yours," laughed Rachelika, who couldn't remain indifferent to her sister's charm.

"I dream that as soon as I'm married, the first thing I do is move to Tel Aviv. I'm not staying here in this hole! Since the first day we visited I've dreamed about living in Tel Aviv. Tel Aviv's young, easy, free, Tel Aviv's me! Jerusalem's old, it takes everything to heart, it thinks too much. Jerusalem, Rachelika, is you."

"I'm old?" Rachelika was hurt. "Is that how you think of me?"

"You sit in Papo's shop all day, and then you come back from the shop and sit at home. Since you stopped going to school, you've become an old frump."

"What do I have left? They took me out of the gymnasium, they took me out of the Scouts, so what can I do?"

"Do! If I were in your shoes I wouldn't have given up. I'd have argued with Papo, I'd have made his life a misery until he gave in. But you, Papo tells you to stop going to school and work in the shop, and like a little Goody-Two-Shoes you go and do what he tells you."

"I can't disobey him. Even you don't."

"The trick, my dear sister, is to make Papo feel that you're listening to him, giving him respect, but not giving up on what you want. The trick, Rachelika, is not asking permission to do every little thing. You just say good-bye and go out, and if he asks where to, you say I'll be back soon. By the time you get home he's already snoring."

"But how can I go to school when he wants me to work in the shop? And how can I go to the Scouts if I'm not at the gymnasium?"

"You can't go to the gymnasium if he won't allow it, and he really needs you in the shop because he's sick. It's not like before when he wanted you there to punish you. Now that you're his right hand, forget the gymnasium. But if you want to study so badly, why not take high school evening classes? And who said you have to go to the gymnasium to be in the Haganah?"

My God, Rachelika thought, how her coquette of a sister could sometimes surprise her.

"Where did you get so many smarts from all of a sudden?" she said and hugged Luna.

"From you," Luna replied. "We're the same blood, aren't we?"

At dinner the following day, Gabriel was in a good mood and joined them at the table. They ate in a pleasant silence, though every now and then the girls' gay chatter and Gabriel's request for someone to please pass the salt broke the quiet. The only unheard voice was Rosa's. In general, her mother had become almost invisible lately, Rachelika observed. Since Gabriel had fallen ill, it was as if she had been fading together with him. She considered telling her mother what she'd heard recently from her friend Temima, a member of one of the Lehi youth groups, about Tio Ephraim, who was now going by a new name and was an important commander. But ultimately she decided to keep it to herself. If she wanted to return to the ranks of the struggle, she had to keep quiet. Nobody, not even Luna, could know about her plans.

"Where are you, *querida*? Where have you gone, to America?" Her father's voice cut into her thoughts. She smiled at him, glad to see he was feeling better. She worried about him very much. Lately the rheumatism had had a bad effect on his mood. The tremor in his fingers was still there despite his efforts to conceal it, but the smile and the gentleness were back. Seizing on his good mood, she said, "Papo, I want to go back to school. I can take evening classes so it won't interfere with my work in the shop."

Gabriel was silent for what seemed like eternity to her, and then said, "I'm not a well man, Rachelika. I hardly go to the shop, I sit at home. So why don't you take over the shop from me, you and your future husband?"

"What future husband, Papo? I don't even have a boyfriend."

"There will be, Rachelika, there'll be a young man, with God's help, and there'll be a wedding, and this is your dowry, querida. Luna and Becky will marry and be at home for their husbands and children, but you, you've got the head to run a shop. You've learned from me everything you need to know."

"Papo querido, is that what you want for me? To work in the shop in Mahane Yehuda? Didn't you say you wanted me to have an education? Didn't you say you were working to give us the opportunity you never had?"

Gabriel seemed to reflect on this point.

"Heideh, querida," he finally said with a big smile, "go and enroll yourself in evening classes."

She jumped into his arms, kissed him again and again, and danced around the table. Luna looked on amazed at the sight of her always serious sister now deliriously happy, happier than she'd seen her in a long time. She got up from the table and joined her, dancing and laughing, and Becky joined in too, and the three of them danced around the table with their arms around one another's waists. Gabriel watched his happy daughters and his heart swelled. His gorgeous girls, his wonderful girls, the joy of his life. He didn't even notice Rosa, looking as if she'd seen a ghost.

She was sitting at the end of the table watching her happy husband and laughing daughters and thinking about her father and mother who died from that cursed disease, about her brother Nissim who'd lived in America so long that she'd forgotten what he looked like, about her brother Rachamim hanged by the damned Turks at Damascus Gate, and mostly about Ephraim, whom God only knew where he was and whom she missed desperately. *Ya rabi*, oh God, look at her. She had a family, a husband, daughters, but at moments like these not only didn't she feel close to them, on the contrary, she felt further away. And the more she thought about it, the angrier she got. He has managed to distance my daughters from me. It isn't enough that in all our life together he's been aloof from me? Now my daughters are too? Luna, his twin soul, I can understand, I've gotten used to it, accepted it, but Rachelika? Becky? What terrible act did my soul commit before it entered this body of mine? And why am I paying such a painful price in this life for what happened in that one? She shoved the chair back and got up from the table. The noise of the chair tipping over onto the floor silenced the girls' celebration.

"Mother, what's the matter?" Rachelika asked.

"Nothing's the matter. Carry on dancing and leave me be!" she snapped and went out onto the balcony.

It was freezing cold, but she didn't feel it. Insult had seared her body. Her eyes filled with tears as she leaned against the balcony railing and for a fleeting moment considered throwing herself onto the street below, thought about dying and ridding herself once and for all of the pain, of the feeling of not belonging, the feeling of orphanhood that had been with her since the day her mother and father died and left her, a ten-year-old girl, with her five-year-old brother, alone in the world.

Right after work the next day Rachelika enrolled in evening classes. She decided that she would pay the tuition from her wages and wouldn't even ask her father for the money. Afterward she ran straight to Zacks & Son so Luna would be the first to know. Rachelika watched her sister stand barefoot in the window display as she pinned a dress to a mannequin. A handsome young man walked up beside Rachelika and looked at Luna as if mesmerized. Rachelika smiled to herself and tapped on the glass to catch Luna's attention. On seeing Rachelika, she gave that big white-toothed smile and beckoned her into the shop.

"*Ya rabi*, my God!" the young man said either to himself or to Rachelika. "I don't know which is the real doll, the mannequin or the doll dressing it."

Rachelika laughed and said, "If you ask me, it's the doll dressing the mannequin, and she's my sister."

"And what's your sister's name?"

"Luna, like the moon."

"Well, tell your sister I'm moonstruck."

"Good luck!" Rachelika laughed again and entered the shop.

Luna came out of the window display. "Who was that outside?"

"How would I know? Just a boy. He asked your name. I told him it's Luna like the moon, and he said he's moonstruck."

"Is that what he said?" Luna laughed. "He seems nice."

"Very nice, but I'm not here for that nice boy, but to tell you I've been accepted to the high school evening classes!"

"That's great, hermanita!" Luna said cheerfully. "At long last you're starting to get back on track."

"It's all thanks to you, Lunika. If it wasn't for you I wouldn't have even thought of evening classes."

When she got home from work that evening, Luna seemed different. Her usually glowing skin seemed to glow even more, her eyes were shining, and she cast melting smiles in all directions.

At the first opportunity she pulled Rachelika into their room. "As I come out of Zacks & Son and kiss the mezuzah, the boy who spoke to you while I was in the window is standing there with a rose in his hand. He holds it out to me and says, 'This is for the doll who's more beautiful than the one in the window.' I thank him, take the rose, and start walking, but he follows me. I say, 'Thanks for the rose, but why are you following me?' and he says, 'From today on I'm your shadow. Wherever you go I'll be right behind you.'"

"And you didn't get rid of him?"

"Why get rid of him? He's charming! He escorted me all the way home until we reached the bench at the entrance to the Gan Ha'ir park. We sat down, and he told me his name's David Siton and he was in the British army and just got back from Italy. He's a Spaniol like us. He was born in Misgav Ladach hospital in the Old City, he went to school at the Sephardi Talmud Torah, and from one minute to the next I'm liking him more and more. Then he suddenly brings his lips to mine and kisses me. Bells, I swear to God, Rachelika, I heard bells! Would you believe, hermanita, that was my first kiss!"

"I haven't been kissed yet," said Rachelika shyly.

"Don't worry. David's got friends from the British army. We'll find you somebody who'll kiss you."

"What's this we, you're already a couple? Did he propose?"

"Of course he did. He proposed we get married."

"Today, on the park bench? He's only just met you!"

"He said that from the moment he saw me he knew I'd be his wife, so why waste time."

"And what did you say?"

"I laughed, what could I say? Love at first sight, would you believe it?"

As Luna and David got to know each other better, she was pleased to discover that like her, David too loved life. They spent a lot of time in cafés, in clubs, at the cinema.

"Just look at what fate is," he whispered in her ear one evening as they sat on their bench at Gan Ha'ir. "The day after I get back to Jerusalem after three and a half years in that damn war, I'm walking down Jaffa Road and I see you."

Luna blushed. She couldn't believe this was happening to her. She couldn't believe that at long last her knight on a white horse had come. She hadn't the slightest doubt that she'd found the man of her dreams, the man who would be the father of her children. She was so sure of the future of their relationship that she invited David to her home. She introduced him to Gabriel, who was happy to learn that he was the son of Victoria and Aharon Siton, his former neighbors who had "bought" his late son Raphael. A short time after baby Raphael died, the Siton family had moved from Ohel Moshe to Romema and they'd lost touch. Now, thanks to Luna and David, the two families had reconnected, and since the Ermosa and Siton families had known each other for a long time, the relationship between Luna and David quickly became an engagement.

Every evening when Luna finished work at Zacks & Son, David would pick her up at the shop and they'd go and see the early showing at one of the city's many theaters. After the film they'd walk with their arms around each other to their bench at Gan Ha'ir and talk. Luna told David about her sisters and of her great love for her father. He observed that she hardly ever mentioned her mother, but didn't ask why. He talked about himself sparingly, but she continually urged him to tell her about his life, and he eventually gave in. Once he started talking she could hardly stop him. He told her about his family, the British army, and the war, and mainly his mother, with whom he had a special bond.

Since their engagement, Luna became one of the family in the Siton home. She couldn't help but notice the big age difference between David's parents. "My mother," he started to explain once after they went dancing, "met my father when she was a child. Even though she was only fourteen, she was already a widow. A short time after she was married for the first time, her husband died in the cholera epidemic, and what man would take a widow? Only a widower like him with children. Where could she find a young widower? So they found her an old one who was thirty years older than her and they got married. My father hasn't worked even one day in his life. His sons who fled from the Turks and went to America sent money, but it was never enough, and we, the small children my mother bore him, as soon as we reached the age of twelve, we were taken out of the Talmud Torah and put to work. I worked in my elder brother's butcher shop in Mekor Chaim. Afterward, when he moved to Haifa and opened a butcher shop downtown near the port where, forgive me, the prostitutes and the sailors' bars are, he took me with him. I saw the sailors from the ships, I listened to their stories about faraway countries, and I wanted it too. When I was seventeen I heard they were recruiting men for the British army and putting them on the ships. I wanted to travel overseas. I didn't think about there being a war overseas. I falsified my age from seventeen to eighteen."

"How did you do that?"

"I came back to Jerusalem and went straight to the mukhtar of Zichron Tuvia. The mukhtar, may he be healthy, if you gave him a few grush he'd do whatever you asked, so I gave him a few grush and he changed my age from seventeen to eighteen. I joined up at the Sarafand camp and they posted me as a guard at the Royal Air Force station at Al-Bassa near Ras al-Naqoura. I soon realized I'd only see overseas in my dreams and the sea from Ras al-Naqoura.

"But one day a guy who introduced himself as Gad came to the camp. He said he'd come on behalf of the Haganah to look for volunteers for the British army's Jewish Brigade, and that we'd be going to Europe to fight the Germans. I knew that this was my chance. For me it was an adventure, the opportunity to go overseas. I was recruited into the Royal Engineers and sent on a course where we learned how to build army camps and dismantle bridges. Moise Bechor, my friend from the neighborhood, was with me."

"Did he want to go overseas too?"

"No." David laughed. "He wanted to get away from his mother, who nagged him a lot. We'd come home at night and she'd be waiting for him by the door and yell at him, 'What happened to your grandmother that you've come home at this hour? The sun's already shining!' When he told her he was joining the British army she ran after him down the street, pleading with him to stay home. I'll never forget how the miskenica sat down in the middle of the cobblestone street and wept. Believe me, at that moment I thought that our Moise had a heart of stone."

"And your mother?" asked Luna, who was fascinated by his story. "What did she say?"

"My mother, may she be healthy, was busy looking after my old father, who worked her like a slave."

"And does Moise really have a heart of stone?"

"A heart of stone?" David laughed. "Moise has a heart of margarine. He's a great guy. I love him like a brother. We were together the whole of the war. We were with Montgomery's 8th Army at El Alamein, in the 1st Camouflage Company. We fought Rommel's Afrika Korps that was on its way to conquer Palestine. After the conquest of Egypt we were loaded onto boats for the invasion of Sicily. We built an entire camp in northern Italy, and the next day it was attacked by German planes and completely destroyed. Dogfights like in the cinema.

"Then we moved on to Monte Cassino. The Italian fascists were dug in on the mountain and we were down below. Every day we tried to move up the mountainside and the Italian fascists pushed us back until the American bombers came and reduced Monte Cassino to rubble. The fascists surrendered right away. They didn't have the will to fight, those lazy Italians. They always put their hands up.

"The army advanced on Rome and our battalion stopped in Siena. While we were in Siena, Gad came to see us again, this time with a new assignment: to steal equipment from the British and take it to the cargo ships carrying refugees to Palestine. We hid refugee children in the camp and from there sneaked them to the ships, and that's how we helped the Haganah."

"And all that just for the adventure?" Luna asked.

"Well, in the war it wasn't just an adventure. Praise God, Lunika, what we went through in the war. But don't think, heaven forbid, that I'm making myself into a bigger hero than I was."

"But you're my hero," she said, melting into him.

"And you're my princess," he replied, pressing his lips to hers until it seemed she was being swallowed into him. She could kiss him again and again, never sated with the taste of him. She loved the tickly feeling of his mustache, the fragrance of his Yardley aftershave, the way he always wore elegant suits with a matching tie. David Siton was charming, sophisticated, handsome, and most important, interesting. She could never have enough of his war stories, and he was always happy to tell them. But when he came to the story of the time he spent in Venice, she felt he was holding back. Again and again she urged him to tell her about the city where instead of streets there were canals, and instead of cars, gondolas, but he swiftly changed the subject.

"Tell me, my lovely," he said. "How is it that so far nobody's snatched you up?"

"From the day I turned sixteen," she told him, "my mother wanted to see me married. One day they brought a wealthy prospective husband from Argentina. As soon as I saw him I ran out of the house. Not a day goes by when she doesn't tell me, 'Get married already. Let somebody else take care of you.'"

"Your mother's right. It's time somebody took care of you."

"When my mother loses her temper with me," she went on, "she tells me, 'I hope that your children do to you what you do to me.' The first time she said that I wanted to run to my Nona Mercada in Tel Aviv so she would do a livianos for me and cure me of my mother's evil eye. I began screaming like a lunatic, and then my mother said, 'We'll find you a husband whether you like it or not. It's time you were a bride!'

"Then some old guy came along, he was maybe twenty-seven, God knows where she found him."

"And who was the old guy?"

"My father said that his father owns a big bakery, that they're very wealthy."

"So why didn't you marry him?"

"A man of twenty-seven who isn't married yet? There's got to be something wrong with him!"

"So what did you do?"

"What do you think? I ran like the wind out of the house and to this bench in Gan Ha'ir until I saw the old guy and his father leave our building. When I got back, my father wasn't home. My mother said he was so ashamed he'd gone for a drive to calm down. She shouted that nothing would help me. I could run out of the house as many times as I wanted, but in the end they'd find me a husband, if not the easy way, then the hard way. She wanted me to marry a man I don't love the same way my father married a woman he didn't love."

"Luna, what are you saying?"

"I'm speaking the truth! My father's become ill because he doesn't love my mother."

"Luna," David was shocked, "she's your mother. An angel like you shouldn't be saying things like that."

"My mother brings out all the demons in me. On the other hand, my father, may he be healthy, loves me even more than he loves my sisters."

"And I love you more than I love your sisters." He laughed and hugged her.

Luna pulled away, pretending to want to be released from his embrace, and in a conciliatory tone said, "Enough of my mother, tell me about Venice, the city that has canals instead of streets!"

"Ach . . . Venice." He sighed and looked skyward dreamily. "There's no place like it. It's the most divine city in the world. We lived near the Lido, in villas abandoned by the rich people who fled and left their houses as though they'd be coming back shortly: food in the pantry, rows of bottles of red wine. Did you know that the Italians drink wine with every meal? It makes them happy, and we, who before Venice had drunk wine only for Kiddush and on Seder night, learned from the Italians and began drinking wine until we were completely drunk. We danced on the tables, sang in the streets. We were as happy as kings. After the damned war, after so much death, we were finally living!"

"What else happened there?"

He looked at her as if seeing her for the first time. "Didn't you listen to anything I told you? What more did we need? Life, that's what happened there, life."

"And girls?"

"Endless girls! They'd go with us for a pair of stockings. For food they were prepared to do anything! Not only them, their whole family. The father not only pimped for his daughter but for his wife too. He'd sell his womenfolk for bread and cheese."

"So you had a lot of women?"

"A thousand, like King Solomon." He laughed.

"Didn't you have a special one? A one and only?"

"Why do you want to know?"

"I want to know everything about you!"

"Luna, my love, if there's one thing I've learned in life, it's never to tell the whole story. Not you to me and not me to you. We should tell each other only things that we want to hear."

6

Even before the marriage terms were agreed on and the wedding date set, Luna decided that if her firstborn was a son, she would name him after her father. "Nobody," she told Rachelika, "will take from me the honor of giving Papo's name to my son."

Shocked, Rachelika said, "Surely David will want to name his son after his father, may he rest in peace."

"So he'll have to want!"

"Luna!" Rachelika said, holding herself back from screaming at her sister. "It's the custom! The firstborn son is named after the husband's father."

"Since when have you been interested in custom? These days people give their children modern names. It's not up for discussion! My son will be named Gabriel!"

"Fine, let's see you go head-to-head with David."

"If we have a daughter, he can name her after his mother. I don't care. I'd never name a daughter of mine after our mother."

"God help us, Luna. Now that you're almost married you have to be careful of words that kill, so stop it already. What's become of you?"

"What's become of me? Compared to you, I'm an angel. Was it me who put up Etzel posters in the street while my father thought I was studying?"

"Talk quietly, Luna. If Papo hears I was putting up Etzel posters behind his back, it'll be the end of me."

"So what's your issue with me when all I want is to name my firstborn son after Papo and give him the respect he deserves?"

I hope Luna has a girl, Rachelika prayed. Otherwise there will be a third world war.

Each day brought fresh news of Arab ambushes, of snipers killing Jews. The British police favored the Arabs. They would not allow the establishment of new Jewish settlements or the landing of illegal immigrants from the ships bringing refugees from the DP camps in Europe. The threat of danger hung in the air. Every other day there was a curfew; entire areas were cordoned off with concertina wire and no one was allowed in or out. And Rachelika, God help her, almost got caught hanging posters near the public restrooms in Zion Square. Luckily she'd had her wits about her and hid in a stinky stall in the men's bathroom. For twenty minutes she stood in there, one foot on either side of the bowl, holding on to the filthy tiled walls, waiting for the English bastards to go away.

Only when she was sure that the English had gone had she dared to emerge from the stall. It was pitch-black outside, and due to the curfew, Jaffa Road and Zion Square were deserted. Fear gripped her chest and she struggled to fill her lungs. Her partner had vanished into thin air. They always went out in pairs and were supposed to stay together, except when they encountered British police. In that case, they'd been instructed to look out for themselves, and that's what she'd done when she'd hidden in the bathroom.

British police vehicles were patrolling Jaffa Road and Ben-Yehuda Street. The last time she was out after curfew, she'd miraculously reached Tio Shmuel's house, but what could she do now? She feared the moment she'd be arrested. All she needed was for her father to find out she was a member of the Etzel. At least she hadn't joined the Lehi, despite her friend Temima urging her to do so. Most of her friends at evening classes supported Lehi, but there were also a few Haganah supporters and a large group of Etzel supporters too. At every opportunity there were passionate debates in the school yard over the right way to drive the British out of Palestine. In the end it was her classmate Moshe Alalouf, to whom she was secretly attracted, who convinced her.

"Menachem Begin says it's a fight to the end!" he had said to a group of students.

"The Etzel are robbers and thieves!" someone yelled.

The discussion became heated. "The Etzel doesn't take the money for itself. It robs banks that hold British money and uses it for the struggle!" Alalouf said.

"The Etzel murders and kills without mercy!" shouted one of the Haganah supporters. "When they threw a bomb at the high commissioner's car, his wife was in it too. What's she guilty of?"

"She's there with her husband, so she's guilty," Alalouf retorted.

When classes were finished that day, he came over and handed Rachelika a rolled-up newspaper. "If this is of interest to you, talk to me," he said and went on his way.

At the top of the front page was the Etzel emblem: a rifle against a map of the Land of Israel on both sides of the River Jordan, rendering it a big country whose border reached Iraq. At the bottom were two words: "Only Thus!" The lead article attacked the Labor Movement leadership, calling them "liars, cowards, and traitors." A particular target was Moshe Shertok, who had suggested to the high commissioner that a special unit be formed to combat Jewish terrorist organizations.

When she'd taken part in Haganah youth activities, Rachelika's instructors had heightened her opposition to both Lehi and Etzel, but she never opposed them as fiercely. She'd noticed the posters stuck on trees and buildings by the organization known as Mishmar Ha'uma, the nation's guardian, which warned that Jews donating money to the terrorist organizations were undermining the community's security and hopes of Zionism. The posters were printed in big bold letters and called upon people to report any such case to a public institution or reliable public figure.

"Do not give in to blackmail and threats!" the black letters warned. Now she saw Etzel's response in the paper that Alalouf had given her: "No more restraint! We shall not be intimidated by persecution or death! We are prepared for any suffering and sacrifice! We shall strike the Nazo-British enemy!"

Rachelika was deeply affected by what she read. She met Moshe Alalouf the following day and told him she wanted to join. When he shook her hand, a shiver ran down her spine. She was excited. She had never experienced such a thrill, the feeling of exhilaration mixed with danger. Luna would probably know what she meant.

As he walked her home after school, a distance that for her seemed far too short, Rachelika felt light on her feet. Being with Moshe Alalouf invigorated her. She was quiet for most of the time, and when she did speak, she had trouble finding the words. He, on the other hand, talked and talked, enthusiastically lecturing her on Menachem Begin's doctrine—to establish a Jewish state through struggle, not passivity.

"My father thinks that isn't the right way," she said, trying to get a word in. "My father thinks that the Haganah's moderate approach is the right one."

He barely let her finish the sentence before his face flushed and he waved his fists. He said defiantly, "They've spilled our blood! They've tortured our comrades! They've handed our people over to the Nazo-British enemy! They kidnapped and beat them half to death, and we held back. And why did we hold back? Because Begin said we should for the sake of national unity, but no longer! From now on it's an eye for an eye, a tooth for a tooth!" Rachelika knew he was quoting from the article in the paper, speaking a language and using words that weren't his own.

When they had almost reached her house and before they said good-bye, he asked, "So what do you say? Are you willing to swear allegiance and join the struggle?"

Rachelika was a tall girl, but Moshe Alalouf was a head taller. She raised her face to him and her eyes met his, which were half closed as if he was praying. She so much wanted him to bend his head and kiss her, but he made no move to. Disappointed, she came back to earth and said, "I need time to think about it."

All at once he seemed to wake up. "What do you have to think about when the Land of Israel needs you?"

"I'm still not sure I'm ready to die for anything, not even the Land of Israel!"

"First of all," he replied with infinite seriousness, "people don't die so quickly. And they're not accepted so quickly either. You have to prove yourself first." He raised a clenched fist and proclaimed, "Only thus!" and went on his way.

That night Rachelika was so excited she couldn't sleep. Moshe Alalouf, the Etzel, all whirled in her mind. She tossed and turned until Luna, who had shared her bed since they'd been forced to move from the big apartment on King George Street back to Ohel Moshe, gave her a kick and said, "What's the matter with you? You're keeping me up."

"I can't fall asleep."

Luna sat up. "Has something happened?"

"Keep quiet, you'll wake Becky," Rachelika whispered.

"Becky's snoring like a pig, nothing wakes her up. What's happened? Why can't you sleep?"

Rachelika told her.

"Are you out of your mind?" Luna whispered. "If Papo hears about this, he'll lock you up in the house for life. You won't even have a wedding."

"Nobody must know! It's a secret!" Rachelika leapt out of bed and stood facing her sister. "If you tell I'll never tell you anything ever again, and I won't let you tell me anything either." And Luna, who was scared to death by the thought of her sister not listening to her secrets, swore she would keep her mouth shut.

After classes the next day, Rachelika waited for Moshe Alalouf by the school gate. Without a word he motioned for her to walk with him. Unlike the previous day, when he hadn't stopped talking, now he was silent. They headed down King George Street, and she felt a tiny pang as they went by her former home. They passed Gan Ha'ir, continued toward the Rehavia neighborhood, and went into the garden on Ramban Street. Moshe took her elbow and led her to one of the benches. As soon as they sat down, he put his arm around her shoulders and embraced her intensely. Her heart skipped a beat. "Pretend you're kissing me," he whispered in her ear.

"Pretend?" She was confused. "What do you—" but she didn't manage to finish the sentence because he pressed his lips to hers hard. She wanted to open her lips, kiss him properly, but the way he was pressing her mouth to his made her realize that he really was only pretending. Disappointed, she pushed him away and moved to the end of the bench. He slid over to her and whispered, "What are you doing?"

"What are *you* doing?"

"Didn't you see the kalaniot passing?" he said, and from behind a bush he took out a tube and a tin.

"These are the posters," he whispered. "And this is paste. We're to stick the posters onto trees and buildings."

"And what do we do with the posters and paste if kalaniot come along?" Rachelika whispered fearfully.

"We hold them between our bodies and hug each other tight. They won't notice. I've done this a thousand times!" he said in a tone meant to boost her confidence, but which only heightened her anxiety.

They didn't see any more kalaniot that night. There was no need to embrace and kiss like a couple on a park bench. When they reached the Shaarei

Hesed neighborhood he said good-bye with "Only thus!" and walked off, not even offering to escort her home. Disenchanted and angry, she started toward Ohel Moshe, and only when she made it home was she able to get her breath back.

"What's the matter, querida, why are you out of breath?" Rosa asked her.

"It's dark out and I was scared, so I ran home."

"Maybe going to your classes is too dangerous, mi alma. Perhaps you shouldn't go at a time like this?"

"Enough, Mother!" Rachelika replied in an assertive tone that left Rosa agape.

"I'm sorry," she quickly apologized to her mother. What was happening to her? She couldn't recognize herself, kissing a strange boy, putting up posters after dark, fleeing the kalaniot, being nasty to her mother. This game wasn't for her. Starting tomorrow she wouldn't be sticking up any more posters. Basta, it wasn't for her.

But she didn't stop, not the next day or the day after that. She simply could not.

Rachelika now belonged to a group of boys and girls in the service of the underground and was increasingly absent from her classes. She didn't think about what would happen if her father found out, didn't *want* to think about it. She wanted to carry on putting up posters, work her way up through the ranks so she could be assigned the more dangerous tasks that were spoken of only in whispers and total secrecy.

As on previous occasions, this time too she hadn't known her partner for the mission. He was a bespectacled boy who said very little, and they walked hand in hand as they'd been ordered, two strangers pretending to be a pair of lovers. He held her little finger with his own crooked around it. "It's how my kibbutznik brother walks with his girlfriend" were the only words he uttered. They walked in silence until they reached Haneviim Street and stopped outside the English Mission Hospital. Opposite was a small garden surrounding the house where Rachel the Poetess had once lived, and they easily found the posters and paste under the garden bench and didn't even have to pretend to kiss. They'd been told to put up the posters in Zion Square near the cinema's box office so that the posters would be in the faces of people buying tickets. They walked quickly so they could finish the job before curfew, but they didn't make it. As they passed Dr. Ticho's house on Rabbi Kook Street, British police vehicles driving down the streets announced the start of the curfew. Rachelika had been putting up posters after classes for weeks now, but never during a curfew. She'd told her family that she was studying for exams at Temima's.

At first her father was against it. "You're not going out at that time of day!" he'd said.

"But, Papo querido, when can I study? I'm in the shop until late afternoon. When else do I have time?"

Fortunately, her father had bought her story. But what would happen when exam time really did come around? When would she study then? She knew that no one would believe that she, Goody-Two-shoes Rachelika, was the one putting up Etzel posters. But the way she felt when she was putting up posters—the adrenaline coursing through her veins, the sense of purpose—was addictive and had clouded her judgment.

A cat jumping out of a dumpster shook her from her thoughts. She clung to an outer wall of the public restroom like a shadow. In a quick decision she threw the posters and paste into the dumpster. She'd pay the price for it tomorrow, but right now she had to save herself, so she started walking home. If the kalaniot caught her, so be it. She could tell her father that she was at school until late and didn't make it home in time. *Wai de mi sola*, I'm more frightened of my father than I am of the British police! When did I start thinking like Luna? She prayed she'd be able to lie to her father's face, but before she could plan her lies, she found herself having to lie to the British policemen approaching her from their vehicle. "What are you doing out? Don't you know there's a curfew?" one shouted.

"Yes, sir," she said, putting on the expression of an innocent lamb. "I was at school until late and didn't notice that the curfew had begun. Sir, I've got to get home, please help me. My parents must be worried sick."

But instead of softening, the English policeman hardened and ordered her to take out the contents of her bag. Luckily, all she had were homework books and textbooks. She silently thanked Luna, who had advised her to cut the Etzel newspaper into shreds and flush them down the toilet. She thanked God that she rid of the posters and paste.

The policeman instructed her to put her books back into the bag and then ordered her into the vehicle. Quaking with fear she did as she was told, imagining being dragged to the Kishle and locked up behind bars. Papo will never forgive me, she thought. He'll imprison me in the house. And worst of all, he'll think I've become like Luna. She knew how hard life was for him and was afraid of disappointing him. She saw how he'd been aloof, ravaged with worry, bitter. But he always kept his anger bottled up, didn't shout, didn't get upset, and that was far worse.

"Address," snapped the policeman.

Rachelika gave him the King George address and immediately corrected herself. It'd been almost ten months since they'd moved back to Ohel Moshe and she still hadn't gotten used to it.

To her horror, the driver turned on the siren. The noise sliced through her ears, and it became clear to her that they would stop at the police station and she'd be kept in a cell for who knew how long. But the vehicle passed the police station and stopped at the Ohel Moshe gate, and Rachelika was ceremoniously escorted to her house by two British policemen, one on either side.

What happened in the next hour Rachelika could never have imagined even in her wildest dreams. The policemen banged on the door. "Open up, police!" they shouted. And Rachelika, terrified, knew all the neighbors were now spying from their windows and seeing her, Senor and Senora Ermosa's quiet daughter, escorted by two English policemen, and rubbing their eyes in amazement.

Her mother opened the door. "Thank God, you've given us a heart attack again! We thought something had happened to you." And before she asked the policemen what they wanted, she pulled Rachelika inside. "Gracias el Dio, Gabriel, Rachelika's home."

Her father got out of his chair and turned off the radio. He staggered slightly, held on to the back of the chair, and looked questioningly at Rachelika and the two policemen. Luna and Becky came out of their room as well.

"Forgive me, gentlemen, I'm very sorry," Gabriel said, moving heavily toward them. "The bane of raising daughters. I'm sure you know how difficult it is to raise daughters these days." To his daughters, who were standing as if nailed to the floor, he said, "Why are you standing there like dummies? Introduce yourselves to the gentlemen." Then he turned back to the Englishmen and with exaggerated politeness introduced the girls: "This, gentlemen, is my eldest daughter Luna, our baby Becky, and you've already met my middle daughter Rachel. She's a good girl, but a bit of a dreamer. This isn't the first time she hasn't come home in time before a curfew. I forgive her, and I hope you will too."

The policemen smiled at the sight of the three lovely girls, and Rosa, who until then had been standing rooted to the spot by the door, suddenly came to life and offered the policemen seats at the table. She hurried to set a bowl of fresh bizcochos on the table while urging Luna to serve the guests. Gabriel went to the carved wooden cabinet, took out a crystal decanter of fine cognac, and poured it into crystal glasses. He and the policemen toasted the troubles of raising daughters.

The policemen swigged the cognac, and as soon as their glasses were empty, Gabriel refilled them. Rosa fluttered around the guests, who seemed to have forgotten they were on duty and were enjoying a lively conversation with Gabriel as if they were all old friends.

"Dio santo, they don't want to go," Rosa said to the girls when they were alone in the kitchen.

"Why should they go? Three beautiful girls, fine cognac, why would they leave?" said Rachelika contemptuously.

"Shut up, *calabasa*, you pumpkin, they'll hear you," Luna whispered.

"If we don't do something to get rid of them," Rachelika went on, "they'll end up sleeping here."

"Better they sleep here than you sleeping in prison," Luna retorted.

"Quiet, both of you! I don't want the Ingelish hearing you. Go and serve them some more borekitas," Rosa ordered.

The girls went back into the living room and served the policemen the oven-fresh borekitas.

"Do you have just the three girls?" one of the policemen asked.

"Three that are like thirty," Gabriel chuckled, doing his best to make his laugh sound genuine.

"That's quite rare," said the English policeman. "I know that Sephardi families have lots of children."

"We had more once," Gabriel replied. "But they died. What can you do, The Lord gives and the Lord taketh away, blessed be the name of the Lord."

Much to his surprise, Gabriel found that he was quite enjoying his chat with the English policemen, who admitted they were homesick and missed their families. But it was getting late, and he needed them to leave so he could settle accounts with Rachelika.

Luna took advantage of their presence and asked their permission to use the privy in the yard. During a curfew they usually relieved themselves in tin chamber pots they kept under the bed. In the morning they'd empty them in the privy, wash them out, and hang them by their handles on the wall of the house, next to the iron laundry bath they also used for bathing.

God, Luna thought, where have the happy days in the King George Street apartment gone, when we had an inside toilet and tiled bathroom and brass faucets? How happy those King George days had been, and how brief. She still was in awe of the modern amenities by the time they had to return to the old neighborhood with the old neighbors and the gossiping women who to this day were *still* talking about Tio Ephraim and how he'd shot Matilda Franco.

The policemen allowed Luna to use the privy and Becky and Rachelika after her. "But one at a time, not all together," one said, suddenly transformed from the nice man drinking cognac with their father back into an intimidating English policeman.

When the girls came back inside, the two policemen stood up, thanked Gabriel and Rosa for their hospitality, warned Rachelika about being out after curfew, and left.

"At long last, thank God," said Gabriel with a sigh of relief. He thought the nightmare would never end and that the damned Englishmen were going to move in. They must have enjoyed the idea of three lovely girls and fine cognac. And Rosa, may she be healthy, hadn't shut her mouth the entire time. His silent wife's mouth had opened and refused to close as if her lips were stuck that way. He didn't know if she hadn't stopped talking because she was scared that something terrible would happen the moment she shut up, or because she was just proud of her good English. Thank God she hadn't said a word about having been a housemaid for the English. And lucky the damned Englishmen hadn't asked where her good English came from.

After they left, he sat down in his chair and with a shaking hand lit a cigarette and drew the smoke into his lungs. He glanced at his daughters, who seemed to be purposely zealous with the tidying up. His wife, who since the Englishmen's departure had fallen silent again, was now sitting at the far side of the room embroidering one of her tapestries, which she hung on the walls as if they were works of art, as if their house was the Louvre and not a wretched dwelling in Ohel Moshe.

Gabriel sighed and a sharp pain lanced through his chest. How? How had it happened that after living in the splendid King George Street apartment right next to Rehavia he'd had to bring his family back to Ohel Moshe, and in condition far worse than they'd left it? How had it happened that from being a wealthy, respected man who owned a car and a flourishing delicatessen, he now didn't have a grush to his name? The Ermosa family had never been very rich, but they'd never been poor either. Why had he been sentenced by the

Almighty to be the one to lead his family to the edge of the cliff? It couldn't be his mother's curse. She had removed it the day she did the livianos for him, cleansed him of his sins, forgiven him, and ordered him to start afresh. So who had put the evil eye on him now? And what terrible sin had he committed that he and his daughters deserved such a punishment, to fall from so high to so low? How much longer could he carry this burden before he collapsed under its weight? And if he did collapse, what would become of his daughters? They were still unmarried and didn't have homes of their own. He had to see them married and know that they were well provided for before he raised his hands and surrendered to his fate. Until then he had no choice. He had to go on shouldering the burden.

The girls had finished cleaning up and were about to go to their room. "You," Gabriel told Rachelika, "you stay here." Rachelika looked at Luna, but not only did her sister not soothe her, she made a throat-cutting gesture with the flat of her hand as if to say, Papo's going to slaughter you.

Rosa fixed her eyes on her embroidery. If she could, she would have disappeared. She couldn't bear the thought of Gabriel being angry with Rachelika. Rachelika was pure gold, hija de oro. She worked like an ox in the shop all day, she did everything for her father, and he, he saw only that spoiled Luna. Rachelika did all the hard work. Even now, who washed the dishes? Rachelika, who else? Would Luna dirty her polished nails? Whatever the flaca did, he forgave her, but Rachelika miskenica, was it her fault she got stuck in the curfew? Now he'd shout at her and punish her. What kind of father had he turned into?

"Draw up a chair and sit by me," Gabriel told Rachelika, and she complied. She sat, head bowed, and waited. To her disbelief, he said softly, "Rachelika querida, hija mia, of all my daughters you are the only one I can depend on. You're a serious girl, querida, you're responsible. I know I did you an injustice when I took you out of school and put you in the shop, but you can see for yourself how much I need you. What would I do without you there? How can I rely on Tio Matzliach, may God forgive me, who is just the opposite of his name, 'successful'? How can I rely on Avramino who's not only a troncho de Tveria but also not family? I rely only on you, querida. Only you with your intelligence can save the shop, and you're the only one who won't rob me. And that's why I'm putting you in charge of the shop from now on. I'm sick, querida. My legs don't carry me to Mahane Yehuda anymore, they don't carry me anywhere, so you have to look after the shop for me, for your mother, your sisters, for our family."

Rachelika was silent, trying to absorb the magnitude of the responsibility that her father had just placed on her shoulders, and wondering why he wasn't angry with her for being caught after curfew. Her mind raced like crazy. How can I look after the shop if I'm working and studying? And as if her father had read her mind, he said, "You'll have to stop going to your classes."

She could hardly breathe. She was only a few months away from graduation. She had to graduate so she could go on to teacher training. For the first time when facing her father she dug her heels in. "I'm sorry, Papo, but I don't want to stop."

"You don't want to stop?" he repeated as if he had misheard. "Is that because the studies are so important to you, or perhaps there's another reason?"

Here it comes, she thought to herself. My father must know about Etzel. But he didn't say a word about the Etzel. "Do you think I was born yesterday? That I really believed that you go to study for exams with your friend every day? Your school is close to Zion Square where Café Europa is, where Café Vienna is, where the English bastards hang out."

"God forbid, Papo, I swear I never go to cafés, certainly not the ones the English go to."

"All right," he said, mollified. "But still there's no choice. You have to look after the shop, and if you can't do that and study at the same time, there's no choice, querida. You'll have to stop studying."

"I'll do anything you say," Rachelika plead. "Just don't make me stop studying."

"We have no choice. If you don't, the shop will go to hell and I won't have food to put on the table."

"What am I going to do?" Rachelika asked Luna, who was waiting for her in their bedroom.

"You have no choice," Luna replied gently and stroked her hair. She knew how determined Rachelika was to complete her studies and become a teacher, but she also understood her father and knew that if Rachelika didn't take charge of the shop, then Mordoch the Kurd would take it over the way he did with the halvah factory, and their family would be finished. She wanted her sister to stop endangering herself with escapades that brought English policemen to their house. She wanted Rachelika to have ordinary dreams, to find a husband and have a family, not big dreams like driving out the British and establishing a state. Anyway, she should leave the big dreams to men, Luna thought.

"You have to do what Papo tells you," she said to Rachelika softly. "There's too much at stake. What do you think, that I don't understand what's going on here? You've got the luck of the devil that Papo doesn't suspect you. After he forbade you to be in the Haganah, you join the Etzel?"

"I'm not doing it to spite him. I want to be part of the national struggle."

"You have to be part of the family struggle. If Papo heard you're in the Etzel, he'd throw you out of the family! You're the good girl in the family. It would break his heart."

"He won't hear about it if you don't tell him, so swear you won't."

"Of course I won't tell him, but you have to stop. They'll catch you one day and you'll end up in prison. And especially now Papo needs you to manage the shop."

"Luna, what am I going to do? I don't want to run the shop. I can't stand that dumb Tio Matzliach and that stammering Avramino, and as for the Kurd, I hate him."

"I hate the Kurd too, Rachelika. I felt that from the moment Papo went into partnership with him that he put a hex on us."

"That dog Mordoch," Rachelika said, "he comes into the shop as if he owns it, looks around as if it's going to be his soon, touches things, moves them, asks questions."

"It'll be his over my dead body!" Luna's blood rushed straight to her head. "I'll stand in the shop myself and block him from coming in."

"That Kurd is Amalek, Luna. He's just waiting for the right moment to take over the shop and get rid of Papo and bring in his thousands of children to our place."

"And that's precisely why, hermanita querida," Luna said as if she'd won the argument, "you have to do what Papo asks!"

"But why me?"

"Because you have a good head on your shoulders like Papo. You're the cleverest of all of us, that's why."

Deep down Rachelika understood that she had no choice, but how could a sixteen-year-old girl stand up to Amalek Mordoch? And how could she give orders to her Tio Matzliach and Avramino, who's old enough to be her father?

The next evening at school, she didn't even ask Moshe Alalouf if he knew what happened to her partner the previous night. And when he came over to her with fresh orders for the night's activities, she ignored him and went straight home, preparing herself for another hard talk with her father. She had no idea what she was going to say to him. Her father had always told her that an education was the most important thing of all. How angry he'd been with Luna when she wanted to drop out of school and work in the dress shop! And now what? If her father was asking her to stop studying, then things must be really bad.

Although it was only eight o'clock, she found her father asleep in his bed. Well, at least she could put off the difficult conversation another day.

"He's not feeling well," Rosa told her. "He didn't touch his food. He said he was tired and went to bed."

"And Luna?"

"She went out with David."

"And Becky?"

"Out and about."

Rachelika, who'd gotten used to being busy every evening, didn't know what to do with herself.

"Come and sit here next to me," Rosa said, and she drew up a stool next to her mother in the yard. "Rachelika, hija mia, I heard what your father asked of you. Do what he tells you. Your father isn't the same. He's sick. Today he sat in his chair all day and didn't move. It's as if his whole body is broken."

"Why doesn't he go to the Kupat Holim clinic?"

"He did, querida. He went, and the doctor told him the same thing as Dr. Sabo—rheumatism. Didn't we go to the Tiberias hot springs? We did. Nothing helps. It's not rheumatism, Rachelika. His hand trembles, haven't you seen? He can hardly lift a spoon to put food into his mouth. He tries to hide it, but he can't. When he gets up from his chair, if he doesn't hold on to the table, he'll fall over. Sometimes he starts speaking to me and then he loses his train of thought and doesn't remember what he wanted to say. His moods, Dio mio, one minute he's happy and the next minute he's sad, one minute he's calm and the next he's irritable. He's sick, your father. If he wasn't, would he be left without a grush to his name? If he wasn't sick, would we have come back to Ohel Moshe?"

Rachelika looked at her mother, surprised. "I thought you were happy that we came back to Ohel Moshe. You didn't like King George. You missed the neighborhood, your neighbors."

"Mashallah, querida, what neighbors? Do you see any neighbors here? Even Tamar who was like a sister to me doesn't come here. Ever since Matilda died, it seems I don't have any neighbors."

"So you're not happy that we came back to Ohel Moshe? That was my small consolation, that at least you'd be glad."

"I am, I won't say I'm not. I didn't like living on King George. The neighbors shut the door so nobody could come in without calling ahead, God forbid. I was so shy I didn't even ask for a glass of water from any of them. I won't tell you I didn't suffer when I couldn't go and sit outside like we're sitting here now, and that the noise of the cars didn't give me a headache and that the elevator didn't scare me half to death. But seeing my girls and your father so unhappy because we've come back to Ohel Moshe? It breaks my heart."

"Don't let your heart break, we'll manage."

"We'll manage, of course we'll manage. But it's been long enough since they killed Matilda, may she rest in peace, and to this day not one neighbor has treated us like before. There was a time when they only had to see me outside and right away they'd come, we'd sit and talk, eat and laugh. Now if I go outside and there's a neighbor in the yard, she goes right back into her house, slams the door. No, querida, I haven't got anyone in Ohel Moshe. I'm alone."

Although Rosa didn't actually mention Ephraim, Rachelika heard what her mother left unspoken.

"Have you heard anything?" she asked Rosa. "Have you heard anything from Tio Ephraim?"

"Ah," Rosa released a pain-filled sigh. "Nada, I haven't heard a thing. I wish I had. There's nobody to tell me, and Sara Laniado, whose son is there with him, once I'd talk to her about him, but since Matilda's death, may she rest in peace, she doesn't let me come to her house. God help me, how much I think about Ephraim, how I worry about my little troncho. Who knows if he's alive or dead."

"Maybe he's in the prison in Acre?" Rachelika said. "Maybe the English have caught him?"

"God forbid, *tfu,* don't say things like that so los de avashos don't put the evil eye on him."

"So why doesn't he send you a sign of life? You're his only sister. Doesn't he care about you?"

"He cares, of course he cares, but he knows I'm not alone, that I have my daughters, and I have your father, may he be healthy. But he, who does he have? Miskenico, who does he have to care for him?"

"Maybe he got married? Maybe he has children?" said Rachelika, trying to calm her mother.

"I hope so, from your mouth, mi alma, to God's ears, I hope he did stand under the wedding canopy even though I wasn't there to see him break the wineglass. I hope he has a wife who cares for him. I hope so."

"You know, Mother," Rachelika said, deciding to ease her mother's heartache, "there are rumors that he's a big commander in the Lehi, that he's well-respected."

"Where did you hear that, querida? How do you know what the Lehi is doing or isn't doing?"

"There are boys and girls in my school who know, and they told me that he's doing important things for the Jewish people."

"Hija de oro!" Rosa wrung her hands emotionally. "How is it that you always know how to calm me! What a heart you've got, may you be healthy, and it's because of that heart of yours, querida, that you must do what your father asks, so that we don't find ourselves like the poor people from the market, collecting scraps of food from the floor, and so that, God forbid, we don't get to a state where your father, *pishcado y limon*, won't get out of bed for shame. Listen to me, hija, what your father asked of you is a call for help, so don't disappoint him. Don't let us down."

"Why so unhappy, my lovely?" David asked Luna and hugged her. "Why so downhearted? You haven't smiled at me even once today, not even a little."

"I'm worried about Rachelika. That's why I didn't enjoy the film at all."

As they did every evening, they'd gone to see a film, this one starring Hedy Lamarr, and now they were on their way to have coffee at Café Atara before he took her home.

"What's the matter with Rachelika?" David said indifferently.

"Two kalaniot brought her home during curfew yesterday."

"Rachelika? Kalaniot?" She had finally caught his attention.

"They picked her up outside during curfew."

"They should go to hell, them and their curfew. Did they bring her home in one piece? Is she all right?"

"You don't understand, David," she whispered. "It's much more complicated than that. I'm going to tell you something, but swear you won't tell anyone."

"I swear!"

"She was putting up Etzel posters, but thank God she was able to dispose of them just before the kalaniot picked her up. I don't even want to think what would have happened if they'd caught her red-handed."

"Rachelika's in the Etzel? Well, I'll be damned. Who'd have believed it?"

"Believe it, believe it. She was in the Haganah at first and now she's in the Etzel. We have to get her out of the mess she's in. We have to find her a boy, one of your friends from the British army."

"Lunika, Rachelika isn't for any of my friends. How can I put it gently? It won't work."

"Why not?" she asked angrily. "Rachelika's not picky and she's pure gold. She's got brains like my father."

"Lunika, my lovely, brains like your father isn't enough for any of my friends to want to go out with her."

"Why not?"

"Don't get angry, mi alma, but your sister isn't exactly Greta Garbo."

"What nonsense you're talking, David! My sister's better looking than all the girls your friends go out with. She has a beautiful soul and that's more important than anything else!"

"Bonica, you know it's not more important than anything else. Otherwise you wouldn't be wearing this dress that drives me crazy. Lunika, if anybody knows that beauty is everything, it's you."

On most occasions she would have blushed at the compliment, but not this time. This time she got angry. He took her hand and she pulled it away.

"Lunika, what did I say? Do you know what beauties my friends had in Italy?"

"Like you had?"

"There were as many girls as we wanted, one more beautiful than the next . . ."

"And was there a particularly beautiful one?"

"Did I say a particularly beautiful one? There were beautiful girls there," he said, smoothly evading her question. "It was long before I met you. You know that all my friends are jealous because I've caught the most beautiful girl in Jerusalem."

Luna put her hand back into his. He had softened her with his flattery. She was lucky to have found the handsome man of her dreams. She was happy, but her concern for Rachelika gnawed at her happiness. Tears welled in her eyes.

David noticed the cloud that hung over her delicate face and an idea came to him. "Maybe we should introduce her to Moise," he said. "Our Moise isn't all that particular about good looks anyway."

Luna didn't find it easy to persuade Rachelika to meet Moise. "Am I such a good-for-nothing that I need a matchmaker?" Rachelika grumbled.

"It's not as if his father is sitting with Papo and deciding for you and setting the terms. It's David and me introducing you to his friend. You like him—fine. You don't like him—that's fine too."

"I don't like being set up with boys like this. It embarrasses me."

"It embarrasses me that instead of meeting boys you're getting into trouble with the British police. Enough, don't be an azno, what can happen? At worst you'll have a coffee together, and if you don't like him, you say good-bye nicely and never see him again."

"I don't know, Luna. It's a headache. It stresses me out. I don't want to!"

"Then what about a foursome? What if David and I go out with you?"

"That'd be better," Rachelika said. "Fine. I'll go."

Later that week, the four of them went to Orion to see *Children of Paradise* and afterward to Café Zichel. Unlike David, Moise was a shy man with little experience with women, but Rachelika found that despite the fact that he didn't talk much, he was polite and courteous, and so at the end of the evening when he suggested they meet again, she agreed.

And just as Luna hoped, from the moment that Rachelika started going out with Moise, she ceased her Etzel activities. When Moshe Alalouf demanded an explanation, she told him her father was sick and she had to get home right after school to look after him. When he tried to press her, she evaded him, rebuffing his pleas to talk.

Not long after they started going out, Rachelika brought Moise home and introduced him to her father. "Papo, I'd like you to meet my boyfriend Moise."

Gabriel raised his face to the big dark-skinned man facing him, and his eyes met large brown ones. Later he'd tell Rachelika that he'd never seen so much kindness in someone's eyes.

"It's an honor to meet you, sir," Moise said and held out his hand.

That evening Moise joined them at the dinner table. Gabriel was overjoyed on seeing his good manners, and Rosa was equally overjoyed with Rachelika's happiness. At long last, dear God, at long last you've put a smile on the child's face. At long last she's getting something good, gracias el Dio.

Luna, who felt like the matchmaker in chief, didn't stop prattling and telling over and over how she had made up her mind to find a boy for Rachelika and how her delightful David had chosen his best friend for her. Of course she didn't mention the conversation that had taken place before David suggested Moise. She was happy for her sister, who almost from the start had confided that their relationship was serious.

After dinner, Gabriel sat down in his usual chair, turned on the Zenith radio, and took a cigarette from his silver case. Moise swiftly lit it for him and sat beside him.

"Senor Ermosa," he said in his deep, pleasant voice, "with your permission I would like to have a few words with you."

"My pleasure," Gabriel replied.

"I know, Senor, that I am new to you, but Rachelika and I have known each other for several weeks and I have the greatest respect for her," Moise said in his beautifully accented Hebrew. Gabriel's curiosity was aroused. Was he going to ask for his daughter's hand? Should he consent? After all, this was the first time he'd met the boy. What did he know about him except that he had good manners?

"In one of our talks, Senor," Moise went on, "Rachelika told me that you want her to stop studying and take charge of your shop."

"There's no choice." Gabriel sighed. "I'm not what I used to be and I need her to run the shop in my place. She's the only one I can trust."

"Senor, I don't want to interfere in other people's business, and I hope you don't see this as such, but with your permission I'd like to make a suggestion. Rachelika continues with her studies and I help her in the shop."

"Help her in the shop?" Gabriel didn't even try to conceal his amazement. "First of all, I can't afford to pay you, and second, I don't know who you are, young man, I don't know your family, and I don't know what your intentions are regarding my daughter."

"My intentions are good and serious, Senor Ermosa. And with regard to payment, you need not worry. I'll work without pay until we get the shop back on its feet, until there's money in the till. And regarding Rachelika," he went on, "we're only just starting to get to know each other, but in a few months' time, if Senor Ermosa gives us his blessing, with God's help we shall stand under the wedding canopy."

"No time soon," Gabriel muttered, but he was pleased with the young man's answer.

"Senor Ermosa," Moise said, "my father is from the Maghreb, a Maghrebi, but my mother is one of yours and I'm half-and-half. I look like a Maghrebi, but I speak Ladino like a pure Sephardi, my mother insisted on it, and I know enough so that no one can cheat me in Ladino."

"That's very good," Gabriel said, "especially if you want to work in the shop. We have a lot of Ladino-speaking customers, and it's also important you understand what the staff are talking about among themselves."

"I promise you, Senor Ermosa," the excited Moise said, "I promise you that Rachelika and I together will turn the shop around! I give you my word!"

I hope so, Gabriel prayed. I hope that Rachelika and Moise succeed. But as much as he was impressed by the young man and as much as he believed in his daughter, he doubted they would be able to do anything. How could they cope with the stupidity of Matzliach and with old Avramino, who couldn't even lift a sack, but he, Gabriel, didn't have the heart to let him go and take on a young man in his place? How could these two pure souls stand up to that brute Mordoch? God almighty, how could Rachelika and Moise deal with the Kurdish snake with all his smooth talk, the razor-sharp words that dripped from his lips like honey? Cursed was the day he met the Kurd and succumbed to his sweet talk and agreed to be his partner in the halvah factory. How had that bastard pushed him out of the factory without him even noticing? Why hadn't he listened to his brother Matzliach, who for the first time in his life had tried to give him sound advice: "He's not one of us, Gabriel," Matzliach had said. "How will you get along with him? He thinks black and you think white; he thinks day and you think night."

"Don't worry, Matzliach," he'd told his brother. "An apple tree can't threaten a fig tree." What he hadn't taken into account was that the apple was rotten, and if it fell near the fig tree, it too would rot.

One day Mordoch the Kurd had come to Gabriel and said, "Gabriel, we have to close the factory."

"Close it? Why?"

"*Halas*, it's seen enough," the Kurd said. "We're losing money. We're deep in debt. We have to close it down and repay the debts."

And so it was. Gabriel's head wasn't firmly on his shoulders at the time. He was already feeling unwell and his mind had suffered for it. Otherwise, how could he explain that without asking for any documents and without looking into it, he gave Mordoch his consent and Mordoch sold the factory to another Kurd?

"Where's my share?" Gabriel had asked, and Mordoch, without batting an eyelid, replied, "What share? There isn't a grush left. With all the money I got for the factory, and that was about a quarter of what it's worth, I paid off the debts."

Gabriel was stricken and defeated and sick and didn't ask for any proof. In a strange way he'd been glad to be rid of the Kurd and the halvah factory, which were like a chain around his neck. He'd hoped he'd never see Mordoch again, but the Kurd hadn't disappeared from his life. On the contrary, he'd stuck to him like a leech and continued coming by the shop and the King George apartment, talking business as if Gabriel hadn't known the Amalek had cheated him.

And then he lost the King George apartment too. He hadn't had enough money to pay the rent, and so with a heavy heart he'd told his wife and daughters to pack up their belongings. They were going back to the old house in Ohel Moshe.

The girls, especially Luna and Becky, tried to protest, but one look from him stopped them in their tracks. Normally he would have sat down with the girls and gently explained the situation to them, but times weren't normal. He had lost his money; he was losing his health and strength, and more to the point, his renowned patience. Rosa didn't say a word, but he knew that inside she was happy. She'd never felt at home in the big King George Street building, and only his good Rachelika, only she with her kind expression, gave him the sense that he was doing the right thing.

Before deciding to move his family back to Ohel Moshe, he'd endured many sleepless nights. He understood that it meant admitting to neighbors and relatives that his financial situation was as bad as could be. He thought about his mother Mercada, what she'd have to say about her good-for-nothing son who instead of taking one step up had taken ten down.

But when she'd heard the news, his mother fully believed that her son was still paying the heavy price for his father's death. Even though at the end of the livianos treatment she had blessed him and made her peace with him, deep in her heart that stubborn old woman would never find room for true forgiveness.

And now they'd been back in Ohel Moshe for ten months, and as he'd expected, things had not gone back to what they were. The neighbors had not forgotten Matilda Franco's death. His borracho brother-in-law had sullied the family name forever. All that was left for Gabriel was to shut himself up within his four walls and sit in this chair. The constant contact he'd had with scores of people in Jerusalem had been reduced to contact with just his close family. Mashallah, even so, we're fighters, thank God, he thought. And if that's how it has to be, then so be it.

He was tired and his head was reeling. Tomorrow, *ras bin eini*, he'd get up out of the chair and go to the shop, even if he had to have Moise carry him. He'd go to the shop and sit by the door so that all the market merchants, all the shoppers, could see that Gabriel Ermosa was still alive and kicking.

Apparently Mordoch had been walking around the shop like a *khanzir*, a pig, sniffing here, sniffing there, asking questions, taking bags full of goodies without paying, as if the shop belonged to *him*. Well let's see the Kurd, the big hero when faced with Rachelika, let's see him now when I show up.

"Selichot, selichot." In the dead of night, the voice of the synagogue beadle called the people to prayer before Yom Kippur. Rosa went over to Gabriel's bed, touched his arm lightly, and whispered, "Gabriel querido, it's time for selichot. Are you getting up?" He groaned in his sleep and didn't answer. She shook him gently and whispered again, "Gabriel, the beadle's called selichot three times already. Aren't you getting up, querido?"

Gabriel opened his eyes and gave her a glazed look. "I'm not feeling well," he told her. "They can ask for forgiveness without me."

"Por Dio, Gabriel, you're not getting up for selichot? What will people say?"

All at once he was fully awake. "What do I care what they'll say? I'm telling you I don't feel well, and I'm not going to selichot!"

Rosa went back to her bed. Dio santo, what's happening to my husband? First he doesn't go to the synagogue on Shabbat, now he's not going to selichot. In the end he won't fast on Yom Kippur, God forbid. Nothing is as it once was. This week when she'd asked Gabriel for money to buy meat from the butcher's, he'd told her from now on no more meat, just chicken. Buy meat only for holidays and special events. For months now she had feared the day when Gabriel would tell her that there was no money, and now that day had come. She could feel the memories of the time she was poverty-stricken returning with force, her nightmares threatening to blacken her life. She would often wake up in the night from one recurring dream. In it she was a little girl poking in dumpsters, looking for food, and then the little girl would morph into the old woman she was today, continuing to scavenge in the garbage. She would wake up in a panic and pray, Dio santo, don't take me back there. Don't take me back to where I came from.

One night she woke up from a nightmare and with a heavy heart got out of bed and went into her daughters' room. All three were sleeping soundly. On the cabinet beside Luna's bed she noticed perfume in a crystal bowl. The sight of it made her blood boil. Times are so hard and yet Luna carries on with her luxuries, buys perfume, clothes, shoes. She doesn't even think of putting something aside for the family. All the money she earns at Zacks & Son goes into her own pocket. Once we didn't need it, but now with the situation so bad? What, hasn't the brat got eyes in her head? Can't she see that things aren't what they used to be? She decided she'd swallow her pride and speak to Luna.

The next day she went into the girls' room as Luna was studying herself in the mirror, apparently pleased with her reflection. She was wearing a black suit that set off her hips, silk stockings that accentuated her lovely legs, and the latest fashion in shoes.

"Where are you going?" Rosa asked.

Luna was surprised. Since when had her mother taken an interest in where she was going?

"To meet David," she replied somewhat apathetically.

"Let him come here. You're not going out."

"What do you mean, not going out? Since when have you told me what to do?"

"I'm your mother and maybe it's time I did."

"Don't you think it's a bit late for that? I'm going to be married any minute."

"So long as you're not married you'll listen to what I have to say to you."

"And what do you have to say to me, Mother querida?" she asked, drawing the words out mockingly.

With all her might Rosa restrained herself and replied, "Only this week there was shooting in Talpiot and Givat Shaul. It's dangerous to go out at a time like this."

"David will look after me," Luna said, attempting to put an end to the conversation.

"You're not going anywhere," Rosa said and stood in the doorway.

"Oh yes I am!" Luna insisted, trying to push her mother aside.

"You should be ashamed of yourself! A girl about to get married does that to her mother? You should know that there's somebody up above who sees everything, and everything you do to me, your children will do to you with interest!"

"Oh, stop it. Enough of your threats. My children, Mother querida, will love me and I'll love them, unlike you, who's never in all her life loved me!"

"How could I love you when from the day you were born, every time I tried to touch you, your body was all thorns? How could I love you when from the day you learned to talk, every time you spoke to me your words were as sharp as knives?"

"All right, what do you want, Mother?" Luna asked and sat down on the couch. "That all of a sudden we start being friends? It won't happen. It's like you and I aren't mother and daughter. It's as if they swapped me in the hospital."

"What are you saying? May God forgive you. If you weren't such a big donkey I'd fill your mouth with hot pepper! I raised you, I watered you, I cultivated you, and look at what a prickly bush you've turned out to be!" Rosa said and left the room.

Luna remained on the couch, her eyes filled with tears. Why, God? Why were she and her mother not like all the other mothers and daughters? Why wasn't she like her sisters with her mother, and why was it only she who didn't get along with her? What had gone awry between them and when? Was it when she was still in her mother's womb? Because she couldn't remember one day in her life when they'd gotten along, when they'd exchanged words of affection, when they'd spoken, period. Only shouting, only anger. In God's name, she swore, when I have a daughter, God willing, I'll do everything to bring her close to me. I'll hug her and kiss her and tell her how much I love her, unlike my mother who's never uttered words of love to me in her life, my mother who most of the time gives me that look of hers that says, Get the hell out of my sight!

She hadn't managed to dry her tears when Rosa came back and stood in front of her.

"What now?"

"There's another thing I haven't spoken to you about," Rosa said. "You have to put some money on the table."

"What money? What are you talking about?"

"The money you earn. What, can't you see that your father is barely bringing any money home? Are you so busy with yourself that you can't see anybody else? You go on living like a princess when your father stopped being a
king a long time ago."

Luna felt the anger rising in her throat. "Don't you talk about my father
like that! My father was born a king and he'll always be a king! Never, do you
hear, never say even one bad word about my father!"

"What did I say?" Rosa mumbled, ignoring the insults her daughter had
hurled at her. "All I tried to tell you was that your father doesn't have money
like he used to."

"How do you know what my father has or hasn't got? Since when has he
told *you* anything? When has he ever spoken to you about the shop? When did
he talk to you about how hurt he is that Nona Mercada hasn't set foot in this
house since the day she ran away to Tia Allegra in Tel Aviv *because of you?* You,
you're good for only one thing for my father, cooking and cleaning. You who
used to be a servant in the houses of the English, now you're a servant in the
house of Gabriel Ermosa!"

Rosa's hand came up involuntarily and she slapped her daughter's cheek
hard. Her hand hurt from the force of the blow, and the sound of the slap resonated in her ears.

Stunned, Luna put a hand to her cheek, and without thinking, started hitting Rosa mercilessly.

"Stop it!" Becky ran into the room and tried to separate her mother and
sister. But Luna didn't stop. She grasped Rosa by the hair and pulled it hard,
yelling to high heaven as her mother tried to free herself from her grip. But she
was holding on tight, and at any moment she'd scalp her completely. Little
Becky was between them, crying out, "Stop, stop it, Luna. Stop!" and "Basta,
Mother!" until she succumbed to tears.

Becky's weeping eventually separated them. Mother and daughter retreated,
each to a different end of the room, leaving Becky sprawled on the floor between them.

"Don't cry, Becky," Luna said, bending over her sister and forgetting the
anger that had engulfed her only moments ago, completely ignoring that, God
help them, she had dared to raise a hand to her mother.

Becky shoved her off roughly and yelled, "Don't touch me!"

"Becky, I'm sorry," Luna said instead of begging her mother for forgiveness. "I didn't mean it. I'm sorry."

"No, you're not!" Becky shouted. "You're never sorry! You have no respect for anybody, for anything! You're horrible!"

Rosa left the room and took a seat in the yard. Her heart went out to little Becky, but she was hurt and wounded and unable to extend a hand to anyone. God help them, how could it have happened that her daughter, the flesh of her flesh, had raised a hand to her as if she were a woman from the street?

Becky followed her mother outside and sat on her knee. She put her arms around Rosa's neck, and the two of them wept on each other's shoulder.

This was how David found them when he came to pick up Luna. "What happened?" he asked, frightened.

"Ask your fiancée," Becky said.

When Luna came to the door, David said, "Luna, what happened to Becky and your mother?"

"We had a quarrel," she said.

"Who, you and your sister?"

"No, me and my mother."

"You quarreled?" Becky interrupted. "Tell your fiancé the truth. Tell him so he knows who he's marrying!" Becky shouted through her tears.

"What happened?" David asked again as he followed Luna inside.

"Enough, David. Leave me alone."

"I'm not leaving you alone or anything else! What happened to make your mother and your sister cry?" He looked at Luna, confused and ashamed.

"I'm ready now. Let's go," Luna said, turning to the door.

"We're not going anywhere until you tell me what's going on."

"What does it matter? We're always fighting. We've been fighting since the day I was born."

"Apologize to your mother."

"Never!"

"Luna, she's your mother. Apologize to her."

"I'm not apologizing to her. She should apologize to me."

"Luna, we're getting married in a month's time. I don't want a situation, God forbid, where your mother won't come to our wedding."

"She'll come, don't worry. She won't let people talk."

"Luna!" he said, raising his voice. "If you don't go back into the yard right now and apologize to your mother, I'll walk through that door and I won't come back."

"What?" Luna was shocked.

"You heard me. I don't like your behavior. I've never heard of such a thing, a daughter acting like this with her mother! What does it say about you?"

"What does it say about her? She's my mother. She's the one who makes me lose my temper."

"Go and apologize now."

"But David . . ."

"Now!"

Luna realized that she had no choice. If she didn't want to lose David, she had to swallow her pride and apologize to Rosa. Reluctantly she went back into the yard, and at the sight of Becky and Rosa with their arms around each other, she tried to turn and retrace her steps, but David was blocking the doorway and prodding her. The words stuck in her throat as she went over to Rosa and barely audibly said, "I'm sorry."

Rosa raised her eyes to her daughter's, but there was no remorse there, only a glassy, remote expression.

"May God forgive you," she said and turned her back to her.

Luna stood there not knowing what to do next. David came to her aid and said, "Senora Rosa, I don't know what happened, but believe me, Luna is very sorry and I promise you it will never happen again."

Rosa nodded. "Thank you, David, thank you. Now take your fiancée and go to wherever you're going. It's best that Luna isn't here when her father gets home from the shop."

Rosa never told Gabriel what happened between her and Luna. Together with all the family she prepared for her eldest daughter's wedding, but she couldn't join in on the great excitement that filled the house. She drew strength from the fact that, gracias el Dio, Luna would soon be gone to her husband's house and she would no longer have grief because of her, just as her neighbor Tamar had told her all those years ago.

But no one in the Ermosa family knew that the wedding Luna was so excited about was built on quicksand. Nobody had any idea about the talk David had had with Moise before the wedding.

"She's not such a paragon of virtue," David told Moise when they met after the incident between Luna and Rosa. "She has the face of an angel, but if you saw her face when she talks to her mother, I'm not all that sure I'm getting a good deal."

"Come on, David. There isn't a guy in Jerusalem who doesn't envy you for catching Luna."

"I'm scared I'm buying a pig in a poke," David confided. "I thought my problems were solved when I met her, but now I'm not so sure."

"The fact that she doesn't get along with her mother doesn't mean that she won't with you."

"She doesn't respect her mother, and I think that's unforgivable."

"David, stay out of it. You don't know what goes on between mother and daughter. It's none of your business. Your future mother-in-law won't be living with you and Luna, and her relationship with her daughter won't affect yours with Luna."

"I thought I'd finally met a girl who'd get Isabella out of my mind, but now I just don't know."

"Maybe she'll get Isabella out of your mind," Moise said quietly. "But the question is, amigo, whether she'll get Isabella out of your heart."

In the weeks that followed, apart from absolutely necessary communication, Rosa and Luna avoided speaking to each other. If Gabriel suspected that something had happened between his daughter and wife, he gave no hint of it. He was very preoccupied with the shop and the arrangements for Luna's wedding. Becky chose not to tell him about the terrible fight either, and spoke about it only to one person, her boyfriend Handsome Eli Cohen.

"If I hadn't gotten there in time they would have killed each other," she told him, and he'd advised her not to interfere, and more important, not to tell her father. She didn't speak again to Luna about what had happened, and Rachelika, who was deeply immersed in her new romance with Moise, hadn't even noticed the rising tension and distance between her mother and older sister. After all, Luna and Rosa had never been close.

As the day of the wedding approached, Luna and her sisters' excitement reached a new frenzy: Luna's wedding dress, Rachelika's and Becky's bridesmaids' dresses, the invitations that the three sisters delivered by hand to relatives and friends. Only Rosa was not involved. Not with the wedding dress, not with the invitations, not with any of the arrangements. She sometimes struggled not to burst out and spoil the mood.

Rosa wasn't always able to control herself either. One evening when they sat down for dinner, Gabriel noticed that she hadn't touched her food.

"Eat," he told her. "Why aren't you eating?"

"I don't want to eat!" she replied angrily. "Your daughters have ruined my appetite."

Gabriel glanced at his daughters, not understanding what she was talking about. "What's happened, Rosa? Is there something I don't know?"

"What you don't know you don't want to know!" she answered, getting up from the table and hurrying into the yard.

She was greeted by a starry night. Another thirty days until Luna's wedding, she thought as she took a seat on the stool. How would she be able to stand under the wedding canopy and pretend she was happy when her heart had been pierced by a thousand knives? She closed her eyes and wished Ephraim could be there to stand beside her and give her strength. She sat for a long time until she got the feeling that she was no longer alone. She opened her eyes and saw Tamar.

"Dio santo, you startled me," she said to Tamar.

"Why are you sitting outside like this all on your own?"

"Well," she said, "it's a bit crowded in the house."

"Yes," said Tamar, "mashallah, you've become a big family what with Luna's and Rachelika's fiancés."

"And Becky's boy," Rosa added.

"Becky has a boy?"

"She's not yet fourteen and she already wants to marry him," she said, managing a smile.

"Well, with God's help."

Tamar took a stool next to Rosa's. They sat there side by side for a long while, not talking about the rift between them, not saying a word about either Matilda Franco or Ephraim. They didn't talk about the long, difficult period that had passed. They sat in silence, each listening to the beating of the other's heart.

Perhaps there is a God, Rosa thought. Perhaps all isn't lost. Here, in the midst of all the sorrow, one good thing had emerged: Her soulmate vizina Tamar had come back to her.

Calmer, she went inside, but now it was Gabriel who was scowling. "This boy of Becky's," he hissed at her, "he came in the morning, now it's nighttime and he's still here! Doesn't he have a home?"

"Don't get angry, Gabriel," Rosa soothed him. "He's a good boy."

"I don't like him being here all the time. Becky's still a child."

"They want to get married."

"Married? What are we, Arabs? She's not even fourteen. I'm going to kick him out!"

"No, querido, don't do that. Now that Luna's getting married and Rachelika will also marry, God willing, Becky will be all on her own, the miskenica. It's good she's got Handsome Eli Cohen around."

"What's this Handsome Eli Cohen? What kind of a name is that?"

"It's what the girls call him. They say he's as handsome as a movie star."

"Looks aren't important, woman! The main thing is what a person does with his life."

"He has a job, Gabriel. He's a good boy, may he be healthy, industrious. He works as a clerk at the post office, and in the evening he's learning clerical work and accountancy at the Nachmani School."

"Whatever, but I don't want to see him in front of me all the time. I don't want him getting too close to Becky."

And why not? Rosa thought to herself. Wasn't it better than them roaming the streets? Out there, God help them, it was dangerous. There were signs of war. It was best that Becky and Handsome Eli Cohen be at home where she could keep an eye on them.

In the winter of 1946, Jerusalem was cloaked in white. Heavy snow fell on the city, covering its houses and streets with what seemed like a white down quilt. The preparations for David and Luna's wedding were at fever pitch, and once the sky cleared, the sun came out from behind the clouds, and the first birds heralded the start of spring, the wedding day had finally arrived.

Luna had chosen her wedding dress with extra care after going through dozens of *Burda* magazines devoted to bridal wear with endless patience and deliberation. It was a stunning white silk dress that fell to the floor, with tiny pearl buttons at the front and down to the waistline.

Her beautiful hair was gathered into a fine white lace net at the nape of her neck, gleaming in hues of gold and red around her heart-shaped face. Her white veil flowed from a tiara inset with precious stones, and in her white-gloved hands she held a bouquet of white carnations. She looked royal.

When David saw her for the first time in a week—as was the custom before a wedding—she took his breath away. He could not have wished for a more perfect bride. She was everything he had envisioned during the long months after he and his comrades had been informed they were leaving Italy and going back home to Palestine. She was the woman he had imagined when he'd decided to get married immediately upon his return to Jerusalem and set up a Jewish home with one of their women.

Luna too couldn't take her eyes off the handsome man who was about to become her husband. He was wearing an elegant black pinstripe suit, a starched white shirt with a stiff collar, and a bow tie that complemented his shirt. From the top pocket of his finely tailored suit peeped a white carnation like the ones in her bouquet. There wasn't a hair out of place in his dashing mustache. Together they were a beautiful couple, the perfect bride and groom.

The wedding took place early on a Friday afternoon at the Menorah Club on Bezalel Street, which they had decorated with all of Luna's favorite flowers. At the entrance, the bridesmaids, Rachelika and Becky, stood in matching dresses made for the occasion, handing out white tulle bags containing sugared almonds from Gabriel's shop. As was standard at the time, the refreshments were modest. On white-clothed tables along the walls were jugs of lemonade and raspberry juice, cream cakes, borekas, and fruit trays.

Gabriel felt immense joy at the sight of his beautiful daughter and her handsome husband, and only one thing cast a pall over his happiness: the frugal refreshments. Ach, almighty God, he thought to himself. In normal times the tables would have been laden with dried fruit, almonds, raisins, sweets, a selection of cakes, all the bounty of the world and the country. But what can you do? Times are not what they were. Thank God that he could even afford to book a hall for his daughter's wedding. He wouldn't be able to rent a house for them, and certainly not buy one. The young couple had been invited to spend their first year of marriage at his table until they were on their feet and could move to their own home. This was the custom of *mesa franca*, the king's table.

Gabriel looked around the hall. All his close relatives were there, even his mother Mercada. She had come from Tel Aviv with his sister Allegra, brother-in-law Elazar, and all their children. His brothers, sisters, brothers-in-law, sisters-in-law, and even neighbors from Ohel Moshe, among them Tamar, who had attended despite Senora Franco's dirty looks—they had all accepted the invitation to celebrate Luna's wedding. Even his Kurdish partner Mordoch Levi was there with his wife and all their eight children. He was the only guest whom Gabriel wasn't glad to see. He'd invited him because he'd felt he had no choice.

Gabriel had been growing gradually weaker. His body was betraying him. He found it difficult to conceal the tremors and hard to walk, so he had to use a cane. He had been forced to sell the car he loved so much because its upkeep was costly, but mainly because he could no longer trust himself to drive. His foot trembled on the pedal, his hands shook on the wheel, and now he had to take a taxi to and from the Mahane Yehuda Market.

The financial situation was as bad as it could be, and the state of the shop was going from bad to worse. Matzliach hadn't gotten matters under control, and even the dedicated Rachelika and Moise couldn't make a silk purse out of a sow's ear. How could you make money if there weren't any customers, and if there were some, there was hardly any stock left to sell them?

He looked at Luna, radiant in her bridal gown, the smile not leaving her flawless face. He looked at Rachelika and Becky standing with their mother at one end of the hall. Rosa, mashallah, it'd been a long time since he'd seen her so happy, as if Luna's marriage had taken a weight off her. She was even wearing a pretty dress, not like the shmattes she always wore. He turned his eyes from his wife standing at one end of the hall to his mother sitting at the other. The two women, he noticed, hadn't exchanged a single word. As soon as Mercada came in, he'd hurried over to her and kissed her hand. She had nodded, greeted him, and walked as erectly as a proud young girl to sit at the far end of the hall. His daughters had rushed to their grandmother to kiss her hand, and Rosa had taken a deep breath and she too joined the long line of relatives making the pilgrimage to the sour old woman.

Gabriel looked at both of them—his wife standing with her daughters at the entrance to the hall, his mother surrounded by her children and grandchildren on the opposite end—and his heart lurched. For the thousandth time he asked himself how his mother could have become so cold that she'd married him to a woman he hadn't loved for even one day of his life.

He didn't contemplate it further, for the lovely Luna was approaching him, linking his arm, her beauty lighting up the darkness of his thoughts. Arm in arm he walked with his beloved daughter to greet their guests and receive their blessings. As he gazed proudly at his Luna, who on the day she was born was illuminated by the moon and God had restored love to his heart, a thought flit through his mind: Perhaps it isn't so terrible that Mother married me to a woman I have never loved, for it is she who bore me Luna, she who bore me Rachelika and Becky, my wonderful daughters, my very soul. Suddenly flooded with great tenderness, Gabriel passed Luna into her sisters' arms, took Rosa's hand, tucked it under his arm, and said to her, "Heideh, Rosa, let's go and see our eldest daughter get married."

Six months later Rachelika and Moise were also married in a modest ceremony held in the yard of Moise's parents' home in the Maghrebi Quarter. Gabriel was heartbroken, but the more he had examined his financial situation, it became clear that he couldn't afford to rent a hall for them as he had for Luna and David.

"God forgive my sins, there's no justice in the world," Rosa said to Rachelika. "You work like a horse in the shop, you abandon your dream of being a teacher in order to help your father, and who gets a princess's wedding? Luna, who doesn't do anything for anyone except herself."

"Mother, why do you say things like that? If I'd been married first I would have had a wedding in a hall too."

"You, mi alma, you are oro, gold. You've never been jealous of your sister, but if God forbid it had been you who was married in the Menorah Club and she had to get married in a yard in the Maghrebi Quarter, *wai wai wai*, what a scene she would have made. She would have turned the world upside down."

"Well, it's not her who has to get married in a yard, it's me. And for me, even getting married in a synagogue with only a quorum present would have been enough. So why get angry when there's no need?"

"Miskenica Rachelika, even when you deserve to be number one you're number two, that's why I'm angry."

"Basta, Mother, if it weren't for Luna I wouldn't have even gotten married. It was she who introduced me to Moise. It's all thanks to her and David."

7

GABRIEL LAY IN HIS BED listening to the silence of the house. He was still unused to the emptiness. He missed the commotion that had filled it when his
three daughters had all lived there. But they'd grown up and that was the way
of the world. The fledglings left the nest, that's how it was. At one time young
people would carry on living with their parents for the first year of marriage at
least, but young people had become modern. They rented a room and embarked on their lives. Perhaps it was better that way. It hadn't done him any
good, living with his mother. His mother—it'd been a long time since he'd
heard from her. He hadn't seen her since Luna's wedding. She hadn't attended
Rachelika's. She'd said that traveling all the way to Jerusalem was hard for her,
and Allegra had apologized on her behalf.

In the past, once a month he'd receive a letter from Allegra with an update
on the family and his mother, who'd become a cantankerous old woman. But
now the mailman brought letters from Allegra only infrequently. How long
had it been since he'd last heard from her? Two, maybe three months. Today he'd
sit down and write her despite his shaking hand. What once took him five
minutes to write now took an hour, and he'd get annoyed. He couldn't stand
not having control of his hand, of his life.

The situation with the shop was bad. It was difficult to obtain stock, nobody went to Lebanon or Syria anymore, and commerce with the local Arabs
had also ceased. Even the women from the Arab villages had stopped coming to
the market with cheeses and olive oil. The scarcity of goods and customers alike
had brought the shop to the brink of total disaster. Despite their ambition,

poor Rachelika and Moise hadn't been able to restore the shop to its former glory. Yesterday they'd come to see him with more bad news.

"Papo," Rachelika said, "Moise and I have to talk to you about something important."

"Then talk, queridos, say what you have to say."

"Senor Ermosa," Moise began, "times are hard, there are no customers in the shop, and even when there are, we don't have anything to sell them. We've finished everything that was in the sacks and we have nothing to replace it. Today we had about five customers and they left empty-handed."

Gabriel sighed. He didn't want to hear this. He couldn't bear it. The shop had been his father's and grandfather's before him. Why, why had it fallen to him to bring the family business to ruins? He couldn't even pass it down to the next generation.

Rachelika and Moise were silent, conscious of Gabriel's pain. Rachelika embraced her father and kissed him. "Papo, these aren't only hard times for us. The market stalls are all empty."

"Don't tell me that the market's empty," Gabriel said.

"It's empty, Papo. People come and go but there's nothing to buy. People come to our shop, a delicatessen, to spoil themselves, not for bread, not for a tomato, not for meat. Ask the butchers, Papo, ask the grocers. There's nothing."

"What can we do?"

"Mordoch came with an offer," Moise replied.

"The devil take him, don't mention his name to me!"

"There's no choice, senor. Nobody will make us a better offer these days."

"What has that son of a whore got to say? What's he offering, the thief?"

"He wants to buy the shop."

"I'm not selling!"

"Papo," Rachelika said, "if we don't sell, we'll lose the shop anyway. The shop will be closed. How can we pay taxes? Where will the money for food come from?"

"That shop," Gabriel said, "is the pride of our family. There never was and never will be one like it in all Jerusalem. My mother, your Nona Mercada, will never forgive me if I sell it."

"With all due respect to Nona Mercada, Papo, when was the last time that Nona Mercada showed us respect? When did she show any interest in the shop, in her son and granddaughters?"

"Silence!" Gabriel rebuked her. "How can you speak like that about your grandmother?" But in his heart he knew Rachelika was right. For years now his mother had neither considered nor respected him. Yet his upbringing had prevented him from repaying her in her own coin. "Honor thy father and thy mother"—how many times had they pounded that into him until it was deep in his blood? He wished that his mother would demand of herself what she had demanded of him all his life.

"Papo, if we don't sell the shop to the Kurd, tomorrow we can start begging in Zion Square," Rachelika's voice shook him out of his reverie.

"You're exaggerating, querida," Moise remarked gently. "Begging? I'm young. I'll find work."

"Where? Tell me, Moise, where will you find work now? What will you be? A balaguleh pushing a handcart? A plumber putting his hands into people's shit?"

"I wish I was a plumber. Do you know how much money a plumber makes? I beg your pardon, Senor Gabriel," he said, turning to his father-in-law with a smile, "but Rachelika's right. Putting my hands into people's shit really wouldn't suit me."

"And now you have to clean up the Kurd's shit. The Kurd who from the day I first met him has put *me* deep in shit. Tell me, hijos, why would the Kurd want to buy a shop that's not making money? What's his interest? That man doesn't do anything without good reason. I don't trust him. I wouldn't even if my life depended on it."

"We'll meet with him, Papo, you, Moise, and me, and we'll ask Luna's David to come too, and we'll all face him in a united front. We'll hear what he has to offer and then decide."

And so it was. A few days later Rachelika invited Mordoch to Gabriel and Rosa's house. He came as if butter wouldn't melt in his mouth, smiling in every direction, smooth-talking Rosa, complimenting her on her borekitas. "On my life, Madam Rosa, there aren't borekas like these in all Jerusalem. Why don't you sell them in the shop?"

Rachelika felt he was just pushing her buttons. He knew that they hadn't been selling anything in the shop for a while.

They sat around the big table with Gabriel at its head, the Kurd at the other end, Rachelika and Moise on one side, and David and Luna on the other.

"Go ahead," Gabriel opened the proceedings. "What are you offering?"

"Gabriel, my dear friend, times are hard, nobody knows what tomorrow may bring. The English bastards are in cahoots with the Arabs, every day there's a new trouble. Maybe war will break out tomorrow, maybe the Arabs will massacre us all, perhaps we'll slaughter the English. It's impossible to know what will happen, isn't that so?"

"Get to the point, Mordoch," David said impatiently. "We all know what's happening around us, so why are you beating around the bush?"

"Patience, habibi, I'll get to it. With your permission, first allow me to explain the situation to Mr. Ermosa, who hasn't left the house for a long time."

Gabriel felt the blood draining from his body. How dare this Kurd insult him in his own house, at his own table. How dare he present him as a worthless object. But before he could bring his thoughts to his mouth, Luna burst out at the Kurd: "Who are you to tell my father that he hasn't left the house in a long time? How dare you sit here in our house and insult my father!"

"I'm not insulting him, God forbid. Did you hear me insult him? All I said was that it's been a long time since the honorable Mr. Ermosa was in the shop."

"He hasn't been to the shop for a long time because we've been there instead," said Rachelika, quickly coming to her father's defense. "A man reaches an age, Mr. Mordoch, when he has to stop working, and now we young ones are continuing in Father's footsteps."

Hearing his daughters springing to his defense, Gabriel couldn't contain himself any longer. "You're being far too delicate with our guest," he said. "I have never thrown anyone out of my house, but now I want you to get up and get out!" He pounded the table with his fist.

Silence descended on the room, but the Kurd had seemingly not heard Gabriel and went on. "Why get angry, Mr. Gabriel, it's bad for the health. All I meant to say was that times are hard and there's no point in holding on to a shop that's like a bottomless pit. Not only is it not bringing in any money, it's taking money you don't have. So all I want to suggest, Mr. Ermosa, is that I buy the shop and get you and your family, may you all be healthy, out of trouble. Believe me, Gabriel, I'm doing this in the name of our partnership in the halvah factory. I'm doing it out of respect for you, because I want you to live the rest of your life with dignity and with enough money to provide for your wife and marry little Becky, may she be healthy."

Something in what the Kurd said calmed them all down. Ever so slowly Gabriel recognized that despite his smooth talk the Kurd had a point, that he really had no choice but to sell the shop. Rachelika and Moise had already understood this, while David couldn't have cared less. He hadn't understood why he was being involved in a family matter of no concern to him. His father-in-law's shop in the Mahane Yehuda Market had never interested him. But Luna couldn't restrain herself. "We're not selling anything!" she shouted. "That shop is the pride of our family, the pride of our father. It was our grandfather's and our great-grandfather's when it was still in the Old City market. There's nothing for you here, so go and scout the other market traders."

Nobody said a word. Nobody dared contradict what Luna had said. They had been taught not to argue in the presence of strangers, and for Rachelika, that upbringing was even stronger than her fierce desire to shut Luna up. But as soon as Mordoch stood and took his leave, not before asking them to reconsider his offer, Rachelika could no longer hold back. "Since when have you been such a big maven about the shop?" she fired at Luna. "When was the last time your beautiful feet walked through the market? It's beneath your dignity to sell smoked fish, and all of a sudden you talk about respect?"

"The fact that you work in the shop," Luna retorted, "doesn't mean that I don't have a say. I grew up in the shop, and if we have to sell, then it would be better to sell it to an Arab than to the Kurd! He's been plotting to buy the shop for a long time, you said so yourself, and now you want to sell it to that snake?"

"Why, do you know of anyone else who wants to buy it?" Rachelika replied. "Who'll buy a shop today except that stupid Kurd, another useless merchant."

"Rachelika querida," Gabriel said, finally intervening, "he's far from stupid and even further from being a useless merchant. Forgive me, querida, but it's your father who's stupid. It's your father who's the useless merchant."

"God forbid, Papo, it's because of the hard times. Why are you putting what's happening in the shop on yourself? You made Raphael Ermosa, Delicatessen, the most splendid shop in the Mahane Yehuda Market." Rachelika's voice was choked with tears, and Luna's eyes too became watery.

"Listen to me carefully, hija mia," Gabriel replied, his voice shaking, "and all of you listen: Your foolish father lost the halvah factory to the Kurd without getting a grush in return. Your worthless merchant of a father didn't check where the money from the factory was going. He listened to all the 'good' advice from the Kurd, who told him not to come to the factory so as not to confuse the workers, who told him not to trouble himself about the factory because he's got his shop in the market to worry about and he should let the Kurd manage things for both of them. And what happened in the end? Your fool of a father got the worst of both worlds. That's how it is. If you lie down with dogs, don't be surprised if you get up with fleas."

"So you don't want to sell the shop to the Kurd either?" Rachelika asked.

"What's this either? Me especially! What was it that Lunika said? It's better to sell to an Arab than to a Kurd."

"Well, that's settled then, we're not selling," David summed up impatiently and got to his feet.

"Just a minute," Moise stopped him. "We haven't finished here."

"If David's not interested, let him go," Luna said. "He didn't really want to come anyway."

"Luna!" David fixed her with a glare that frightened Rachelika. What was with that look? she thought. Not a year had passed since her sister's wedding to David Siton and that was how he looked at her? What was going on between those two?

"David," Moise went on, "unless you want to hear what I have to say, you can go."

David went back to his place and sat down. Rachelika couldn't help but notice that Luna had slid her chair away from his.

"Senor Ermosa," Moise continued in his soft voice, "everything you say about the Kurd is true, and I understand why you don't want to sell him the shop."

"He's a snake in the grass," Gabriel interjected.

"I know, senor. Unfortunately I've come to know him. But who else will buy the shop at a time like this? Who's doing business right now? Because of the situation the shop is liable to stand empty for the next few years. He's right about one thing: We don't know what tomorrow will bring, and maybe war *will* break out and all the men will have to go off and fight, and maybe the market will be closed down because of the war, and maybe and maybe and maybe. So please forgive me, Senor Ermosa, but even if you're right, we have no choice. We have to sell the shop to that dog."

"Can I say something?" asked Handsome Eli Cohen, who was sitting on the couch with Becky and so far hadn't taken part in the discussion. They all turned toward him. Over the past year he'd become like one of the family.

"Yes, young man, what do you have to say?" said Gabriel, who had come to like Becky's boy.

"I couldn't help listening to you all, and with your permission I have to give you my opinion."

"*Tfadal*, please do," Moise encouraged him.

"It seems to me that the Kurd is a smart businessman," Handsome Eli

Cohen said as he rose from the couch and stood by the table. "He doesn't want to buy the shop right now with the situation so bad for no reason. He's got plans, he knows what he's doing. He'll buy the shop cheaply now in order to sell it at a profit when things get better. I'll bet he's got dirty money stashed away. If you decide to sell the shop, you should find out first what his plans are and act accordingly."

"So what do you suggest we do, young man?" Gabriel asked, indicating with a hand that he should take a seat at the table.

"If you agree, Senor Ermosa, I'll run a few checks of my own on the Kurd and get back to you with some answers."

"Wonderful, anybody can make decisions about the shop now," David said.

"He's not anybody!" Becky said, annoyed. "He's my boyfriend! And when I turn seventeen, with God's help, he'll be my husband!"

"After Senor Gabriel and Senora Rosa agree to give me your hand, of course," Handsome Eli Cohen added quickly.

"No time soon," said Gabriel. "First Becky will finish school, and then if you want to get married, we'll talk about it."

Gabriel was pleased with Becky's response to David, he was pleased with her boy's good manners, but he was not so pleased with the strange behavior of his son-in-law, Luna's husband, who acted as if everything that was happening around him was a waste of his time. He made up his mind to speak to Luna as soon as possible and find out what was going on between her and David.

"The very least you could have done with my father was behave like a normal human being, not someone who can't wait to get out of there," Luna told David when they got home. "Aren't you interested? Don't you care what happens to my father's shop?"

"Luna, what do I know about shops? What do I know about selling or buying? Not only doesn't it interest me, it bores me."

"And what doesn't bore you? Going to visit my sister and brother-in-law bores you, going dancing at Café Europa bores you, having coffee at Atara bores you. Ever since we got married, nothing interests you."

"What's happening in this country interests me, unlike you, whose only concern is the clothes at Zacks & Son and magazines with all their Hollywood nonsense. You should be grateful I let you go on working."

"Well, thank you, really. If I wasn't working, how would we have any money?"

"How would we have any money? I walk my feet to the bone every day looking for work. I take whatever I can get, whether it's in construction or with my brother the butcher. I come home stinking. It takes hours of scrubbing to get rid of the smell. And all that so we'll have money. The money you earn goes to your perfume and your coffee at Atara and the idiotic magazines you read. So it would be best for you just to shut your mouth!"

Luna was dumbstruck. David had never insulted her before, never spoken coarsely to her. His behavior had changed since the wedding, but until now he had never spoken to her like that. Tears welled in her eyes. Was this the knight she had been waiting for all her life? Was this the man of her dreams whom she'd married? God, what had become of her? She, who all the boys in the city had fought over for just one glance from her, Luna the loveliest of all the girls, humiliated like this by her own man.

She turned her back to him and started getting ready for bed. He went out onto the balcony and lit a cigarette. Since their wedding they'd lived in a small studio apartment in Mekor Baruch with an enclosed balcony that also housed the kitchen and toilet, which they'd shared with their neighbors. There wasn't a shower, so they bathed using a tin bath and a pail in the kitchen. She'd boil water in the kettle and then fill the pail, but by the time it was full, the water would already be lukewarm. She liked bathing in lukewarm water, but David would get angry each time, as if it were her fault that they lived in an apartment without a shower, as if it were her fault they didn't have a bath with taps for hot and cold water and a wood-fired boiler like the one in the big apartment on King George Street. She hadn't imagined things would be this way. She'd been sure she'd marry a man who'd give her a good life, not one who'd get angry with her every time the water she heated wasn't hot enough for him.

Their relationship began cooling as early as their honeymoon, which they spent at the Savoy Hotel on the Tel Aviv seafront. After taking their baggage to their room, Luna had gone out onto the balcony and inhaled the sea air. The sea was as smooth as marble, and the sun emerged from the clouds and caressed her face. It was exactly how she'd envisioned her honeymoon, far from Jerusalem, far from Ohel Moshe and its houses crowded together, far from her family. At long last she was alone with the love of her life, with no need to report on where she was going and what time she'd be back, without seeing her mother's scowling face.

On the beach below the hotel were deck chairs, and reclining on them were Tel Avivans who were undeterred by the relatively cool weather. She was amazed each time anew on discovering how different Jerusalem was from Tel Aviv. The two cities were like two different worlds.

"David," she called to him, "let's go down to the promenade." But he'd already taken off his shoes and was lying on the bed immersed in a newspaper.

"David." She joined him on the bed, wheedling, planting tiny kisses on his cheeks, his head, his nose, his lips. He pushed her away and said, "Not now, Luna, I'm reading."

"David, we're on our honeymoon. Let's do something together. You'll have lots of time to read the paper."

"Just a minute. Let me finish this page."

Luna went back out onto the balcony. How she wanted to go down to the street in the hat she'd bought specially for her honeymoon, the black dress with the white belt that highlighted her waist, the patent leather high-heeled shoes. To put on lipstick, roll a curl on her finger, and pin it to her head. To glance in the mirror and know that she was the loveliest of all, and then go out and enjoy the looks of passersby. And maybe David too would see how beautiful she was and be jealous because of the other men's stares.

David was still deep in his paper, and she began to lose patience. "*Nu,* David, when are we going down? We're on our honeymoon! Let's go for a walk."

"All right, nudnik," he said reluctantly. He got up, put on his shoes and jacket, and only then looked at her. She was breathtaking. There was no doubt at all that his wife was the most beautiful of women, so why was it that from the moment she'd accepted his proposal of marriage, his heart had closed to her? Why wasn't he mesmerized by her like he had been at the beginning? Had he ever been attracted to her? Or had he simply convinced himself that he was in order to fulfill the promise he'd made the moment the ship departed Mestre Port: to find a woman and set up a Jewish home in the Land of Israel.

"What?" she said, expecting a compliment as he continued staring at her.

"Won't you be cold without a coat?" He opened the door to leave.

"How do I look?" she asked.

"You look lovely," he said languidly.

"In that case I won't be cold," she said and handed him a white angora fur cardigan to drape over her shoulders.

They went out, and though she wrapped an arm around his waist, he didn't put his arm around her shoulders. Never mind, they didn't have to walk with their arms around each other like they had before they were married, she consoled herself as she linked her arm with his instead.

As she'd expected, the passersby couldn't take their eyes off the striking couple. They went into a café and ordered milk shakes. At Café Atara they made milkshakes the way she liked, with mountains of whipped cream on top. In Tel Aviv the ice cream melted too quickly and the cream turned into water, but this didn't tarnish her enjoyment. The blue sea, the pleasant sun, the people strolling by or sitting on the café's terrace, the euphoric atmosphere—she was so happy. Even the English policemen at a table near theirs didn't spoil her good mood. When David said, "What, doesn't anybody work in Tel Aviv?" she laughed and laid a white-gloved hand on his arm.

"Are you happy?" she asked him. "Are you as happy as I am?"

"I'm happy," he replied, but his tone was unconvincing.

She decided to ignore it. She wasn't going to let anything ruin her honeymoon, not even her husband.

"Your lady is very pretty," the waiter said to David.

"Thank you," Luna quickly responded in David's place. "We're on our honeymoon."

"Mazal tov," the waiter said, and when he returned to their table he brought them a Savarina with a colorful umbrella on top. "This is to celebrate your honeymoon," he smiled. "Compliments of the house."

Poor Luna, she's so happy, David thought to himself. She has no idea how much I want this honeymoon that's barely begun to end. He didn't know how he'd get through the next seven days. He was supposed to be happy, to hug and kiss her, take her to cafés, for walks on the beach, the cinema, restaurants, and at night he was supposed to make love to her. How could he survive the first night when his heart and body still belonged to another woman? The woman he'd left behind in faraway Italy, the woman from whom he was now separated forever. No, he wouldn't let the memories from Venice ruin the honeymoon in Tel Aviv. He wouldn't let Isabella come between him and Luna. He'd forget her. He'd force himself to forget her. He loved Luna, and he'd continue to love her as if Isabella didn't exist. He'd give her a dream of a wedding night. He'd do everything in his power to make this radiant woman happy.

That night, true to his promise, he was gentle with her, very gentle. She loved kissing him, running her fingers through his tousled hair, stroking his back. At first she felt she was melting in his arms, but then each time he'd try to touch her body, she'd recoil. He'd reach for her breasts and she'd move away. He'd try to stroke her belly, but her body would go rigid.

"Is everything all right, my love?" he whispered.

"Yes," she replied shyly.

"So why are you running away from me?"

"I'm not running away."

"Come closer, I won't bite."

She took a deep breath and moved closer. She could go on kissing him for hours, but when he tried touching her in her most intimate places, she felt herself freezing up.

"Luna, I won't hurt you. I promise."

She kept silent and bit her lip. He moved closer to her again and slowly took off her nightgown. He tried to look at her body, her small, firm breasts, her flat belly, but she lay curled up like a fetus, trying to cover herself with her hands.

"Luna, let me see how beautiful you are."

David was very experienced. The thousand women he'd had in Italy and the one Isabella had made him a skilled lover. He liked sex, and once he'd discovered it he'd found it hard to abstain, but he hadn't been with another woman since he'd met Isabella. He knew he had to have intercourse with Luna because that's what you did on your wedding night, and even if he didn't enjoy it as he had with Isabella, it would happen all in good time.

"My lovely," he said with a gentleness that surprised even him, "my beloved, help me. Open your legs." But she was incapable of separating them. "Lunika, we won't be able to do it if you don't help me," he went on with infinite tenderness even though he felt he'd lose patience any minute.

She didn't say a word. Tears oozed from her eyes. This wasn't how she'd imagined her wedding night. She was sure that they'd kiss and suddenly it would happen, suddenly he'd be inside her. She hadn't anticipated that her body would resist so strongly and that she'd be so terrified.

He slid his hands under her body and undid her bra, and she shut her eyes. Even though it was dark he could see her blushing like a tomato. He caressed her small breasts. God, the thought flashed through his mind, where are Isabella's breasts, big and heavy and mature? My dear wife has two like a girl's.

Luna continued to be uncooperative. Her body was stiff, and she was shy and scared. Gabriel decided he'd had enough, rolled away, and turned his back to her.

Luna was horrified. God almighty, what have I done now? Was this what her honeymoon was supposed to be like? Her husband tries to make love to her and she is like a block of ice, so he turns over and goes to sleep? She burst into tears and whimpered like a wounded cat.

Her sobbing tore at his heart. What a son of a bitch he was! What was he doing to his beautiful wife? How the hell had he dared to harden his heart to her? How had he given up on her so quickly? David took Luna in his arms, rocking her back and forth, kissing her, trying to soothe her. He felt her slowly relaxing, and this time when he tried to penetrate her, she didn't resist. She groaned in pain, but he was good to her, speaking words of love. And with each word her body melted even more until he was inside her and streams of blood dripped down her thighs. He got up, fetched a towel from the bathroom, and gently dabbed away the blood.

"What will we tell the reception clerk?" she whispered giddily. "How embarrassing."

The feeling of embarrassment was almost as strong as the sense of relief she felt now that they'd finally done it. She'd lost her virginity on her wedding night just like any normal bride, and now she could start living.

The week-long honeymoon came to an end, and they returned to Jerusalem. They hadn't made love much during the week. They kissed, hugged, walked along the promenade, shopped on Allenby Street, sat in cafés, and ate in restaurants. They even went to the cinema and saw *Casablanca* with Ingrid Bergman and Humphrey Bogart. When they'd get back to their room, they'd lay side by side on the bed, he reading a newspaper and she *Cinema World*. Then they'd change into pajamas, embrace, and go to sleep. She was surprised that he didn't want to make love every night, but she was also relieved.

After their honeymoon their life entered the routine of a married couple. She continued at Zacks & Son, and he found work at a carpentry shop near the Rex Cinema at the end of Princess Mary Street. After work he'd sometimes go and see a cowboy film at the Rex. The theater's audience was a mixture of Jews and Arabs, and Luna didn't like it there, so whenever he went to the Rex she'd go to her parents' house and visit her sisters, and afterward David would escort her back to their studio in Mekor Baruch. Some evenings they went to the cinema with Rachelika and Moise, and then they'd go out to a café. On Fridays after Shabbat dinner with Luna's parents they'd meet David's friends from the Jewish Brigade and their wives, and with the big group of Luna's friends and cousins, they'd all get together at a different apartment and spend the night talking about the situation and cracking sunflower seeds. They'd spend Saturdays with the family, and after the Shabbat hamin at lunchtime, the men would go to a soccer match, and Luna, Rachelika, and Becky would stay and chat in their parents' house.

Every now and then David would remember that he had to observe the "be fruitful and multiply" precept, and he'd come to her. She'd lie on the bed in silence and wait for him to finish what he was doing, and then she'd flutter her lips over his cheeks, run her hand once or twice over his back, and wait for him to fall asleep. After, she'd get up, go into the kitchen, and wash her body with soap and water, scrubbing her skin hard. She couldn't stand the stickiness on her thighs. It roused a feeling of dirtiness and disgust in her that she couldn't ignore.

In Jerusalem, where women got pregnant right after their wedding night, the fact that Luna and David had been married for a few months and she wasn't yet carrying a child was cause for concern.

"Dio santo, Gabriel," Rosa said to her husband, "how is it that she still doesn't have a child in her belly?"

"Don't interfere," Gabriel said. "Everyone at their own pace."

"But God forgive my sins, Gabriel, it's been seven months since the wedding."

"Rosa," he said assertively, "haste is of the devil. All in good time."

Rachelika too was worried by the fact that her sister wasn't pregnant. When she'd discovered she was with child a month after her own wedding night, she'd decided not to tell anybody so as not to embarrass Luna. But when she began to show in the third month, she couldn't conceal it any longer.

Luna had showered her with kisses and wished her mazal tov, and to Rachelika's surprise, she couldn't discern even a hint of envy in her sister.

"I don't understand," she said to Moise afterward, "how Luna isn't pregnant yet."

He sighed.

"Do you know something I don't?" Rachelika asked him. "Does your friend David have problems?"

"Problems?" Moise laughed. "Who knows how many children he left behind in Italy."

"Did you find out anything about the Kurd?" Gabriel asked Handsome Eli Cohen.

"No, Senor Ermosa, unfortunately I haven't found anything. He doesn't have an account with our bank. He probably keeps his money under the floor tiles. But I'm still convinced there's something behind his wanting to buy the shop."

"We'll sell him the shop," Gabriel said wearily. "Later, when Rachelika and Moise come, we'll decide on the price. But Eli, I'd like you to be here too. You're like family now."

"Yes, Senor Ermosa, with pleasure."

They held the family meeting after dinner. Becky and Rachelika cleared the table while Luna remained seated, her low spirits on full display.

"You get up too, princess," Gabriel told her. "Help your sisters and mother."

When the girls finished and were about to help Rosa wash the dishes, Gabriel called them over. "Come, queridas, leave the dishes till later. Come and sit down with us. You too, Becky."

Becky was stunned. She'd always been treated like a baby, the family's little girl. She knew her father had invited her because of Eli, her Eli who was now helping determine the future of the shop. She felt a surge of pride. What a boy she had. She loved him. How would she survive the three-year wait until they could stand beneath the wedding canopy?

"You too, Rosa, come and sit with us," Gabriel called to his wife who was still at the sink.

She turned around, a towel in her hand, and looked questioningly at him.

"Come, querida, you too should have a say in the decision."

Rosa felt that her heart would burst out of her chest. This was the first time in her life that her husband had shown her such respect, and in front of the girls and sons-in-law too, the first time he was including her in a talk about the family's future. *Ya ribon*, the Days of the Messiah have come, she thought. He must be very sick, miskenico, if he's asking me to take part in a discussion about the shop. She took off her apron and sat down next to Rachelika.

"Come and sit next to me," Gabriel said. "You are the senora of the house. You should sit next to the senor."

She got up and Moise gave her his place. "My pleasure, Senora Rosa, my pleasure."

She liked Moise. He was like the son she never had, and in her heart he filled the place left by Ephraim. Ephraim, she'd almost forgotten what he looked like. Her yearning and concern for him had given way to ire. She was angry at his lack of consideration, that he didn't even send a sign of life. After all, he knew how much she worried about him, and he—nada—he behaved like he had no family, so he could go to hell. If that's what he wants then so be it. He has no family.

Every now and then Rosa was alarmed when she heard about underground operations and arrests. She didn't even know the difference between Lehi and Etzel. They were one and the same for her. Her heart almost stopped beating when she'd heard that twelve members of Lehi disguised as Arab prisoners and British policemen had attacked the Ramat Gan police station, blowing open the armory door, taking the weapons, and loading them onto a waiting vehicle. She was sure that Ephraim was one of them, and it was only when the names of the casualties and captives were announced that she heaved a sigh of relief. Who knew how many times she and Gabriel had argued after he quoted Ben-Gurion, who'd said he wouldn't lift a finger to help free Dov Gruner, the commander of the operation who had been captured.

"He didn't take the weapons for himself," Rosa insisted. "He took them to liberate us from the Ingelish."

"And killed innocent people along the way," Gabriel retorted angrily. "If Ben-Gurion doesn't want to help a Jew, then things have reached a low point."

"Dio santo, Gabriel, that Ben-Gurion has addled your brain. He's made you blind."

"Silence, woman! I don't talk from emotion like you. I read the papers before I talk. I understand the situation. And you, without reading, without knowing, without understanding, talk nonsense. Do you think I don't know it's because of your brother the borracho who's with them?" And with that he put an end to the conversation.

Now the Days of the Messiah were here, and God be praised, her husband was showing her respect in front of the whole family.

"I've given this a lot of thought," Gabriel began. "Rachelika and Moise are right. There's no point in holding on to the shop, which, as that dog Mordoch said, is a bottomless pit. We're spending money we don't have to pay taxes to the municipality that cheats us shamelessly, and we're not bringing in a single grush. But I don't want to sell to the Kurd. I thought that if we advertise in the market that we're selling the shop, then perhaps we'll find other buyers."

"Senor Ermosa," Moise said, "please don't be angry, but I've already spoken to some people about the shop, and believe me, at a time like this nobody has the money to buy property. They all want to sell and there aren't any buyers."

"So if everybody wants to sell, why doesn't the Kurd buy somebody else's shop? Why does he want ours?" Luna burst out.

"A good question," Gabriel replied. "Why is he so insistent on buying our shop?"

"Forgive me, Senor Ermosa," Eli Cohen interjected, "I don't want to contradict my future brother-in-law, but although times are hard, nobody's selling their shop. People are holding on to their property as if their life depends on it."

"I was talking about the few who do want to sell," Moise persisted.

"Where are their shops located in the market?" Handsome Eli Cohen asked.

"One's on Agrippas Street near Rachmo, another's in the alley by the Iraqi market."

"And where is Senor Ermosa's shop?" Eli said. "On Etz Ha'Haim Street, the market's main street, the best location with the largest number of customers passing by. That's why the Kurd wants this particular shop."

"There's a lot of sense in what Eli's saying," Gabriel said.

"So what do you suggest we do, Papo?" Rachelika asked.

"I suggest we listen to Eli. What do you say, habibi?" he asked the young man, and Becky felt herself blush as her heart swelled with pride.

"The best thing," Eli said, "is to hear what Mordoch's offering and go from there."

But when they heard the Kurd's offer, it was so low that they rejected it on the spot.

The sound of a huge explosion catapulted Luna from her place behind the counter at Zacks & Son. The shop was empty, and only a few minutes earlier Mr. Zacks had walked across Jaffa Road to deposit the morning's takings in the bank.

Within minutes the street was filled with the wail of sirens from British police vehicles driving by the shop at high speed, passing Zion Square and on toward Princess Mary Street. Thick smoke rose into the sky from the direction of Mamilla and the entire area seemed engulfed in chaos. Soon enough the street had emptied. Alone in the shop, Luna was scared to death. A sense of foreboding gripped her. She wanted to get out of there as quickly as possible and run to her parents' house, but how could she? She couldn't leave the shop open and unattended. The keys were with Mr. Zacks, who hadn't yet returned from the bank. But before she could decide what to do Mr. Zacks came running in, out of breath. "There's been an explosion at the King David," he said. "Run home before the curfew starts."

"God help us. David, what about David? The carpentry shop's right next to the Rex Cinema. It's only five minutes from the King David."

"David's a man, he'll look after himself. Run home before the English put up concertina wire all over the city and you can't get anywhere."

Luna hurried toward Agrippas Street, her high heels catching in the cobblestones and making her stumble. In the end she took them off and ran barefoot. When she got to her parents' home, her father was already sitting at the radio surrounded by neighbors who'd come to listen to the news. "Thank God you're here," he said to his daughter. "And David, where is he?"

"He probably can't get over here."

Panting, Moise and Rachelika arrived a few minutes after Luna.

"We closed the shop," Moise said. "The whole market's closed. They're saying the Etzel blew up the British offices in the King David."

"Where's Becky?" Rachelika asked.

All of them were anxious about Becky. Rosa restlessly paced from one room to another. Not only was she worried about Becky, but whenever a disaster happened that evidently involved members of the Lehi or Etzel, despite her anger she was scared half to death that something had happened to Ephraim, God forbid.

Gabriel turned up the volume on the radio. The Voice of Jerusalem newsreader announced that at 12:37 an explosion in Jerusalem shook the city. An entire wing of the King David Hotel had been destroyed, leaving shattered masonry and clouds of dust behind. "The number of dead is still unknown, and whether there are Jews among them," the newsreader reported.

Gabriel turned off the radio and the arguments for and against the action began in loud voices. Luna blocked her ears, went into the other room, lay down on her childhood bed, and buried her face in the pillow.

The door opened and Rachelika stood in the doorway. "What's the matter, Luna?"

"Enough, enough, I've had enough! I can't take anymore! I can't take this tension! Every day there's shooting. Every day there's explosions. Every day there are people killed. And who knows where Becky and David are? Who knows where they're stuck with all this danger out there?"

"David probably went to look for you at Zacks & Son," Rachelika tried to calm her sister. "And when he sees that the shop's closed he'll come here, and Becky will be here soon. Calm down, Lunika, now's not the time for hysterics."

"What do you want me to do? I'm dead scared that something will happen to me, dead scared that a building will collapse on me when I'm walking down the street, dead scared I'll be shot by mistake. I'm living in fear all the time!"

"Tell me, hermanita, what's really frightening you? Is it the situation out there or your personal one?"

"What are you talking about?"

"Luna, I'm your sister. I look at you and I see that your lovely eyes are sad. What's the matter, Lunika?"

"Nothing's the matter. You're talking nonsense."

"Lunika querida, please talk to me. I don't want to interfere in your business, but if there's something you want to tell me, if there's something troubling you, talk to me."

"The only thing that's troubling me right now is you. Just leave me alone!"

"All right, if that's what you want, but I know that something not good is going on. You can't hide it from me. You can put on a show for Papo and Mother, but not for me."

"Mother doesn't even look at me, so I don't have to hide anything from her."

"So it's true? There's something you're hiding?"

"I'm not hiding anything. Just get out of here!" she screamed as if possessed by a dybbuk and threw a pillow at her sister. "Get out of here! If you weren't pregnant I'd throw a shoe at you!"

The shouts brought Moise rushing in. "What happened?"

"Nothing happened," Rachelika replied. "Let's go."

Luna buried her face in the pillow and began weeping uncontrollably. She cried for a long time, her sobs turning into gasps. She wept for her life that had lost its meaning, for her youth lost forever, for her husband who she now knew for sure she shouldn't have married. How had it happened that she of all people, to whom so many men were prepared to give the moon, had married a man who didn't love her?

She suddenly felt that she wasn't alone. She opened her eyes and saw

Rachelika sitting silently on the bed beside her. Rachelika stroked her head and brushed her tears away.

"Why are you crying, Lunika, why are you crying?"

She felt she could no longer go on living the lie. She had to tell her sister.

"I'm crying over my life, hermanita, my wasted life. I waited for my knight on a white horse for so long and he came, but he's not a knight or anything like it."

"What are you saying? What's happening with you and David?"

"Tell me, Rachelika, how often do you and Moise do it?"

"Do what?"

"You know, do *it*."

"Luna, what kind of a question is that?"

"All right, it's clear that you do. Otherwise your belly wouldn't be swelling, and it's clear that David and I don't do it," she said and lifted her blouse to expose her flat belly.

"Luna, what do you mean, you don't do it?"

"How often do you and Moise do it?"

"Every night."

"Every night since you got married?"

"Every night, and sometimes in the morning before he goes to work."

"Even now that you're pregnant?"

Rachelika blushed to the roots of her hair and nodded embarrassedly. "And you, Luna, how often do you do it?"

Luna lowered her eyes and said dejectedly, "Once on our wedding night, and after that, sometimes, but not all the time, not every night."

"Are you serious, Luna? You haven't been married a year yet. You're still on your honeymoon."

"It's not David's fault. It's me that doesn't like it."

"How can you not like it? Don't you want children? Where do you think children come from, the stork brings them?"

"I don't like it."

"Sometimes I don't like it either, but I never say no. Even if I don't like it at first, I do afterward, and when my husband tells me he loves me, that I'm the love of his life, that he can't live without me, I like it a lot."

"But David never says things like that to me."

"He doesn't tell you he loves you?"

"He doesn't love me."

"God help us, Luna, what are you saying?"

"He doesn't love me. Instead of coming home after work, he goes to the Rex Cinema. He goes to the Rex on purpose because he knows I don't like it there because of the Arabs from the Old City. He plays cards with his friends twice a week, and once a week they go for a drink at the bar over the Edison where only men go and no decent woman would step inside."

"And you're at home on your own? Why didn't you tell me?"

"What would I have said, that my husband leaves his wife alone in their first year of marriage?"

"But you don't like being on your own."

"I hate being on my own. I'm scared of being on my own, and in Mekor Baruch too, so far away from everything I know."

"What about your neighbors?"

"I told you, I don't want the neighbors knowing that I'm on my own. If I don't talk about it, then nobody else will know."

How naive she is, Rachelika thought to herself. The nosy neighbors must notice the unusual times that David gets home. Luna is surely the subject of malicious gossip.

"Once," Luna said, "our next-door neighbor asked me why my husband comes home so late at night, and I told her that there are things you don't talk about, so she probably thinks he's in the Haganah."

"Miskenica." Rachelika hugged her sister. How dare that bastard David treat her sister like this. She'd show him, her stupid brother-in-law. She'd open his eyes for him.

"Eli, God be praised, Eli," they heard Rosa burst out from the other room. Luna quickly dried her tears and the two sisters ran to greet Becky.

"When I heard the explosion at the King David I got on my motorbike and raced to Becky's school," Eli explained.

"Eli drove like a lunatic," said the excited Becky. "Even if the English had wanted to, they wouldn't have caught him. He drove like the wind."

"May you be healthy," Rosa said. "May you be healthy, Eli. I won't forget that you brought our Becky home safely."

"All my life I'll bring Becky safely to anywhere," he promised Rosa, who knew that he would keep that promise.

Gabriel nodded and beckoned Eli over to him.

"Well done," he told him. "I'm liking you more and more. With God's help, when Becky turns seventeen we'll announce your engagement, but in the meantime I want you to know that I consider you one of the family, that you're my son-in-law no less than David and Moise."

"I'm honored, Senor Ermosa, greatly honored. I thank you from the bottom of my heart."

"Don't thank me, may you be healthy, just look after my daughter. Now she's home safely at last, it's time to eat. Heideh, Rosa, some food on the table."

Gabriel noticed that Luna and Rachelika had shut themselves in the other room for some time. Luna's behavior had worried him recently. She had lost a lot of weight and the radiance she always displayed seemed to have dimmed. He didn't know why his daughter was sad, but he was glad she had Rachelika. That she didn't have to endure whatever it was alone.

The number of dead in the King David bombing reached ninety-one: forty-one Arabs, twenty-eight British, five foreign nationals, and seventeen Jews. That night David stayed in the carpentry shop and slept on the sawdust together with the owner and the other workers. It was impossible to leave the shop. Had there been a telephone in his father-in-law's house he would have called from the public phone in the adjacent post office and assured them he was all right. He recalled Luna telling him that when they lived in the big apartment on King George Street, their neighbor who was a doctor had a phone, but that didn't help now.

Much water had flowed in the streams around Jerusalem since the Ermosa family left King George Street, mainly muddy water. His father-in-law's health was bad, his business situation even worse. The question of selling the shop was still in the air, and he himself had no opinion. With all due respect to his marriage to Luna, David didn't feel close to his father-in-law, nor did he feel close to his wife. How had he thought that everything would work out if he got married? How had he thought that another woman, even a stunning beauty like Luna, could replace Isabella in his heart?

He missed her. There hadn't been a night since he'd left her weeping on the Mestre pier that he hadn't thought about her, recalling over and over the first time he saw her riding her bike in shorts that showed off her long tanned legs. Her white shirt tied at the waist revealed a tanned, rounded belly, and her large breasts seemed like they were about to burst from the buttoned shirt. David remembered her striking, dark-skinned face and almond eyes, her long hair that she secured with a ribbon.

"*Ciao, bella*," he'd called to her. She'd stopped and gotten off her bike, and from that moment his life had changed. He, whose friends dubbed "Solomon" because he had a thousand wives, he, who spent every night with a different woman, had fallen head over heels with the gorgeous Italian woman who introduced herself as Isabella. How could he have thought that he would be able to forget her? He hadn't forgotten her even when he was courting Luna. Back then he'd repressed his feelings, determined to marry, have children, a family. But how could he have children when he hardly made love to his wife? Moise and Rachelika married after them and were already expecting. And for he and Luna, where would children come from, the milkman? He had to make love to his wife, he had to give her a child; otherwise there'd be talk. Luna didn't deserve to be talked about. She was a good girl. He had to change. On my life, just let us get through this night, and starting tomorrow things will be different.

"We have to talk," Rachelika said to Moise.

"We talk all the time, my love," he replied and kissed her belly.

"It's serious. It's about Luna and David."

Moise tensed. "What about Luna and David? What's happened now?"

"Do you know that they don't have marital relations?"

"What are you saying?"

"What you're hearing. That 'Solomon' of yours who's had a thousand women, the famous lover, doesn't have intercourse with his wife."

"Rachelika, that's none of our business."

"It most certainly is. We got married after them and I'm already pregnant. I feel terrible for my sister. Soon people will start talking."

"And I still say, my love, that it's none of our business."

"Is there something you're not telling me about David, Moise? You're not behaving as if you can't see or hear for no reason. I know you."

"My love who is more precious to me than life itself, what I know about David is between me and him. I can't talk to you about my best friend."

"It's long since not been between you and him." Rachelika became annoyed and got up from the couch. "From the moment he marries my sister and doesn't make love to her at night, it's no longer a kid's game."

"My heart and soul, with all my love for you and the respect I have for you, I'm not prepared to talk about other people's marriages."

"And you think I am? Do you think it was easy for me to talk about it with my sister? Do you think it was easy for her to talk about it with me? We don't talk about things like that in our family. No one ever explained to us what you do or don't do on your wedding night. Once upon a time mothers would explain to their daughters, fathers would explain to their sons, but with us, nada. My mother didn't tell me a thing."

"So you didn't know what to do, querida mia?"

"Moise, not every woman has a husband like you who's considerate and gentle and loving. Not everyone loves the way we do. We're very lucky."

"I thought that Luna and David were lucky as well," Moise replied.

"Shit is what my sister's got, not luck. Your dreck of a friend is breaking her heart, and if you don't tell me what's eating him, I'm going out that door to my mother."

"Calm down, my precious, you mustn't excite yourself. Think of the baby."

"Then start talking!"

Moise mulled over telling Rachelika the truth about David. Would she be able to keep his love for Isabella a secret from her sister? She was his beloved wife, and he wanted to share it with her, to reveal what lay behind David's behavior, but words had their own way of always reaching the wrong ears. Words had the power to destroy, even when uttered with the best of intentions. He decided it would be better to keep it to himself. Perhaps the situation would change in time and the words would not hold the power they had now.

"Are you going to tell me or am I leaving?" she roused him from his thoughts. Moise cleared his throat and said, "When we were in Italy, David really did have a thousand women, maybe more. He'd change girls like he changed his socks. He was pretty wild, that David."

Rachelika noticed that Moise was squirming in his chair. "Spit it out, Moise. What aren't you telling me about David?"

"Don't you understand anything I've just told you?" he replied. "How could you not understand, my lovely? I thought I married Senor Gabriel Ermosa's smartest daughter."

"I don't understand because you haven't explained it, troncho de Tveria. How is David having a million women in Italy connected with him not making love to his wife?"

"He's used to being free, a butterfly. He's not used to being with just one woman. He needs time to adjust to it."

"God help us! What are you saying, that he's cheating on Luna?"

"Heaven forbid, Rachelika! Did I say he's cheating? God forbid anyone hears you. I'm saying he's like a little boy, he needs time to get used to being married. He'll grow up and you'll see what a wonderful husband he is. I promise you we'll be hearing good news before the month is out."

Rachelika bought his story, and Moise breathed a sigh of relief. Now he had to have a talk with David and give him hell. He had to get the stupid ass in line before a disaster erupted and destroyed the whole family.

Luna brushed her bronze hair with her fingers, rolling a curl around one finger, then putting the finger into her mouth to wet the curl. She gazed at the mirror. She was still beautiful; it was just a pity that her husband couldn't see it.

It was early evening. A short while ago she had come home from work, since Mr. Zacks had closed the shop early. He had been very depressed lately. The situation in Jerusalem had gotten to him, and even she hadn't been in the mood to buy new clothes.

Instead of going to her parents' home as usual, Luna had decided to head for her and David's studio in Mekor Baruch. Her conversation with Rachelika weighed heavily on her. She shouldn't have talked to her sister about their intimate life. That was a secret nobody else should know, not even her sister. And anyway, what had come of spilling her heart to Rachelika? What had come of seeing her sister's horrified expression when she'd told her that David didn't make love to her? How could her dear Rachelika help? She had only hurt her sister with what she had confided. And what if Rachelika couldn't restrain herself and told Moise, and what if Moise told David, and what if David decided she had a big mouth and left her?

God Almighty, what had become of her? She who'd had it all, suitors just waiting for her to toss them a word, who stopped breathing as she passed, who swooned at a smile from her, now married to a man who hardly looked at her? How had such a disaster befallen her of all people? Perhaps it was because she had too high an opinion of herself? Because she felt she was queen of the world? Had she behaved badly toward people because she was so full of herself? Forgive me, God, forgive me for forgetting the upbringing I was given by my father.

Modesty in all things, that's what her father had always taught her. Never be boastful, do not be prideful about what God has given you, always remember that there are people who have less than you. But she had forgotten and committed the sin of arrogance, which, so her father had told her more than once, was the most terrible of them all.

Despite the oppressive heat in the room, Luna was shivering. She put on a sweater over her dress, but it did not warm her. She went to the gramophone on the sideboard and put on a record. "Bésame, bésame mucho," Emilio Tuero sang in his mellifluous voice, managing to thaw the cold that enveloped her. She began moving her body side to side to the rhythm, closing her eyes, her feet carrying her of their own volition lightly across the room. When the record finished, she put the needle back on and continued dancing, hugging her body, overcome by loneliness and a longing for the man who had not touched her in such a long time, longing for love of the kind she'd dreamed about but didn't have. She danced and danced until she became exhausted, dropped onto the bed, and fell asleep.

That's how David found her when he got home late that evening, at a time when young husbands were already making love to their wives. He'd gone to see a cowboy film and waited until it was late so that by the time he got home he'd find his wife asleep.

She was curled up on her side, so small in contrast with the wide bed. He brushed a red curl from her eye and studied his beautiful wife. He felt badly for her, miskenica. She'd probably waited and waited for him until she'd fallen asleep. The needle was still scratching the revolving record and he lifted it, switched off the gramophone, and replaced the record in its sleeve. What's happening to me? He asked himself the question that had so troubled him since their wedding night. Why has my heart turned to stone? He took a blanket from the closet and covered Luna, then quietly changed into his pajamas and lay down beside her. She was lying in the middle of the bed, not leaving much room for him, and he was afraid to touch her accidentally. What would happen if she woke up? Would he have to talk to her? Would he have to hug her? Make love to her? He was so ashamed of himself. What would the guys from the brigade say if they knew he didn't touch his wife?

"I have to talk to you," Moise said to David when they went out to the yard for a cigarette after Friday-evening dinner at Gabriel and Rosa's house.

"I can't help with the shop," David said quickly. "I don't understand anything at all about it, so whatever you and our father-in-law decide is fine by me."

"I don't want to talk about the shop, David. I want to talk about Luna."

"Luna? What do you have to say to me about Luna?"

"Not now, David. Just the two of us need to talk, without all the family close by."

"There's nobody here now, there's just you and me. So talk, Moise."

"What's going on between you and Luna?"

"Everything's fine, thank God."

"Are you sure everything's fine, amigo?"

"Why wouldn't it be fine?"

"Because her sister thinks that nothing is fine."

"Her sister? Since when has her sister interfered in our business?"

"That's it, she's not interfering, I am. I think you're ruining your life. I think you'll bring down disaster on the family."

"Hold it, Moise, stop right there! With all due respect to you being like a brother, I won't let you speak to me like that!"

"Come on, David. What, you think that I *want* to interfere? I'm saying this because I care. You think that people can't see that something's not right between you and Luna? That people don't have eyes?"

"If you mean that you're ahead of me and got your wife pregnant first, then well done you, Moise, but I'm not competing with you. You've evidently forgotten that there are methods that prevent pregnancy."

"Stop with the stories, David, I know exactly what's going on. Get this into your head: There's no more Isabella! Your life with her stayed in Italy! You're married to Luna now, and listen well, amigo, you start behaving like a man, respect her and do your duty as a husband, be the father of her children, because if you don't, you'll have me to deal with. On my life, David, if you don't come to your senses and get things back on track, I'll break every bone in your body!"

David was stunned. Moise, his quiet, gentle friend, had never spoken to him so vehemently. Moise had always respected him, and it had always been David who had told Moise what to do, who had given advice, arranged things, taken him under his wing and even found him a wife.

But Moise was dead serious, and although his words had surprised and angered David, he knew there was truth in them. He knew that if he didn't start behaving with Luna as a husband behaves with his wife, there would be a disaster and God only knew how it might end.

He stubbed out his cigarette and followed Moise back into the house.

"Heideh, Lunika," he called to his wife. "Let's go home."

"What did you say to David?" Rachelika whispered to Moise.

"Me?" he asked, playing dumb. "I didn't say anything to him. We just had a cigarette together."

"Sure, sure," she said and hugged him.

For many days the shop had been devoid of customers. Moise repeatedly cleaned the half-empty shelves, and Rachelika must have swept the floor a thousand times. They had stopped setting the larger sacks outside. They were empty and there was no way of refilling them, and even if there was, where would they have gotten the money to buy fresh supplies? They had let Avramino go. Gabriel had almost dug his heels in when she and Moise had told him there was no choice.

And times were so hard that shortly after they had to let Uncle Matzliach go too. And that was much harder. Matzliach was deeply hurt.

"After all I've done for my brother?" he told his niece. "After I've given my heart and soul to this shop you're sending me home?"

"Forgive me, Tio," Rachelika lowered her eyes to the floor. She couldn't find the courage to look at her uncle. "We don't have the money to pay you."

"Does my brother Gabriel know that you're throwing me into the street?"

"Papo is broken by it, Tio. We had to let Avramino go, we're letting you go, and soon we'll be left with no choice but to go as well."

"You should be ashamed of yourself," Matzliach said, fuming. "I carried you in my arms when you were a baby. You should be ashamed that you're throwing your old uncle out like this."

"I *am* ashamed, Tio," she said, wishing she could disappear, "but there's no choice."

Tio Matzliach spat on the floor, threw his apron at Rachelika, and left the shop. Her eyes filled with tears and she collapsed into Moise's arms.

"Shhh . . . shhh, my sweet one. Think of the baby. This isn't good for it," Moise said in a soothing voice.

"I wish my father had done it and not given me this loathsome job."

"Your father kept Matzliach on for many years even though he was a lazy worker."

"And he never stopped complaining," Rachelika added.

"And took home a tithe from the goods, and not only on the first of the month," Moise went on.

"You saw that?" She laughed. "I thought I was the only one who noticed."

"Your father knew about it too but turned a blind eye. Don't feel bad. I'm sure that as soon as the situation improves your father will help. It'll be all right."

But nothing was all right. Matzliach was so angry at being let go that he broke off relations with Gabriel and his family. "I don't want any favors from them," he told Allegra when he went to Tel Aviv to vent his rage and inform his mother of Gabriel's disrespect.

"Blood is thicker than water," he said. "And if Gabriel treats me like water, he can go to hell."

"Heaven help us, what are you saying, *tfu-tfu-tfu!*" Allegra said, upset.

"He threw me into the street like a dog. It's as if he killed me!"

"Are you sure Gabriel knows that his daughter fired you?" Mercada asked, stepping in.

"What do you think, madre querida, that Rachelika would do something without her father knowing about it?"

"You never know," Mercada said. "Gabriel is at home sick. He hasn't gone to the shop in a long time. Now it's Rachelika and her Maghrebi who are running it. Perhaps they sent you home on their own. The Maghrebis," she said, spitting contemptuously, "are Scots, they're misers. You go to your brother's house now, tell him that they've left you without food! Do you hear me? You won't give in to his daughter and the Maghrebi. You'll talk to your brother, your flesh and blood. One brother doesn't go against the other. Behaving like that with family is not in our blood."

"It's not in our blood? Madre querida," Allegra intervened, "if it's not in our blood, how is it that for years you haven't been to Jerusalem to see how your favorite son is and you haven't shown any interest in his health, when now, God forgive my sins, it's as bad as ever?"

"Don't be insolent!" the old woman scolded her, but Allegra, who had long since lost patience with her irritable mother, went on. "You have to go and see Gabriel in Jerusalem yourself. Tell him you've forgiven him, and maybe he'll get out of the chair he sits in all the time, go back to the shop, and together with Rachelika and the Maghrebi he'll get it back on its feet, and then he'll take Matzliach back."

"I'm not going to Jerusalem even if the Messiah comes!" the old woman retorted, banging her cane on the floor.

"If you don't go and see Gabriel, then don't send Matzliach to him. I'm sure that Rachelika consulted him before firing Matzliach, so why send him now? To rub salt in his wounds?"

"Why are you defending him?" Matzliach asked angrily. "I gave him years of loyal service. For years I carried sacks on my back, I worked with the broom, with dusters. I covered for him when he took his afternoon nap, looked after the shop so nobody would steal, God forbid, and now look at me—a man who'll soon be a grandfather left without a livelihood. Is that how a brother behaves?"

"I'm sure it's because he has no choice. You said yourself that the shop's in bad condition, that there's almost nothing to sell and no customers to sell to," Allegra said, trying to defuse his anger.

"Well, at least he could have kept me on out of respect."

"His respect for you doesn't allow him to keep you on without paying you. You have to go to him, kiss his hand, and ask him to forgive you for your behavior."

"*Bukra fil mishmish*, out of the question. *I'll* ask *his* forgiveness? He won't hear a single word from me. Not from me, not from my wife, and not from my children! I'm finished with my brother, do you hear, Mother? I'm finished with Gabriel!"

"Do what you want," Mercada said. "I have nothing to say in the matter. Nobody respects my opinion."

"And you've brought that on yourself, madre querida," Allegra said and flounced out of the room.

The falling-out with his brother hurt Gabriel very much, but his body hurt him more than anything. From day to day it became harder for him to move, and he stumbled with his speech, on many occasions choosing to keep quiet rather than utter such heavy, clumsy words.

Rosa too was not the woman she had been. Even though Gabriel was increasingly engrossed in himself, he could not help but notice how old age had crept up on her, how wrinkles now furrowed her face. It pained him to see that not only had her relationship with Luna not improved since his daughter's wedding, it had worsened.

For years he had ignored how his favorite daughter treated Rosa as if she were nothing. After Luna married and left the house, he'd hoped that she would change her attitude toward her mother. He'd thought that now she was a wife herself and had her own home to run, and with God's help would become a mother and give him and Rosa a grandchild, she would finally grow up and stop being the child who bickered with her mother about every little thing. But Luna didn't change. Even though it vexed him, he was in such pain and so weak that he was unable to speak to her about it, and his heart filled with great sadness. The child who had restored light to his life, the joy, the love who had filled his most difficult times with happiness, who had to some extent eased the pain of longing for that woman whose name he didn't even want to remember, had grown into a woman whose personality he despised, a woman whose only interest was clothes and having a good time, who lived in a world of her own as if people weren't getting killed every day, as if war wasn't on the horizon, as if the whole world was her stupid magazines and Hollywood. She wasn't even carrying a child in her belly yet, and it had been months since the wedding at the Menorah Club that had cost him almost all the money he'd had left.

Rosa had been right: Luna was different from all other people. She wasn't like her sisters Rachelika and Becky. They'd all come to their house, sit around the radio, and she, she wouldn't be interested in hearing what they'd have to say. She'd go into her childhood room and occupy herself with nonsense. Rachelika had made him very angry when she'd gone to Haganah activities without his permission, but at least she'd cared, at least she'd wanted to be part of establishing a Jewish state in Palestine. But Luna, nada. Her magazines and lipstick were her culture. He felt he had failed in her upbringing, and what hurt most was that he had been slowly drifting away from her and now preferred the company of his clever, good Rachelika.

Gabriel tried to ease his position in the cushioned chair, but every movement hurt him. He turned up the volume on the radio. Lately he'd also had difficulty hearing. The radio was permanently set to the Voice of Jerusalem station, and it had become the center of his life. From the moment he'd open his eyes in the morning he'd switch on the radio and not turn it off until he went to bed. Since he'd stopped leaving the house, the sound of the radio had become his pipeline to the outside world. He'd learned from the radio that the curfew imposed on Shabbat had been dubbed Operation Agatha by the British, and the Black Sabbath by the Yishuv. More than a hundred thousand soldiers and policemen had surrounded Tel Aviv and Jerusalem and imposed a curfew on dozens of settlements and kibbutzim. Some three thousand Jews had been arrested, including members of the Jewish Agency. He'd also heard on the radio about the hanging of three British sergeants. Everything announced on the radio immediately became the talk of the day.

The situation in the country seemed to be changing quickly. Rachelika told him about a bunch of children who encountered English soldiers as they exited the Alliance School near the shop. The children stood facing the soldiers and began singing "Kalaniot," which had become a song of mockery of the British soldiers. The soldiers lost their temper and started chasing the children, cursing them in English, but the children evaded them to the joyful shouts of the vendors and merchants, who all gave the English the finger.

"They're not scared of the kalaniot anymore, Papo. I actually heard somebody yell 'Gestapo' at them."

Gabriel was sorry he was not able to be in the Mahane Yehuda Market at a time like this. He would have spat in the faces of the English himself. And when the big demonstrations erupted, with masses of people carrying banners and shouting, "Free immigration, a Jewish state!" he was deeply saddened that his physical condition did not allow him to participate. Fortunately he had his radio and Rachelika to keep him abreast of the situation, and happily the neighbors came and sat with him by the radio and exchanged views. That at least made him feel included, that he wasn't completely cut off from what was happening outside. Each day Rachelika had brought him a paper from the fat newspaper seller who always asked after him, but due to the family's finances, she'd started buying only one copy per week.

The newspaper seller, who noticed that Senor Ermosa's daughter wasn't coming every day, would pass by the shop and give her a copy of the previous day's paper.

"Give it to your father," he'd tell her. "Yesterday's news is good today as well."

Gabriel silently thanked his newspaper seller friend for yesterday's paper but still felt a twinge in his heart. If things didn't get any better, tomorrow the market stallholders would start sending him fruit and vegetables, and the butcher would send him meat. He was deeply ashamed that he was in such dire straits. He, who had always given freely to others, now felt like a beggar.

"Gabriel querido"—he heard Rosa's voice from the other room—"heideh, the food's on the table." How could he get up out of his chair and go to the table in this state? "Querido, the food will get cold," she went on. He tried to get up but couldn't.

"Do you need help, Papo?" Rachelika was beside him. How the child read his thoughts!

"May you be healthy," he told her as she helped him up and linked her arm in his.

They walked slowly to the table, and although it was only a very short distance, Gabriel found it difficult. They stopped for a moment so he could gather his strength.

"Mi alma," he whispered to her as if sharing a secret, "a few days ago Luna was here and she asked me if I love her. I told her I love her very much, but she said, 'You love me more than anyone, don't you?' I could see her spirits were low, that she was sad and that I had to strengthen her, and so I told her, 'True.' But the truth, Rachelika, hija mia, the truth is that I love you most of all."

Luna came back from work very upset. "Mr. Zacks sent me home," she told David, unable to conceal her emotion. "The shop's as dry as the desert. Not even a stray dog comes in. For whole days I've been sitting behind the counter doing nothing. I was so bored I started playing with the mannequin in the window—undressing it, dressing it, undressing, dressing. Mr. Zacks got annoyed, but what could I do, David? If I'd sat there all day like an idiot I would have gone out of my mind. Mr. Zacks hardly comes to the shop anymore. I open up, I close. He doesn't even come to check the takings. There's nothing to come for, there's no money. Today he paid me my last wages and told me not to come back." She sobbed. "What am I going to do, David? What will I do now without my job?"

He took her into his arms and stroked her hair, and with the tenderness he had recently adopted when speaking to her, he said, "Don't worry, Lunika, you'll soon be very busy. We're working on it, right?"

She smiled at him through her tears. Ever since they'd come home from Shabbat evening dinner at her parents' house a few weeks before, he had changed completely. He'd stopped going to the cinema after work and came right back to their rented studio in Mekor Baruch. She was usually home already, but if not, he'd meet her at her parents' house and they'd walk home together from there.

Rachelika noticed a change in her sister. She was happier now, she laughed more.

"You did a good deed," she told Moise, nodding at David and Luna, who were sitting close together on the couch in her parents' house. "Look at them, a pair of lovebirds."

At the first chance she had of catching Luna alone, Rachelika asked her, "Is everything with you and David all right now?"

"Everything's wonderful!" Luna replied, smiling from ear to ear.

"And David, he's good to you?"

"Good? He's as good as gold. He's trying to make up for the hard period we went through, and he's like he used to be before the wedding, like he was when I first met him, when we'd go to Gan Ha'ir and sit on the bench and kiss till I saw stars."

"At this rate, Lunika, you'll be having a baby together with me."

"From your lips to God's ears, amen!"

After his talk with Moise, David was determined to fix what he had almost broken. When they entered their little studio apartment, he'd hugged her, turned off the light, and undressed her in the dark. He'd kissed her gently on her forehead and ran his fingers down her back very slowly, lingering on each muscle and tendon. His lips were hers, his tongue hers, and then he kissed her eyes, her neck. She lengthened the kisses, the embraces, putting off the moment when he would try and penetrate her. No, she didn't like that. It hurt her and made her feel uncomfortable, especially when he'd whisper in her ear, "Hold it, help it," and groan as if he was laboring to breathe. She felt the shame burning her cheeks, amazed by the revulsion she felt when she took his penis, as slippery as an eel, in her hands. She was frightened when the eel stiffened almost as soon as she touched it and grew in her hands.

And when he took her hand, guiding it up and down, holding her fingers on its crown, moving them as if they had a life of their own, as if they didn't belong to her hand, to her body, her soul, she thought that at any moment she'd die of shame and nausea. She could feel the veins pulsing in it, but she never dared to look down and see what was in her hands.

"Now put it inside," David whispered, giving himself up to the pleasure, not noticing her disgust. She tried to insert his penis, which seemed to have grown even bigger, but without success. Even though she opened her legs as wide as she could, the garden was locked and the gate refused to open.

"Hold it," he whispered. "Hold it, don't let it go." When he eventually managed to penetrate, gripping her shoulders tightly and rocking above her forcefully, she shut her eyes and prayed for him to finish. He hurt her so much her body screamed, but she bit her lip and held back. He forced himself into her again and again, his eyes shut tight, completely in thrall to pleasure, and she lay beneath him like a log, not knowing what to do, whether to move at his pace, make sounds like him, pretend she was enjoying it. God, she hoped it would work this time. She couldn't stand people's questioning looks at her flat belly, she couldn't stand the whispering behind her back. She knew that the whole of Ohel Moshe was talking about the fact that Rachelika got pregnant before her even though she was married after her. She hoped she'd get pregnant and put this nightmare behind her.

After finally releasing a choked shout, he slackened and lay on top of her. She felt like she was suffocating. She wanted to go to the sink and wash herself, but Rachelika had told her she mustn't move, because if she did, God forbid, and if she washed her thighs, she'd spoil her chances of getting pregnant. Despite the discomfort, she remained on her back, pressing her thighs together, following the instructions Rachelika had given her.

David fell asleep on top of her, his body heavy. Luna gently slipped from under him, hurriedly put on her nightgown, and moved over to her side of the bed. She closed her eyes but couldn't fall asleep. She felt disgusted. Tears began to flow from her eyes. God, what's wrong with me? I'm supposed to feel happy, I'm supposed to be hearing bells, soaring to heights, and instead I feel hurt and humiliated. The thoughts were running through her head like scenes from a film. How she'd wanted him to make love to her, how she'd wanted them to bear children. How she'd looked forward to the moment he would treat her like a husband treats his wife, and now it was finally happening and all she wanted was for it to be over. Did every woman feel this way? Maybe it was only the men who enjoyed making love. Maybe it was the world's biggest lie that women enjoyed it as much as men. Maybe it was a secret shared by all the women in the world. It wasn't possible that only she lay there with her legs apart and prayed for it to be over. And why did you have to do it so many times to get pregnant just once?

Luna got out of bed and shuffled to the sink to wash her body in the ice-cold water. Pregnant or not, she couldn't stand this repulsive stuff on her body any longer. She scrubbed and washed with soap and water. Now there's no chance I'll get pregnant, she worried. I'll never be a mother. But the compulsion was stronger than her; she was incapable of stopping. She scrubbed and scrubbed, almost peeling the skin from her body. It was only when her skin was reddened and scratched that she finally felt clean, and she threw her night-gown into the laundry basket and took a clean one from the closet. The scent of laundry soap soothed her. She put on the nightgown and went back to bed. What a crazy woman I am. David will leave me, I'll be on my own, and I'll never hold a baby in my arms.

Luna's next period didn't arrive, but a few weeks later the morning sickness did. She was excited, and even before David she told Rachelika, who jumped for joy and hugged her.

"Our children will grow up together. Mine will be six months older than yours, they'll go to school together. They'll be best friends."

"Am I really pregnant?" Luna asked her excitedly. "I'm not imagining it, am I?"

"If you're nauseous and your monthly present hasn't arrived, you're pregnant," Rachelika replied matter-of-factly.

"Should I tell David?"

"Of course, who else should you tell! Run and tell him, go make him happy!"

And she did make him happy. He hugged her and lifted her in the air, twirling her as he danced around the room.

"Put me down, put me down. I'm feeling sick as it is," she said through her laughter.

He put her down, cupped her chin, and kissed her. "I'm mad about you," he said. "You'll be the most beautiful mother in Jerusalem." Once again she noticed that he didn't say, "I love you." Since the day he'd started courting her and even when he'd proposed, he had never said, "I love you." He'd say, "I'm mad about you," express his affection for her, but never did he declare his love. And again, like on the previous occasions, she let the thought pass without further ado. She was going to be a mother, and that was the important thing.

David did his best to fulfill all Luna's odd pregnancy requests, and thank God, because she had a lot. She hadn't yet spoken to him about the baby's name, but it was clear to her that it would be named after her father. There was just no other option.

"How many times do I have to tell you that the firstborn son is named after the husband's father?" Rachelika told her angrily. "I'm done arguing with you about this."

"I'm arguing?" Luna replied, playing dumb. "You name your son after your husband's father. I'm naming mine after Papo."

She is so breathtaking, pregnancy suits her, Rachelika thought. I'm as fat as a bear, and on her, except for a small belly, you can't see a thing. The legs, the arms, the face are all perfect. *Ya ribon*, how is it that you gave all the beauty in the family to her and didn't spread it out among the three of us?

Unlike Rachelika and all her friends who couldn't stop complimenting her on her pregnancy, Luna hated being pregnant. She felt clumsy, hated her swelling breasts, her bloated thighs, this weight that had suddenly landed on her. She felt robbed of her beauty and had already discovered several dark blotches on her pale skin. Even the visit to the seamstress who made her new maternity dresses from *Burda* patterns did nothing to cheer her up. Rachelika made do with two dresses that she alternated, while Luna had ten and still wasn't happy. She felt like an elephant. The only good thing about the pregnancy was that David stayed away from her at night.

"So we shouldn't lose the baby, God forbid," he had said. She knew that they wouldn't stop at one child and that they'd have to do it again after the first one was born, but they didn't have to do it right away. They could wait a year or two. In the meantime, with God's help, the first baby would be born with all his fingers and toes, and he would be named Gabriel.

8

GABRIEL WAS SITTING in his chair, his ear to the radio. The news wasn't good. The English had intercepted another boat carrying illegal immigrants and transferred its passengers to an internment camp in Cyprus.

The children would be here soon. They wanted to talk, and he knew what about: It couldn't be helped, they had to sell the shop to Mordoch the Kurd. Very soon now there wouldn't be enough money for food. It was all over. The shop was finished, his health was finished, and very shortly his life would be finished too. This way at least there would be enough left for Rosa after his death. She'd been so quiet lately, he hardly heard her. She tended to him as if he were a baby and didn't complain. She helped him up from his chair and into bed, dressed him and undressed him. He was unable to do anything himself and was totally dependent on her. And she, in her quiet way with a force he never knew she possessed, worked around the clock just for him. She'd wake up before him in the morning, make him tea with bizcochos, help him hold the cup so it wouldn't fall from his shaking hand, and wipe his drooling mouth. Then she'd take off his pajamas and put on a new pair. Lately he wore pajamas all the time. He was uncomfortable in tight-fitting clothes and needed something loose. Yes, he was now officially sick. He'd stopped fighting the disease. He'd stopped trying to seek relief. Anyway, in times like these, it was impossible to travel to the Dead Sea and the hot springs in Tiberias. There, in the warm, oily water, he could feel a little better. If only it were possible to bring the Tiberias springs to his home.

When the children arrived, he'd instruct them to do what they deemed fit and sell the shop to the Kurd. His grandfather was probably turning in his grave. It was as clear to him as today was Sunday that he was being punished for his sin against his father, that Raphael had not forgiven him even from the grave. It was clear to him that his mother's damnable curse was still haunting him. She hadn't come to visit him even once since he'd become ill, hadn't even sent messengers. He would die before her, he could see that. She would bury him and only then would she rest. Don't worry, madre querida, I'll soon be gone and your soul will finally find peace. Your darling son is going to die.

They sold the shop to Mordoch the Kurd for five hundred lirot, a price which, in normal times, would have been considered a bad joke. They knew he was ripping them off, but what choice did they have? Nineteen forty-seven was a bad year for business. Nobody was buying or selling except for thieves like Mordoch who had gold under their floor tiles. The heavily pregnant Rachelika and her good Moise negotiated the sale as toughly as possible. She was no fool. She went from shop to shop in the market on her swollen legs, checking the value of their shop with the various merchants. Rachelika knew they were selling to Mordoch for less than half the shop's value, but he'd known how desperate their situation was and wouldn't budge from his original offer. "If you don't like it, try and sell to somebody else," he'd said, knowing that nobody else was doing business at a time like this.

"You go and close the deal with him," Rachelika had said to Moise. "I can't do it." Tears flowed from her eyes and she sobbed like a little girl.

"Basta, querida," Gabriel told her, "you're breaking my heart all over again. We've no choice. If we have to sell then we'll sell, but without tears."

"We're selling him the shop at a loss, but who'll pay us the cost of our shame, Papo, who'll pay it?"

"Enough!" All at once Rosa's voice stopped her crying. "Enough crying, go and close the deal with him and behave with dignity. He's won our shop, but he will not win our respect. Go, queridos, go and get it over with and let Papo rest now. Heideh, go."

"Mother, I'm not going," Rachelika said. "I'm not going even if you force me."

"You're not going where?" said Luna, who had just come in, surprised to see Rachelika crying. She hadn't seen her sister cry since she was five. "What's the matter, hermanita?" she asked anxiously.

"We're selling the shop to the Kurd," Rachelika replied through her tears. "And at a loss. He's robbing us, the bastard, robbing us shamelessly."

The hurt in Luna's eyes was so palpable that it paralyzed Gabriel. "Over my dead body! Starving to death would be better than selling to him. If anything, give it to Tio Matzliach for nothing, but not to that Kurd who from the day he came into our life has turned everything black. Papo, it's our great-grandfather's shop. We grew up with that shop, Papo!"

"Stop it, stop it, Luna, you'll harm the baby. What's all this outburst about?" Rosa said, trying to pacify her. "It's only a shop. Your father's health, your and Rachelika's health are more important."

"Only a shop?" Luna yelled at her. "For you it's only a shop, but for us it's our life!"

"Silence, Luna!" Gabriel raged. "How dare you speak to your mother like that! What's this 'for you' and 'for us'? Who are you to be so insolent to my wife? Who put words as sharp as daggers into your mouth, who put a stone in your chest instead of a heart?"

An intense silence followed. Rosa couldn't believe her ears. Gabriel was defending her against Luna. The anger she felt toward her pregnant daughter was now replaced by a gentleness toward her husband. The Days of the Messiah had come. He was finally seeing her.

Very quickly Luna regained her composure and headed for the door.

"Where are you going?" David thundered.

"I'm going home," she said, her voice choked. "My father doesn't want me here."

"You're not going anywhere," her husband ordered. "Not before you kiss your mother's hand and beg her pardon. Not before you kiss your father's hand and beg his forgiveness."

"You keep out of this," she replied from the doorway. But David quickly blocked her path.

"Let her go," Gabriel said, "so she doesn't harm the baby. Let her go home, lie on the bed, and think about the words that come out of her mouth."

David moved out of Luna's way and she left, but to everyone's surprise he didn't follow.

"Papo," Rachelika said, defending her sister, "she didn't mean it. She's upset, you know how much she loves the shop."

"She never did anything for the shop," Gabriel said. "She was too proud to sell in the market, and now she cares?"

"Papo querido, that's Luna. She likes working with clothes, but she loves you and the shop as much as she loves herself. For her, as for all of us, if we sell the shop, it's as if we're selling the family's honor, and to the Kurd yet, whom she, more than any of us, hated right from the start."

"Mi alma, what a heart you've got," Gabriel said, beckoning her over and kissing her forehead.

"You're a fortunate man, Moise," he told her husband.

"I know, Senor Ermosa," he said and hugged his wife close.

From the day the shop was sold to Mordoch the Kurd, the Ermosa girls stopped going to the Mahane Yehuda Market. None of them had the strength to pass by the shop. Mordoch hadn't bothered to take down the sign over the door of the shop, which had been padlocked and bolted since he'd bought it from Gabriel.

"I hope he ends up without a grush to his name and never opens the shop," Luna said when she heard the rumor that the shop was closed. "I've never hated anyone the way I hate that Kurd. He's ended Papo's life, he's taken away the little dignity he had left, and for that I'll never forgive him."

"Why are you taking it so hard?" Rachelika asked. "The shop's been sold and that's that. Life goes on. Now you have to stay calm and get ready to have your baby."

"How can I stay calm when I see Papo fading away from day to day?"

"He's sick, Lunika. It has nothing to do with the shop. He's sick and nobody can help him."

Luna had forgiven her father for reprimanding her in front of the whole family. She'd gone to her parents' house the next day, kissed his clenched hand that he could no longer open, straightened the beret on his head and the cushions behind him, and helped him drink some tea. And he, seeing the sorrow and remorse in her eyes, didn't say a word about what had transpired the previous evening. Except for David, who scowled at her, everybody else acted as if nothing had happened. And to Rosa's surprise, even she felt for her daughter. Poor Luna, even when she loves, it doesn't come out clean. It's always dirtied with hate, miskenica.

As Gabriel's illness worsened, Rosa's standing in the household was enhanced. Now that Gabriel was unable to run the family's life, the burden fell on her. Her daughters Rachelika and Becky and her sons-in-law Moise and

David showed her immense respect, and though her rebellious daughter Luna had not changed her stripes, she had at least studiously avoided friction with her mother. It's better this way, Rosa thought. Better she doesn't say a word to me rather than be how she was before, when she only had to see me and her skin would become a porcupine's.

For Rosa, each day became as long as the Exile. She'd get up early in the morning, and after washing her face and before drinking a cup of mint tea, she'd go to Gabriel's bed, help him sit up, plump the big cushions behind his back, bring him a cup of tea, and hold it to his lips until he'd taken the last sip. It was sad to see the handsome man sinking ever deeper into his illness.

Yet into all this sadness shot a ray of light that brought a little joy into the Ermosa family's house: Gabriel and Rosa's first grandchild, Yehuda-Boaz, whose first name was given to him after his paternal grandfather Yehuda, and the second chosen by his mother because it had been a fashionable biblical name.

"Why didn't you give him Gabriel as a second name?" Luna had asked her sister.

"How could I name my second child Gabriel, troncha, if his big brother's second name is Gabriel?"

Rachelika was grieved not only because she couldn't name her son after her beloved father, but also because she couldn't give Gabriel the honor of being her firstborn's godfather at his circumcision, since tradition held that it was given to the father's father.

But on the eighth day after Yehuda-Boaz's birth, when the whole family gathered for the circumcision ceremony, Rachelika's husband surprised her. After he took the baby from her, instead of giving him to his own father, he laid him in Gabriel's arms. Rachelika's heart swelled on seeing her father's joy. She looked at her husband and for the thousandth time thanked God for her good fortune. When she'd first met Moise she hadn't thought she'd like him. After all, her dream man had been a Palmachnik, salt of the earth, a brave fighter, handsome and tousle-haired. She hadn't believed that she could learn to love a simple, kindly boy with almost no education, heavily built and balding. But she loved him with every fiber of her being. She had no idea how he'd convinced his father to confer the honor of being her son's godfather on Gabriel, but she was grateful and proud.

The baby's cry as the mohel circumcised him pierced her heart and she hurried out into the synagogue yard, her sisters consoling her in her wake.

"Miskenico, only eight days old and already being cut." Rachelika wept. "It must hurt him terribly."

"He can't feel it," Luna comforted her. "They dip the pacifier in wine. He's as drunk as a lord."

"Miskenico, only eight days old and drunk already." She sobbed.

"He won't remember anything. Do you know a boy who was cut when he was eight days old and remembers it?" Becky said, surprising her sisters with her logic.

"You, how do you know what a boy remembers or doesn't remember, little one? When did you become such an expert on boys?" Luna laughed, and Rachelika wiped away her tears.

"Stop it, enough. I haven't been little for a long time. I have a boy."

"*Wai de mi*, don't tell me your boy tells you what he remembers or doesn't remember from his circumcision." Luna laughed.

"If you weren't pregnant I'd slap you, you idiot," Becky replied.

Rachelika's weeping mingled with their laughter, and they all felt like three little girls again, sharing a room in their parents' house, when life had been simple.

And that's how Rosa found them when she came to call them in to toast the new baby. As she looked at her three daughters, she thought, Ay, Senor del mundo, you have been good to me. Perhaps I should thank you every day, every hour, for marrying me to Gabriel and giving me three daughters and now a grandchild too, and with God's help another one soon. Perhaps my life hasn't been all that bad. God be praised, you've finally remembered me, Rosa the poor orphan from Shama, and even given me a little joy.

Six months later, on November 29, 1947, the family and all their neighbors gathered around Nono Gabriel's radio and listened to the broadcast from the United Nations in New York. The fifty-seven member states were about to de-cide on the partition of Palestine. Everyone was entranced by the announcer's voice. Though he was speaking English, there was no need for translation: the United States of America . . . Yes. Australia . . . Yes . . . With the name of each country, hearts skipped a beat. Thirty-three times the announcer said yes, and thirty-three times yells erupted from the Ermosa house in Ohel Moshe. Ga-briel, who could barely move, was so overjoyed he jumped up from his cush-ioned chair. And once it was clear that there was a majority in favor of the resolution to partition Palestine into two states, one Jewish and one Arab, it also became clear that the English, may their name be erased, would finally be leaving Palestine, and the Jews would finally have a state of their own.

While everyone went running out of the Ermosas' house and through the Ohel Moshe gate toward Zion Square, where thousands were already celebrating in the street, Luna felt her baby kicking in her belly. And Luna, who wanted nothing more than to join them all and dance till dawn like she loved to do, was instead forced to go to Hadassah Hospital on Mount Scopus in an ambulance. There, after seventeen hours of painful labor, her firstborn, a daughter, finally emerged into the world.

Luna was far too exhausted to feel happy when they laid the baby on her breast. All she wanted was to close her eyes and sleep. She wasn't interested in the fact that she had just brought a living, breathing creature into the world. She was not interested in her husband, who was crying like a baby, almost collapsing onto the tiny body of his new daughter. She was not interested in the fact that while she was in labor, the Jewish people were celebrating their rebirth. She just wanted to be left alone to sleep.

The next morning when they brought the baby to feed, Luna refused to nurse her. She was too tired and in too much pain to even open her eyes.

"You have to try and feed your baby," the nurse told her. "She has to eat."

But Luna couldn't.

The nurse helped Luna sit on a pillow and put the baby into her arms. But instead of feeling sublimely happy and bursting with love, she didn't feel a thing. And when the nurse undid her gown and exposed her breasts, she was filled with terrible shame.

"Bring her mouth to the nipple," the nurse told her, trying to bring the baby's lips to her mother's nipple. But the baby wouldn't take the nipple and started to cry. Luna closed her eyes and prayed that they would take the baby away and let her sleep.

"God almighty, don't drop the baby," the nurse said as she quickly retrieved it from Luna's lax arms. She lay back in her bed, covering her head with the sheet, trying to find a less painful position for her aching body.

Rachelika, who had just arrived, hurried after the nurse who had removed the baby from Luna's room. "Where are you taking her?" she asked.

"If we don't want her to starve to death, we have to feed her," the nurse replied dryly.

"Why isn't my sister feeding her?"

"In some cases the mother's too tired and in too much pain to care for the baby. But don't worry, your sister will be back to her old self in a few hours, and in the meantime we'll give the baby a bottle."

"A bottle?" Rachelika was shocked. "Giving a baby a bottle isn't healthy."

"So what do you want us to do, let her starve?" asked the tired nurse.

"Give her to me," Rachelika ordered.

"Excuse me?"

"Give me the baby!"

She took the baby from the astonished nurse, sat down on a chair in the busy corridor of the maternity ward, took out a breast, and brought the baby's mouth to her nipple. Only when the warm milk from her aunt's breast had satisfied her hunger did she stop crying.

When she'd finished, Rachelika laid the baby on her shoulder, pressing her tummy against it, gently patting her back until she heard the welcome burp.

"Aaach," said Rachelika, pleased with herself. "Now we feel better, now we've had a good burp we're calmer." She kissed the infant's forehead, handed her back to the nurse, and told her, "I'll pump my milk until my sister can feed the baby herself."

After filling several bottles with her milk, Rachelika went back to Luna's room. David was sitting at the side of his wife's bed.

"What's happening?" Rachelika asked.

"She's not speaking to me," he replied. "She's not talking at all."

"Go outside, David, leave me alone with my sister."

He got up and headed for the door, stunned by Luna's behavior. He couldn't fathom why she hadn't even given their daughter a glance.

Despite the fact that he hadn't welcomed a son into this world, the emotion David felt when he'd held his daughter in his arms had erased any disappointment. He was filled with a love he couldn't contain. For the first time since he had parted from Isabella, he felt happiness had reentered his life. He felt that the baby was reparation for the lost love he had left behind in Italy.

After David went out, Rachelika sat beside Luna and stroked her hair.

"I want to die," Luna mumbled. "My whole body hurts, my down below is on fire. It was a nightmare, Rachelika, a nightmare. Why didn't you tell me it'd be such a nightmare?"

"Would it have helped if I'd told you?"

"Did it hurt you like this too?"

"It hurts everyone. It hurt Mother too, and it'll hurt your daughter as well.

It's the curse that God gave our Mother Eve when she tempted Adam to eat the forbidden fruit. In sorrow thou shalt bring forth children. You won't remember a thing by tomorrow. It's pain you forget. Otherwise would we have babies again and again?"

"I'm not having any more!" Luna said. "This is the first and last."

"Lunika," Rachelika laughed, "you'll see that by your next pregnancy you won't remember a thing. Your baby's exquisite, a princess."

Luna didn't reply.

"Don't you want to see her, Lunika?"

"Not now. I'm tired."

"She's the spitting image of you. She has green eyes and red hair like yours. You'll love her."

"I want to sleep."

"All right, Lunika, go to sleep, but soon, when you wake up, they'll be bringing her to you and you'll see how she takes all the pain away."

But I didn't manage to take away my mother's pain. Every time they brought me to her to nurse I'd scream, almost choke. My lips couldn't hold on to her nipple, and when they did, I sucked and sucked, but the few drops of milk yielded by my mother's small breasts didn't satisfy my hunger, and I'd scream to high heaven. My tiny face, swollen from crying, turned red, and my frightened mother would call for the nurse to take me from her. And so, three days after I was born, it was clear to everybody that Rachelika would have to carry on providing me with her milk.

Hadassah Hospital was situated on the eastern slope of Mount Scopus, a Jewish enclave in the heart of an Arab area that from day to day had become increasingly hostile. As soon as the United Nations passed the resolution on the partition of Palestine, traveling to and from Mount Scopus had become dangerous. Luna, who was in pain and depressed after a difficult birth, was deathly afraid of traveling the road from Mount Scopus into Jerusalem, and when the time came for David to take her and the new crown princess home, she adamantly refused to leave the hospital.

"I'm not going in a taxi with the baby, it's dangerous!" she told David.

"They won't give us an ambulance," David tried to reason with her. "You're not critically ill."

"Then I'm not going! I didn't survive seventeen hours of hell so I could get killed by an Arab sniper."

She wouldn't get out of bed, and not even the staff nurse who'd been called to her room and demanded she vacate the bed could do anything.

"You can shout at me from now till tomorrow," she said in an icy voice. "You can bring Ben-Gurion here in person. I'm not going down from Mount Scopus without protection. As far as I'm concerned"—turning to David—"you can find us a room and we'll move here."

And David, who had been waiting for the minute when he could bring Luna and the baby home and finally get away to the war that was about to break out and join the forces defending the homeland and the struggle to establish a state, almost lost his patience. Each additional moment with his wife became an even more unendurable punishment.

He had behaved impeccably since Moise had pulled him aside for a talk ten months before. He'd realized that if he wanted to hold his marriage together and not become, with Luna, the leading players in a scandal that would threaten not only their future but that of their family too, he would have to do everything he could to father a child, even though it would be hard for him, even though it would demand tremendous mental effort. After all, he was a rational man and wouldn't give in to his emotions at his family's expense.

Only one time in his life—when was it? way back while he was in Italy, in a life so different from his life today—had his heart caught him by surprise and overtook his common sense. He'd become quite the Don Juan when they'd been posted to Mestre near Venice at the end of the war. As soon as he and his comrades had settled into the houses of the wealthy people who'd abandoned the town in panic, he embarked on a mad pursuit of the pleasures of life. The war years had left him with a hunger for life. The Italian girls shamelessly offered themselves, and he happily accepted, two or three women of all ages every day. He would never forget the day he'd unknowingly slept with a mother and her daughter. How could he have known they were mother and daughter? The mother had looked like her daughter's older sister. They weren't whores. They were simply hungry for food and attention. He'd left them a larger wad of bills than usual and took off. Nothing like that had ever happened to any of his comrades. They'd all slept with lots of women, but none had done it with a mother and daughter one after the other.

Since then David Siton's reputation had preceded him. Of all the guys, he was without a doubt the Don Juan. And so it went on for many weeks—women, women, women—until he'd met Isabella.

He and the guys had been sitting as usual in a café in the piazza. Slowly the number of men around the table dwindled as they left with their arms around Italian girls who'd been awaiting their chance to have a good time with a soldier. He and Moise were the last ones left at their table: David, because he didn't fancy any of the girls that day, and Moise, who was always the last to leave. He was shy and introverted, and David almost had to force him to take a girl out. Just as he was thinking of getting up and trying his luck at a club, David saw her riding her bike.

Moise had absolutely no idea that while he was leaving the field to his friend, as he had dozens of times before, David the Don Juan was about to lose his head and fall in love with an Italian girl. From that moment on, no other woman existed for him. David spent every free moment with her, riding bikes through the alleyways of Venice, gliding in a gondola and paying the gondolier an extortionate sum to serenade her. He took her to restaurants and cafés, went dancing with her in clubs, pampered her with boxes of chocolate, silk stockings, and the perfume she loved.

David quickly became one of the family at her parents' home, a rural stone house surrounded by a garden. While Mestre's markets were suffering shortages, the army canteen was fully stocked, and every weekend he'd bring the family a basket of provisions. "God bless you," her father would say as they sat at the big table in the yard for a feast fit for a king.

Years later he would try to retrieve the taste of the pasta and tomato sauce that Isabella and her mother had cooked, the taste of Parmesan cheese melted into the sauce, the taste of Isabella. Throughout his life he would miss the fragrance of the basil and thyme that grew in big clay pots in her parents' yard, the beauty of the bougainvillea that blossomed in hues of bright red. The big wooden table, the noisy family around it, the fine wine that was so different from the sweet Kiddush wine of Shabbat eve in Jerusalem.

"I'm in love," David had told Moise. "I've never felt this way. This woman has stolen my heart."

"Don't exaggerate," replied the always serious Moise. "We'll be going home in a few months. What will you do then?"

"I'll take her with me. I'll bring her to Jerusalem."

"How can you bring her to Jerusalem? Your father will never accept a Christian daughter-in-law."

"She'll convert. Stranger things have happened."

"Are you out of your mind? Where are your brains? There's not even the slightest chance that your father will accept her. Your family will disown you."

"We'll see," David said. "Meanwhile we have time, and until it's time to make decisions, I'm celebrating love."

Isabella became an inseparable part of his life. They went everywhere together. Even when he went out with his comrades he brought her along and introduced her as his girlfriend. One evening as they lay naked on a secluded beach they'd discovered a few months earlier, David told her, "I'll give you the moon and the stars if you ask for them." The lights of Venice glimmered in the distance, and the sky was strewn with stars. They swam naked, and afterward she spread out a blanket and they'd made love. Isabella was a passionate lover. He'd never met such a sensual woman. She loved pampering him; she taught him things he didn't know, leading his fingers along the hidden curves of her body and instructing him in how to pleasure her. He loved to hear the moans that escaped her sweet lips. Who would have believed that he could enjoy pleasuring a woman so much?

Then came the day of their parting. Their officers informed them that their mission was complete and they would be going back to Palestine. Isabella begged David to take her with him. He was beside himself. On the one hand, he wanted to be with her for eternity, to marry her, have children with her, but on the other, he knew that his father and his family would never approve. He knew that a devout Catholic like Isabella could never become Jewish, even if she did convert. Deep in her heart she would always be seeking a church where she could kneel before the crucified Christ, and in Jerusalem there were churches on every corner. His heart wanted it, wanted it so much he thought it might explode, but his head told him no.

"I love you more than life itself," he told her painfully. "I don't believe I will ever love a woman the way I love you, but we have no chance. My father will never accept you."

Even though he did his best to harden his heart, David almost collapsed onto her shoulder and wept with her. He was unable to change the way of his world. He had to return to Jerusalem, find himself a decent woman, and get married. He could never marry an Italian Catholic even if she was the love of his life.

On the boat to Haifa, he shared his plans with Moise. As soon as David arrived in Jerusalem he'd look for one of their women and marry her. "A new love heals the wounds of an old one," he told Moise. "My heart's broken into pieces, but I'll put it back together and forget Isabella. There's no other way."

"How can you forget her when your kit bag's filled with photographs of her and you spend all your time looking at them?" Moise asked him. "If I were you, I'd throw them into the sea."

"I'm not throwing anything into the sea. Those photos are a memento from the most beautiful time in my life."

By the next day he was already back in his parents' home in Jerusalem. Each day he went out looking for work, and in the evenings he'd go out with the guys, flitting from one of the city's cafés to another, and then to dance clubs. And it was there, in Café Europa, that David first spotted Luna. He asked about the good-looking girl doing the tango like a Spanish dancer, and was told her name, that she came from a good, well-to-do family, that her father Gabriel Ermosa had a shop in the Mahane Yehuda Market, and that she worked as a saleslady at Zacks & Son, ladies' clothing, on Jaffa Road. He knew what he had to do and began spinning his web to snare her. He learned that she was a prize catch, that she rejected all her suitors with a flat-out no and didn't give herself up easily.

"So who does she go dancing with?" he asked.

"Her sister and cousins and a few friends from Ohel Moshe."

David conducted in-depth research on Luna Ermosa. From his mother he learned that there was a schism in the Ermosa family between the mother, Mercada, and her son Gabriel, Luna's father, and that Gabriel, who was very wealthy, was not a well man and his businesses were not doing well. None of this really interested David. He wasn't going to marry her father's businesses, he was going to marry Luna. He'd chosen her for his wife almost from the moment he first set eyes on her. It would be she who removed Isabella from his heart, once and for all.

Every day he'd go to Jaffa Road, stand between the building's columns, and observe Zacks & Son. Occasionally he'd see her come outside for a break and lean against the door, dressed to the nines, elegant and well put together. Sometimes he'd watch her go into Barashi's seed and nut shop in the adjacent alley and come back with a bag of sunflower seeds. Once a week she'd climb into the shop window holding a pincushion in her teeth and change the mannequin's clothes. That, David knew, was his opportunity. He would stand by the window and catch her attention.

Luna had no idea that for weeks now David had been planning to woo her. She of course thought that he'd passed the shop window by chance and was flattered when he'd told her he didn't know which of them was the real doll, she or the mannequin. She hadn't known that he'd been rehearsing that line for a long time. And as he'd expected, she fell right into his hands like ripe fruit.

Luna wasn't shy when David kissed or hugged her in front of other people. On the contrary, she encouraged his public displays of affection, much the same way as she showed her love for him. But between the sheets she was as frightened as a tiny bird. Unlike Isabella, who was a bubbling spring, his young wife was a shy, inexperienced virgin.

If he'd harbored hopes that she'd loosen up with time and let her natural instincts take over, he was disappointed. Unlike Isabella, who was all fire and brimstone and smoke, who writhed like a snake under him, who moved her body to the rhythm of his, who climaxed with a shout that threatened to perforate his eardrum, his wife was quiet and remote.

When Luna finally became pregnant, he, like she, was relieved. He wasn't surprised that she was happy to cooperate when he'd told her that they shouldn't make love until after the baby was born. The months of pregnancy were hard, and her moods had made him spend more time at work and at the cinema. It was lucky that she liked being at her father's house more than in their own home, lucky that she preferred her sisters' company to his. It was lucky that soon war would break out and he'd be able to join the army and do what he loved best, be a soldier.

But David's plans to take off as soon as possible ran aground. He fell in love with the baby. Who would have believed that the baby would restore the light to his eyes, that the baby would give renewed meaning to his dull life? How much beauty God had given her, and what sweetness! Why didn't her mother want to hold her? Why didn't she want to nurse her? His wife had gone crazy. She didn't even look at the baby, and now she didn't want to leave Mount Scopus and go back home to Jerusalem.

Seven days after I was born my mother was finally forced to vacate her hospital bed for another expectant mother, and much against her will consented to leave Mount Scopus in an armored convoy. The convoy drove slowly, the journey seeming to take an eternity to Luna, and even though the windows of the bus were armored and there were soldiers driving in front of and behind it, she didn't feel safe and clung tightly to my father.

She wasn't mistaken, my mother. When the convoy reached Sheikh Jarrah, the bus was hit by a volley of stones. She shrank and tried to hide under the seat, but every movement hurt her, and when she bent down she felt that her insides were being torn apart.

My father, who was holding me wrapped in a blanket, didn't say a word about the fact that she'd first protected herself and not the baby, but he decided then and there that he'd take us straight to her parents' house and leave us there. "Your mother and Becky will help you with the little one," he told her, concealing the fact that as soon as they got there he was going to enlist for the war.

My mother was terrified. She had absolutely no idea how she'd manage with me. She didn't know how to feed me, how to change my diaper, how to hold me. Who would have believed that she had to be *taught* to be a mother? She thought it'd have come naturally, but not with her; nothing came naturally with her. Nobody had told her that her body would be ripped to shreds when she gave birth, that she'd be sewn up with a needle in her body's most sensitive place, the place where every touch caused her to shudder. Who would have believed that her body would resist giving birth like this, so much so that instead of having a few contractions and giving birth in no time at all like Rachelika, whose baby had just slid out of her, her baby would refuse to come out and tear her insides apart for seventeen hours? Who would have believed that her body would resist her becoming a mother to the point that her breasts didn't produce milk and that her baby would have to nurse on her sister's breasts?

These thoughts ran through Luna's mind and gave her no peace. As the bus drove through the poor Arab neighborhoods, she closed her eyes and prayed they would make it safely. David didn't stop kissing the baby, clicking his tongue and talking to her. But what would happen if he gave the baby to her to hold? She couldn't, she was afraid she'd drop her, and the shooting that could be heard from all around, and the vehicles all around, she'd never seen so much traffic in the streets of Jerusalem. British police cars with their sirens wailing, groups of soldiers laying out concertina wire. Any minute there'd be a curfew and they'd be stuck on the bus with the baby and wouldn't be able to get home.

She calmed down only once they reached her parents' house in Ohel Moshe. In the yard the neighbors were waiting to throw sweets at them and shout, "Mazal tov! *Mabrouk! Sano que 'ste!*"

David immediately put the baby into Gabriel's trembling arms, and Luna's heart stopped. Just don't let him drop the baby, she prayed. But once she saw Gabriel's smile, her heart melted.

"*Preciosa*, she's beautiful," he said. "She's just as beautiful as her mother." Luna saw a spark of happiness in his eyes, and she recalled how he'd loved her when she was little. Her heart swelled even more, and at that moment she made her decision.

"Gabriela," she told her father. "Her name's Gabriela."

David's eyes widened in shock. Rosa, who was on her way to the kitchen, halted. Rachelika, who was nursing Boaz, shook her head in disbelief. Only Becky clapped her hands in pleasure. "Gabriela," she said, "what a pretty name!"

"Thank you," said Nono Gabriel. "Thank you very much. I'm honored."

And that's how I was named Gabriela.

About what happened next between my father and mother, Rachelika told me about it many years later, after my mother died.

"Are you out of your mind?" he'd yelled at her. "How can you give a girl a boy's name, and without even asking me?"

"I wanted to give my father the respect he deserves."

"But why didn't you consult me? She isn't only your daughter, she's mine too!"

"It just came out, straight from the heart. I saw my father so happy for the first time in so many months and it came out spontaneously."

"Spontaneously? What will you tell my mother? How will I look now when I go to see my mother and tell her that I haven't named my firstborn daughter after her?"

"Your mother, praise God, has already got five granddaughters named after her. Isn't that enough for her?"

"It's customary to name the first child after the father's father or mother, and you know it."

"So give her a second name, Victoria, your mother's name."

"Not a second name. I'll give her a first name, Victoria, and the second name will be after your father."

"In your dreams! My father's name first, and then your mother's."

"Don't talk crap! I've decided and that's that!"

"Excuse me," said my mother, "is that any way to speak to me? What do you think, that I'm one of your buddies from the brigade? I've just given you a baby after seventeen hours of agony and that's how you speak to me?"

"I'm sorry, I didn't mean it. I apologize, forgive me," he said and tried to put his arm around her shoulders, but she shook it off and left the room angry and hurt. She was already irritable and restless and couldn't bear the sight of the new body she'd been given.

"Just look at these tires," she wept to Rachelika, revealing her waist that had thickened slightly. "Look at these tetas," she sobbed, cupping her breasts. For years she'd been called "the airfield" because of her flat chest, but she had liked her breasts and pitied Rachelika for her heavy ones. Now she had to carry her own watermelons, yet with all their size they didn't even produce milk.

"Do you realize that a cow has an advantage over me?" she cried to Rachelika. "Do you realize that a cow gives milk and I don't?"

"It's all mood," her sister said. "There isn't a woman who doesn't have milk. You just have to calm down and release it."

"Release what? The milk? What, I'm locking it up in my tetas?"

"You need to relax your mood a bit. You've been as tense as a spring since you had the baby and you're being foolish. I told you it isn't customary to name the first child after the mother's father, but you went right ahead so you could fight with David. Why did you have to name the baby Gabriela?"

"Because that's what I decided, that my child would be named after Papo."

"But your child's a girl."

"So what? Gabriela's a nice name, an angel's name. It'll protect her."

On May 15, 1948, a few months after I came into the world, the Ingelish, may their name be erased, finally left Palestine, and Nona Rosa practically danced on the table in delight. But the immense joy my nona felt on the departure of the hated Ingelish was mixed with immense anxiety regarding the future.

The previous day, David Ben-Gurion had announced the establishment of the State of Israel and the War of Independence that would determine the fate of the Jewish people. My nono's radio didn't stop spewing news. My father joined Ben-Gurion's army without consulting my mother, and when he told her of his decision, she was so frightened, she almost dropped me.

"Please, David, don't leave me alone with the baby," she begged him.

"You're not alone, you're with your mother and sisters."

"Let him go," my nono said. "Don't make a scene. Everybody's enlisting. We have to be part of the effort."

Gabriel was proud of the fact that his son-in-law had enlisted and wished he could have joined up himself. He was a man of forty-seven who felt like a one-hundred-year-old shuffler, and his health would not allow it. A short time after David, Moise enlisted, and now his two sons-in-law had become fighters in the Israel Defense Forces.

Immediately after Moise enlisted, Rachelika also moved back to her parents' house with baby Boaz. The house was small and crowded, but Nono Gabriel was happy that all his daughters were with him at such a fraught time, and even happier with the babies that filled the house. The little ones' voices somewhat assuaged his pain, and at long last he could sit at a *mesa franca*, a king's table, with his girls.

And then what Nona Rosa called "the miracle" occurred. One morning the gate opened and into the yard strode a stocky, tanned man, his head crowned with curls, a thin mustache on his upper lip. "Dio mio! Ephraim!" Rosa screamed and fell into his arms, almost fainting. Years after his disappearance, Ephraim had returned. He was so different from the young drunkard who had left the house and slammed the door behind him. He'd left a confused youth and come back a real man.

"Rachelika, Luna, Becky, look who's here!" Rosa called. "Look who's here, Tio Ephraim, Tio Ephraim's come home!"

Even Gabriel was happy to see his brother-in-law again. Many years had passed, and despite the animosity he felt toward anyone connected with the Lehi or Etzel, and despite the fact that he had sullied the family's honor following Matilda Franco's death, he was glad to see Ephraim safe.

"You broke our mother's heart, Tio Ephraim," Rachelika said once the excitement died down.

"Shhh, he didn't break it at all. What happened is past," Rosa said. "The main thing is that you're back safe and sound. The main thing is that I'm seeing you with my own eyes." She wanted to take her little brother into her arms, to hug him, kiss his eyes, until something in his look made her hold back. His boyish features now comprised the face of a man. The deep furrows in his cheeks, the wrinkle that formed a path on his forehead told her in one glance that the years that had passed since he'd walked through the gate and not returned had not exactly been paradise for him. Who knew what he'd been through, where he'd hidden from the damned Ingelish, how many times his finger had pulled the trigger. She didn't dare ask him any of the questions whirling in her head, didn't dare penetrate the armor he now wore. She just stood close to him, inhaling his new scent, so different from the smell of alcohol that engulfed him in the last year he'd lived with them.

They sat around the table, the girls quietly holding their babies, still astonished by their uncle's return. Only little Becky chattered away, asking him all the questions that Rosa, and perhaps Rachelika and Luna too, wanted to ask but didn't.

"Where did you disappear to for such a long time?" Becky said. "Mother almost went crazy because she was so worried that we didn't know where you were."

"I was fighting for the Jewish people," Ephraim replied. "I helped drive the British out of Palestine, and they left, thank God," he said and pinched her cheek.

"Did you scare them?"

"Oho, and how I scared them."

"What did you do to them?"

"Not now, querida Becky, it's not yet time to tell. One day I'll tell you, but now it's too soon."

"Leave Tio Ephraim alone," Rosa scolded her. "Stop talking his ears off. It's time to eat."

Ephraim ate ravenously. "How I missed home cooking," he told her. "And how I missed the family. I'd heard that Luna and Rachelika were married and I was sorry I couldn't take part in the celebrations."

"Who told you?" Luna asked.

"I was told." He winked.

"Who?"

"I'll tell you one day," he said. "You're a mother already and you've still got ants in your pants? Paciencia, all in good time."

Afterward he slept for half a day. He was so exhausted that the noise of the house and the babies' crying didn't wake him. Rosa watched him as he slept, stroking his face. He was her fourth child, the son she never had; that's how she'd always felt.

War was raging outside, cannons thundering, and yet she felt a peace she hadn't known for as long as she could remember. Her girls were with her in the house, her grandchildren were with her, her husband was still alive, thank God, and now her little brother had come back to her. God be praised, she found herself thanking God for the second time that week. Gracias el Dio, thank you, thank you for bringing Ephraim back to me. She was curious about what he'd been through, but she knew he'd tell her in his own time. Now they had to make him feel he was wanted here, even if she had to sleep in the yard because there wasn't enough room in the house.

"At least we've got a man in the house now after the men went off to the war," Becky remarked in the girls' room later that evening.

"Some man," Luna snorted contemptuously. "Until I know that it wasn't him who killed poor Matilda I'm not going to treat him like a man."

"Mother says it wasn't him."

"Matilda's mother saw him, and our mother who was fast asleep in her house knows it wasn't him?"

"Drop it, Luna," Rachelika said. "Don't you dare bring it up. What's important now is that Tio Ephraim is back. Did you see how happy Mother is?"

"I don't think that Matilda's death should be swept under the rug. I think he should tell us exactly what happened that night."

"Enough, Luna," Becky said. "Why are you always looking for a fight? Isn't the war outside enough for you?"

"Oho, the child's learned to talk," said Luna. "You dummy, keep quiet. Until you grow up a bit we don't want to hear from you."

"Dummy yourself," Becky retorted and left the room, offended.

"What's the matter with you?" Rachelika asked. "What is it with you that you can't shut up? Why did you speak to Becky like that? And why do you have to sadden Mother when she's got a smile on her face at long last?"

"Are you against me too?"

"I'm against you? I'm for you more than anyone else in this house. I'm always defending you and explaining that your awful behavior is because you've just had a baby and your nerves are still on edge. But enough, Gabriela's already five months old. When Boaz was five months old I was already trying to get pregnant again."

"You're trying to get pregnant again?" Luna was shocked. "Boaz isn't a year old yet."

"He'll be a year old in a month's time, and yes, I want another child. I want my children to grow up together, it's what's best."

"You're out of your mind," Luna said. "You've just gotten back to your weight from before you had the baby, and you want to get as fat as a pig again?"

"It's natural," Rachelika said patiently. "I'll get pregnant, put on weight, have the baby, get pregnant again, put on weight again, and so on and so forth."

"How many children do you want, hermanita?"

"Moise and I want four, God willing."

"God be praised, may you all be healthy."

"And how many do you want?"

"One. I have one and that's enough for me."

"Don't talk nonsense!" Rachelika said, but deep down she feared that her sister meant every word.

Rosa's joy lasted for just one day. The next day, right after he woke up and ate the breakfast she'd labored over for him, Ephraim announced that he was going back to the front.

"Hermano," Rosa pleaded, "you've only just come home."

"I'll be back," he assured her. "But first we have to finish the job. We got rid of the British. Now we have to get rid of the Arabs and establish our own state at long last. In fire and blood did Judea fall; in blood and fire Judea shall rise!" he proclaimed with great determination.

He took his leave of Rosa, kissed Rachelika, Becky, and Luna, patted the babies, and then went to Gabriel in his chair.

"Brother-in-law," he said in Ladino, "I want to thank you for putting me up in your house for the night and to say good-bye again. I'm going to the war."

"Go in peace and return in peace," Gabriel blessed him. He wanted to shake Ephraim's hand but his knotted fingers and trembling hand wouldn't rise from the chair's armrest. And when Ephraim bent down to kiss his hand, Gabriel told him quietly, "Before you go, there's something I want to know."

Ephraim tensed.

"Who killed Matilda Franco?"

"It wasn't me who pulled the trigger," Ephraim replied. Then he turned and went off to the war.

"I knew it, I knew it," Rosa said and sighed. "In my heart I always knew it wasn't Ephraim."

"He didn't say it wasn't him, he said it wasn't him who pulled the trigger. You always hear what you want to hear," Luna said angrily and stormed out of the room.

The question of whether Tio Ephraim had or hadn't pulled the trigger when Matilda Franco was murdered remained a mystery in the history of our family. And Tio Ephraim, who until his death at a relatively young age remained as secretive as if he were still living underground, never provided a straight answer.

But in Ohel Moshe they never forgot or forgave him for Matilda Franco, and they'd talk about the murder over and over. And only my nona would say,

"My little brother *que no manqui*, everything they say about him should happen to *them*. The evil tongues can say what they want. To me he's a hero of Israel."

For many weeks now they hadn't heard a word from David, Moise, and Handsome Eli Cohen, who had also enlisted. Becky didn't stop crying.

"You're playing with your luck," Rosa told her. "You're crying before anything has happened, God forbid. Stop crying right now so you don't have to cry later, God forbid."

But Becky's tears flowed uncontrollably. Eli's photograph was always close to her heart, and at every opportunity she looked at and kissed it. At night she slept with the photograph under her pillow, and inside her bedside table she'd hung a drawing of a huge red heart pierced by an arrow through the middle, and on it she'd written "Becky and Eli Forever."

The only one who brought a smile to her face was Luna's baby, Gabriela. As soon as she got home from school she ran to the playpen and lifted Gabriela out. The baby held out her hands to her and laughed. What amazing dimples the child had when she laughed! Fortunately Luna gave Gabriela to Becky whenever she wanted, and not only that, it sometimes seemed to her that Luna was happy when she took Gabriela.

"Mashallah, look at Becky," Rosa would chortle, "playing with Gabriela like she played with her dolls when she was little."

Still, the atmosphere in Ohel Moshe was bleak and tense. Every day more and more people enlisted. They'd even started recruiting students, giving them a short period of training and then sending them to the front. Danger lurked in the streets. The Arabs destroyed the shops on Princess Mary Street, razed them to the ground, and burned down the Rex Cinema. The schools had been closed, and the youth movements had organized students to clean up shards of glass from the shops.

"You'll leave this house over my dead body!" Rosa yelled when Becky asked permission to join her friends in cleanup. "You're not going anywhere at a time like this! You could get caught in a shelling."

"I'm going to buy bread then," Becky told her mother. She didn't have the strength to argue. She was spent from crying all the time for Eli. Her friends were all taking part in the war effort, and only she was stuck at home.

"You're not going anywhere," Rosa said.

"But we're out of bread."

"We've got flour, we'll bake our own bread."

"There's no flour either," Becky said after searching the cupboard. "We're out of milk too, and cheese, and there's only a bit of rice left."

"We're lucky that Rachelika's got milk. At least we don't have to worry about Boaz and Gabriela," Rosa replied.

The market was almost devoid of goods, and even if there was stock, the Ermosas didn't have the money to buy. Of the five hundred lirot the Kurd had given them for the shop, there was hardly a grush left.

"Did you talk to Papo?" Luna asked when Rachelika shared her concerns regarding the finances.

"I don't want to worry him. He doesn't ask and I don't tell. The money will last for another few months at best, but I don't know what we'll do then."

"Maybe I'll go back to work at Zacks & Son," Luna suggested.

"Don't talk nonsense, Luna, you can't leave the baby."

Luna was silent. For what could she tell Rachelika, that what she wanted above all else was to leave the baby? That she didn't have the strength to hear her mewling like a kitten anymore? Miskenica Rachelika, who had to fill bottles of milk for her. How much could one tiny baby eat? And if she was not given milk, *wai de mi*, what screams, you'd think she was being killed. And worst of all was when Luna tried to pick her up, the baby screamed even more, but when Rachelika or Becky or even Rosa went to her, she calmed down right away. Whoever heard of such a thing, a baby that didn't want her own mother?

"How many bottles have you filled for her today?" Luna asked.

"Better you don't ask," Rachelika replied with a smile. "Your daughter, may she be healthy, eats for three. Even Boaziko eats less than her, God bless him. I just about finish nursing Boaziko and Gabriela's already yelling for her bottle."

"So just give her a teta."

"God help us, Luna, what am I, her wet nurse? I'm her aunt, it's out of the question!"

"What's the difference if she feeds from you or a bottle?"

"Does a bottle have feelings, troncha?"

"All right, don't get angry. I just wanted to make it easier for you so you don't have to fill bottles."

"You're not making it easier, you're making it harder. Go away now, let me be alone with Boaz. Take Gabriela and go out."

"Where to?"

"Outside, the garden, take her for a walk."

"Are you crazy? It's too cold for her outside."

"I don't care where you go, just take her out and give me a little privacy!"

"What privacy? Is there any privacy here? We've gone back to being three little girls, you, me, and Becky."

"Luna, enough!"

Luna went out, forgetting Gabriela, who was lying in the playpen with Boaz.

"Troncha de Tveria, where's her head?" Rachelika muttered.

It really has become too crowded in the house, thought Rosa, who had been eavesdropping on her daughters' argument. Let this cursed war be over, let each of them go to her own house. She hadn't raised girls so they'd be hanging around her neck forever. Not Rachelika, she was like light in the house, but Luna? Until she's finally gone to her own house, praise God. But what was to be done? The men were in the war, and until the war was over they'd live like this, even though the crowdedness sometimes threatened to suffocate her.

That evening Rosa went out into the yard and sat on a stool. A chilly wind was blowing and she pulled her big scarf more tightly around her. The sky was full of stars and everything was so tranquil and serene. Even the echoes of shooting had fallen silent. The babies had been put to sleep in their playpen, her husband had gone to bed, and her daughters were in their room, so why was this quiet so menacing? Why did she have the feeling that something bad was about to happen?

She suddenly saw Luna standing in the doorway. She was so thin, she had the silhouette of a young boy, as if a baby had never been in her belly. Feeling stifled, Rosa hurried back inside and went to bed.

Thank God she's gone back in, Luna thought. I was worried I wouldn't find anywhere to be alone for a moment. Gabriela's inside, my mother's outside, and Becky's crying all the time because of Handsome Eli Cohen. You'd think she's the only one who's worried about her boy. Rachelika isn't worried? She keeps her worries to herself, doesn't let anybody in on her thoughts, keeps herself busy all day with Boaziko and Gabriela. Like a worker ant she runs around and takes more and more tasks on herself so as not to let her worries invade her life. And she, Luna, was she as worried about her husband as her sisters were about their men? God help them, sometimes entire days went by without her even thinking about David. God forgive her, but since he went off to the war she'd finally started breathing again. She'd needed distance from him. If he'd taken Gabriela with him, it would have been even better.

God would repay her for these thoughts, but she couldn't deny them. Ever since Gabriela had been born, Luna's heart had been hollow. Everybody crowded around her like she was the center of the world, a rare and fragile creature, amazed by the rosy-cheeked, green-eyed baby, the one they all said was her spitting image. Only she couldn't see any resemblance at all between them. And Gabriela, she smiled at everyone except her mother. You couldn't fool babies. You couldn't pretend with babies the way she'd pretended over the past year with David. Babies feel more than adults do, Luna recognized. And my baby must sense her mother's heart is empty.

At first she'd thought that it was because of the difficult birth. After the stitches were removed and her body gradually recovered from the trauma, she believed that now she'd fall in love with the baby, but it hadn't happened. She had more of a bond with Boaziko than with her own baby. She wished she could get away and go sit in Café Atara, but all the boys had gone off to the war and all the girls were at home busy worrying about them, so there was nobody left to meet there. Her heart ached with sadness because she was such a bad mother. Miskenica the baby, it wasn't her fault her mother was sick in the head, it wasn't her fault that instead of being happy and proud that the baby enchanted everybody, she didn't feel anything, just the opposite, she got angry. She should be put in a straitjacket and sent to the Ezrat Nashim Mental Hospital. She was surely going crazy. If she didn't find a way out of this madness she'd kill herself. She couldn't stand herself. How could it be that she didn't love her baby, not even a tiny bit?

"Let her go to work," Gabriel said to Rachelika when she shared Luna's proposal of going back to Zacks & Son to help with the family's finances. "She doesn't help in the house, and anyway you and Becky look after Gabriela while she sits with her legs crossed."

"How can she go to work?" said the shocked Rosa, whose voice had been increasingly heard since Gabriel had fallen ill. "Gabriela's not yet six months old. What will the neighbors say?"

"What do I care what the neighbors say," Gabriel shouted. "Let her go to work!"

"Dio santo, Gabriel, whoever heard of a mother leaving her baby before she's a year old and going to work?"

"So what do you suggest, Rosa? That I get up out of this chair and go out robbing for money?"

"God forbid, what are you saying?"

"Mother," Rachelika tried to calm things down, "there's no choice. The money will run out any minute. Somebody has to bring in an income."

"Then I'll go back to cleaning houses!" Rosa said, not quite believing she'd actually uttered those words.

"Wait a while longer until I die and then go back to cleaning houses," Gabriel said. "It won't be much longer—a few months, no more."

"God forbid, *pishcado y limon, tfu-tfu-tfu,* how can you let nonsense like that out of your mouth?"

"I talk nonsense and you're as wise as an owl. Do you hear yourself? The wife of Gabriel Ermosa will clean houses? Do you want to take away the little dignity I have left?"

"God forbid, querido, God forbid, don't get angry, it's bad for you. I only wanted to help so Luna doesn't have to work and can stay home for Gabriela."

"Mother, Luna doesn't even look after the baby. It's you, Becky, and me who do. Luna's in no state to look after the baby right now. We have to let time take its course."

Rachelika knew full well that Luna's chances of getting a job at Zacks & Son were slim. They should pray the shop was even still open and that Mr. Zacks hadn't closed it because of the situation. But it was better that Luna had something to do, healthier for both her and the family.

Luna was beside herself with happiness when Rachelika told her the news, but she forced herself to sit quietly on the couch and not jump for joy. There's a god in heaven who hears prayers, she told herself. And even Rachelika, who warned her not to get too excited before she was sure that Mr. Zacks needed a saleslady at a time like this, couldn't dampen her enthusiasm. Luna didn't understand why a war should stop women from buying clothes. Never mind that there was no food—Jerusalem was under siege, and there was nobody to bring fruit and vegetables and even meat or flour to the market—there were plenty of dresses hanging in the shop. The mannequins in the window were still styled in last year's clothes and were just begging for Luna to come and change them.

That same day Luna put on a tailored gray suit, and although she hadn't regained her figure and had to wear a corset, the cut of the jacket accentuated her slim hips. She looked at herself in the mirror and was pleased for the first time since she'd had the baby.

She slung an elegant black purse over her shoulder, put on a pair of high-heeled pumps that set off her beautiful ankles and legs, and walked through the Ohel Moshe gate, her heels tapping and her head held high as if her whole life lay before her.

It had been a long time since she'd walked down the slope of Agrippas Street toward Jaffa Road and the Pillars Building. The continuous shelling from the direction of Nabi Samwil had put an end to her strolls, and she'd left Ohel Moshe only when she'd had to. She wasn't surprised by the almost deserted streets or the sandbags and sand-filled wooden crates in the doorways of houses and shops. People were being killed every day. One day, one of their neighbors, a draft evader, was walking to the Mahane Yehuda Market when shrapnel from a shell exploding nearby sheared off his head.

"Miskenico," Rosa had said, "if he'd gone to the war perhaps he'd still be alive."

The family of one of Luna's girlfriends from school, seven people in all, were killed when their house took a direct hit from the shelling. The Jews of the Old City's Jewish Quarter were imprisoned in the Quarter and could leave and reenter only in armored vehicles. The relentless shelling and the siege choked the city, turning the lives of its inhabitants into one of constant terror and fear. The soldiers of Mishmar Haam, the Jewish home guard, and Meginei Yerushalayim, the defenders of Jerusalem, could be seen everywhere. Young boys, children almost, and men too old to fight on the front stood shoulder to shoulder and did what they could to protect the citizens from the shelling, which had become a daily occurrence.

As she walked, Luna could hear shelling and shooting from the eastern part of the city. Fear stole into her heart, but her excitement over the possibility of working in the shop again kept her going. Soldiers whistled at her as she passed. "Hey, sweetie pie!" they called out, and she smiled and was as happy as she'd once been, before she'd married David, before she'd had Gabriela, before the war. Fully aware of the glances of the passerby, every now and then she brushed her red curls aside and tightened her suit against her slim frame. And then, just as she reached the Eden Cinema and the junction of Jaffa Road and King George Street, she heard a terrifying whistle that almost tore her eardrums apart, an awful, petrifying noise. She felt a tremendous force carry her like a tsunami wave, and then she lost consciousness.

———————

All at once Agrippas Street was filled with the wail of ambulance sirens. The shelling had been more intense than usual, destroying houses on the street and in adjacent neighborhoods. Clouds of smoke enveloped the street, and ambulances sped over from Bikur Holim Hospital at the center of the city. Shouts and screams and cries could be heard from every direction. The soldiers barely managed to control the commotion as they set up a fence around the area to prevent people from entering it, and then began evacuating the wounded.

Rachelika was at the grocery next door to Rachmo when she heard the explosion and immediately started running.

"Wait a minute," the grocer tried to stop her. "Wait until we know where the shelling's coming from." But Rachelika had already crossed the street, though not without almost being mowed down by a horse and cart. Something told her to hurry, so she ran faster, straining every muscle. She had a feeling that something terrible had happened. Just not Boaziko, just not Gabriela, she prayed. When she reached her parents' house exhausted, people were crowding around the door. Frightened, she burst in, and only when she saw that Boaz and Gabriela were safe did she breathe a sigh of relief. Thank God, she thought. She'd been scared for nothing.

"What are all the neighbors doing here?" she asked Rosa.

"As soon as we heard the noise they all came to hear what happened on your father's radio."

"And Luna?"

"Probably at Zacks & Son. She'll come back soon when they let people through," Rosa replied and scurried back into the kitchen. She didn't want to worry about Luna. She had habas con arroz on the stove and Gabriel to worry about, and Luna, God willing, would arrive soon.

"We need to go and look for her," Gabriel called out.

"Come on, Becky," Rachelika said. "We'll run to Zacks & Son."

"Be careful," Rosa begged them. "It's very dangerous outside. Only walk where the soldiers tell you, don't be heroes." Dio santo, she would have preferred that her daughters stay home and not go out at such a time, but she too understood that her husband would not sit quietly until Luna showed her face. All she could do now was pray and contend with the faces Gabriel made because he'd had enough of eating habas con arroz every day. But what could you do, God forgive her sins, when they couldn't afford anything other than rice and beans?

Rachelika and Becky ran down Agrippas Street. Disobeying their mother and avoiding the soldiers who were keeping people out of the shelled area, they took a roundabout route through the alleys, between the debris of the collapsed buildings, trying not to think about the bloodstains on the sidewalk. Out of breath they finally reached Zacks & Son, only to find that the shop was locked.

As if possessed, they continued running up Jaffa Road toward Bikur Holim Hospital. They stormed inside, looking for Luna in all the wards, but she wasn't there.

"Maybe she's home already," Becky said hopefully.

"Let's keep on looking," Rachelika replied. They crossed the street and then ran to Hadassah Hospital, and that's where they found her.

"She was wounded in the shelling," the girls were told when they arrived. "Badly wounded. She's in surgery. The doctors are doing everything they can to save her."

The two sisters sat down on the cold stone floor and burst into tears.

"I shouldn't have let her leave the house at a time like this," Rachelika sobbed. "I just let her go. I knew that Zacks & Son was closed. I knew that nobody's buying clothes now. I knew it was dangerous outside. Why did I let her go?"

"Papo knew as well," Becky said. "And so did Luna, but she was suffocating in the house. We needed to let her feel that she was doing something. You could see she wasn't bonding with the baby, you could see it was hard for her. It hurt me more for the baby than for her. I could see her sadness. She had to get out of the house."

"That's why I urged Papo to let her look for a job," Rachelika confessed. "That's why he put on a show for Mother as if Luna could save the family with the few grush she earned in the shop, that's why he told me to give her his consent. Miskenica Lunika, I'm sure she felt she was going for nothing too, that deep down she knew the shop was closed and that Mr. Zacks was sitting at home like the rest of us."

"What will happen if she dies? Gabriela's not six months old and she won't have a mother." Becky wept.

They cried in each other's arms until Rachelika regained her composure and said, "We have to speak to the doctors, hear what her condition is, and then we'll have to go and tell Papo and Mother."

"How can we tell Papo?" Becky asked through her tears. "He's hanging on by a thread as it is. If he hears that Luna's seriously wounded it'll finish him."

"We'll worry about that later. Right now let's wait for the doctors."

The hours ticked by and Luna didn't come out of the operating room.

"You go home," Rachelika told Becky. "They must be going crazy with worry. I'll stay here until Luna comes out."

"I'm not going anywhere!" Becky insisted. "If anybody goes, it should be you. You have to nurse Boaziko and give Gabriela her bottle. They're probably so hungry they're turning the house upside down."

"God almighty, I completely forgot," Rachelika said in a panic. "I completely forgot the babies! All right, you stay here, I'll go tell Papo and Mother. I'll feed the babies and come straight back."

"Go and be careful on the way. I won't move from here."

But before Rachelika could get up and go, the door of the operating room opened and one of the doctors came out.

"Is there anybody here from the family of Luna Siton?"

"We are," they said as they jumped up and held their breath.

"We've operated on the patient," the doctor said. "She's very seriously wounded, almost all her internal organs have been damaged, but she's young. She'll live."

While Luna was fighting for her life, Jerusalem was fighting for its life too. The city was under siege and the water supply piped into the city from Rosh Haayin was cut off by the Arabs.

"Thank God there's a cistern in every yard," Gabriel told his daughters. "Without it we'd die of thirst." He ordered them to place empty cans on the roof and in the yard to collect rainwater for washing themselves and the dishes, and then they'd use the dirty water to wash the floor. A short time later the Mishmar Haam would distribute leaflets in the city with similar instructions.

Rosa and the girls emptied a few tins planted with geraniums in the yard and wasted some of the precious water supply to wash them with soap. Then they took the tins to Agrippas Street, where they waited with the rest of the neighborhood for the allocation of water from tankers that went from one neighborhood to the next. Each family was given one can of water for drinking and another for washing, but there wasn't always enough. Gabriel remembered that there was a cistern at the Etz Ha'Haim yeshiva not far from his shop in the market. He knew the man in charge of pumping. Every Friday before Shabbat he used to fill the man's basket with free goodies for his family. It was time to be repaid for everything Gabriel had given over the years, so he sent Rachelika, and the man opened the cistern and filled her can, off the books.

Kerosene was also running out. We'll soon have to light the Primus with arak, thought Rosa. The kerosene the Mishmar Haam give out in glasses is barely enough for a pot of soup! Many families in the neighborhood had resorted to sending their children to stand by the chimney at Berman's bakery with tins to catch the dripping oil.

Life in the Ermosa house revolved around taking care of the babies and Gabriel, whose condition was worsening. His mind was as clear and sharp as it had always been, but his speech was increasingly difficult to understand. They had to bend over him and put their ear to his lips to comprehend him. And yet, though his handsome face was gray, it surprisingly did not bear a single wrinkle. Amazing, Rachelika thought. He has the face of a young man and the body of an old man, and he's not yet forty-eight.

Since he'd been called back from the front after Luna's injuries, David's life was divided between his wounded wife in the hospital, his baby daughter at his in-laws' house, and his guard duty at various posts surrounding Jerusalem. Every morning Gabriela's crying would rouse David from his restless sleep. He'd hurry over, pick her up, and tickle her tummy with his nose, and the child would smile back at him. He'd give her the bottle that Rachelika had pumped the previous evening, change her diaper, play with her a while, and then rush to the hospital to be with Luna.

At the hospital, he'd leap over the sandbags at the entrance and quickly climb the stairs to the second floor. The corridors were crowded with the wounded. Their cries, along with the weeping of relatives and the desperation of the few overworked doctors and nurses who were unable to keep up with the flow of victims arriving every hour, always broke his heart, and the awful stench of urine mixed with ointments and disinfectant made him dizzy.

"Lunika," David whispered to her one morning. She was lying in her bed, eyes closed, hooked up to an IV and other devices which although he'd been told their function innumerable times, he still hadn't understood. She looked so small, a little, broken-winged bird, even the narrow hospital bed too big for her frame. Her face was twisted with pain, her lips, cracked. She was one big wound. He didn't dare touch her, God forbid he break her fragile body.

When she didn't respond, he put his hand under her nose, to her lips. She was breathing, thank God. This he did every morning to make sure she was alive, the way he did at night when he checked on Gabriela.

There wasn't a chair in the room, and he was afraid to sit on the bed in case he grazed her damaged body. "Lunika," he whispered again.

"She's alive," said the man in the next bed. "Barely, but she's alive."

He was a boy of maybe eighteen, maybe twenty, and he was wounded from head to toe, his whole body swaddled in bandages. His face was swollen, and blood had collected on it and in his golden hair. Only his blue eyes burned with the vitality of youth.

"Where were you wounded?" David asked him.

"At Bab el-Wad," the boy replied. "I was in a convoy that tried to break the siege when we were attacked from Beit Makhsir. Luckily they were able to get me out and brought me here in an armored vehicle. The doctors operated and saved my life, but it'll only be after they take off the bandages that we'll see what's been salvaged." He grimaced in a short laugh.

"The main thing is you're laughing, and that's something." David smiled.

"Well, what else can I do, cry?"

"And your parents, the family know?"

"My parents haven't been here yet. They live a long way away, in Nahariya, and the city's cut off, so there's no way they can get here and no way to inform them."

"Is there anything I can do for you? Do you have family in Jerusalem?"

"No, all my family's in Nahariya."

"Well, if there's anything you need, don't hesitate to ask," David said.

"Thanks," the young man said. "I'm Gidi, but the guys call me Ginger. I'm sorry I can't shake hands. And she," he asked, "where was she wounded?"

"In the shelling on Agrippas Street."

"A relative?"

"My wife, Luna. We have a six-month-old daughter. I was on the southern front when it happened. I was only told a few days after it happened and was granted permission to come to Jerusalem. I came with one of the convoys, and now I'm here looking after the baby and my wife."

"They released you from the front?"

"I'm currently serving at the outposts around Jerusalem. I'll go back to the front when my wife's condition improves. I have to go now, I'm due on duty. If a miracle happens and she starts talking, tell her I was here. Tell her I'll be back tomorrow."

Two complicated operations were needed to save my mother, and she barely survived either. My father was there when she had the first, sitting for many hours with Rachelika and Becky outside the operating room, praying for her life. He spent many days at his wife's bedside, and every other free moment he spent with me, his baby daughter. But as sixty days went by and there was no improvement in my mother's condition, he felt that if he continued living this way he'd go insane. He needed to be at the front, taking part in the war. That's what he'd done when he'd fought against the fascists in Italy, it's what he'd done when he'd fought against Rommel's army, and now he wanted to fight against Kaoukji's army. He missed the south, the jeeps, the stocking hat. He missed the battalion's Oras, raven-haired Ora and blond Ora, Ora the kibbutznik and Ora the Tel Avivan. They were always dancing attention on him and he liked to give each of them the feeling that she was the only Ora for him. He'd loved the easygoing atmosphere of his unit, the leather jackets, the goggles, the scarves, the unconditional bond. He loved telling chizbatim, tall tales, and most of all he loved being behind the wheel of the reconnaissance jeep. How he missed speeding between the hills. He'd never forget the fusillade of fire the battalion took near Negba. He'd felt that his life might be over when the jeep's tires were shot out and it came to a halt, but on the other hand, he'd had this feeling of elation. And right then, just as he'd really begun to enjoy the war, Luna had been wounded and he was sent back to Jerusalem.

When my mother's condition improved slightly, Rachelika decided it was time to take me for a visit to the hospital. "Perhaps if Luna sees Gabriela it will improve her mood," she said. But to her horror, she recognized that not only wasn't my mother in the mood to see me, I wasn't in the mood to see her either. When they lay me beside her on the hospital bed I burst into tears and waved my little arms in every direction, and Luna devolved into hysterics. "Take her away, take her away," she said. "And don't bring her anymore. A hospital's no place for children."

It was a hard scene to witness, and my Aunt Rachelika, whom nothing in the world could break, couldn't bear it. Tears flowed from her eyes as she took me from my mother and gazed at her sister. Luna had lost weight and was as feeble as a leaf in the wind. Her beautiful hair had started falling out, and there were bald patches on her pate. She looked like one of the Holocaust survivors whose pictures frequently appeared in the newspapers.

Rachelika kissed her sister and took her leave. "You're right, Lunika, a hospital is no place for babies. We'll wait till you're strong enough to get out of bed and go down into the garden, and then I'll bring her again."

My mother didn't answer, her spirits now so low that she didn't say a word for days on end. My father would plead with her, "Luna, say something?" but she'd remain silent. It sometimes seemed to David that she was punishing him. Only the redheaded boy in the next bed could rouse the occasional smile from her. Despite his condition, which was no less serious than hers, his spirit infected all the other patients in the ward, even Luna.

She was never alone. There was always a family member at her bedside to give her anything she needed. Rachelika, Becky, Rosa, other relatives, and neighbors all took their turn looking after Luna and taking care of me. "Chicitica miskenica," Nona Rosa told me many years later, "how many hands you passed through!"

The war raged on. Every now and then one of the convoys managed to elude the Arab gangs lying in ambush and break through to Jerusalem. Rachelika and Becky would run down to Jaffa Road and together with "the whole of Jerusalem" would welcome the heroic soldiers with cries of joy and love, and then stand in line to receive the ration of food.

On one such occasion a surprise awaited them. From Tel Aviv Tia Allegra had sent a package containing oil, rice, flour, sugar, two tomatoes, a packet of butter, and even some sweets and bizcochos she'd baked specially. That evening the neighbors were invited for an equal portion of the goodies. That was the custom. Anyone who received a package would share it and not keep it, God forbid, all for themselves. They made a point of sharing with families with babies and sick people.

"We had a lot of tricks to invent food," Nona Rosa explained to me many years later. "When the food ran out, your aunts, may they be healthy, would go with the neighbors to the fields behind Ohel Moshe near Sheikh Badr, where the Knesset building is now, and they'd pick hubeiza, mallows, like the Arab women. Then we'd make a fire in the yard, boil water, and add the hubeiza seeds, a little onion, salt and pepper, and we'd have a splendid soup. If there was enough flour and a drop of oil, my dear neighbor Tamar would bake bread, which was her specialty, and we'd dip it in the soup and have a feast for a king."

Rosa did her utmost to keep the household in order, trying to stick to the traditional Spaniol dishes as much as she could, going to great lengths to make something out of nothing. She had long since stopped putting meat in the Shabbat hamin, and instead she made kubebas, bread dumplings that she spiced with salt, pepper, and herbs picked from the fields. Fortunately, the family loved her kubebas, and years later, even when they could afford meat and there was no shortage, my family continued to eat the kubebas that Nona Rosa had made during the war and the following period of austerity.

Three months had passed from the day my mother was wounded, and while her condition had improved somewhat, she was still unable to get out of bed. Most of the time she'd lie on her back, eyes closed. The redheaded boy would try to make her laugh and would just about squeeze a tired smile out of her.

"*Ahalan,* lovely lady"—he smiled at her—"I've been told you have green eyes, but I don't believe it."

She opened her eyes.

"Oh, at long last. I've been lying here next to you for three months and this is the first time I've seen your eyes. You have such beautiful eyes, why do you keep them closed?"

She didn't answer, but deep down she took pleasure in the compliment. It was the first time since she had been wounded that somebody had gotten through to her.

As the situation in Jerusalem worsened, the number of neighbors and relatives who volunteered to sit with my mother dwindled, and the burden fell mainly on Rachelika and Becky. Nona Rosa preferred to look after the babies rather than sit with my mother, who even though she was critically wounded still scowled at her.

Between bombardments the neighbors would sit in the yard to get some fresh air, chat, and enjoy the sun after days and nights cooped up indoors.

"Heideh, querido," Nona Rosa said to her husband, "let's go and sit outside for a while."

"You go. I'm happy inside."

"But querido, it's been a long time since we went outside. The sun will do you good."

"Nothing will do me any good. What point is there in my life when I sit in the chair all day and can't even visit my daughter."

Rosa's heart ached. She knew how much he was torturing himself for not being able to visit Luna. She decided to speak to David. Maybe he'd have an idea for getting Gabriel to the hospital.

And so my father parked an army jeep by the Ohel Moshe gate, carried Nono Gabriel to it, and sat him in the front seat. Rachelika and Becky climbed into the back, and Nona Rosa stayed behind to look after Boaz and me.

When they reached the hospital, my father carried Nono Gabriel up the stairs to my mother's ward. Carefully and gently he lowered him to the floor so he wouldn't fall. Supported by my father on one side and my Aunt Rachelika on the other, Nono Gabriel walked slowly and with measured steps to his daughter's sickbed.

"Lunika, look who's here," Rachelika said.

Luna opened her eyes, and when she saw her father, the dam holding back everyone's tears broke. There wasn't a dry eye when the sick man bent over the bed and kissed his daughter's fevered brow, and Luna's cracked lips whispered, "I'm alive. Don't cry, Papo, I'm alive."

The Arab Legion overran the Etzion Bloc and the defenders who weren't killed were taken prisoner. The Old City fell and its Jewish residents fled to the western part of the city. Arnona and Talpiot, the city's southern neighborhoods, were shelled incessantly. Kibbutz Ramat Rachel was also taken by the legion but was then retaken by the Israeli Defense Forces. There was a cease-fire in late spring, but a month later, as the figs ripened and the sabras, the prickly pears, were bursting with juice, the fighting erupted again in full force. The convoys barely made their way into besieged Jerusalem. People were starving, and infant mortality was on the rise.

One night Nona Rosa was awakened by my crying. She went to the playpen and picked me up. I had a high fever, my diaper was soaked with watery, bloody feces, and my face was contorted in pain. My wails tore at Nona Rosa's heart, and my crying woke the whole house.

"The child has a high fever," Rachelika said. "We have to get her to Dr. Kagan and quickly."

My father wrapped my little body in a blanket and with me in his arms ran all the way to Bikur Holim Hospital.

Dr. Kagan was already there and was being run off her feet. It took only one look for her to say, "She's got dysentery like half the children in Jerusalem. We need to admit her."

Dr. Kagan treated me with devotion as if I were her own daughter, as she treated the scores of children in her care, but my condition didn't improve and the fever didn't abate. I cried and cried until my strength was spent and my crying became a sad wailing, matching that of the rest of the children in the ward.

I was critically ill. My poor father didn't know who to take care of first, my mother or me. Even Rachelika broke down. She could endure anything, even Luna's suffering, but not the suffering of a baby.

Becky moved into the hospital and slept on the floor at the foot of my crib in a blanket she brought from home. She spent hours pacing in the corridors with me in her arms. Nona Rosa found herself pleading to God as she hadn't pleaded since she lost her firstborn son, holding a Book of Psalms and staring at the letters she didn't know how to read, lighting candles and making vows. And Nono Gabriel withdrew into himself more and more. He hardly spoke and even stopped listening to his radio, for what could it tell him that he didn't already know? The cursed war was inside his own home. Who could tell him anything about the injustices of the war when his own daughter and granddaughter were its victims?

"Why aren't you doing anything?" my father pleaded with Dr. Kagan. "Why aren't you helping my daughter?"

"I'm sorry," the doctor replied, "but there's nothing more to do beyond what we're already doing. We're replacing the little one's fluids and salts in the hope it will help. We don't have any penicillin, we're out of drugs. We're waiting for them to arrive with the next convoy."

But the convoy couldn't break through and my condition deteriorated.

"Dio santo, how frightened I was that we'd have to sit shiva for you, God forbid," Nona Rosa told me. Her nightmares returned, all the memories that over the years she'd tried to repress, the pain of her son Raphael's death assailing her anew as if she had just now lost him. Dio Senor el mundo, she begged her god, don't let me lose a granddaughter too.

And while I was fighting for my life in Bikur Holim and my mother was

fighting for hers in Hadassah, Rachelika was fighting to hold the family together. She was constantly rushing around looking after her son and her sister
and her niece. She was unafraid of the danger and would leave the house once
a day and go from one hospital to the other. Even Nona Rosa's pleadings that
she let Becky, who was living in the hospital, look after Gabriela and just visit
Luna were to no avail. Rachelika was out of her mind with worry. She finally
found some small consolation in a letter that arrived from the field, reading it
over and over until she could draw enough strength from it.

"I love you, my soul," Moise wrote. "I love you as much as life itself, both
you and Boaz who I hardly know." He asked about the family and Luna and
only at the end, in one sentence, did he write that he was safe and well. Thank
God. She was calmed on that front, and now she had to do the same on the
others. But how could she while Luna was still fighting for her life and her
baby was at death's door?

One time, before Rachelika went home to Boaz, she told Becky, "Try and
rouse Gabriela's will to live. You have to!"

But how could Becky rouse the will to live in such a little baby? She was
only a child herself, how could she help Gabriela recover? Where was her Eli
now when she needed him so badly? He would have given her strength, he
would have helped her save Gabriela.

"You have to get better," Becky told Gabriela. "Do you hear me, my sweet,
my lovely, you have to drink, because if anything happens to you I'll die. Do
you hear, my honeybunch, I'll die."

She put the bottle into the baby's mouth, and with her last remaining
strength Gabriela pushed it away. As the doctor had instructed, Becky wet the
corner of a diaper and put it between the baby's lips, but she turned her head.

Becky didn't put her down for a moment. She refused to lay Gabriela in her
crib, frightened that as soon as the baby didn't feel her thin arms around her,
something terrible would happen. The responsibility for Gabriela's life was on
her shoulders. Even David was unable to cope and cried like a baby. And Rachelika miskenica, when Dr. Kagan heard that she had a baby at home, she
forbade her to come. She could infect Boaziko. So every day she stood in the
hospital yard and Becky held Gabriela in her arms by the window so Rachelika could see her, and only once she had did she run to Luna's bedside.

Luna knew nothing of Gabriela's illness. The family decided not to tell her.
Anyway, she'd asked them not to bring the baby, and she was so preoccupied
with her own pain and troubles that she didn't even ask. It's better this way,

Rachelika thought. When the war's over, when Luna gets better, God willing, and when Gabriela gets better too, they'll tell her. Everything will be fine. Luna will find room in her heart for Gabriela, and they'll be able to make up for lost time.

Gabriela's condition continued to decline, and pain threatened to tear David's heart from his chest when he held her frail body in his arms. Her sweet face was twisted in constant pain, her expression was apathetic. She no longer laughed aloud when she saw him and didn't raise her arms for him to pick her up. She couldn't even cry anymore. He couldn't bear it. He fell apart, wept like a child. Compared to him, Becky, may she be healthy, a fifteen-year-old child, was a rock. Rachelika, Rosa, each of the Ermosa family women is more of a man than me, David thought. He didn't know which one to worry about first, his wife or his daughter. He didn't know who to pray harder for. So instead of praying he cried, not in the dark and not in secret but openly, holding his dying daughter, clasping her tiny body to his heart, defeated.

Like David, Jerusalem too felt defeated. The city looked like it had suffered an earthquake, smoking ruins, people moving like shadows, seeking refuge from the exploding shells. The city center was shelled daily. The crowded, vibrant Jaffa Road and Ben-Yehuda and King George Streets were deserted now, the shops shuttered, the houses darkened. No one came or went. The Arab Legion had taken Atarot and Neve Yaakov. Kibbutz Beit Haarava had also fallen, the Old City had fallen, and if a miracle didn't happen soon, the New City would fall too.

If the makeshift Burma Road into Jerusalem hadn't been opened a month after I contracted dysentery, it's doubtful that I would have lived. When the siege was broken and supplies reached the city, drugs arrived too. My condition slowly improved, I started eating again and put on weight, and I regained my vitality. Now when my father came to visit me in the hospital I'd burst into shouts of joy, wave my arms, and laugh at him, and he'd sink his face into my tummy and make funny noises, lifting me in the air with a big smile on his face.

Two months after I was taken to the hospital I returned home. My recovery was the only thing that lifted the cloud over the Ermosa family home at the time. My mother's condition had improved slightly, but she wasn't yet out of the woods. She had been in the hospital for many months and the end still wasn't in sight.

My father, who had been forced to give up his duties and become a dispatch rider when I got sick, rejoined his unit defending Jerusalem and spent every night in one of the defensive positions, his weapon cocked. When he was relieved in the morning he'd hurry to the hospital to visit my mother, and when Becky or Rachelika came to take over, he'd rush to Nono and Nona's house to be with me until it was time for him to go back on duty. He scarcely slept.

The convoys that brought supplies to Jerusalem along the Burma Road also brought mail from the front. Becky lived from letter to letter. Each time a convoy reached the city, she'd hurry to Handsome Eli Cohen's parents' house, and he'd never disappoint her. Each time he sent a letter to his parents, there was one for her filled with love and longing. She'd open the envelope excitedly and read the letter over and over, kissing it and staining it with tears. At every chance she visited the home of her beloved's parents. She felt that when she was close to them, she was close to him as well.

Optimistic letters arrived from Moise too, relating the advances made in the south and the approaching end of the war. Yet the more he tried not to worry her in his letters, the more Rachelika worried. She could sense his helplessness. His words of love couldn't conceal his anxiety for her, Boaz, her family, and the wounded Luna, but she tried to repress the pain she felt so she could carry on.

While Handsome Eli Cohen and Moise wrote to their loved ones whenever they could, Nona Rosa didn't receive any sign of life from Ephraim. Despite her concern, she felt sure that just as he'd managed throughout all the long years in the Lehi, he'd manage this time too. Her main focuses now were Luna, over whom the threat of death still hung; her husband, whose condition was constantly worsening; and the maintenance of the household. Rachelika and Becky were a major help and took over all her usual tasks, except for looking after the babies. But the money was running out, and even if Gabriel now agreed to her cleaning the houses of strangers, who would she work for? Who had money for a housemaid in wartime?

My mother was still not aware of the danger to my life. She was so worried about her own injuries and in such pain, so why add grief and sorrow? Every now and then she'd ask how her daughter was, and they'd report on her progress: She'd cut a new tooth, she'd begun standing in the playpen, she'd started crawling. Luna would smile and say, "May she be healthy," and no more.

But one day she said to David, "Maybe you'll bring the little one tomorrow? I miss her."

So the next day Becky put me in a pink dress with pompons that Nona Rosa had knitted, tied a ribbon in my red curls, and handed me to my father.

"We're going to see Ima," my father told me. "Ima, say Ima," and I repeated it like a parrot. "It will make your ima very happy when she hears you say Ima." He laughed, and again I repeated the new word I'd learned.

My father was worried that, God forbid, I might catch a bug or some infection and become sick again, so he and Luna arranged to meet in the hospital garden.

Luna made it down to the ground floor with great difficulty. Every step was very painful for her. Her wounds hadn't yet healed, and she was worried that each step she took might open the stitches and her guts would spill out. But at each step she forced herself to keep going.

"Be careful," the redheaded neighbor had counseled her. "Go down very slowly and hold on to the banister." He wanted to help her, but he himself was bedridden, unable to move his legs. It broke his heart to see Luna making such a tremendous effort for her daughter. She'd grunt in her sleep, groan with pain, weep into her pillow, covering her head with the hospital blanket so nobody would hear her, but he saw and he heard and he hurt for her.

Luna limped from step to step until she reached the lobby, and from there she walked, almost crawled, to the gate. She came out just as David arrived with the baby. When she saw the child, she couldn't believe how much she'd grown. She held out her arms to take her, but the moment my father passed me to her I started crying and kicking, refusing her arms. And Luna, who'd already forgotten the scene I'd made the last time I'd been brought to see her, stood there stunned and hurt.

"She doesn't recognize me," she said painfully. "She has no idea that I'm her mother."

"She hasn't seen you for ages," David tried to console her. "Give her time and everything will be fine."

Luna could not conceal her pain and disappointment.

"It doesn't matter, David," she said. "The main thing is that Gabriela's well and being looked after."

"Don't worry, my lovely, everyone's looking after her. Your mother, your sisters, the neighbors, they all love her. She's a good girl."

"Yes," Luna muttered. "She's a good girl."

"She's the spitting image of you, everybody says so. The eyes, the hair, the dimples, she's a real little Luna."

"Yes, a real little Luna," she mumbled, trying to hold back her tears.

"Go now," she told my father. "Go and come back another time. I'm tired. I'm going back to the ward."

He kissed my mother's cheek, and in a last desperate attempt said to me, "Heideh, bonica, heideh, my little dolly, say Ima like you did before. Say it, good girl."

But I scowled and refused and cried even louder.

"It doesn't matter, David, take her home."

"But Luna, she has to get to know you. She has to know that you're her mother."

"She'll know, David. I'll come home, God willing, and everything will be all right. Take her home now. I don't like her crying like this."

"Look after yourself," he told her. "I'll be back tomorrow."

He kissed her again and went through the hospital gate, disappointed by the encounter between his daughter and her mother but determined not to give up. He would continue bringing Gabriela to visit.

Again with great difficulty Luna climbed the stairs, limped to her bed, got under the blanket, and covered her head.

"Is everything all right, Luna?" the redhead asked.

She didn't answer.

"How was seeing your daughter?"

"She doesn't even know I'm her mother," Luna whispered.

"She hasn't seen you for many months, it's only natural," he said, trying to comfort her.

"No, it's not natural. Nothing between me and my daughter is natural."

9

FOR MANY NIGHTS now Gabriel had been unable to have an hour's undisturbed sleep, night after night waking from a recurring dream. In it he is running, he crosses fields, mountains, seas, and oceans. "Where are you running to, Gabriel?" a woman's sweet voice asks him. He doesn't reply and goes on running. He is breathing heavily but he can't stop, he can't slow down. He runs and runs and runs, and then—always in the same place and at the same moment—her figure suddenly appears out of nowhere, running in front of him, and he tries to catch up with her, the girl he hasn't seen for years, the girl with the golden hair and blue eyes. He holds out his hand to touch her but can't get close enough, and the girl continuously eludes him. And when he is almost there, almost touching her, he wakes up drenched in sweat and with a harsh sense of missed opportunity. He wants to sit up in bed; he is parched, thirsty, but he can't sit up by himself. He would have to wake Rosa to help him, and how can he wake her, how can he look her in the eye and ask her to help him when the reason he needs her help in the middle of the night is the golden-haired girl whose memory has prevented him from loving her all his life in the way a man should love a woman?

He lies with his eyes open, praying to God to end his suffering. It is better for me to die than to live, he thinks. What kind of a life am I living anyway, a sick man unable to move a finger unaided? Dependent on the goodness of my wife, my daughters. I am sick to death of this life.

When Rosa came to wake him in the morning she found him lying in his bed, his eyes open.

"Good morning, querido," she said.

He didn't reply.

"Buenos dias," she tried again. "How are you today, querido?"

He remained silent.

"Gabriel, *que pasa?* Are you not feeling well?" She laid her hand on his forehead. He was frightening her. She sat on the bed, put her cheek to his lips, and the feel of his breath calmed her. He was alive. She stood up and went into the other room.

"Rachelika," she said to her daughter, who was nursing her baby, "your father's lying there like a dead man and isn't saying a word."

"What do you mean?"

"I speak to him and he doesn't answer me."

Rachelika disengaged Boaz from her nipple and he started crying. "Take him," she told her mother and hurried into her father's room.

"Papo, are you all right?" she asked worriedly.

He was silent.

"Papo, stop scaring me. I have enough on my mind as it is."

But Gabriel stayed silent.

"Papo, I'm begging you." She kneeled at his bedside. "We won't be able to stand it if anything happens to you too. Have mercy on us, now isn't the time not to speak, Papo. If something's hurting you, tell me."

"What's going on?" asked David, who had just woken up and stood in the doorway.

"My father's found the perfect time to take a vow of silence," Rachelika replied.

"Go back to the baby, he's screaming like he's being slaughtered. I'll stay with your father."

Boaz stopped crying only when Rachelika put her nipple back into his mouth, and now Gabriela was hungry too and started wailing. Becky took the bottle of milk that Rachelika pumped earlier, poured it into a pan, and heated it on the stove.

"Don't make it too hot," Rosa said, "so it doesn't burn her."

"I know exactly how long to heat it. I can be a mother myself, I'm ready," Becky said proudly.

"May you be healthy, of course you're ready. God willing your Eli will come back from the war and in another two or three years we'll have a wedding," Rosa said, and at the mere mention of Eli's name Becky burst into tears.

Dio santo, they've all gone crazy, Rosa thought. Gabriel's gone crazy,

Rachelika's gone crazy, the babies have gone crazy, and now Becky has too. It's a madhouse! Only she held it together even though she felt her strength draining away each day.

David, who had remained with Gabriel, was at his wits' end. He paced from the window to his father-in-law's bed, not sure how to behave with the old man. He'd never been alone with him.

"Senor Gabriel," he said, "how are you feeling this morning?"

To his amazement, Gabriel, who had remained silent when his wife and daughter had spoken to him, turned his face away from the wall and said, "I feel like my troubles."

"Well, everything's fine then." David laughed. "I feel like my troubles too. I thought that, God forbid, you were going to give us a surprise and be ill too."

"Healthy I'll never be, son-in-law. I'm old and sick and my life isn't worth a damn. I can't wait for the day when I return my soul to Senor del mundo."

"God forbid, Senor Gabriel, what are you saying? You're not that old, you're not fifty yet."

"I'm old, my boy, long in the tooth, a castoff. I can't get out of bed by myself. I even need help to take a piss. What do I have left in this life if God has taken what little dignity I had, when I have to ask my wife to wipe my ass?"

David remained silent, shocked by Gabriel's frankness. He hadn't been prepared for such an intimate conversation with his father-in-law. He thought they might chat about inconsequential things as always. Uncomfortable, he went from Gabriel's bed to the door, praying that Rosa or one of his sisters-in-law would come rescue him. But no one did, and the only words that left his mouth were "What can I do for you, father-in-law? How can I help?"

"You can take care of my daughter," Gabriel replied. "Because I'm no longer able to."

David was relieved. He'd feared that the old man would ask him to perform an embarrassing task like wiping his behind or unzipping his pants and holding his penis so he could urinate.

"I'll take good care of her, father-in-law. I swear on my life that I'll look after her."

"Luna's young, she'll get stronger, she'll recover, she'll go home to you and Gabriela. You've got to look out for yourself so you don't get hurt, God forbid, when you're outside the outpost."

"Don't worry, Senor Gabriel, the war will end, Luna will get well and come home, and you'll live to a hundred and twenty."

"David!" Gabriel stopped his son-in-law in full flow. "Swear to me by everything you hold dear that you'll look after Luna."

"I swear!"

"And as soon as Luna is well you'll have another baby, and this time you'll name him after your father, and afterward you'll have more children and have a big family, may you be healthy."

"I swear."

"You know, David, before Luna came into the world I was more dead than alive. She restored meaning to my life. I don't forget that. Not a day goes by when I don't think about it."

And to his father-in-law, David replied, "Luna loves you more than she loves herself. She named her daughter after you, she loves you so much she gave her a boy's name. She loves you, my dear father-in-law, more than she loves me, more than she loves her own daughter."

When David arrived at the hospital he didn't find Luna in the ward.

"Where's my wife?" he asked one of the nurses.

"In the doctor's office," she said.

He sat down on a bench in the corridor and waited for Luna. The sound of laughter came from inside the ward. The patients were a close-knit group, people who'd come a long way together, and their prolonged hospitalization had shaped them into a family.

"*Ahalan,* my friend," came redheaded Gidi's voice as he parked his wheelchair next to David, rousing him from his musings.

"*Ahalan wa sahlan,*" David replied.

"Are you waiting for Luna?" Gidi asked.

"Yes," David nodded.

"Have you made all the discharge arrangements?"

"What discharge?"

"Luna's."

"Luna's being discharged? When?"

"Today. Didn't she tell you?"

"No," David said, not even attempting to hide his shock.

"The doctor's talking to her in his office, and after that she's going home."

"How long have you known she's being discharged?" David asked, trying to absorb the news that had just hit him.

"Three days. The doctor said we're throwing a farewell party for her."

David was silent. How had Luna known for three days that she was being discharged from the hospital and hadn't said anything to him? Was it because she'd rather be in the hospital than go home? Because she preferred the company of her wounded companions over his and their daughter's? He shut his eyes tight, trying to swallow his frustration. His face reddened and he pounded the bench with his fist.

"Don't take it personally," said Gidi, attempting to pacify him. "It's not about you. She's scared about going home because she doesn't feel strong enough. She probably didn't tell you because she didn't want to disappoint you if she had to stay in the hospital after all."

David took a deep breath. How was it that this redhead knew more about his wife than he did? He didn't know her anymore. He had no idea what she wanted. He could barely even talk to her.

When Luna finally emerged from the doctor's office she was sullen and angry.

"The doctor's discharging me," she said to Gidi, ignoring her husband. "I don't want to go home. I'm not strong enough." She burst into tears.

"Luna"—Gidi's voice was soft—"this is a hospital, not a convalescent home."

"You don't understand," she sobbed. "I'm frightened that the wounds will open."

"They won't, Luna," said the doctor, who had stepped out of his office. "Your wounds have healed. You're still not a hundred percent, but you will be. Go home, start living again, get your strength back, and in time you'll be as good as new, I promise. If you want, I'll arrange a week's convalescence at Motza for you."

And all the while David sat on the bench feeling like an outsider who was present by chance. His wife was ignoring him as if he wasn't there. She didn't need him. She had the redhead, she had her wounded friends. He was just in the way. Only when he stood up and was about to leave did the doctor notice him and say, "Mr. Siton, I'm returning your wife to you."

"My wife didn't tell me she was being discharged," David said.

Luna looked at him as if seeing him for the first time and said to the doctor, "At least let me stay for one more day. I'll go home tomorrow."

"One day, Luna," the doctor said. "One more day, no more."

That evening she said good-bye to her friends in the ward and shed a flood of tears. She insisted on taking her leave on her own, without her husband present to accompany her.

"He wouldn't understand," she told Gidi. "He'd think I'd taken leave of my senses if he saw how many tears I'm spilling here."

"He'd think they were tears of joy," Gidi said.

"But you know they're tears of sadness."

"Why sadness, lovely lady? I wish I was getting out of here."

"I'll miss you," Luna said and quickly added, "and everybody else in the ward. My life won't be the same without you," she whispered.

"Why without me? You'll come and visit, and then I'll be discharged and we'll keep in touch."

"Do you promise?"

"You need me to promise? There aren't many people who share what we do."

"What do we share?"

"Love," he whispered.

"Love like between a man and a woman or love like between friends?" Luna persisted.

"You're a married woman. It can't be like between a man and a woman."

"And if I wasn't married?"

"And if pigs could fly? And if I could walk?"

"It's a serious question. Stop making a joke of everything."

"It's a serious question? Then I'll give you a serious answer. If we'd met before the war, before you were married, before you had a baby, before you were wounded, before I was wounded, before I was told I'd never be able to have children, I'd have married you."

"Of course you'll be able to have children," Luna said.

"I'm paralyzed, Luna, remember? I won't have children. And you have a daughter and a husband and you'll have more children, God willing, so get out of this damned hospital and go back to your life. Remember me, but forget a man's love for a woman. It can't happen, not for me and you, and not for me and any other woman."

They were standing on the hospital balcony overlooking Haneviim Street. This was their place, where they went when they wanted to be alone. It was the place where for the first time since she'd been wounded she'd felt alive again, when her heart had skipped a beat in the face of the only person capable of making her smile. It was the place where she realized that what she felt for him was not feelings of friendship and affection, the way she felt for her other friends in the ward, but something more profound. Deep down inside her an emotion had been bubbling for months, and now the reality of her leaving had brought it to its boiling point and she couldn't ignore it anymore.

"I love you," she told him.

He gave her that jovial look of his and told her, "It's the morphine talking—you're hallucinating."

"No, I love you," she said again.

He shifted his gaze to the street and said in a barely audible voice, "You mustn't say things like that to a man who isn't your husband."

"I love you," she repeated more forcefully.

He tried to hide the tears welling in his eyes. "Never," he told her, "I beg you, never again tell me you love me. I won't be able to survive in this place when you're not here. If you truly love me, then please forget what you told me and I'll forget it too."

But they both knew it was impossible to forget. It was impossible to loosen the bond that had tightened between them. He had breathed life into her wounded body. Her soul was bound to his. It had been many long months since more than her own pain had preoccupied her. She was so worried about him. Most of the time he was happy and humorous, the life of the ward, but there were days, especially when he came back from an examination, when he was depressed and silent. And she, who had been silent for such a long time, imprisoned in her pain and agony, grieving over her ruined body and beauty that would never be what it had been, now that a spark of life had been reignited in her, it suddenly went out in him.

One time when he came back from an appointment with the doctor he climbed onto his bed and closed the curtain between their beds. He refused to eat, refused to talk to anyone. All her efforts to break through were rebuffed. Even his parents, who had come all the way from Nahariya, he sent away. Luna was beside herself. His suffering made her forget her own. Except for her father, she had never been so worried about anybody in her life.

And then one morning he was his usual self again as if nothing had happened. The jokes returned, the laughter and pranks that made him the nurses' favorite and her pride and joy.

She would never forget the first time they'd gone to their place on the balcony. One evening after doctors' rounds, when their wardmates were in bed asleep, a moment before they closed the curtain between their beds, he whispered, "Do you feel like taking a walk?"

"Sure," she replied and quickly brought his wheelchair and helped him out of bed.

"Where to?" she asked.

"The balcony."

When they reached the end of the corridor, she carefully opened the door and they went out onto the spacious balcony. It was a warm summer night, a pleasant breeze caressed their faces, and a robust moon hung in the sky, casting a serene glow on the balcony. Luna felt as if she were in a film.

"You know," she said, "it was on a moonlit night like this, on the fifteenth of Adar, that I was born. My father called me Luna, which is moon in Ladino."

"Luna," he whispered, turning his face to her, "how that name suits you."

Luna didn't take her eyes from his. She knelt beside him, resting her head on his knees, and he stroked the red curls that had grown back. For a long while they stayed like that in silence.

Then he lifted her chin with a finger, raised her head above his knees, and said, "I want to tell you something."

Her eyes sparkled.

"I made the doctor and the nurses swear they wouldn't tell a soul, not even my parents, but I want you to know. It's important to me that you know."

"What?" she asked excitedly.

"You know that the Arab sniper's bullets hit my spinal cord?"

"Yes."

"I'm paralyzed from the waist down, and I'll never walk again."

"The main thing is that you're alive," she said, telling him what she herself had been told so many times. "You're alive and you'll be able to do everything, just not walk."

"I won't be able to do everything, Luna. I won't be able to father children."

"No," she blurted painfully and quickly covered her mouth with her hand as if trying to push the word back in. "Is that final?" she asked, trembling. "It won't pass?"

"No, it won't pass."

"Is that why you've been sad for such a long time?"

"When they told me I'd be paralyzed, I accepted it. I thought, I'm lucky I didn't lose my eyes, it would have been far worse if I'd been blinded. But when the doctor told me I wouldn't be able to have children, it broke me completely. Do you understand what it means, Luna?"

She nodded. "But you can always marry a woman who has children."

"Unfortunately that apparently isn't going to happen."

"Why not? There are lots of war widows who've been left with children."

"Ah, that." He smiled for the first time. "I thought you meant I could marry you."

"I wish," she said sadly. "I wish you could marry me."

From then on Luna wheeled Gidi to the balcony every evening.

None of their friends joined them on their nightly walks to the balcony. They all knew that something was going on between the two, but nobody spoke of it. It became one of the best-kept secrets of the band of patients and nurses. Even if there were those who took a dim view of the closeness between the married woman and the wounded young man, they didn't say a word. That closeness, they noticed, was like a wonder drug for both of them, and it accelerated their recovery.

Luna gradually fell in love with Gidi. Her heart fluttered each time she saw him, and she felt her youth being restored and her will to live rekindled. She asked Rachelika to bring her lipstick and face powder and began wearing makeup as she had before she was wounded. With a headscarf she hid the stubble of what hair had begun growing back and the remaining bald spots. And Rachelika, who was overjoyed by the change in her sister, brought the cosmetics to the hospital, including a file for Luna's nails.

"Thank God," she said to Moise. "My sister's getting back to her old self. Lipstick, face powder, manicure, pedicure. She'll soon be walking around the ward in an evening gown and heels."

The change didn't escape David either. Now when he came to visit her, she wasn't lying in bed like a mummy. He'd sometimes find her on the balcony with her friends, wearing her silk robe instead of the ugly hospital gown. Luna's back to being Luna, he thought to himself. It won't be long before she comes home, and what will happen then? He couldn't ignore the fears that rose in him. They'd been growing apart even before she'd been wounded. They hadn't had intercourse since the day she told him she was pregnant, and when he'd tried to come to her after Gabriela was born, she'd rejected his advances with the excuse that she was embarrassed about doing it when her parents were in the next room. And he hadn't pressed her. It had been over a year since she was brought to the hospital, and since then he'd had to satisfy his drives in secret, with women he met for an evening or two, widows or divorcées, heaven help him, and when neither of the two was available, he did it with women for whose services he paid with money he couldn't afford to spend.

———

On the day Mother came home from the hospital, Becky dressed me in a lovely white muslin dress that had arrived in a package from America. Every day she made me practice saying, "Welcome home, Ima," but I, who at age one couldn't stop talking, stubbornly refused to repeat the greeting until Becky despaired and said, "All right, just say 'Hello, Ima.'"

And as if out of spite I said, "Hello, Abba," and Becky said, "All right, so don't say anything. Just give your mother a hug and kiss."

Mother came home after the war had ended and after Moise and Handsome Eli Cohen had already returned. My father turned in his Sten gun and was released from his duties defending our Jerusalem and went to work as a mechanic at his brother Yitzhak's garage in Talpiot. When she stepped through the door of Nono and Nona's house, holding on to Father's arm and measuring her steps as if afraid of stumbling, she went first to her father. Nono Gabriel, who was sitting more or less paralyzed in his usual chair, his body not obeying his commands to stand up to greet his beloved daughter, wept oceans of tears and for a long time laid his hand on the head of his daughter kneeling before him.

"God be praised, God be praised," he said, murmuring the words like a mantra. Only after she embraced her father, kissed his sunken cheeks and trembling hand, did she embrace—seemingly against her will—Nona Rosa too. Then she sat down in the armchair next to my grandfather, exhausted by the effort. Becky, who was holding me in her arms, came over to her and told me, "Say hello to Ima, say welcome home." But I shook my head vigorously.

"How she's grown," my mother said tiredly.

"Come, sweetie, come, bonica," my father said, taking me from Becky. "Come to Ima." My mother held out her arms, but as always I refused her.

She drew her hands back into her lap and said, "I'm tired. I need to lie down."

And since then my mother lay down at every opportunity. She'd get up only infrequently, mostly when people would come to visit her, and as soon as they'd leave she'd go back to bed. My grandmother, my aunts, and my father continued looking after me, leaving my mother to recover at her own pace.

Every morning David would go off to his job at the garage. He didn't like the work, he didn't like dirtying himself with engine oil, he didn't like working with his hands. He wasn't born to be a laborer. The moment an opportunity came his way he'd get the hell out of this stinking garage and away from his brother, who treated him and the other workers like slaves. A little tin god, David thought to himself, a pompous schmendrick. Only yesterday Yitzhak was a snot-nosed kid and now he was the big shot. David had to get out of this stinking place, he had to find a job that suited his talents, like Moise who joined the police force. Even Handsome Eli Cohen had found a job at Haft & Haft, Accountants, on Ben-Yehuda Street. So why couldn't he find his niche? Why, wasn't he as good as them? When Moise joined the police and he and Rachelika had moved out, he'd urged him to join too, but David didn't want to be a policeman.

"Yuck," Becky always said and made a face when David walked in. "You stink!" Of course he stunk, he worked in a stinking job. What, she expected him to be like her Don Juan de la Shmatte, who went to work in a white shirt and came home from work in a white shirt? He was a laborer! He'd hoped that when Luna returned from the hospital she'd make a quick recovery, get back to functioning like a mother, and life would resume its normal course, but Luna, since she'd come home from the hospital, had only sunk even deeper into herself. She hardly spoke and scarcely ate. He'd plead with her, "Luna, if you don't eat, you won't get your strength back, and if you don't get stronger, they'll put you back in the hospital," and she'd just look at him with that sad expression of hers. His wife wouldn't put a thing into her mouth, and soon there would be nothing left of the beauty he'd married her for.

In the hospital her mood had been pretty good. Redheaded Gidi in the next bed, despite his condition, spread good cheer, told jokes. On more than one occasion he saw with his own eyes how Gidi was able to coax a smile, even a laugh, out of Luna. Almost every time David visited her in the ward, all the wounded guys would be sitting around her bed, like they once did at Café Atara. They had their own life at the hospital, and he sometimes felt as if he was trespassing. One had lost an arm, another a leg, and they'd laugh, and Luna Queen of England would be sitting in her bed, all of them trying to make her laugh, but she—nada. And there were some, *Allah yustur*, God save us, who died of their wounds, and others who lost their sight, they'd never see their wives again or their unborn children, and some who were bandaged from head to foot, but she, his wife, was the saddest of them all, as if all the suffering in the ward rested on her shoulders.

Then at least she'd been somewhat present. He'd sit by her bed, holding her hand, working to carry on a conversation with her. But now her mood was worse than ever and she wasn't speaking. Luna, who always had something to say about everything, was silent. Only with Rachelika did she sometimes exchange confidences. Being in his in-laws' house was becoming more and more oppressive. David needed to get out of there too. As he rose from his place in the garage, he realized he had nowhere to go. Moise spent every moment not at work with Rachelika and their children, happy in his marriage. If there was one good thing that came out of his relationship with Luna, it was the match they'd made between Moise and Rachelika. That and Gabriela, may she be healthy, what a child, what joy, the spitting image of her mother and as different from her as the moon is from the sun. The child was all light. How she laughed with him, hugged him. How he loved to take her in his arms, sing songs to her, and how she talked. There wasn't a word she didn't know how to say. She knew all the names, even the neighbors' names. Only *Ima* she stubbornly wouldn't say. It didn't matter how many times he asked her, she refused. But whatever, it'd pass. She'd say *Ima*. Was there a child who didn't?

That evening Luna got into bed, covered her head with the blankets, and pretended to be asleep. The last thing in the world she wanted right now, David knew for certain, was to be with him. He sat in the yard and smoked a cigarette, watching the smoke drift upward in rings. As a half-moon tried to make its way through the clouds, he got up and walked through the Ohel Moshe gate. The streets were deserted; Jerusalem went to bed early. He still hadn't gotten used to the fact that there weren't any British soldiers, that there was no curfew, no concertina wire, that you could go anywhere at any time without some bastard of an English policeman stopping and questioning you. He walked down Jaffa Road toward Nahalat Shiva. There, in one of the alleys, not far from where the burnt-out Rex Cinema still stood, was Rosenblatt's Bar. He knew he wouldn't encounter neighbors or acquaintances there, only men like himself who went there to dispel their loneliness in the company of strange women and a bottle of cheap brandy.

From the street he heard a warm Italian voice singing "Ti Parlerò D'Amor," and a sharp pain lanced through his heart. Isabella. He made his way down the dark steps, pulled the red curtain aside, and entered. Heavily made-up women wearing dresses that left nothing to the imagination lined the bar with tired-looking men. He sat down and ordered a Carmel 100 cognac and downed it in one. The liquor seared his throat, and he ordered another, hoping the cognac would put out the fire raging in his heart and erase the lie he'd been living. Cursed be the day he'd decided to leave Isabella on the Mestre pier; cursed be the day he'd married Luna out of cold, wrongful consideration. Why hadn't he listened to his heart? Why hadn't he heard Isabella's pleadings? Maybe if he had, today he'd be happily married to a woman he loved. Perhaps he wouldn't be bogged down in a life he didn't want. He ordered another cognac, trying to dull the thoughts pounding in his head.

"Gimme one for the road," he eventually said to the bartender as he gulped another shot and staggered out the door. When he got home, he collapsed fully dressed onto the living room couch, his bed ever since Luna had come home from the hospital.

Instead of growing stronger and recovering, my mother had been steadily getting weaker. She could hardly stand, and when she spoke her voice was barely audible. Every time she had to walk from her bed to the privy in the yard she felt like she was climbing Everest.

"I'll fetch you a chamber pot," Becky had told her, but Luna had vehemently refused. She had to reclaim a little of the dignity that had been taken from her. She was home at long last, but she wasn't prepared for anybody to see her naked, not her sisters, not her mother, and especially not her husband. Although every step she took cost her great pain, she insisted on going to the privy. She had agreed to let Becky help change her clothes but wouldn't let her bathe her. She preferred not to wash rather than have Becky see her scarred body.

Becky became my second mother, taking me everywhere, even when she went for a walk with Handsome Eli Cohen or sat on the steps and chatted with her girlfriends. The only one Luna had patience for was Nono Gabriel. She'd sit beside him for hours on end, feed him with a teaspoon, wipe away the bits of food from the corners of his mouth, plump the cushions behind him, read to him from the newspaper, tune the radio stations for him. Nobody could understand his addiction to the programs about the search for missing relatives, but Gabriel would put his ear to the radio as if he were afraid he might miss a name, as if some relative was hiding inside it. Where will he find a relative among the Ishkenazim who were in the Holocaust? Rosa wondered. She couldn't understand her husband, but then again, she didn't understand much in those hard times.

For instance, when she gave Becky their new ration card to fetch eggs, she brought back three Turkish eggs for each of them, and three for Gabriela.

"Why Turkish eggs?" Rosa asked. "Why not eggs from Tnuva?"

"How would I know," Becky replied irritably. "That's what they were giving out. I had to stand in line for an hour and fight the whole world for them."

"And what about sugar?" Rosa asked her. "Did they say when there'd be sugar?"

"There was a notice from the food controller that they'd be giving out sugar only next month, so until next month only Luna, Gabriela, and Papo will have sugar in their tea, and you, David, and I will go without. There's nothing to be done."

Luna was sitting at the table, all skin and bones, trying to bring a cup of tea to her cracked lips, when suddenly it slipped from her fingers and smashed onto the floor. Her head dropped to her chest, and she lost consciousness. Nona Rosa started screaming, Nono Gabriel sat helplessly bound to his chair, and I, who was crawling on the floor at the time, crawled over the shards of glass and was badly cut. Blood poured from my knees and hands and I screamed with pain. My poor grandmother didn't know who to help first, and she ran madly from me to my mother until my grandfather banged on the floor with his cane and shouted, "Basta, Rosa! Stop running around like a headless chicken and get the neighbors to call Magen David Adom to take Luna to the hospital!"

Nona Rosa went out into the yard shouting, "Magen David Adom! Magen David Adom! Somebody call Magen David Adom!"

"Dio santo, what's happened?" Tamar asked from the doorway of her house. And my grandmother was so choked by her tears that she couldn't reply and simply pointed at the door of her own house. As Tamar ran outside, she ordered one of her children to run to the Assouta Pharmacy and tell them to call Magen David Adom right way. She entered our house and tried to rouse my mother, and my grandmother tried to extract the splinters of glass from my body.

The ambulance arrived within a short time, its siren deafening the whole street, and my mother, who'd regained consciousness, was laid on a stretcher and rushed to the hospital.

It took Nona Rosa a week to take all the splinters out of my small body, and all that time my grandfather didn't speak. He didn't even ask how my mother was.

"Dio santo, Gabriel," Rosa said, "why don't you keep quiet a bit. You're giving me a headache with all your talking."

But he ignored her banter and stayed silent. Even I couldn't get a smile out of him.

My father came home from the garage in the middle of the day irritable and edgy. When Nona Rosa asked what he was doing home, he replied rudely, "Leave me alone."

My nona was shocked. He'd never spoken to her with such a lack of respect. Even my nono, who seemed to spend most of his time immersed in himself, raised his eyebrows.

Father went to the kitchen sink, washed off the engine oil with Ama detergent, put on clean clothes, and sat down at the table.

"What is there to eat?" he asked Nona Rosa.

"Habas con arroz," she replied.

"Beans and rice again?"

"Well, where can you get meat, querido? There isn't any, not even on the black market."

"If you have the money you can buy anything on the black market," he answered angrily.

"So whoever has money will buy on the black market. We don't have any money, it's finished," my nona said. "So eat up. It's filling."

"Beans give me gas and I've become Chinese from so much rice."

"Querido, it's all there is. There's nothing else."

"Fine," my father said and got up from the table.

"Where are you going? Maybe spend some time with your daughter?"

"I'm taking Gabriela with me," my father said. He lifted me out of the playpen, sat me in the pram, and we left the house.

My father walked aimlessly down Agrippas Street, pushing my pram. His stomach was rumbling, and as he walked past the Taraboulos restaurant on the corner of King George Street and Jaffa Road, he was almost tempted to go in. He liked the strawberry-flavored jelly they served for dessert, but he knew that a meal cost quite a few lirot that he didn't have, and he gave up on the idea.

He had to talk to somebody, tell them what had happened that morning at Yitzhak's garage. He had to get it off his chest. He decided to go and see Moise at police headquarters in the Russian Compound. Moise worked as a groom in the stables there.

He pushed the pram down Jaffa Road, passing the Pillars Building and Zion Square, and when he reached the Generali Building, he stopped and pointed at the lion carved into the facade. "Say hello to the lion," he said in a baby voice and told me the story of the lion, who every night, when no one could see, came down into the street, did a peepee, and went straight back to its place atop the building.

He passed the Magen David Adom station and the Russian church with its green cupolas as he continued on toward police headquarters. The policeman at the gate was a friend from the British army days, and Father stopped to chat for a few minutes, letting him shower praise on me. Then he headed for the stables. Moise was standing there in his work clothes and rubber boots, cleaning a hoof of one of the horses.

"What guests! And how's our bonica today?" he said, stroking my cheek. "And you, David, you have time to take the child for a walk in the middle of the day? Shouldn't you be at work?"

"I'm out of work," my father replied.

"What?" said Moise in disbelief.

"I resigned. I told Yitzhak to go to hell, him and his garage."

"You resigned? This is no time to be out of a job."

"I'd rather die of hunger than work for that dog."

"What are you saying? He's your brother!"

"He's my brother? He's Amalek! All of a sudden he's a big shot."

"Have a glass of water," Moise said. "Calm down."

"How can I calm down?" David said angrily. "I feel like I'm going to explode. I've kept quiet for a long time about the way Yitzhak behaves. Almost from my first day there he treated me like an ordinary worker, as if we didn't grow up in the same house."

"Well," said Moise, trying to pacify him, "work is work . . ."

"That's just it, there's no work. There are hardly any cars coming to the garage. Even the Jewish Agency cars that came for regular servicing only come if they're running on their wheel rims. So because there was nothing to do I was sitting reading *Yedioth Ahronoth*, and all of a sudden Yitzhak comes at me, snatches the paper out of my hands, and shouts, 'You damned parasite, as if it isn't enough that I'm keeping you on, you read the paper in the middle of work!'

" 'There isn't any work,' I tell him. 'What do you want, that I pretend I'm working just for show?'

" 'That's right,' he says. 'There's no work, so go home.'

"I look at him, I can't believe my ears, and ask him, 'You're firing me?'

" 'No,' he says, 'you're firing yourself. You said yourself there's no work.'

"I feel like I'm going to blow up at him any minute. The bastard knows what the situation is at home, he knows I'm supporting my wife's family right now, and he says, 'Go home.' But I hold back, swallow my pride, and tell the little nobody I used to carry piggyback, the one I slept in the same bed with when we were kids in our parents' house, 'I need the job.'

"'Money doesn't grow on trees,' he tells me. 'And I'm not Rothschild. If it wasn't for Mother, I'd have sent you packing a long time ago.'

"I'm defeated, he's trampled the little dignity I had left, but I know I can't leave, I absolutely can't be without a job, so I try again, almost begging: 'Izak,' I say, 'for the sake of our father, may he rest in peace, don't do this to me.' And he turns his back on me and says, 'It's only for the sake of our father, may he rest in peace, and our mother, may she live long, that I hadn't already fired you. I'm holding on to you here and you're not ashamed to read *Yedioth* during work hours, and in front of the other workers yet. One rotten apple spoils the whole barrel, and you're spoiling all the workers for me.'

"Now I can't hold myself back any longer. He's standing with his back to me as if I'm nothing. I'm seething. I've never felt so humiliated, and by my own brother. I tap him on the shoulder, and as he turns around, I punch him in the face and break his nose. He starts yelling like a lunatic, but I've already taken off the stinking overalls and thrown them on the floor. I stand there in my underpants and shout, 'If there's one rotten apple in the Siton family, it's you. Our parents raised a whole pile of wonderful kids, each one a success, and you're the only rotten apple in that pile!' And I run out of there. I swear, Moise, I'll never, ever speak to that bastard again. Even if my mother gets on her knees and begs me, I won't speak to him."

"He really is a bastard," Moise said.

"I went home and our mother-in-law, may she be healthy, started in with her questions. She's a nudnik too. Our father-in-law was in his chair, and even though he hasn't said anything for a long time, I felt he too wondered why I was home in the middle of the day.

"I didn't even have lunch, our querida mother-in-law made habas con arroz and I was so edgy I insulted her, miskenica, as if she's to blame for us not having the money to buy meat."

"Are you hungry?" Moise asked.

"Starving."

"Let's go to the cafeteria and get something there. On me."

All this time I was sitting in my pram, engrossed by the horses and garbling happily. In the heat of telling his story, my father had forgotten I was there and I, riveted as I was by the animals, didn't disturb him. It was only after he'd poured out his heart to his friend that he remembered me, bent down, and kissed me on the forehead. "If it wasn't for the child," he said to Moise, "I'd go to Tel Aviv and start over."

"Don't talk nonsense."

"There's more. I'd get on a boat and go to Italy, look for Isabella, and fix what I ruined."

"Halas, enough," Moise said. "Haven't you got that Italian girl out of your head yet? I thought the story with Isabella was over."

"I did too, at least I hoped it was. But I miss her more than ever. From day to day I realize what a mistake I made."

"What are you missing, David?" asked Moise, dropping the horse's hoof to the ground, patting it on the rump, and releasing it to its stable. "The happy days after the war in Venice? When we were young and carefree and had no commitments? When the Italian girls threw themselves at us, when Isabella gave herself to you for a bottle of perfume, a pair of stockings, and the meat and vegetables you bought for her family? If she was one of ours, we'd say she's a slut."

"I loved her, Moise."

"Love isn't taking a girl to the cinema and dance clubs and cafés. Love isn't riding bikes and making love at night without being married and you have to do it quietly so her parents won't hear you."

"*Yahrebetak*, damn you, I shouldn't have told you all that. I shouldn't have let you in on my and Isabella's secrets. Now you're throwing it all in my face as if I've committed a crime."

"I'm just trying to bring you back to reality."

"And I'm trying to forget reality. What kind of reality is it when only less than three years ago I was free and happy and loved a wonderful woman who loved me in a way that Luna never will?"

"Do you know what love is, David?" Moise said quietly. "Love is choosing a wife to be your life companion. Love is building a home together, getting up in the morning, going to work, making a living, raising children—that's love. The love you're missing is a fantasy that was fine for you when you were a young man after the war in Italy. You're missing something that wouldn't have lasted for one day after your discharge from the British army, something that wouldn't have survived for a minute after you brought her to Jerusalem. Wake up, my friend, my brother, stop yearning for something that was never yours. Be realistic, accept what you have."

"That's easy for you to say," David said. "You have a healthy wife who loves you and pampers you and is waiting for you with a hot meal and a kiss when you come home every day. And what do I have? A wounded wife in the hospital, a baby who's growing up without a mother, and a couch in my in-laws' living room. And worst of all, Moise, worst of all is that I can't see an end to it. I can't see that Luna really wants to get better. Sometimes it seems to me that she's happier with her wounded friends at Hadassah than at home with me and Gabriela."

"Basta!" Moise said. "Don't talk rubbish. Who doesn't want to be healthy? What, can't you see how much she's suffering? She can hardly move."

"Maybe I'm wrong," David said painfully. "But every time I went to visit her I had the feeling that she preferred the company of her wounded friends over mine."

"She lived with those people in the hospital for a long time, David. It's only natural that she'd feel close to them. It can't be helped that the damned war ruined your relationship. But both of you, you and her, be grateful she's alive. She could have been killed, and then what would you have done, a widower with a baby? You have a short memory, my friend. It wasn't long ago that you almost lost not only your wife but your daughter as well. You should go to the synagogue every day and say Birkat Hagomel, the blessing of deliverance, instead of fighting with your brother and losing your job."

"I'll look for a new job."

"Maybe join the police? They're recruiting new people all the time."

"It's not for me, Moise. I'd go crazy if I had an officer over me telling me what to do. Don't you remember how many times I got on the wrong side of the sergeant in the British army?"

"David, my friend, you'll go even crazier if you don't have a job to go to and you're under Rosa's feet all day. You'll go crazy and she'll drive you crazy. In the meantime, let's go eat," Moise said. "They have jelly here that's much tastier than at Taraboulos."

The austerity period in Israel did not bring good news for David, who couldn't find work. Every day he'd go off to the employment bureau and sit for hours with the other job seekers, but there were no offers. He told the woman there that he wanted a clerical job and wasn't interested in manual labor.

Yisrael Schwartz, his friend from the British army who'd found work at the agricultural school that had been established in Ein Karem, invited him to visit and pick fruit in the heavily laden gardens the Arabs had left behind. Yisrael lived on the upper floor of an abandoned Arab house.

"What do you think of my palace?" Yisrael asked him.

"It's a real palace!" David agreed. "You got all this from the agricultural school?"

"It comes with the job. If you're interested, they're looking for workers. I can arrange it for you."

"Get me a house and a job? What would I do?"

"We'll find you something, it's a great opportunity. Where else could you get a house and a job?"

"I'll have to speak to my wife," David replied. "But now let's walk to the gardens."

"There's no need to walk," Yisrael said. "They're right here, below the house."

They went down the stairs and through the arched gate into a grand garden overlooking the cultivated terraces and the Church of the Visitation, which stood tall and proud on the side of the hill facing them, its bells ringing loudly.

"My God," David exclaimed. "Just look at this fig tree. It's bending under the weight of the fruit!"

"Go on, help yourself, enjoy. Fill this," Yisrael said, handing him a big straw basket.

As if possessed David started picking figs from the tree, putting one into his mouth for each one he picked. "*Yinal dino*, goddamn, they're so tasty," he told Yisrael.

Vines laden with grapes climbed on latticed fences, and David picked bunches of juicy grapes until his basket was overflowing.

"Here, fill a crate too," Yisrael said.

"What can I do with a crate?" David laughed. "How will I get it back to Jerusalem?"

"I'll take you in the jeep."

"God save us, you have a jeep as well, you bastard? You've really done well for yourself."

"You can too. Just make up your mind."

"I have. Now I'll just have to persuade my wife."

"Talk to her, tell her what a great deal this is."

"Believe me," he told Yisrael, "you've made me a very happy man."

They loaded the crate and the basket into the jeep and Yisrael started it up. On the way to Jerusalem they stopped in the Bayit VeGan neighborhood. Yisrael said to David, "I have another surprise for you. There's a potato field here." David jumped out of the jeep and started pulling potatoes from the ground.

Rosa couldn't believe her eyes when David came through the door with his friend, their arms full of fruit and potatoes.

"What's this?" she muttered excitedly. "Did you rob a bank?"

"No," David laughed, happy to see his mother-in-law's joy. "It's from Ein Karem and Bayit VeGan."

"It's from what the Arabs left behind?" she asked.

David nodded.

"God be praised, miracles still happen in this world."

Yisrael Schwartz wasted no time and arranged for David to meet the agricultural school's manager. David hadn't yet had a chance to talk to Luna, but the more he thought about it, the more he liked the idea of moving to Ein Karem. He saw it as an opportunity to rebuild their life in a house of their own. Even if they paid him a low wage, there would always be fruit on the trees and vegetables in the field.

"We're looking for someone for the school's carpentry shop," the manager told him. "And I understand you were a carpenter before the war."

"That's right, sir, I was. And a good one too."

"In that case, the job's yours. You can start tomorrow. You will, of course, have the same conditions as Yisrael. You can choose one of the houses in the village and live there with your family, and we'll give you a jeep for work and trips into Jerusalem."

David could feel his heart pounding wildly. It was too good to be true. A house, a job, and a jeep!

"You'll fall in love with the place. The scenery's breathtaking, the air's clear, and when the church bells ring it's a dream."

"You've convinced me," David said, shaking his hand. "Now I have to go convince my wife."

David was thrilled. He couldn't wait for the moment he'd tell Luna he'd found a job *and* a house.

In the afternoon, as Luna was about to leave to visit her hospital friends again, David said, "Instead of going to the hospital today, how about a matinee?"

She was surprised. It had been a long time since she'd gone to the cinema and since her husband had invited her to go to a matinee.

"Heideh, Luna," he urged her, "nothing will happen if you don't go to the hospital for once."

"All right," she said. "They're showing *Singing in the Rain* with Gene Kelly and Debbie Reynolds at the Edison. I hear the song on the radio all the time."

Luna was in a fine mood when they left the cinema later that day.

"Did you see how he dances, Gene Kelly? How he sings? 'I'm singin' in the rain,'" she sang and imitated Gene Kelly's dance steps, forgetting her pain.

David laughed and clapped his hands. "Bravo, Luna!" This was the Luna he remembered. Although money was tight, he'd made the right move by asking her to go to the cinema. He'd have to cut down on cigarettes and shopping in the market for Rosa, but it had been worth it. Luna was in just the right frame of mind for what he was about to tell her. Now he'd take her for coffee and cake at Atara, which had been their favorite haunt before the war. The good old days. All that now seemed so far away as if it had happened ages ago, not just a few years. So much had changed since the last time they'd had coffee at Atara, since they'd danced the tango at Café Vienna, since they'd been married at the Menorah Club.

Luna held his arm and they walked from Zion Square up Ben-Yehuda Street, stopping to look in shop windows until they reached the café. Tziona the waitress welcomed Luna as if she were greeting a regular patron. David was amazed that the elderly waitress showed no surprise at Luna's return after such a long absence. He had absolutely no idea that Luna visited the café every day to meet her friends from the hospital who had recovered and gone back to their lives, many working as taxi drivers out of the station on nearby Lunz Street. Like Gidi the redhead, who'd been discharged a few months after her and right away had become a dispatcher at the station, a stronghold of disabled war veterans. Luna had never told David that when she went on her daily visit to the wounded, she went to the taxi station and at the end of his shift pushed Gidi's wheelchair to Café Atara, staying there for a long time with him and the others before coming home.

She and David sat at one of the tables on the second floor and ordered tea. He wanted to order her a hot sandwich he remembered she'd liked, but he didn't have the money.

The café was almost empty at this late afternoon hour, but David couldn't ignore the fact that even the few people sitting there were staring shamelessly at his wife. Luna's famed beauty had been restored as if it had never left, her angelic face as white as snow, her lips plumped with scarlet lipstick. On any other woman it might have looked cheap, but on his wife it was wonderful. He studied her long fingers holding the cup of tea to her lips, the perfectly manicured nails, the tweed suit that set off her waist. From beneath the jacket peeped a white blouse, and around her neck glowed the string of pearls he'd given her as an engagement present.

He was married to the most beautiful woman in Jerusalem, so why the hell wasn't he happy with her?

"Aren't you going to drink your tea?" She roused him from his thoughts.

He sipped the tea and placed the cup down on the table.

"Luna," he said, finally mustering courage to broach the subject, "I've received a wonderful job offer."

"Really? Where?"

"In Ein Karem."

"The Arab village?"

"There aren't any Arabs there anymore. They fled and the village is abandoned. Now there's an agricultural school there. My friend Yisrael Schwartz works there, and he set up the interview for me."

"What kind of job?"

"A carpenter, in the school's carpentry shop."

"And how will you get to Ein Karem?"

"They've offered me a house there too."

"A house in Ein Karem?"

"That's what I said."

"Great!"

"Great?" he asked, astonished by her reaction.

"I'm happy for you," she said. "It really is a wonderful opportunity."

"And you don't mind leaving Jerusalem to live far away from your sisters, your parents?"

"Who said anything about leaving Jerusalem? You're leaving Jerusalem, me and Gabriela are staying with my parents, and you can come and be with us on Shabbat."

He felt anger stirring inside him. Once again his dear wife had managed to humiliate him.

"Luna, don't you think it's time we had a home of our own, just you and me and the child?"

"In Ein Karem?"

"In a big house, a palace."

"Not in a palace or anything else! Ein Karem's the end of the world. What would I do there on my own with Gabriela, without my father, without my sisters? You can go to Ein Karem and work there. I'm staying in Jerusalem."

He barely swallowed the insult. "You were in the hospital for such a long time," he said quietly. "At long last you're out and I want us to live in a house of our own like any normal couple, and you want me to live in Ein Karem alone while you stay at your parents'? It'd be better if we got divorced and ended it!"

"Are you crazy, David, who's talking about divorce? What, do I look like a slut to you? Why get divorced? Today lots of men work a long way from home to make a living. There's no work in Jerusalem. It's no secret."

"Why not come along and see the place for yourself?" he said. "And then decide. Yisrael Schwartz and his wife live there in a mansion with a huge yard. There are a lot of houses like that there—we can pick and choose. They promised me that a jeep goes with the job, so we could drive to Jerusalem whenever you'd want."

"It's out of the question! You want to hide me away in some abandoned Arab village? You want to cut me off from my family? I know exactly what will happen. You'll be working and I'll be on my own with the child all day. If I haven't already gone crazy, you want me to go crazy now? How can you even think about something like this? Why do you think only of yourself?"

"I'm thinking about our future. I'm thinking that if we don't take this offer, we'll never have a home of our own."

"What kind of a man are you who can't give me a home?" she asked tauntingly.

David was silent. What kind of a man *was* he? A man whose wife repeatedly humiliated him, a man who submitted to his wife's every whim? He had to force her to come with him. A wife must follow her husband. Why was he even asking her? He should be stating a fact. *Ras bin anaq,* she'd go with him to Ein Karem come hell or high water!

"In the morning," he told her, "I'll go and see the school's manager and tell him, 'Thank you for your generous offer, but my wife's not interested.'"

"Exactly," she replied, ignoring his sarcastic tone. "Now let's stop talking about it. It's been so long since we went out and you had to go and spoil my good mood."

As with everything else, my mother eventually got her way. Father bent to her will and declined the job offer, but not a day went by in my mother's life when he didn't remind her that he'd missed the chance of a lifetime because of her. As the years went by Ein Karem became an artists' village and house prices there soared. The distance between the village and Jerusalem was shortened, and the village was annexed to the city as a northern neighborhood.

"Why, why did I listen to your mother like an idiot?" he'd say again and again. "Why didn't I accept Yisrael Schwartz's offer? His house is worth millions today and I have zilch."

Living in Nono and Nona Ermosa's house became unbearable for my father. He'd had enough of sleeping on the living room couch, seeing my grandfather sink ever deeper into his illness depressed him, and he was sick of hearing the nitpicking of his mother-in-law, who'd become more irritable from day to day and whose arguments with Luna were exhausting.

I was two and a half when they enrolled me in the prestigious Rehavia school. My mother simply wouldn't stand for enrolling me in the one in Ohel Moshe.

"I want the best there is for my daughter," she told my father.

What a strange woman, my father thought. She hardly takes care of the child, barely pays her any attention, but she wants the best there is for her.

And my mother got her way again. The only time I spent with her during those years was when she took me to school and when she picked me up. Every morning we'd go in through the iron gate, and Mother would say good-bye by the big ficus tree. In a desperate attempt to gain a little attention from her, I'd create heartrending parting scenes. I cried, threw myself on the ground, and held on to her legs and didn't let go, and my mother would be helpless.

"Stop it," she'd say angrily. "Stop making a scene." The angrier she became, the more I'd scream, embarrassing her in front of the other mothers.

"You take your daughter to school," she finally said to my father. "I don't have the strength for her scenes. She humiliates me in front of all the mothers in Rehavia. The children from the Kurdish Quarter are better behaved than her."

Whenever my mother associated something with the Kurdish Quarter, it was a sign that all hope was lost, her way of saying that she'd had it up to here!

How my mother hated the Kurdish Quarter, which before the Kurds came with their thousands of children, so she'd say time and again, was called the Zichron Yaakov Quarter and was a Spaniol neighborhood. And as much as my father told her again and again that she was talking nonsense and the Kurds had always lived in the Kurdish Quarter, it made no difference. As far as she was concerned, the Kurds had taken over a neighborhood that once belonged to the Spaniols, just as Mordoch had stolen my grandfather's shop.

Soon the hard times forced Nono and Nona to leave the house in Ohel Moshe and rent it out. With the money, they rented two rooms in the Barazani family's house in the Kurdish Quarter, and we lived on whatever was left over.

How my mother wept when we moved to the Kurdish Quarter. "Only poor people live here," she told my father.

"That's not true," David replied. "The Kurds that live here aren't poor at all, only the Spaniols are, and we're poor now."

Even more than she hated the Kurdish Quarter, my mother hated their landlords, the Barazani family. Ever since Mordoch the Kurd had robbed Nono Gabriel and got his hands on the shop for a miserable five hundred lirot, all Kurds were the same for her. She held Mordoch to blame for all the bad things that had happened to the family since he'd become Nono Gabriel's partner.

Almost from the day the Ermosa family moved into the Barazani family's house, the feuding began. Rosa in particular suffered, for except at the time of Matilda Franco's murder, she'd always been on friendly terms with her neighbors. And now with the Barazanis every little thing sparked a tiff. She'd wash the cobblestone yard, and they'd complain that she threw out the dirty water on their side. Mrs. Barazani would hang out her washing, and Rosa would complain that she was hanging her rags on her clotheslines. Mrs. Barazani would light a fire under her tabun and make the traditional kada, cheese and spinach pockets, and Rosa would shout at her that the smoke was coming into the house through the windows. Not a day went by without the neighbors arguing about something.

"Dio santo," Rosa cried out one time, "I can't even quarrel with her like a normal person. She doesn't speak Ladino and I don't speak Kurdish." On more than one occasion her throat became sore from shouting, and she had to call for Luna's help. And she, mashallah, what a mouth she'd run. Then they'd scramble back inside and shut the windows.

The Barazanis loved Gabriela, and as if to spite her family, the child loved them back. At every opportunity she'd ride into their yard in the little green pedal car David bought her.

"If I hear that you've gone to the Kurds with your car again," Luna once shouted at Gabriela, "I'll break your arms and legs."

"What do you want from her," David had intervened. "What does she have to do with a neighbors' dispute? She's only a child."

"Child or not, my daughter will not go to the Kurds' side. I want you to put up a fence between their yard and ours."

The next day David brought some barbed wire and separated the two yards.

Mr. Barazani threatened to throw the Ermosas out, but in the end he too realized that the right solution was the fence that now separated the two families.

"If it wasn't for the little girl I'd throw you all into the street," he said, making sure he had the last word.

"That's how it is, he who pays the piper calls the tune," said Becky dejectedly. "And there's nothing to be done. The Kurds pay the piper."

"They pay the piper?" my mother retorted angrily. "Why, they were rich when they came from Kurdistan? They didn't have a shirt on their back or shoes on their feet!"

"So how did they get rich?" Becky asked.

"They found money in Sheikh Badr," Luna said and laughed.

"Before the Arabs fled," said David, joining the conversation, "they hid their gold in tins, dug holes in the ground, and buried the tins. They were sure they'd win the war, and when it was over they'd throw all the Jews into the sea and return to their village. But we won the war, and they, thank God, didn't come back. And the Kurds, who were new immigrants, took over the abandoned property in Sheikh Badr, found the tins with the gold, and became rich. They opened businesses, butcheries, kiosks."

It was lucky that Uncle Moise was a policeman. If it hadn't been for him, the dispute between the Ermosas and the Barazanis would never have come to an end. One day he put on his uniform, ironed the sergeant's stripes on his sleeve, polished the badge on his cap, and knocked on the Barazanis' door. Despite my mother's pleadings he refused to say a word about what went on behind the door, but from that day on the fighting stopped.

And yet I continued to sneak into the Barazanis' yard. I liked sitting on Mrs. Barazani's knee, laying my head on her large bosom, and falling asleep.

"You're not your mother's daughter," she'd tell me over and over. "How did a woman with a guttermouth have a sweet child like you?" My mother, who'd be out measuring the streets all day, as my father called it, didn't know about my daily visits to the Barazanis, and Nona Rosa, if she knew, chose to turn a blind eye. She was busy with her household chores and looking after my nono, who became more dependent on her from day to day. Inside she was probably happy there was someone to take looking after me off her hands. When I'd come back home as usual with the toffee that Mr. Barazani had given me in my mouth, she'd say, "Just be careful you don't tell your mother you were at the Kurds' house so a third world war doesn't start."

Father finally found work at a bank on Jaffa Road. Handsome Eli Cohen had told him that the bank was looking for clerks, so he went for an interview, received an offer, and started work as a teller. His brother Yitzhak begged his forgiveness and offered him his old job, but as my father said to Moise, even if he'd offered him the garage for free, he wouldn't go back to working for him.

For a long time after Mother was discharged from the hospital and had recovered, and after Father started work at the bank, we lived with Nono and Nona in the Kurdish Quarter.

"It's not normal that you and Becky sleep in the same bed and your husband sleeps on the couch," Rachelika said to Luna one afternoon.

"Well, what do you want, that I sleep with him and she sleeps next to us? It's shameful!"

"You have to get out of Father and Mother's house. You need to have a life of your own."

"Becky will be getting married to Eli Cohen soon and then there won't be a problem," Luna replied.

"What, you're waiting for Becky to get married so you can sleep with your husband?" Rachelika yelled. "How long do you think David's patience will last? In the end he'll throw you out and find another woman."

The condition that Mother stipulated to Father was unequivocal. If they left her parents' house, then they'd need to move close to Rachelika's. She was incapable of moving away from her family and was connected to her sister with every fiber of her being. Rachelika was her confidante, the only one privy to the secret life she'd been living behind David's back.

On the day Gidi was discharged from the hospital, Luna began leading two lives, dividing her time between him and her husband without anyone—except for their small group of wounded friends—knowing about it. And their friends kept the relationship between Gidi and my mother a closely guarded secret, as if it were their own, not even talking about it among themselves.

Every day Luna would go to the taxi station and sit inside the dispatcher's booth with Gidi. Even if she was a distraction at work, none of the drivers dared say anything, so in the end it was Gidi who said to Luna, "I don't think it's entirely appropriate for you to sit here with me in the booth all day."

"Why?" she asked.

"You're a married woman and people will talk."

"Why, can't I visit my friends from the hospital?"

"We're in the middle of Jerusalem, people are passing all the time, they'll see you. It's not smart."

She, of course, continued going and sitting with Gidi until his shift ended. Afterward, she'd push his wheelchair to Café Atara, where they'd be joined by their driver friends who'd also just come off their shifts. These were her most beautiful hours. Every day she waited for the time she could spend with Gidi and her friends. She couldn't imagine life without those hours far from her family, her husband, her child, and in the company of the people who'd become her second family, people with whom she felt a profound connection. Nobody could understand, not even Rachelika, whom she'd bound with a thousand oaths never to tell a soul about her secret meetings.

"You're playing with fire," Rachelika warned her.

"But we're not doing anything," Luna said, feigning innocence. "We just sit and laugh with the guys."

"If David doesn't know you're meeting Gidi and your friends at Atara, it's a secret, but secrets come out in the end."

"I can't tell him. He won't let it continue."

"If all you're doing is sitting with the guys and talking, why wouldn't he? Do you know what cheating is, Luna? It's when you betray someone's trust."

"Cheating's if somebody touches you," Luna replied. "And Gidi's never touched me and I've never touched him."

"Don't worry, that'll come too. It's only a matter of time, and then that'll be the end of you. Remember what I'm telling you—you'll ruin your life. David will never forgive you for the shame you'll bring down on him. He waited for you to come out of the hospital, he sat at your bedside, he prayed for you to stay alive, he provided for Father, Mother, and Becky, he took care of Gabriela on his own, and this is how you repay him?"

"What am I doing? All I'm doing is meeting my friends from the hospital."

"Then why don't you tell him?" Rachelika taunted.

"Anyone who wasn't with us wouldn't understand. Anyone who didn't go through the horror with us—the operations, the pain, the death of friends who lay beside us in the ward and didn't survive their wounds, the fear of our own death—they wouldn't get it."

"I'm worried about you, Luna. There's no way this is going to end well."

"We're not doing anything we shouldn't," Luna insisted.

"And in your heart are you doing anything you shouldn't?"

Luna was silent for a long time before she replied. "The heart has its own ways. I can't tell my heart how to feel."

"Do you love Gidi?"

"Like I've never loved any man in my life."

"God help us, don't you dare let those words out of your mouth ever again. Don't you dare tell anyone else!"

"What can I do, Rachelika, he's reached into my heart."

"And what about David? You married David out of love. Nobody forced you to marry him."

"Maybe I didn't love David at all. Maybe I just imagined I loved him. Maybe I wanted to get married so much that I convinced myself I loved him. I've never felt with David what I feel when I'm with Gidi. I've never cared for David the way I care for Gidi. Every time he doesn't feel well, I'm scared to death. Every time he goes into the hospital for another procedure, my knees are knocking until he comes out."

"Lunika, my dear, what are you going to do?"

"Don't worry, hermanita, I'm not going to leave David, I won't leave Gabriela. I don't have the guts! I'm a coward. I'll remain a married woman. But you can't ask me to stop seeing Gidi; you can't tell me to stop going to the station, stop sitting with him at Atara. Because even if you do, I won't listen to you. I'll go on seeing him."

"Does he really not touch you?"

"Touch me? I wish he would. Sometimes he strokes my head. Sometimes he holds my hand for a moment, never more than a moment, and then he pulls his hand away as if he's been burned. And I want to hold him, kiss him on the mouth, caress his handsome face, but I don't have the courage. I know the moment that happens I'll have crossed a line and there will be no way back. So I hold myself back, you see, I restrain myself!"

But Luna didn't know how much longer she'd be able to restrain herself, how much longer she could go on meeting Gidi when her body cried out for his touch.

In the end it was he who made the first move. One afternoon when his shift ended, she pushed his wheelchair toward Café Atara as she did every day. After they crossed the street he touched her hand and said, "Stop." She did, and he pointed to a small hotel nearby and said, "Let's go there."

Without a word she pushed the wheelchair toward the hotel, which during the Mandate period had been frequented by British soldiers and their slutty Jewish girls. The receptionist was sitting in a small room off the entryway. He came out and greeted them and told Luna to push Gidi's wheelchair to one of the ground-floor rooms. He showed them in, took his leave, and Luna closed the door behind him. The room was big. The floor was covered with painted tiles, and from the high ceiling hung a chandelier made from four stained-glass bowls. Dark drapes covered the windows overlooking the street, and most of the room was taken up by a wide iron bed with a thick wool quilt. Beside it stood a small dressing table with a mirror that had seen better days.

"Help me," he said, indicating the bed. She held him around the waist and he leaned against her, and with a strength she didn't know she possessed, she transferred him to the bed. Then she took off his shoes and socks and lifted his paralyzed legs onto the bed. Using his elbows, he lay down, and she lay next to him. He turned to her, his blue eyes looking into the green ocean of hers, and began unbuttoning her dress very slowly as if they had all the time in the world. Excited, she lay beside him and shut her eyes tight as he took off her dress, revealing her white silk camisole.

"Look at me," he whispered. She opened her eyes, and as they met his a flame kindled in her heart. His hands traced her body, his fingers tenderly stroking her face, down the length of her neck, around her nipples. She shuddered as he caressed her through the silk garment and felt a wave of heat between her thighs, a feeling of pleasure she had never experienced with David.

"Take your camisole off," he whispered, and she shrank. God, how could she lie there naked before him? How could she expose the scar that had disfigured her body?

"Don't be shy," he said.

"Look." He lifted his shirt. "I have a scar just like yours. Feel it." He took her hand and ran it along the scar that marked his wound.

"Now let me touch yours," he whispered. He shifted his body and put his lips to the scar that crossed hers, kissing the length of it. She felt as if his lips were healing her, as if with each kiss the scar was fading and her body was as whole as it had been before she was wounded. She pulled him to her, pushing her body against his as if wanting to be engulfed by it, clasping him as if afraid of letting go.

"Can you feel," he whispered, "can you feel your skin against mine?"

"I love you," she whispered back.

"I love you more than my life," he promised.

"Turn around," he said, and she turned her back to him. He unhooked her bra and removed it, and she faced him once again, her upper body bare, her perfect breasts revealed to him. She took off the rest of her undergarments and lay beside him, not trying to hide her nakedness.

His breath caught in his throat at the sight of her beauty before him. "Come here," he said, "close." She moved closer and he held her face, not taking his eyes from hers. He brought her lips to his and kissed her in a way she'd never been kissed.

His hands felt her body from her waist upward—her belly, her breasts. He brought her nipples to his mouth and kissed them, and then began sucking them like a baby. She stroked his head, grabbing his hair, praying he wouldn't stop. He pleasured her with his lips for a long time, moving over her as much as his body allowed. She couldn't believe the groans that escaped her. She wanted him to touch her in that intimate place, the place she'd always hated David touching, and she didn't believe it when she took his hand and guided it between her legs. With his fingers he roamed inside her, his hands drowning in the nectar of her body, and she started trembling. Her back stiffened and her heart began pounding wildly, almost leaping out of her chest. She shouted like a madwoman and only his strong embrace could calm her shivering body. God almighty, she thought, what was that? She'd never experienced such a sensation and only with difficulty managed to regulate her breathing.

They lay in silence side by side, tears welling in her eyes. Of all the places in the world, this was exactly where she wanted to be, alone with him. There was no world outside. Everything happening outside the room had nothing to do with them: not the nearby taxi station, not their friends from the hospital, not David, not Gabriela, not Rachelika, not Becky, not her mother, and not even her father. She wanted this moment to last forever.

She opened her eyes to find him staring at her.

"How long have you been looking at me?" she asked with a smile.

"For all the time in the world," he replied.

"I've never felt this way before. I've never been so happy."

"Me too," he said.

"I want to do to you everything you did to me. I want you to feel exactly what I felt," she whispered.

"That's impossible, my love, I'll never feel the way you feel. I can't feel anything down there." He took her hand and guided it to his flaccid body. "But I can feel here." He pulled her hand to his chest. "Here I feel like I've never felt before. I love you, Luna. I love you, light of my life."

"I love you too. I've never loved anyone the way I love you, and I never will."

He kissed her again and again, their tears, their hands, their hearts mingling. She was beside herself with love. God, she thought, don't let this end, don't let this ever end.

Split into two parts, Luna's life moved between her time with Gidi and her regular life with her husband, daughter, and extended family. She was unable to avoid her daily chores, and on the contrary, she functioned as the perfect housewife and turned the studio apartment they'd moved to into a real gem. On the balcony she cultivated pots of white and red geraniums, cacti of various types, and pansies. She gradually added more and more pots until there was no more room on their side of the balcony and she'd encroached onto the neighbors' side, much to their delight. And to extend their living space, she put a small table and chairs on the balcony, covered the table with colored cloth, and set a plant pot at the center.

"Luna's apartment looks like a gift box," her sisters laughed. "Just like her."

As her relationship with Gidi deepened, Luna did her best to be a better wife to her husband and a better mother to Gabriela, though she found it hard. Almost everything the child did, almost every sentence her husband uttered, angered her. In David's case she'd bite her tongue and get over it, but with Gabriela, it was far more difficult.

"You don't understand that when you get frustrated with her, she annoys you more out of spite," David told her. "You have to talk to her gently, kindly, show her you love her. That's the only way she'll behave nicely. If you carry on yelling at her, it'll only get worse."

"But she starts it," she complained. "I haven't even entered the room and she's already irritating me."

"She starts it? Can you hear yourself? Where's your head, Luna? Who's the child here, you or Gabriela? She wants your attention, she wants you to see her. That's why she does everything she can to annoy you, because it's the only way you take any notice of her."

"I don't notice her? Who takes her to school every morning? Who dresses her, brushes her hair, feeds her?"

"And who gives her a bath every evening and who puts her to bed? You?" he asked, raising his voice. "When have you sung her a lullaby before she went to sleep, when have you told her a bedtime story? Don't talk crap. The child shouts so you'll see her, and you, nada!"

The conversation with David depressed Luna. There was truth in what he'd said. She did all kinds of maneuvers so she'd be with the child as little as possible. Actually, she was often busy trying to find an alternative arrangement for Gabriela. She bribed Becky to collect her from school and bring her back to their parents' house so that she could run to Gidi. She always made sure to be back in time to pick Gabriela up before David got home from the bank, just as she made sure she was home at noontime with a hot meal when he took his afternoon break. Sometimes they'd meet for lunch at her parents' house, and sometimes she'd meet him at the bank and together they'd go for hummus at Taami. After lunch David would take a short nap and head back to work. And although she'd be counting down the minutes until Gidi finished his shift and they'd meet in their usual room in the hotel, she never left the house before David. She waited patiently for her husband to finish his afternoon break, and only then got herself ready for the love of her life.

She had a precise ritual. First she'd wash her body with a wet towel; then she'd dry her damp body with a dry towel. When she finished, she'd spray herself with perfume from the crystal bottle that stood on the dressing table, squeezing the bulb once or twice but not more so as not to overdo it, then put on one of her silk robes and go to the drawer where she kept her silk lingerie with sprigs of dried jasmine and lavender in muslin sachets she'd sewn herself. With her delicate manicured fingers she'd take out a matching set of underwear, bra, and camisole and lay them one beside the other on the bed. From her stocking drawer she'd choose a pair of fine nylons and place them beside the underwear. She'd take the time to slowly massage her feet with cream until it was fully absorbed and they softened, and then would sit in front of the mirror and start making up her face. After peering into the mirror again and again, pleased with the result, she'd start getting dressed. She'd gently roll the nylons over her feet and legs, making sure that the seam ran exactly up the middle of her calf and not, God forbid, deviate one millimeter to the right or left. She'd put on the delicate lace garter belt and close the clips on the top of the stocking, taking care not to pinch the flesh of her thighs. After making sure her stockings were perfect, she'd put on her silk camisole, and then would come the most difficult task of all: choosing the right dress. She'd try on a dress, discard it, try another and take it off until she'd been through her entire wardrobe and was finally satisfied with her choice. Once she was dressed, she'd sit down in front of the mirror again and apply lipstick. The lipstick was always the last link in the chain of preparations. After came another light spray of perfume and she'd be off.

Her heels tapping, she'd walk toward Jaffa Road. It would have been easier to take the Hamekasher bus that went the whole length of the street to Zion Square, not far from the hotel, but Luna didn't like being crowded on a bus with strangers. Until Gidi finished his shift she'd have time to dawdle by the shop windows on Jaffa Road and glance at the listings at the Eden and Zion cinemas to see what was showing and what was coming soon. Time would pass slowly, too slowly.

She could have walked to the taxi station and waited for him, but lately Luna had avoided going there as much as possible. She trusted her driver friends, but since she and Gidi were now lovers, she felt somewhat uncomfortable around them.

She knew that their relationship was forbidden, and that if her husband heard about it, he'd throw her out and she would bring down shame on her family. No woman she knew, not in her immediate or even distant circles, had divorced. The only divorcée she'd heard of was Vera, a very good-looking Hungarian woman who worked at the bank with David and was raising two children on her own.

At the same time, Luna never even thought about putting a stop to her affair with Gidi. It was the only point to her life, the perfect world she inhabited every afternoon. Just him and her in a shuttered room with dim light coming from a single lamp. Even the noise of the busy street outside didn't come through the walls. All that could be heard was their whispering voices, the sound of quiet breathing, and the beating of their hearts.

Luna couldn't get her fill of the feel of his hands and his lips, his company.

He saw her as no one had seen her before. He saw all of her, inside and out, and was the only one who didn't judge her, the only one who understood who she really was. They talked about everything except her other life with her family. As soon as she'd try to tell him about what was going on in her home, he'd gently place a finger on her lips and say, "Here it's just you and me. You don't have another life except for this moment. I don't have another life. It's just you and me," and she'd fall silent right away.

Luna too loved the feeling of being in a bubble, though she sometimes felt the need to share her feelings about the trouble Gabriela caused her. Only Gidi would understand that she felt helpless, that she didn't know how to be her daughter's mother. After all, she hadn't had time to be a mother. When she was wounded, she'd left Gabriela as an infant, and when she'd come home she'd found a ready-made child who was attached to her father, Becky, Rachelika, Rosa, Gabriel. Luna was the only one the child didn't want. She hadn't been there when Gabriela had learned to stand, hadn't held her hand when she'd learned to walk. She hadn't been there when Gabriela had begun saying her first words. It was as if she'd given birth to a two-year-old child and could not bridge the chasm of those two years apart. Dio mio, she wanted to talk about it with Gidi, she wanted to so much. But Gidi was firm, absolutely refusing to allow others into the room they rented by the hour. Not her husband, not her child, not her sisters, not even their friends from the hospital. Whenever she mentioned one of them, he'd cut her short and say, "Just you and me, remember?"

But there was one thing Luna had to talk to him about. She had to tell him she was having sex with her husband. For many weeks after they'd moved into their own home and slept in the same bed, which during the day was folded up and hidden behind a curtain to give them more space, David hadn't touched her. Every night they'd say good night, turn their backs to each other, and fall asleep. Until one night, without warning, he snuggled up to her back. Her body tensed, but she didn't move. He lifted her nightgown and began stroking her thighs, and she, who didn't want to prolong the moment, turned over onto her back and let him take off her underwear, spread her legs, and penetrate her. She shut her eyes tightly, trying to detach herself from what was happening. Her arms lay at her sides, her fists clenched involuntarily. The moment she noticed her position, she placed her hands on his back and moved them along its length, as if they were the hands of another woman lying beneath her husband's body. Happily for her he climaxed quickly, kissed her lightly, and fell asleep.

She lay next to him in silence. Her body had just been defiled by her husband, a stranger to her as if he were not the father of her daughter. She hadn't wanted to have sex with him, but she knew that just as she took Gabriela to school, just as she did laundry, washed dishes, cooked lunch and dinner, she had to have sex with her husband. She got out of bed, went into the kitchen, and washed her thighs with a wet towel as she had in the past. She wasn't hurting, she wasn't grieving, she had no regrets. She didn't even feel she was betraying Gidi. She didn't feel a thing.

The next day when they met in their hotel room, Luna told him. She didn't want secrets and lies to come between them. She wanted her relationship with Gidi to be as pure and clean as the way they made love. To her surprise, he held her tightly to his chest and told her, "It's all right, my lovely. Just don't tell me again, okay?"

She nodded and never told him about other times. If he was jealous, he showed no trace of it. He just didn't want to hear and didn't want to know.

Luna wanted to explain that this way, the way that she and he made love, was the only way she liked it: a kiss, a touch, a caress, a word, a look, accelerated heartbeats, the feel of his lips on her body, his skin against hers, her soul in his. How she wanted to tell him that she didn't need his penis inside her the way her husband did it. She didn't like it that way at all. She wanted to swear on her life and his that this was the whole truth, but Luna knew Gidi like she knew herself. She knew he agonized over losing potency, and she knew that anything she might say would hurt him even more. I'll go on loving him, she decided. I'll love him till I die, like no woman in the world has ever loved a man, and with the power of my love he'll overcome the pain. She vowed to protect Gidi, look after him, make him feel like a man, because for her he was a man among men.

Nine months after she had sex with David, Ronny was born, named after Aharon, David's father. When she'd discovered she was pregnant, Luna had wept. She hadn't known how Gidi would take the news. But to her amazement, he'd kissed her belly and congratulated her, and she'd hugged him, snuggling up to him as if he could shield her from the whole world.

10

AFTER MY MOTHER DIED, I escaped to gloomy London, far away from Rachelika and Becky's endless fussing and my uncontrollable anger at my father. At first I fled just to Tel Aviv, but it turned out Tel Aviv wasn't far enough. I had to move to a place where I wouldn't get a daily phone call from Rachelika or Becky, a place where Father wouldn't turn up on surprise visits. If it had been up to me, I'd have gotten on a plane and vanished without saying good-bye. But even I didn't dare do things like that in our family.

When my mother died, I didn't mourn, I didn't cry, I didn't hurt, but I was angry. I was terribly angry with my mother, who'd left me before I could make peace with her, and with my father, who before even a year had passed had already brought his Hungarian lover Vera and her children into the house. The woman who almost caused my mother to divorce my father was now sleeping in my mother's bed and cooking in my mother's kitchen and watering my mother's plants on the roof.

But I didn't wait for Vera to move in with my father to flee to Tel Aviv. Even before my discharge from the army I'd rented a room in Amnon's big apartment on Motzkin Boulevard behind the Dizengoff Street police station, which he'd inherited from his grandmother. He was my only friend in Tel Aviv. I settled into the little room, with its bed, table, and closet, and hardly went to Jerusalem. I even spent the Passover Seder with Amnon and a few other refugees from their families. We called it an "orphans' Seder." Everyone there had their own reasons for not being with their family. I told my father and aunts that I was on duty at my army base, but the truth was that I couldn't bear a Seder without my mother. I couldn't imagine a Seder without the annual competition between the three Ermosa sisters—which one of them made the best haroseth. My mother had now dropped out of the race, and I knew it wouldn't be interesting without her.

After my discharge from the army I moved from job to job. I was a waitress and got fired. I was a go-go dancer at Tiffany's, the discotheque under the Dan Hotel. I was an extra in the crowd scene in *Blaumilch Canal,* which was shot at Herzliya Studios, and the secretary of an aging film producer who had tried to feel me up every chance he got. And I did all this with one aim in mind: to save enough money to get the fuck out of Israel and go to London, the center of the world, the city of the Beatles and the Rolling Stones, of Pink Floyd and Cat Stevens and Marianne Faithfull, Sex and Drugs and Rock 'n' Roll and "Lucy in the Sky with Diamonds." Each time I accumulated a decent sum of money, I'd run to the travel agency on Frishman Street and deposit my savings in an account with the agent so I could eventually buy the ticket.

When I began thinking about my daily rush from one nonbinding job to another, I realized I was in constant flux. Fleeing for my life from everything I'd known, from everyone who knew me, fleeing to forget my old world and adapt to a new one: a world without a mother, with a father so incapable of being alone for one second that he was already bringing a new woman into our home, with aunts whose grief was so oppressive that it made me want to scream, and with a young brother I'd left to cope on his own. But what could I have done? I couldn't have soothed Ronny's pain as well. I couldn't have allayed the pain of Rachelika and Becky, who had begged me not to go back to Tel Aviv after my discharge.

"We haven't yet parted from your mother and you're already going," Becky wept.

"My mother's dead," I said every time anyone mentioned her. "I'm not dead, I'm only going away. It's not the end of the world."

My father didn't ask me to stay. He hugged me and slipped some money into my pocket, to start off with, and made me promise to ask for help if I needed it.

Regardless of Vera, I didn't want to live in Jerusalem. Ever since I was a little girl and we'd visited Nona Mercada and Tia Allegra on Rothschild Boulevard in Tel Aviv, I'd decided that just as soon as I was my own woman I'd live in Tel Aviv. I said as much to my father, I tried to explain it to him, but he wasn't prepared to listen. He was hurt and didn't come see me.

Rachelika and Becky brought Ronny to Tel Aviv to visit, along with pots overflowing with food, baskets full of vegetables they'd lugged all the way from Jerusalem as if there wasn't a market in Tel Aviv, and borekas and bizcochos they'd baked specially for me. From the moment she stepped inside, Rachelika took over and started cleaning. Becky put the pots in the fridge and made a fresh salad, and only when they were sure I had enough food for a month and sat down with me and heard that I had a job and friends and ascertained that I wasn't lonely, miskenica, and that there was somebody who'd share the food they'd cooked for me, they went back to Jerusalem, not before each had surreptitiously shoved some money into my hand without her sister seeing how much, and made me swear that if I was short, God forbid, I wouldn't be ashamed to ask.

"First you come to us," Rachelika said, "so you don't have to ask a stranger, God forbid. We're your first call, remember that."

We stood at the door and they showered me with hugs and kisses so I shouldn't go short if by chance, God forbid, I wasn't kissed or hugged until the next time we got together. And just before I closed the door and they were already in the hallway, Rachelika came back and whispered in my ear, "My Gabriela, isn't it time you made peace with your father? Do you know how sad he is because of you? He's not sleeping."

"He's sleeping very well," Becky burst out from behind her. "He's sleeping with his Hungarian woman in my sister Luna's bed and isn't ashamed of himself."

"Basta!" Rachelika said. "Don't add ammunition to the fire. David's a man, that's how it is with men, they get on with their life."

"As far as I'm concerned, Gabriela, you can carry on not speaking to him for the rest of your life," Becky said. "I don't speak to him either. He should be ashamed of himself!"

"Aunt Rachelika," I asked my kind and always considerate aunt, "aren't you angry with my father for bringing that woman into my mother's home?"

"Of course I'm angry with him, but what's to be done? Your mother isn't coming home, your father needs a new wife, and perhaps Ronny needs a new mother."

"A new mother!" Becky exploded. "Just listen to yourself! What, Ronny's a baby? He's grown up already, he'll be in the army soon. And he has you and me, thank God. He doesn't need a new mother."

"He needs a father who's a good man," I said quietly, "who doesn't bring his Hungarian whore into our home."

"Shhh, sweetie, don't curse," Rachelika said.

"There's no other word for the Hungarian," Becky interjected, "just that one! I hope she gets . . . Every time I think of David, I get mad. How isn't he ashamed of himself, how could he do something like this to Luna?"

"Don't let me start saying things I'll regret," Rachelika said softly.

"It really is best you don't open your mouth, sister. I hope for your sake that Luna isn't watching you right now."

"What are you talking about?" I asked them, confused. What wouldn't my mother want to hear? What bad word would Rachelika have to say about my mother, her beloved sister, especially now, after her death, when both of them had elevated her to sainthood?

"Nothing, my sister's just chattering," said Becky. "Ignore what she's saying, it's all from grief. And you, Gabriela, sweetie, look after yourself and call, and remember, whatever you need, anything, we're here for you. Remember, Gabriela, if anything happens, God forbid, the first thing you do is call us."

I got on with my life. Work, parties, drugs, sex. If my aunts had known the tiniest bit about my lifestyle, if my father had known—but they didn't. I didn't stay in touch with my father, and when I called my aunts once a week as I'd promised, I told them what they wanted to hear: that everything was fine.

One day when I was sitting with Amnon and some friends in the apartment rolling joints, the doorbell rang.

Amnon went to the door and peered through the peephole. "Cops!" he yelled in panic.

All at once we started getting rid of the suspicious paraphernalia. Some we flushed down the toilet and some we threw into the yard. All our friends hopped over the ground-floor balcony and took off through the backyard, leaving Amnon and me to deal with our visitors.

When I opened the door and saw the cop standing before me, I burst into hysterical laughter. Uncle Moise in his policeman's uniform had come to visit with Father. I almost choked as I invited them in, ignoring Amnon's stunned expression as he fled to his room and locked the door.

"What's so funny?" Uncle Moise asked as he followed Father into the messy living room.

"No hello for your father?" my father asked. "No kiss?"

I brushed a kiss onto his cheek.

"Are you still angry?" he asked.

"I don't want to get into that," I said and moved away from him, avoiding his outstretched arms.

"That's not nice, Gabriela," Uncle Moise said.

"So now you've brought help?" I said to my father in an icy tone. "You can't deal with me on your own?"

"No, Gabriela, I can't deal with you on my own anymore. I don't know you. My girl got lost and I can't find her. You're a stranger I don't know."

"If I'm a stranger, then what are you doing here?"

"I really don't know. Come on, Moise, let's go," my father said and turned to leave.

"Hold on a minute," Moise stopped him and turned to her. "You're throwing your own father out?"

"I'm not throwing anyone out. If he wants to go, he can go."

"Your father swallowed his pride and came all the way from Jerusalem to see you," Moise rebuked me. "He's missed you. Tell her, David, tell her. Don't be ashamed."

"I'm not ashamed," my father said. "There's no shame in a father missing his daughter. I don't sleep because of you," he continued painfully. "I know you're angry with me, Gabriela, but please, before you interrupt, listen to what I have to say."

"I don't want to hear it," I raised my voice. "I don't want to hear anything."

"I've come all the way from Jerusalem to talk to you, and whether you like it or not you'll hear me out!"

"No! No!" I put my hands over my ears. "I don't want to hear it, leave me alone!" I was on the verge of hysteria. "Go back to your Hungarian girlfriend!"

My father looked shocked and helpless. "I'm going," he said. "Just calm down, I'm going."

I started crying, and my father took my hands from my ears and despite my resistance held me in his arms. His familiar smell filled my nostrils as his strong arms encircled me. I lay my head in the hollow between his neck and shoulder, the place I loved so much, and for a moment I felt as I had when

I was a little girl and he'd protect me from the whole world, from my mother's rage.

"Pretend you're crying," he'd say with a wink when he was supposed to be punishing me, and afterward he'd sing me a lullaby. I needed him to sing to me now. I wanted to fall asleep and wake up to find my mother alive, as angry with me as ever, fighting with my father as always, sitting at her dressing table and applying lipstick to her heart-shaped, puckered lips, smoothing her dress over her fabulous figure, and click-clacking on her heels to Café Atara. Her death was no more than a bad dream and now I was waking up in my father's arms. But it wasn't a dream, because he was crying with me.

Even as I shouted about his relationship with Vera and my mother's humiliation, my father continued clasping me to him, not letting go when I tried to free myself from his grip.

I wailed, and he let me go on for a long time until the well of my tears dried up. Only when I calmed down did he begin to speak. "Your mother wasn't a wife to me for many years. We were like a couple of strangers long before she became ill. We lived in the same house, we functioned as parents to you and Ronny, but we were not man and wife in the way a man and wife should be. I'm a man, Gabriela, I have needs, and Vera loves me. She's good to me."

"Father, I don't want to hear about you and Vera."

"Before you judge me, it's important that you know that the only reason I didn't leave your mother was you, you and Ronny. I wanted you to grow up with a father and mother in the same house."

"How generous."

"If you knew only a quarter of the truth, then perhaps you wouldn't judge me, perhaps you'd understand."

"Understand what? That my mother's body wasn't yet cold and you're already bringing your lover into her home? Tell me, Father, now that she's sleeping in Mother's bed, is she also wearing her clothes? Is she wearing her jewelry?"

"All of a sudden you're defending your mother's honor?" he asked, his eyes full of pain. "Why didn't you defend her honor when she was alive? All those years all she got from you was grief. You made only trouble for her, only arguments, and all that time I was defending you and fighting with her over you, and all of a sudden it's all the other way around? All of a sudden I'm the bad guy?"

"If it was the other way around, Mother would never have brought another man home, never!"

"There's a lot you don't know about your mother, Gabriela. Don't let me open my mouth about it." And at that he turned his back and left the apartment.

Uncle Moise, who all this time had been standing silently by the window, looked at me for a long time. Before following my father out he said quietly, "Before you lose your father too, ask your Aunt Rachelika to tell you a few things about your mother Luna, and do it quickly so you don't die a fool."

I of course didn't ascribe any importance to what Uncle Moise said and didn't ask my aunt to tell me things about my mother. I was determined to move forward with my life, not go back to Jerusalem. I stood at the window and watched my father and Moise walk away down the narrow street. My father's back was bowed, Moise's hand on his shoulder, and for a moment I wanted to run after them and call my father to come back, tell him I didn't mean it, I was just being difficult—after all, I've always been a difficult child—that I still love him the way I did long ago, when I loved him more than anything else in my life. But it was as if my feet were stuck to the floor and I couldn't move.

Amnon came to stand beside me and asked in amazement, "What was all that about?"

I turned my head and looked into his kind blue eyes. I touched his hand as he stroked my cheek, and I knew then that he really cared. Tears started running down my face, and he hugged me as I cried my heart out. He didn't say a word, just held me, and afterward we fell into bed and made love all night.

We slept late in the mornings and went to the beach in the afternoons, lying for hours on the warm sand until the sun set, unable to keep our hands off each other. When it was time for me to go to my waitressing job at the Red Teahouse, he'd walk with me as far as Mapu Street, head back to the apartment from there, and then pick me up at the end of my shift.

It could have gone on forever or until I got bored and had had enough of him, but Amnon had his own plans in life. He enrolled in an architecture program in London and prepared to leave his apartment and me and move on with his life. He hadn't asked me to join him because he'd understood without my telling him that I was with him just so I didn't have to be alone. I hadn't even attempted to remove the barrier blocking my heart, somewhere between my belly and my breasts, where my Aunt Becky had told me you're supposed to feel love. Because I didn't want to love. I just wanted not to spend the night alone, not to confront a new day alone each morning, so I wouldn't have to feel or remember, so I wouldn't have to face my life.

I thought I could fool the whole world into seeing in me what I wanted to see in myself: a young, liberated, carefree woman who didn't have to answer to anybody, not even herself. And maybe I succeeded in fooling everyone, just not Amnon. He saw that all the show and bluster was hiding an unhappy young woman who couldn't find her place. He saw my inside, but when he'd tried to get in there, I rebuffed him.

"I don't want to fuck," he told me one time. "I want to talk."

"Not with me," I replied. "With me you fuck, not talk."

He threw me off him, got out of bed, and slammed the door.

After a few days in which he didn't utter a word to me, he suggested I start looking for someplace else to live. But then, when he no longer wanted me, I couldn't leave him.

"Leave me alone," he pleaded. "I can't take it anymore. I have to get ready for London and you're distracting me."

The more he begged me to leave, the more I wanted to stay. He stopped picking me up from work, and when I came home I would sneak into his bed. One night he grabbed my shoulders and shook me. "What's wrong with you?" he said in a voice as tough as steel. "When I want to, you don't. When I don't want to, you don't leave me alone. Go already, just go! If you don't go, I'll throw you out."

He left for London the next day, not before giving me the key and making me promise to stay in the apartment until I found somewhere else to live.

His first letter arrived a week later in a flimsy blue airmail envelope and stamps bearing the image of Her Majesty Queen Elizabeth II. The paper was as thin as the envelope. I held it in a trembling hand and read:

> *My one and only impossible love,*
> *It's so cold in London and I miss you. As much as I try, I can't get you out of my head. Unfortunately, you touched me in a place no woman has touched before. I don't understand why it was you, because we both know you're a fool, such a fool that you can't differentiate between who really loves you and someone who just wants to have fun. But maybe it's you who just wants to have fun? Maybe it's you who doesn't want to love? And in spite of it all I'd still be happy if you were here with me now.*
> *Amnon*

Three months after Amnon flew to London, I joined him.

I insisted on going out my first night there. I was curious and wanted to devour the new world I'd entered, taste every last thing in it. Tel Aviv's Lod airport, my first time there; the flight; the landing; the vast Heathrow Airport, which scared me so much; Amnon, who was waiting for me outside the arrivals gate, and only when I saw him could I relax; the Underground train that took us to Victoria Station; the people crowded into the train without touching each other—it was all new and exciting and I felt I was at the start of the greatest adventure of my life.

Amnon took me to his local smoke-filled pub, ordered us beers, and led me to an empty table. My eyes roamed all over the place, unable to get their fill of what was happening around me, the music, the noise, the usually restrained English people talking in loud voices, the TV screen showing a soccer game, the young girls, knockouts in miniskirts and thigh-high boots, the boys with their long hair and jeans. I saw hands wandering, I heard rolling laughter. I was high. I'm in London, a thousand light-years away from Jerusalem, swinging London, London of the liberated world, I thought to myself. Everything is so foreign yet familiar. The happy atmosphere of the noisy pub is like the pub at the end of Dizengoff Street in Tel Aviv. The men and women are so different, but they're wearing jeans and minis just like the young people in Tel Aviv.

"I can't believe I'm here, it's crazy! I'm at the biggest party of the seventies, the world of 'Lucy in the Sky with Diamonds,' Jean Shrimpton, and Twiggy," I yelled through the haze of alcohol and the loud music. I felt free to dance to the hypnotic sound of Jimi Hendrix's guitar, free to chug beers, free to be like Julie Christie. The more I drank, the more I brazenly flirted with the guy sitting next to me at the bar, completely ignoring Amnon.

Over the next few weeks, when I came to him from the beds of strangers and asked him to hold me, Amnon forgave me again and again. And I thanked him silently, for I too was unable to be without him. We consoled each other, and it sometimes seemed to me that a scrap of happiness was suddenly insinuating itself in me and calming my troubled soul. I'd snuggle into his arms and feel they were protecting me from the unease inside me and the noise outside.

Once, after we'd made love and lay sweating in his water bed, trying to get our breath back, Amnon asked, "What's my place in your life?"

"Don't start with that," I said. "Leave it."

"I won't leave it," he persisted. "You don't tell me how you feel about me, so at least tell me how I fit into your life."

"I don't want to play this game."

"Why not?"

"Because I'm scared."

"Of what?"

"I'm scared of saying you're important to me. I need to have a way out."

"Why do you need a way out?" he asked, caressing my breasts.

"So I can escape just before you leave me."

"Who's leaving you, my little fool," he said and held me tight. "If anybody's leaving it'll be you. If anybody's going to get hurt it'll be me, and we both know it."

"There's something broken in me," I told him. "I don't know how to be in a relationship."

"You're breaking my heart," he said.

"I don't mean to."

"I don't understand you. I don't understand why you won't let me love you."

"Maybe it's because of the curse," I said quietly.

"What curse?"

"The curse of the Ermosa women. My Grandma Rosa told me that the Ermosa women are cursed with men who don't want them, and vice versa."

"I know that you sleep with other men," he said.

"And you still want me?"

"More than any other woman."

"Why?"

"Look me in the eye," he whispered, and I drowned in the sea of love I saw in his eyes. "Because of this."

But instead of staying in a place where I was loved, I banged my head against the wall and drove him away. Amnon couldn't take any more and got up and went to India. After this time, I knew, I wouldn't get another chance.

After Amnon left me in London and flew to India to heal his broken heart, I sat in a smoky London pub crowded with drunks. If people were talking to me, I didn't hear them. I was drinking one beer after another so I didn't have to think or feel. A long-haired young man I hadn't noticed before was sitting next to me. For every glass of beer I drank, he downed two. A short time after we were both sufficiently drunk, he tried to kiss me. I was tipsy when he invited me to go outside and smoke a joint.

Maybe it was the joint, maybe the beer, but it was mainly because of the loneliness that I later found myself rolling around in bed with him. Not long afterward, I moved into Phillip's flat on noisy Finchley Road. Its windows were always closed because of the cold and the unbearable racket of the traffic outside. At night we'd turn on the gas heater, inserting a five-penny piece into the meter, and I'd lie on the rug close to the heater and cover myself with an old fur jacket I'd bought at the flea market.

Phillip was moody and wore a permanent scowl. He drank himself senseless and smoked like a chimney. The gloomier the weather turned, the more my fear of loneliness took over, and I felt I was helplessly becoming dependent on his presence.

He was a reclusive character, Phillip, a loner. On numerous occasions he'd leave me alone in the apartment and come back wasted in the early hours of the morning. Some nights he'd ask me to go to the pub with him, and when I did I felt like a fifth wheel, that he didn't actually want me there. He didn't drink with me, didn't dance with me. I'd sit at the bar like a wallflower, watching him flirt like crazy with English girls whose skin was pallid and wrinkled.

But the more he distanced himself from me, the more I hung on to him. The more he rebuffed me, the more I felt like I needed him. Phillip didn't even notice how desperate I was for his attention. He'd sit in the room chain-smoking and staring at the ceiling, and I'd try to talk to him but he wouldn't answer. He treated me like I was worthless.

Desperate, I began following him everywhere. I clung to him like a shadow in the narrow Soho alleys when he went looking for the young boys who sold him hash. I followed him when he went drinking, always beside him, never with him. If he noticed that I was following him, he didn't let on, and I liked the game. It added drama to my boring life.

One night when we came home drunk from the pub he began undressing me on the front steps, and we crumpled onto the freezing ground. I couldn't keep it in any longer and yelled, "God, I want you!" I bent over him and brought my mouth to his and my eyes to his and asked in a seductive voice, "Do you want me?" And when he didn't answer after what seemed like an eternity, I realized he'd fallen into a drunken stupor and hadn't heard me at all.

The next day he didn't remember anything that had happened, and I, deeply mortified, all I wanted was to go to India and look for Amnon. Restless, I decided to go out for a walk.

The cold wind sliced my face and threatened to blow me over. Eventually I gave in and hurried inside a small church. Sitting down in a pew, I was a little girl lost in an unfamiliar place. What was this dependency I'd developed for Phillip? Me, Gabriela Siton? How had it happened that I needed a guy who didn't want me, who saw me as no more than a flatmate who paid rent? What did I even really know about Phillip? Apart from his muttered yes and no, he'd never told me anything about himself. There I sat in a church, lusting after a man who didn't even know the color of my eyes.

I had once asked him, "Why are you like this?"

"Like what?"

"You're either drunk or sleeping."

"Why not?" he answered slowly. "Do I have anything better to do?"

"Talk, for instance. Tell me why you're always running away to drugs or drink."

He laughed in my face. "I'm not running away. I'm in the here and now. It's where I want to be. I want to smoke and drink and fuck and sleep. That's me, take me or leave me." He shrugged. I wished I'd had the strength to leave him, and a wave of yearning swept over me: for our house on Ben-Yehuda Street; for Nono and Nona's house; for the Shabbat macaroni hamin; for the Seder when they'd open the doors between the rooms in Nono and Nona's house so there'd be enough space around the table for everybody, and they'd read the Haggadah in both Hebrew and Ladino; for the old pioneering songs they'd sing at the end of the Seder; for Uncle Jakotel, who'd get drunk and climb onto the table and drum with knives and forks. And most of all I longed for my Nona Rosa to hug me and tell me, "The Ingelish, may his name be erased, he should go to hell. He isn't worth the ground you tread on, mi alma. He's not worth you being sad for a second."

Nona Rosa's words about the fate of our family's women passing from generation to generation, her belief that the men they loved didn't love them back, resonated in my mind as I sat in the church. I'd never thought that my life would be like the unfortunate lives of the Ermosa women who'd come before me. Throughout my short life I'd done everything possible to break the thread binding me to my mother. All my life I'd tried to escape the fate of Rosa and Mercada.

And suddenly I was tired from that journey, from the winding road I was walking along that seemed to be leading me nowhere, tired of the apathy that gripped me, of the crazy obsession I'd developed for the strange Englishman.

I thought about Amnon and wondered where he was right now, and if he still thought about me or whether he had healed his heart with a new love. I recalled how he'd eagerly wait for me after work each evening, hugging me so tightly that he almost broke my bones. I missed his eyes, which laughed with his mouth, his big body, so different from Phillip's skinny frame.

Amnon wanted me with him all the time, like air. "Let me sniff you," he'd say. He let me be whomever I wanted, and sometimes he could even make me forget my dead mother and my suffocating aunts and father. How I'd clipped my own wings, and how, instead of continuing to be as free as a bird, I'd become a willing captive in a relationship that existed only in my mind. How could I have replaced Amnon with this impossible character who hadn't the faintest idea that he was hurting me, this zonked-out, skinny Englishman who muttered words I didn't understand? And only because he didn't want me I stuck to him like a sore.

I hadn't heard a word from Amnon since he'd left, but a friend of his had told me he was in Goa, living in a commune of hippies, that he had a black-haired American girl who loved him very much. I felt a twinge in my heart, but I was glad for him. If one of us deserved to be happy, it was surely he.

As I left the church I was greeted by torrential rain. I spread my arms out wide and let the rain wash away the pain of my humiliation and loneliness. When lightning flashed, in an instant I knew what I had to do: I had to go back to being Gabriela Siton, the girl who'd sworn she'd never be like Rosa and Luna, the young woman who'd decided to break the chain of unhappy women in her family. But would it be possible to break away when their blood flowed in my veins?

London no longer seemed glamorous to me. The cold, rainy weather, the bad economic situation, the trade unions' strike, the political rallies held every other day, the images of police breaking their batons on demonstrators' skulls, the hatred of colored immigrants from Jamaica and Asia, the immigration authorities who made their lives a misery—all of this had turned London into an alienated city, light-years away from the London I'd dreamed of when I was saving up to buy a ticket.

To scrape by, I waitressed at a cheap Greek restaurant in Camden Town and spent most of my time there. One night I came home exhausted after a hard day at the restaurant, my ass red from being pinched and my soul dulled from the insults of strange men. All I wanted was to smoke a joint and collapse into bed. All the lights in the house were on, a Pink Floyd record was playing at full volume, and the acrid smell of hash hung in the air. People were rolling around on the mattresses, men and women, men and men, everyone with everyone, and only I felt like an outsider, like I didn't belong in my own home. Nobody had noticed that I'd arrived. I could have hanged myself from the rafter and nobody would have given a shit. I went to the record player and lifted the arm, scratching the record as I did.

"What the fuck d'you think you're doing?" yelled somebody I'd never seen before.

"Get the hell out of here!" I started shouting. "All of you, get the hell out!"

The bedroom door was open, and on my bed was a tangle of naked bodies. I burst in, ranting and raving like a possessed woman. "Get out of here!" I shouted and hit the naked bodies. Phillip raised himself up from under the body of the man on top of him, or maybe it was the woman lying under him, a puzzled expression on his face. I was completely hysterical and fell onto the floor crying and screaming. The man and woman fled for their lives, and I went on crying. I couldn't stop myself.

"Mother," I cried out, "where are you? I need you so much, Mother, just look at what's become of me." That was the first time I'd cried for my mother, the first time I'd admitted to myself that I missed her, that I needed her love to protect me from the chaos of my world, from myself.

"Mother," I wailed, "come and get me out of here." I sank into self-pity, curling up like a fetus on my defiled bed, and wept for the little girl I once was and for the wretched woman I'd become, for the dreams my mother had probably had for me, dreams I had surely shattered. How I wanted her to come and take me to our house on Ben-Yehuda Street, to Father and Ronny and her plants on the roof. The tears flowed down my cheeks, and my heart ached. I hugged my body as if my mother's arms were around me, the perfectly manicured hands that in all my life had never embraced me.

My mother is standing by her dressing table and applying red lipstick with an artist's hand. And she's mad at me again, God knows why, and now Father's home from work and Mother has presented him with the list of problems I caused her that day. Father removes his belt, winks at me, takes me into the other room, and whispers, "Now yell so Mother thinks it's hurting you."

But instead of hitting me with the belt he holds me close, and I can hear my mother in the other room saying, "Cry, cry. Better you cry now than Ronny cry later."

Miskenica, my mother, how she didn't have the head for me or for Ronny, how she wasn't suited to be the mother of two children, how she wanted to get rid of us every chance she got and go to God knows where.

She did everything she could to restore the youth that had been taken from her the day she'd married my father; she did everything to restore the splendid body that had been ruined the day she'd gotten pregnant and brought me into the world, I'd heard her tell Rachelika. How the damned war had ruined her life and health! How nothing had gone back to the way it was before the war, before she was wounded, before the birth, before the wedding. When she was Beauty Queen of Jerusalem. And now not only did she hate her body and her face, she also had two children on her head and a husband who drove her nuts.

Rachelika, so she told me later, had tried to silence her, but my mother got angry. "I've had enough of this child. She chatters all the time and gives me such a headache."

"Really, Luna," said Rachelika, trying to soothe her sister, "you should thank God that you're walking on two feet, that you have two children. Who'd have believed when you were lying in Hadassah like a corpse that we'd see you come home healthy and in one piece and have another baby?"

"I didn't come home healthy and in one piece! That's what you, David, and nobody else in this family understand! My body's ruined. I have a zipper across my belly, and what's inside my belly, the liver, the kidneys, will never be healthy, and that's what you call coming home healthy and in one piece!"

"Lunika, some came home without an arm, without an eye, without a leg. Look at the redhead, that poor miskenico in a wheelchair. You, thank God, came back whole. You're back to being as beautiful as ever. Why don't you thank God for that miracle? Why are you always angry with the whole world, especially your daughter, who hasn't done anything to you!"

"She doesn't love me, my daughter," my mother said sadly. "And she does everything to spite me all the time."

"How can your daughter not love you? Give her time. Don't forget that for two years she didn't know you. We'd bring her to the hospital and she'd be frightened to go to you. Then when you came home you hardly had time to adjust to each other before you had another child."

"Enough, Rachelika, why are you on her side? Why aren't you on mine?"

"God almighty, Luna! Can you hear yourself? What, you're competing with a little girl?"

"I'm competing with her? She competes with me. The moment her father comes through the door she jumps at him right away, kisses him, hugs him. She wants me to be jealous because her father kisses her and doesn't kiss me!"

"Luna! You've gone completely crazy! Put your ego aside for a moment and look at the child. She's fabulous! People are constantly amazed by her."

"It's because she's so fabulous that she drives me crazy. I'm irritable, Rachelika, I've had a hard day."

Everybody irritated my mother. Nona Rosa irritated her, I irritated her, Ronny irritated her, and my father especially irritated her. She'd lose her temper with him most of all, slamming doors, yelling, throwing herself onto the bed and crying, and Father would tell her, "If you make a scene like that again, I'm leaving!"

"Go to hell and don't come back!" she'd scream, and he'd leave the house.

I'd hug Ronny, and together we'd hide under the bed, waiting out another fire drill.

The strong smell of cigarettes and dampness hit me as I opened the door to the flat. The quiet almost propelled me backward. I'd never been alone in the flat before. At any hour of the day and night there were people in it, music blaring from the speakers standing on both sides of the record player. Now there was nobody here. I searched desperately for a joint and found a bit in a small box on the dining table. I started rolling with the cigarette papers I always carried in my purse, and put on a Three Dog Night record. "One is the loneliest number," my favorite band sang, and again I was crushed by a wave of self-pity and childhood memories.

I thought about the strained relations between Nono Gabriel and his mother Mercada, the hostility between Nona Rosa and Mercada, who had never tried to conceal the fact that she despised her daughter-in-law. Things that Nona Rosa had mentioned about the speed with which Mercada had married her to Gabriel, and how of all the virgins in Jerusalem she had chosen her, the poor orphan, to be her handsome son's bride. I loved Nona Rosa profoundly, but I too, whenever I looked at the photographs of her and Nono from when they were young, I wondered how my handsome and well-to-do grandfather had married such a heavyset, penniless orphan. And I thought about Mercada: What a heart of stone she must have had when she'd forced Nona Rosa onto Nono Gabriel to keep him away from the woman he loved. I wanted to ask Rachelika and Becky if they knew anything about it, or my mother. If only she'd still been alive I would have called her.

Though would I have? While she was alive I never called her. Our conversations were brief, matter-of-fact. I never poured my heart out to her, never asked her advice. I never cried on her shoulder; she never held me close and whispered comforting words. I could never shake the anger and disappointment at my mother, who laughed and touched everybody but me. Why hadn't my mother known how to show me love?

I never cried with my mother, not even when she told me she had cancer. "It's not that bad," she'd said. "You can recover from it." But she didn't recover, and the sicker she became, the further I moved away from her. I was in twelfth grade and spent every free moment with Amnon, even Rosh Hashanah eve, and in our family that was unforgivable. Despite my father's forbidding me to go, for the first time in my life I disobeyed him and went with Amnon to visit his aunt and uncle at the kibbutz. In the middle of the night, a few hours after the meal had ended, I suddenly awoke to shouts. Amnon's Aunt Dvora had returned her soul to her maker.

I'd run away from my dying mother, but death had pursued me. I spent New Year's Eve in the house of a dead woman I'd met only a few hours earlier.

A few months before she died, when she was in remission from the awful disease, for the first time in her life my mother left Israel and with my father went on a cruise to Europe. It was her last wish. She wanted to see the world before she died, so Rachelika told me. And my aunt, though she had serious concerns, let her go. Father too wasn't keen on the idea. He was afraid of being alone at sea with his sick wife. But the preparations for the trip excited my mother so much that everyone else became infected by her excitement. The ship was to sail from Haifa and the whole family went to see them off.

Mother couldn't wait for the trip. The day before they sailed she went to the hairdressers' on Koresh Street and even bought a new wine-red jersey suit, which was very flattering despite her thinness. The pink rouge she'd used on her cheeks even succeeded in hiding her pallor. When they boarded the ship, there was no woman as elegant as her in sight.

The ship moved out of the harbor, and Mother stood on deck waving good-bye until she disappeared into the distance. At that moment Rachelika felt as if my mother was saying good-bye to her for good, that perhaps she'd never see her again, and she collapsed into Becky's arms. All that time she hadn't allowed herself to cry while Mother was around, and now that Mother was sailing away, the tears burst forth and she couldn't stop them. Becky cried with her, and so did Ronny, who tried hard to put on a brave face but couldn't hold back his tears. The three of them stood there hugging, releasing the months of anxiety and worry in which they'd buried themselves. And only me and Handsome Eli Cohen, who'd driven us to Haifa in his black car, didn't cry.

On the road up to the Castel, when we were not far from Jerusalem, Handsome Eli Cohen opened his mouth for the first time and said he thought that the trip would do Luna good. The sea air and enchanting places she'd visit would help her forget the illness, and who knew, perhaps they would even make her better. But the sea air didn't do my mother any good. She felt so horrible that at their first port of call in Piraeus she and Father got off the ship and flew home, and Mother was taken to the hospital.

When I got to the hospital, Rachelika, Becky, Ronny, and Father were at her bedside. She gave a faint smile when she saw me but stayed very quiet.

"What's up, Mother?" I asked nonchalantly as if everything was fine, everything was as usual. Rachelika was sitting close to her bed doing her nails—even on her deathbed it was important to my mother that her nails were manicured—and Becky was sitting in the hallway smoking like a train. I went out and sat beside her.

"What are you doing here?" she asked. "Go and sit a while with your mother."

"I need air," I replied.

"You've only just gotten here and you need air already? You should be ashamed of yourself."

"All right, all right," I said and went back inside. I stood by the bed, not quite knowing what to do. I blocked out my emotions. I didn't want to feel the pain that pressed on my chest. I behaved as if my mother's illness was nothing but a spring fever that would pass in a few days, refusing to admit to myself that she was dying.

"*Ya ez*, you nanny goat," Ronny said and slapped me on the back of my head. He was now a boy of fifteen, handsome and skinny as a beanpole. How I loved him. When he was little I'd tease him and pull his hair. "Just like your mother," Rachelika would say. "When we were children she also liked pulling my hair." Now too, when we were already grown up, every time Ronny and I were together we'd pick up where we'd left off. Barbs, slaps, shoves. "Like two little kids," my mother would say angrily.

And now as I looked at my little brother, I saw that although he was doing everything he could to conceal his pain, he was vulnerable. His eyes shone as if he was about to cry.

"Come outside," I said.

"I'm not moving from here."

"How long have you been sitting here like this?" I whispered.

"Since Mother was brought here in the ambulance."

"Let's go outside for just a few moments," I said.

"Poor Mother," he said as we walked down the hallway toward the exit. "She so much wanted to see Piraeus like in that Aliki film, and in the end she didn't get to see anything."

I recalled how much my mother had loved the vivacious Greek actress and how she never missed any of her films, just as she hadn't missed a film starring Rock Hudson or Paul Newman. I didn't know anyone who loved films or admired Hollywood stars more than my mother did.

"She should have lived in Hollywood," I told Ronny.

"It's too late for her," said my little brother in a serious tone. "Let's go back to the ward."

"I can't be in there," I replied.

"It's no secret that you have a heart of stone."

"Why would you say that? I hate hospitals."

"I'm not exactly crazy about them either, but I can't leave Mother," he said.

"You're closer to her than me."

"Maybe I'm a better person than you."

"You're definitely a better person than me."

My brother was silent for a long moment and then said, "You don't hate hospitals. You've been *scared* of them since you were a baby, when they used to bring you to visit Mother."

"When did you get so smart?" I asked.

"Since Mother is dying."

"Shut up, don't talk like that."

"And if I don't talk like that, she won't die? These are our last days with her and I suggest you stay with her a while. Otherwise you'll regret it all your life."

My sweet fifteen-year-old brother, how right he was. How I'd regret not taking his advice and staying with Mother until she closed her eyes. What a fool I was, what an obtuse fool. How I'd let the one chance I'd had to forgive and be forgiven slip through my fingers.

"Father," Ronny finally spoke again, "Father's a miskenico. Mother makes his life miserable."

"We're all miskenicos, Ronny."

"Yes, but him more than the rest of us. Mother doesn't speak to him, and he does everything for her, runs around her just waiting for her to say something, and she's silent. She doesn't say a word to him."

"Does she speak to you?"

"She only speaks to me and Rachelika and Becky. She asked that nobody visit. She doesn't want people seeing her this way."

My mother passed away a short time after. She spent her last days with the nuns in the Notre Dame Monastery Hospice on the border of East Jerusalem, the same monastery the whole family would visit every Saturday before the Six-Day War, when the Old City was on the other side of the border. We'd climb up onto the roof and try and see the Western Wall that was enclosed by the Old City's walls.

The day before she died, I went to visit my mother at the hospice. She was very weak. My father was trying to feed her with a teaspoon, but she spat out everything he put into her mouth. "You must eat, Luna," he pleaded. "You have to get stronger."

Mother stared at him and didn't respond. Father pushed her wheelchair onto the veranda overlooking the road that led down to the Old City.

"Do you remember, Luna, how we'd walk to the Western Wall before the War of Independence?" he said. "Do you remember the time when we both wrote on the same scrap of paper a request to God to give us a long life . . ."

"I also asked for a happy life," she whispered in a barely audible voice. "God didn't fulfill all my requests."

I looked at my mother, who even on her deathbed was the most beautiful woman I'd seen in my life. Her high cheekbones accentuated her chalk-white face, the pallor highlighted her big green eyes with their dark lashes, her lips painted in the shape of a heart stood out against the white background, and only her red hair, her great treasure, was sparse, missing her famous curls. I wanted to hug her, but I couldn't. I was unable to move and take that first small step that perhaps might have saved me from my torment forever, that would have released my mother and me from the pain.

"I'm tired," Mother said to my father. "Take me back to my room."

He took her back inside and I hurried out. She died the next day.

I could have gotten up and left, looked for another place to live, away from scowling Phillip and the wretched Finchley Road flat forever. But I stayed. I didn't have the mental fortitude to go. I was incapable of action, so I carried on with my pathetic life at Phillip's side, continuing my slide down the decadent, empty slope we lived on. The money my aunts and my father sent was barely enough, and I was too ashamed to ask for more. I was such a bad waitress that even the people in the miserable Greek restaurant weren't prepared to keep me on.

I decided to turn to the Jewish community and scanned the want ads in *The Jewish Chronicle.* I went to a splendid house in the Marble Arch area, walked into the spacious lobby, and announced myself to the concierge. After notifying the lady of the house, he instructed me to go up to the floor where she lived. I walked to the elevator and pressed the button, but just before the door slid open, the concierge stopped me.

"This one isn't for you, young lady," he said and pointed to the adjacent elevator. "You use the service lift."

God almighty, if my mother could see me now going up in the service lift she'd turn in her grave, I thought. Everything in London is determined by class, and right now I'm the servant.

That day I cleaned three toilets, three bathrooms, three bedrooms, and one living room. I scrubbed, vacuumed, and cursed, but all the time I kept in mind what Nona Rosa had told me: "Remember, Gabriela, there is no work that is beneath a person, and if ever, God forbid, you find yourself in a situation, *tfu-tfu-tfu,* where you have no choice, there's no shame in cleaning toilets for the Ingelish."

11

Life could have gone on this way if a letter hadn't arrived from my Aunt Rachelika informing me that if the mountain wouldn't come to Muhammad, Muhammad would go to the mountain. She was coming to London to check on me.

Until I actually saw her I hadn't realized how much I'd missed her. I fell into her arms and she hugged me, cradling me like a baby.

"Let me look at you. Why are you as thin as a rail? God help us, what, they don't feed you in London? What are these dark circles under your eyes? And why are you so pale? Maybe you've got anemia? Have you seen a doctor?"

"Hold it, Rachelika, let me get my breath. You've just arrived and so many questions already."

I hailed a taxi and we headed to Rachelika's hotel.

"So how are you, child?" My aunt continued bombarding me with questions. "What have you been doing here in London for such a long time? Have you enrolled to study something?"

"No," I replied shamefacedly, "I'm not studying."

"If you're not studying, then what *are* you doing in this freezing cold?"

"Living."

"Living?" Rachelika looked at me, scrutinizing me from head to toe. "This is living? You're all skin and bone. Who are you living with?"

"A flatmate."

"Israeli?"

"Not an Israeli, not even Jewish."

"That's all we needed."

"Enough talking about me," I said and quickly changed the subject. "Tell me how everybody is."

"Everybody's well, except for going crazy missing you. We don't understand why you've been away for so long. Your father's gone half insane."

I didn't reply.

"Are you still angry, Gabriela? Hasn't your anger faded? Why be angry? Life is too short. You saw how your mother went and didn't get to see you married. You have to live, Gabriela, and your father wants to live. Let him. Forget it. It's better that you accept it."

The driver dropped us at the hotel, and after she'd checked into her room and freshened up, my aunt was as eager as an inquisitive young girl to see the sights of London. It was the first time she'd been abroad, and she wanted to taste everything: Hyde Park and Buckingham Palace and Big Ben and Trafalgar Square.

Each day we walked through a different part of London. Some days I even slept over at her hotel. Phillip didn't go off the deep end to impress her and it was clear that Rachelika wasn't keen about him. She also wasn't exactly impressed with our flat, to put it mildly.

"Disgusting!" she'd said and immediately sent me to buy cleaning materials and spent half a day on her knees scrubbing.

"If your father saw how you're living, he'd come and drag you home by your hair. And your boyfriend, *wai de mi sola*, what's up with him? A scarecrow's well dressed compared to him. What kind of fashion is this hair down to the backside, and anyway, why an Englishman? Why don't you have an Israeli boyfriend?"

"I had one," I said, thinking of Amnon. "I think he's back in Israel."

"It's a pity you didn't come back with him," she said and told me she wouldn't step foot in the apartment again. "What I saw was enough for me. I don't want to lose my temper."

We crisscrossed the streets of London, stopping at all the big stores. She emptied entire shelves at Marks & Spencer and bought me a dress at Miss Selfridge. I took her to all the tourist attractions. My feet were killing me, but she didn't tire.

"I think you're wearing me out on purpose," I told her.

"If I can't get some sense into you through your head, maybe I'll manage it through your feet."

"What do you mean?"

"The fact that you look like my troubles. You're as thin as a stick, as pale as the angel of death. Maybe if you walk, move your body, you'll work up an appetite and eat something."

"Oh, come on, Rachelika, is that why we've been plowing the streets of London? So I'll work up an appetite?"

"For that and because I'm a tourist."

"You've killed me, my feet are hurting. Let's sit down."

"If we sit down will you listen to what I have to say and not stop me?"

"I listen to what you have to say all the time and don't stop you."

"I think you're looking for trouble," she dove right in. "I think that your *demiculo* good-for-nothing boyfriend isn't for you. What are you doing with him?"

"I'm with him until I find somebody to love."

"Until you find somebody to love, you need somebody who'll love you," said my aunt, that wisest of women. "Isn't this a waste of your time? Why eat crow with a man you have no future with? Come home, Gabriela. You're not doing anything here. Come back to Jerusalem, be with people who love you. My heart aches seeing you like this. I haven't seen a smile on your face since I got off the airplane. When was the last time you laughed, Gabriela? Tell your aunt, when were you happy? I've known you since the day you were born, and now that your mother's gone, I'm the mother you have, me and Becky. With God as my witness, I won't let you stay in London. This city has turned you into a sad girl. You don't deserve that, Gabriela, nobody deserves to live in a city that makes them sad."

Trafalgar Square was crowded with pigeons but empty of people. We sat on a bench and Rachelika didn't stop talking. "Here." I gave her a handful of the birdseed I'd bought. "Feed the pigeons."

"Don't change the subject, Gabriela."

"Did you come to London to preach to me or enjoy yourself?"

"I didn't come to London to enjoy myself. I came to bring you home."

"I don't want to go home," I said.

"Of course you don't. If it was up to you, then perhaps we wouldn't see each other for another ten years. What is family for you, Gabriela? Nothing?"

"I'm not coming back. I have a life here!"

"What kind of a life is that? With a hooligan who looks like a scarecrow, God help you? Cleaning houses for the English?"

"Nona Rosa herself told me there's no shame in it."

"Nona Rosa's turning in her grave just from the thought of you doing work she was forced to do because she was a poor orphan."

"I'm an orphan too."

"*Pishcado y limon*, Gabriela. Your father's still alive and you're breaking his heart. Come back to Jerusalem, enroll in university, find a good boy who's one of ours instead of this hippie you have. If you were happy with him I could maybe ignore the fact that he's a goy, but you're not happy!"

"Enough, Rachelika," I told my aunt impatiently. "How many times do I have to tell you, I'm not marrying him. I'm just passing the time with him."

"You're as stubborn as your mother. I look at you and I can see Luna."

"Oh, come on, Rachelika."

"I don't only see Luna," she persisted, "I can hear her too. You don't just look the same, you talk the same."

That was something I wasn't prepared to hear. I hadn't abandoned my previous life to escape everything that reminded me of my mother so my aunt could come and tell me I resembled her.

"I don't look like my mother, I don't talk like my mother, and I don't resemble my mother," I said angrily. "I resemble myself."

"Not only talk, you behave like your mother too," she went on as if she hadn't heard me. "You're a carbon copy of her."

I was losing my patience. "I am nothing like my mother. If I didn't look like her, nobody would believe we're mother and daughter."

"How wrong you are, Gabriela, how much you don't know your mother, and yourself even less. Just like you, your mother was as stubborn as a mule. When she wanted something, she wouldn't listen to anybody. Just like you, she looked for trouble, and when that wasn't enough, she'd charge forward with full force, especially when it was related to one thing."

"What?"

"A man. In anything to do with a man, your mother wouldn't listen to anybody. She did what she wanted to the bitter end."

"What man, what bitter end, what are you talking about?"

"Your mother suffered a lot in her life, and I'm not just talking about the two years she was ill. She suffered from the day she married your father."

"Suffered? They didn't get along all that well, they argued, fought, but suffered? I didn't see she was suffering."

"You were a little girl, what did you know? What did you know about what happened behind closed doors?"

Over the next few days my mother was ever-present in my thoughts, her image appearing relentlessly before my eyes. I remembered her beautiful and tall in her tailored suits, her red hair meticulously coiffed, slipping on her high-heeled shoes, giving me and Ronny a perfunctory kiss, leaving us with either Nona Rosa or Becky. She was always hurrying off, always had something to attend to. Things that Ronny and I knew nothing about.

I remembered that my mother suffered from her wound even after she'd recovered. She complained frequently about pains in her stomach. There were days when she shut herself in the bedroom and Ronny and I walked on tiptoe because making noise was forbidden. We were sent outside to the roof to play so we wouldn't disturb her.

One day when she went to rest, I discovered a more exciting game than playing on the roof. I poked around in Father's cabinet in the living room and found what I was looking for: a brown wooden box that had always piqued my curiosity. What treasures was my father hiding in it? After opening the box, he always made sure to lock it and put the key into his pocket. But to my surprise, this time it wasn't locked, and I eagerly raised the lid. Inside were Father's British army medals and the badge he'd received for taking part in the War of Independence, as well as various documents and letters and lots of photographs. I sat down on the floor and began going through them. My father looked so young in his British army uniform. There was a photograph of him with a young woman holding a bike, my father's arms snaking around her waist. This beautiful woman—black-haired, big eyes adorned with long lashes, lips full, teeth white, smiling happily at the camera—appeared in almost all the photographs.

Before I could ask myself who the woman was and why she was smiling so happily, my mother was standing over me, shouting, "Nosy girl! You and your little hands are everywhere!" Then she took a photograph and turned it over, trying to read the handwriting on the back. Ignoring me, she sat down on the couch and began feverishly going through the contents of Father's box, looking at all the photographs. I stood beside her trying not to breathe so she'd forget I was there. Suddenly she stood up.

"Son of a bitch!" she said. "The lying son of a bitch! And you," she screamed when she noticed me, "go straight to your room, you nosy little thing, you pack of trouble. Get out before I beat you to death!"

My mother never beat me to death, but when she threatened, her green eyes would flash and I'd be paralyzed with fear.

"Get out!" she screamed again, and I fled for my life to my room and sat on the bed until Father got home.

Usually when he came home from work we'd all have dinner together. An omelet and salad, sour cream, cream cheese, and fresh white bread. But today wasn't an ordinary day. As soon as Father walked through the door, Mother started yelling at him and crying. She repeatedly called him a liar and asked why he had married her at all. I heard her ask about the black-haired woman in the photographs. Multiple times she said the word *amore,* shouting that the word was written on the back of all the photographs, and even she who didn't speak Italian knew full well what it meant because it was the same in Ladino. He couldn't tell her stories, feed her lies.

Father spoke quietly. I heard him say that he wasn't telling her stories and that he'd met the black-haired woman during the war, long before he'd met Mother, so what was the point of her getting upset now about something that had happened before they'd even met, before the children had been born?

"Then why did you hide the photographs from me? Why lock them away in a box? Why haven't you ever told me about the woman who called you amore?" she said.

"I told you when we met," Father replied in the same quiet, chilly tone, "you don't have to share everything. There are things that you should keep to yourself, and things I should keep to myself."

"Is that what you want?" my mother asked in her threatening voice. "That you keep things to yourself and I to myself?"

"Yes," my father said calmly, "that's what I want."

"Fine," Mother said. "Just don't be surprised down the road. Don't come complaining to me."

My mother never forgave me for opening my father's secret box. She didn't forgive me for discovering the secret of his love for a woman who called him amore. I actually heard her telling Rachelika that if I hadn't been such a nosy child she wouldn't have known about the Italian woman at all and her heart wouldn't have been broken.

"What does your heart have to be broken about?" Rachelika asked. "It was a long time ago before you met. What does it have to do with you?"

"And how it has everything to do with me!" my mother replied. "David has never stopped loving that woman. This explains everything!"

"Don't talk nonsense," Rachelika said. "You're looking for trouble where there isn't any. That one's in Italy, and you're here and you have two children."

"I was innocent when I married him," my mother said. "I thought he loved me and all the time he loved another woman."

"But he married *you*. Enough, Luna," Rachelika said, trying to mollify her. "Halas, it's over, she's probably married and has children of her own."

"What difference does that make?" my mother asked angrily. "He lied to me. Before we were married he was as sweet as honey, and then after the wedding he suddenly became distant. So it's no wonder."

I didn't know what wonder my mother was talking about. Rachelika cut her off and stopped her, but after the day I opened my father's secret box, nothing was the same. Father and Mother argued all the time. I heard them through the wall separating their bedroom from the room Ronny and I shared. I'd scrunch up in bed and cover my head with blankets so I didn't have to listen to it, hoping that Ronny was fast asleep and not troubled by it like me. I'd stick my little fingers into my ears and dive into a world of silence until my fingers got tired and I'd take them out and again hear the fight on the other side of the wall.

Having macaroni hamin for Shabbat lunch with the whole family wasn't fun anymore. It wasn't fun going to Clara and Jakotel's house to watch a soccer game at the YMCA stadium, and it certainly wasn't fun driving in Handsome Eli Cohen's car for a picnic in the Jerusalem hills. The tension between Father and Mother almost always hung in the air.

But at some point the arguments stopped, the fights stopped, and instead Father and Mother hardly exchanged a word. The words were replaced by a tense silence. On the face of it, life went on as usual. Father would come home from the bank at noontime every day and the family would eat lunch together. Later in the afternoon he'd go back and either Mother would take us to Rachelika's or Rachelika and her children would come to our house. We'd play outside while they'd talk in the kitchen, often with Becky or another relative as well. We had dinner either at Rachelika's or at our house, and Father would join us when he finished work.

Our house was still a magnet for all our relatives and friends. Anyone passing through the triangular intersection of Jaffa Road, King George, and Ben-Yehuda would pop in for coffee and cake. What can I say, my father and mother were good company. They liked people, they liked entertaining, and most of all, they liked having a good time. Even during the difficult period, they didn't stop going out. Several times a week Nona Rosa would babysit Ronny and me when they went to a late showing of a film or out dancing with friends at the Menorah Club. As time went by, the anger subsided, and it seemed to me that everything was back to normal.

Until one time when I got sick and Father volunteered to take me to the clinic, but instead of the clinic he ended up taking me to a colleague's house. That was the first time I saw Vera. When we arrived at her house, they sent her two children and me to play downstairs, and only after a long while my father called me to go home. Just as we were about to go up the steps to our apartment, he crouched down to my height, cupped my chin, and said, "Gabriela, sweetie, if Mother asks where we've been, tell her at the clinic."

As soon as we entered my mother said, "What, you went to invent medicines? How long does it take to go to the clinic?"

And before my father could respond, I said, "We weren't at the clinic."

"So where were you?" my mother asked.

"At Vera's from the bank," I replied.

Why did I break my promise to my father? I think I was just being rebellious. My mother always said I was a difficult child, and that time too my behavior caused a terrible fight between my parents, and produced the venomous hatred my mother harbored for Vera from that day until she closed her eyes. Vera from the bank, whom my father was now sleeping with in my mother's bed. Their affair had gone on for years, and now he was flaunting it in public. Just the thought of my father and Vera turned my stomach. I still couldn't forgive him for his betrayal of my mother, even if it had been me who'd maliciously revealed it.

Rachelika's trip to London was coming to an end, but she had no intention of going home empty-handed. She wanted to bring me with her as a Rosh Hashanah gift for the family.

"I went to the El Al office today," she informed me. "I bought you a ticket."

"You wasted your money. I'm staying here."

"There's nothing to discuss," Rachelika stated. "I'm not asking you if you want to or don't want to. I'm telling you, you're coming home with me."

I dug my heels in, but in a few days' time, I would change course. Rachelika was reluctantly in the flat, trying to have a heart-to-heart talk and convince me to go home, when Phillip came out of his room and yelled, "Get the hell back to your own fucking country with your aunt. Piss off already, so we can finally have some peace and quiet around here!"

Before I could say a word, Rachelika got up, squared up to him, and said, "Show some respect when you speak to my niece. Who do you think you are, you English punk, using foul language like that? Apologize right now!"

Phillip was speechless and looked ridiculous standing there, an idiotic expression on his face. After a few moments of silence he rudely turned his back on her and left the room.

"Give me a minute," I told Rachelika and went into the other room, took my backpack down from the top of the closet, and began stuffing everything I could lay my hands on into it. Most of my clothes and other belongings wouldn't fit, so I left them there and zipped up the backpack. All that time Phillip lay on the bed, contentedly smoking his joint. He didn't say a word, didn't even glance in my direction. I went out and slammed the door behind me.

The El Al plane was far from London and on its way to Tel Aviv. "I need a cigarette," I told Rachelika, and made my way to the rear of the cabin, where smoking was permitted. I went into the bathroom and reached my hand deep into the pocket of my jeans. In a scrap of aluminum foil I'd hidden a couple of lines of cocaine. I sat on the toilet, trying to arrange the line on a small mirror I took from my purse, and just as I brought my nose to it, the plane suddenly jolted. The mirror fell to the floor and smashed into pieces, and the white powder scattered in all directions. That was a sign, I was sure of it. It was a sign that if I carried on sniffing, I'd never find peace, I'd never find forgiveness. I breathed deeply, took the foil with the remnants of the cocaine, emptied it into the toilet bowl, and flushed. With a foot I swept the small shards of glass behind the toilet, blew away what remained of the cocaine, washed my face and hands, and went back to my seat.

"I feel a whole lot better now," I told Rachelika.

"I can see." She smiled.

I didn't even try to pretend I was happy to see the large delegation awaiting my arrival at the airport. All of my close family were there: Father and Ronny, Becky and Handsome Eli Cohen, Moise and all the cousins big and small.

They were holding balloons and a sign that said in colored letters: WELCOME HOME, GABRIELA. Ronny was the first to run to me, almost squashing me with a big hug. He'd grown into a handsome young man. "Let me look at you a minute," I said, holding him away from me. He'd changed so much! I'd left him as a child and now found him a man. His button nose had grown and changed his whole face, which now bore stubble.

"How can I pinch your cheek now? You're all prickly," I said. An army buzz cut was all that remained of his lovely hair. "And how can I pull your hair?"

Out of the corner of my eye I saw my father hesitate momentarily before he came over and hugged me, crushing me against his chest. I lay my head in the nook between his neck and shoulder, like I had when I was little. "I've missed you, my little girl," he said. "I've missed you terribly." But unlike in the past I quickly freed myself from his embrace. My anger hadn't dissipated.

I hurried to hug Moise and Handsome Eli Cohen, and then fell into Becky's arms. She wouldn't let me go and hugged me and kissed me and then held me at arm's length and said, "God almighty, what's this, isn't there any food in London? I can almost see right through you. You're almost transparent."

Hollow, I thought to myself, is probably a more accurate word.

"Where am I staying?" I whispered to Becky so my father wouldn't hear.

"What do you mean, where? At your house."

"I'm not going to Father and Vera's house."

"He got her out of the house," she whispered back. "He told her to go to her own apartment so you wouldn't have to see her."

"How long will she be staying at her own place? For the next two hours?"

"Gabriela, your father went crazy missing you. We all did. He's prepared a welcome for you. Don't disappoint him."

I didn't disappoint him. I got into his car, declining to sit in the front and instead preferring to crowd into the backseat with Boaz and Ronny. We drove all the way to Jerusalem, Father in front like a chauffeur and me, Ronny, and Boaz squished in the back. The few questions they asked I answered with yes and no, and the three of them quickly realized there was no point in pushing me.

As Becky had promised, Vera wasn't in the house, but I found signs of her everywhere, mainly because I was looking for them. There was a bottle of Nina Ricci perfume in the bathroom, and my mother didn't like Nina Ricci. She called it an old woman's scent.

Hanging in the closet were some dresses that weren't my mother's.

"Where are Mother's dresses?" I asked my father who had followed me into the bedroom.

"In the hall closet," he said. "You can take whichever ones you want."

"You think I'd wear one of Mother's dresses?" I replied with disgust. "What, I'm from the twenties?"

"Gabriela," he said in a tired voice, "you just got back, you haven't been here for two years, and you already want to start a fight? Don't you think you should lay down your weapons? I'm not asking you to love me the way I love you. I'm not asking you to tell me you missed me the way I've missed you. I'm asking for a truce."

He sat down on his and Mother's bed and looked so vulnerable it was as though he was the child and I the parent. I wanted to hug him, I wanted to tell him I loved him, that I'd missed him, that I'd missed him so much. But then I remembered that he'd defiled my mother's honor in the bed he was sitting on, and my heart hardened.

"I'm terribly tired," I told him and ran to my childhood room, which to my surprise was exactly how I'd left it.

"Hasn't anyone slept in here?" I asked Ronny, who'd joined me.

"Father didn't let Vera's children sleep in your room."

"Where did they sleep?"

"In the small living room."

"And where did you watch television, where did you eat dinner?"

"In the big living room."

"Wow, Mother probably died all over again just from the thought of you using the big living room not for guests. So where are they?"

Ronny became serious. "Father wanted you to come home, so he told Vera to take the children and go back to her own place."

"For good?"

"No, just until you get used to the idea, until you accept her. I think he wants to marry her."

"What?"

"Stop being a baby, Gabriela, accept Vera already. She might as well be Father's wife now and she's good to him. She's also good to me. She cooks for me and washes my uniforms when I come home on leave. She takes good care of me."

"Traitor," I told him. "I wouldn't have believed it of you."

"Mother's dead, Lela." His voice softened as he called me by the name he'd used when he couldn't yet pronounce mine.

"Don't you miss her?"

"I miss her, but I'm realistic, and in reality, Vera is now Father's wife."

"That's just it. She was Father's wife even while Mother was alive. He cheated on Mother all the time."

"I don't want to hear this. Life's too short. Look at Mother, she died so young. Why do I need to face all that right now? I'm just starting my life and I suggest you do the same. There's no point in being angry and hanging on to the past."

But nothing helped, and I carried on being angry. I was so angry that the next day I went to Rachelika's and told her I wanted to move in with her.

"No, Gabriela, you can't live with me. You can't insult your father like that. Grow up, it's time you did. Accept your father and Vera. Believe me, it'll make life easier for you."

"Thanks for the good advice, but I don't need it. I'll get by," I said and turned to leave.

"Where do you think you're going?"

"To look for a job waitressing and rent a room in Nachlaot."

"You're not renting a room in Nachlaot. You're going back home to live in your own room. Find a job, enroll in university, and then look for a room in Nachlaot. But until then you're going to live at home."

"Rachelika, since when have you told me what to do?"

"Tell me, what did that good-for-nothing Englishman do to you that's made you spit such venom on the whole world, and mainly on your father?"

"What does any of this have to do with Phillip?"

"If it has nothing to do with him, then what do you want, tell me? What do you want, that we bring your mother back to life? And what for, so you can make her life a misery just as you did when she was alive?"

I was silent. And encouraged by my silence, Rachelika continued pouring out everything she'd wanted to say to me from the moment she'd arrived in London. "She didn't get one moment of happiness from you. You never got along with her, you always misbehaved with her. You were always complaining to me that she was a bad mother, she didn't understand you, didn't see you, she thought only of herself, nothing interested her except her clothes and her lipstick and her Hollywood, isn't that what you said? So why are you turning her into a saint all of a sudden? And your father into Amalek? All of a sudden you've forgotten how good he was to you, how he looked after you all those years, how he was your rock when you cried on his shoulder because your mother didn't understand you? All of a sudden you've forgotten who sang you 'Sleep, sleep, my baby' every night? Who took you to the zoo, the Medrano Circus, who showered you and put on your pajamas and went to school with you when you got into trouble?"

"What's happened, Rachelika?" I asked in awe. "You're defending Father and disrespecting Mother?"

"Disrespecting? You should be ashamed of yourself for saying things like that, Gabriela. I'm just reminding you of how things always were. I'm just saying that God knows why you've made your mother a saint since she died, when we both know she wasn't."

"We both know? I felt that you thought she was perfect. You always loved her more than anyone else in the world."

"Like my life, like Moise, like my children," Rachelika said quietly. "But that's not to say I didn't see her worst qualities. She was my beloved sister. After Moise, she was the person closest to me in the whole world. I'd tell her all my secrets and she'd tell me hers. But that doesn't mean I was blind. I saw very well that she didn't have patience for you, how she looked at you but didn't see, how she held you but didn't touch. How, from the moment she came home from the hospital after two years there, she wanted to get away and did everything she could to leave you with me and Becky and Nona Rosa. What do you think, that my unconditional love for my sister blinded me?

"And you weren't exactly a paragon of virtue either. Do you know what it means for a mother to know that her daughter, her own flesh and blood, doesn't want her? Do you know what it was like for her when she was lying broken in the hospital, and with great difficulty, with a superhuman effort, she went downstairs to the garden to see you, and you saw her and started screaming like you were being slaughtered? Do you know how long it took you to call her Ima? You, who at two years old knew the Even-Shoshan dictionary backwards? There wasn't a word you didn't know how to say, except for one: Ima. Do you know when you said Ima for the first time? When you were three, and you went with your mother to Freiman & Bein's shoe shop and the saleslady asked you who the beautiful woman who brought this beautiful little girl to buy shoes was, and you said, 'Ima.' And that day your mother danced in the streets. She was as happy as if she'd won the lottery."

"I don't remember," I said. "I don't remember her dancing in the streets when I said Ima. I don't remember her being happy. I don't remember her ever hugging or kissing me."

"Well, your mother always had an issue with kissing and hugging. Even when I gave her a kiss, she didn't like it. Your mother didn't like being touched too much."

"She actually hugged and kissed Ronny quite a lot. She loved Ronny, but not me."

"She raised Ronny from the day he was born. He was such an easy baby. He ate, slept, and smiled. You were just the opposite. You gave her hell."

"A mother should love her child even if it's not an easy baby," I said.

"I know, my child, I know. Your mother had a hard time with you. She loved you and cared for you, but she simply didn't know how to talk to you, how to approach you. Every time someone told her that you looked like her, she'd say, 'Gabriela's better looking than me!' And do you know what it meant for your mother to say that someone was better looking than her? Even her own daughter? She was so proud of you, Gabriela. Every time you came home with good grades, every time somebody complimented you, she'd beam with pride. She just didn't know how to show you. She loved you a lot. Believe me, my child, you must believe me so you can forgive her, so you can forgive yourself, so you can get on with your life without so much anger inside you."

I listened to Rachelika, I tried to believe her, but I was unable to soften my heart. I couldn't forgive, not my mother, not my father, and certainly not myself. Instead of letting myself sink into my aunt's arms, I said coldly, "This conversation is starting to get heavy. I'm going."

Rachelika took a deep breath. "Go, then, Gabriela, but straight home. Your father made a big gesture to you when he asked Vera to leave the house after four years and go back to her own apartment. You should appreciate it."

"Appreciate what? That he took his lover into my mother's bed? It's not that he found her after Mother died. She was in the background the whole time. She was his lover while he and Mother were married."

Rachelika stood at the window and waited for a long moment before replying in a quiet, barely audible voice, "It's not that simple, Gabriela."

"It's very simple. He cheated on Mother."

"Life isn't black and white, Gabriela. And after two years of living in London, you should know that."

That reminded me of what Uncle Moise had said when he came to visit with Father in Tel Aviv: "Ask your Aunt Rachelika to tell you a few things about your mother Luna, and do it quickly so you don't die a fool."

"Rachelika, maybe it's time to tell me what you've been keeping from me?"

"I don't think it's my place, Gabriela. Maybe it would be better if you asked your father why he went to look for love with Vera, why your mother's love wasn't enough for him."

"He's my father. A daughter doesn't ask her father questions like that."

"And perhaps not her aunt either," she said softly.

"You told me after my mother died that you're like my mother now, you told me that you were my first call for anything at all. So now I'm asking you, my dear Aunt Rachelika. You want me to rid myself of my anger, to move on with my life, but how can I move on with the secrets you're all hiding from me? I know there are secrets, and I'm ready to hear them."

My aunt gathered me into her arms. "My sweet girl, my precious, I don't even know where to begin."

"At the beginning, and don't keep any of the painful details from me."

And so, cradled in my aunt's arms, I finally heard my mother's story.

"Your mother, miskenica, had dreams. She thought she was a princess who deserved a knight on a white horse, until life came along and her dreams blew up in her face. Your father, what can I say, wasn't the knight on the white horse she'd been waiting for. She realized that not long after they'd gotten married, but it was too late by then, and Luna had to accept what she'd been given. In fact, it was me, who'd never had big dreams, who'd gotten a dream man, not a knight on a white horse like the one Luna dreamed of, but a knight with the biggest heart, and Becky, may she be healthy, found a boy who worshipped the ground she walked on, and only Luna, the Beauty Queen of Jerusalem, got the wrong man. There was never a grand love between your father and mother. At first she thought she could hear bells, but quite quickly the sound of bells became the sound of a hammer hitting her head.

"When you were born she hoped that now, after the birth of a daughter, their life would finally change for the better. But then the war broke out and she was wounded and was in the hospital for two years. And it was there in the hospital that something happened that changed her life."

"What happened?"

"She found her knight on a white horse."

"My mother found her knight while she was lying wounded in the hospital?"

"He was more badly wounded than her. At first they just talked. They'd share the pain of their wounds, their dreams of a healthy life. They were friends. But after they were discharged, they began meeting in secret every day. And that was when your mother finally came to understand what true love was, what it meant to care for somebody else before yourself, what it meant when your soul connected with the soul of another."

"My mother met her lover every day? So Ronny could be his child?"

"God forbid, Gabriela, Ronny isn't his. He couldn't have children, he was paralyzed from the waist down. Now do you understand what pure love is? Your mother loved his soul more than she loved his body. She was happier than she'd ever been in her life, and though I warned her that she was skating on thin ice, that she was endangering herself and her marriage, she wouldn't listen. Every day she'd leave you and Ronny with Nona Rosa and Becky and go meet him. Then one day he died—he'd never completely recovered from his wounds—and when he died, your mother died too. That was the day your father realized that your mother's heart was broken because of another man, that throughout almost all the years they'd been married, your mother had loved another man.

"The night her lover died, your father knocked on my door in the middle of the night and asked me to come to your house and be with her. She was so shattered that he was afraid she might try to kill herself. He asked me to look after her so she wouldn't hurt herself.

"Your father forgave her in the end, but things were never the same. From the day her lover died she was never the same woman. Something died in her heart. And she missed her beloved until her dying day. Do you know what she said to me before she closed her eyes? She said, 'I'm not frightened of dying, Rachelika, I'm going to meet Gidi.' That was his name. And your father, what was he to do if his wife didn't want him? Seek comfort in another woman. And that's how he found Vera. And Vera loves him and gives him everything that Luna withheld from him, so don't punish him. It was your mother who pushed him into Vera's arms."

At long last another thread in the tapestry of Ermosa family secrets had been woven before my eyes. Who would have believed that my mother had had an affair? That her cool, proper facade concealed a volcano?

My mother had led a double life. On the one hand she was a wife, the mother of children, and on the other a brokenhearted woman who'd never recovered from the death of her one true love. It wasn't surprising that she'd accepted Vera's presence in my father's life all those years.

Suddenly I saw my mother in a different light. Human, vulnerable, misunderstood. And strangely, serenity descended upon me.

Har Hamenuchot in Jerusalem is a bald, sad hill. Row after row of graves hang on the mountainside without a single flower or tree between them. The stony hill overlooks the road into Jerusalem, a menacing and frightening reminder to all those who pass. It is to here that the people of Jerusalem are brought when their time comes. Here is the end of their road. Men, women, children, young and old, Sephardim and Ashekenazim, each of them is laid to rest in their community's section. Nono Gabriel and Nona Rosa were brought here, and here, in the Spaniol section, my mother was buried too.

Had my mother been alive to see it, she would have loved her gravestone. A slab of white marble, and on it, in raised lettering, the words:

HERE LIES MY WIFE, OUR MOTHER AND SISTER
THE DEARLY BELOVED LUNA SITON,
DAUGHTER OF GABRIEL AND ROSA ERMOSA
MAY HER SOUL BE BOUND IN THE BOND OF EVERLASTING LIFE

Yet it is a very simple gravestone for a woman who had so much style and good taste. My mother loved flowers, and there isn't even one blooming by her grave.

How many unfulfilled dreams did my mother have? How many places did she want to visit but never got the chance? She didn't manage to become an elderly woman. Her face had not yet become furrowed with lines, no gray streaked her hair. She didn't live to see her children beneath the wedding canopy, and her grandchildren will know her only from photographs.

It's the fifth anniversary of her death. I'm standing at her graveside holding a bunch of red carnations, her favorite flower. My father and Ronny are reciting Kaddish; Rachelika and Becky are weeping silently, each in her husband's arms, their children beside them; and dozens of relatives and friends are clustered around the family. It looks like a funeral rather than a memorial service, I think, so many people here to love and honor my mother.

People move to the grave, place a stone on it. The more distant ones say their good-byes and leave. Only the close relatives are left. Rachelika takes a cloth and Becky fills a bottle from a nearby tap and they quickly and gently wash the gravestone as if they're washing my mother's body. They pay special attention to the letters of her name, carefully running their fingers over each one as if caressing it.

I'm standing to the side, not part of what they're doing, waiting for them to finish, wanting them to leave, ashamed they might see that I'm on the verge of tears. I want to be alone with my mother, press my lips to the cold stone and say good-bye. I want to hug her in death as she had never let me hug her in life, as I'd never let myself. I want to make peace with her, rid myself of the ache in my chest. Why hadn't I said good-bye to her while she could still feel? If my mother could see me now from her place in heaven she would probably shrug her angel's wings in disbelief: I, Gabriela, the most different child of all, I, the street girl, the one who was always misbehaving, is now standing by her grave and yearning for her.

"We have to get going, Gabriela," Becky says. "It's getting late."

"You go," I reply. "I'm right behind you."

Becky walks away with Handsome Eli Cohen's arm around her, and I remember how, when Nono died and Becky fought with Mother and left the shiva, and I ran after her and we sat on the wall of Wallach hospital, she told me, "You'll find yourself a boy like my Eli and marry him and be happy. Don't search right or left." But I haven't yet found my Handsome Eli Cohen, and the one time in my life when there was perhaps a faint hope I'd found him, I didn't listen to my heart. I ignored the signs and pushed him away. I didn't see the gift that had been presented to me. And now it's too late, for since then, the narrow gap that he had opened in my heart has closed, and my heart is shielded by a rampart that even a thousand cannons can't bring down.

It's becoming gloomy and starting to rain. I pull my coat around me and recall autumn last year. Autumn in London, where I crossed Regent's Park, treading carefully on the golden leaves so as not to crush their beauty, enjoying the orange-gold vista of the park. I raised my eyes to the sky, inhaled the fresh, chilly air, glanced at the treetops as the leaves were carried in the wind. I'd never witnessed such a magnificent sight. My twenty-second birthday was just around the corner, and I was standing at the height of my youth, a yellow woman shedding her leaves, defeated.

I sat down on the carpet of golden leaves and played with them, taking fistfuls and sprinkling them over my head, my face, my body like rain. There

I was, another link in the chain of cursed Ermosa women: Mercada, Rosa, Luna, Gabriela. Luckily, Rachelika and Becky had been saved from the curse; luckily they'd had sons. Luckily I was the only daughter born to that generation of Ermosas, the only and last daughter, because the curse would end there. I would not have children, I'd decided. The woman who'd marry my brother, the women who'd marry my cousins, would not carry the curse. I would be the last woman of the Ermosa tribe so the curse could be removed.

The rain's stopping, and a patch of blue sky is revealed from behind the clouds. I raise my eyes heavenward and fill my lungs with the good smell that comes after rain, the rain that like Rachelika and Becky also washed my mother's grave. With the hem of my coat I wipe the raindrops from the stone.

I'm alone. My family has gone down the steps to the road where Handsome Eli Cohen's black car and my father's white Studebaker Lark are waiting, and into which everybody will pile like sardines and drive to Rachelika's house for the customary meal.

It's a bit frightening in the cemetery, and a shiver runs through my body. I look right and left to make sure there's nobody around, and only then, once I'm sure that no one can see what I'm doing, I take a red lipstick from my purse and carefully apply it to my lips in the shape of a heart the way my mother used to, drawing the lipstick in careful strokes, trying to keep within the lines. I bring my mouth to the gravestone and kiss it gently, leaving the print of my red lips on the cold white stone, breathing a little life into it. I remove the cellophane from the bouquet of flowers and spread the red carnations all over the slab.

"Ima," I whisper, and kiss the stone again for the last time.

I go down the steps to where my family are all standing by the cars.

And that's when I see him. I'm stunned, not quite believing my eyes. "What are you doing here?" I ask as he walks over.

"I saw the announcement in the paper."

"And you've been here the whole time?"

"The whole time."

"Are you coming?" Ronny calls to me before he gets into my father's car.

"You go ahead," I tell him. "I'll be there shortly."

The cars drive off and Amnon and I are left on our own.

"You know," I say, "when I was standing by my mother's grave I was think-ing of you."

"Really?" he asks. "What were you thinking about?"

"I was thinking that once upon a time I had the opportunity to love and I blew it."

"There isn't a day in my life," he says quietly and looks into my eyes, "when I don't think about that missed opportunity."

I stare into his big eyes and fall into his arms. Then he holds me away from him a little and says, "So how are you?"

"I'm good now, but it's been unbelievably bad."

I tell him about Phillip, about my mother and her dead lover. And I tell him that I know my mother has brought him back to me because I've stopped being angry.

Amnon doesn't say anything. He just hugs me and it's as though I'm exactly where I should be.

It's pitch-black on Har Hamenuchot. The dead have gone to sleep. Below us on the Jerusalem–Tel Aviv road a swarm of cars is flowing, their headlights dancing. We sit down at the foot of my mother's grave.

"And you," I whisper, "what have you been up to all this time?"

"I ran away from you as far as India," he says. "I was on a long journey with myself. I searched for relief from the pain, from the sense that something was missing. At first I was angry with you. Afterward I became angry with myself. I asked myself over and over why I hadn't fought for you, why I'd given up.

"I traveled all over India. I went to Manali and Dharamshala, the Himalayas, Kasol and the Parvati Valley. I went south to Rajasthan and in the end I reached the paradise called Goa. And there, where the tide's ebb and flow soothes one's soul, where the jungle kisses the golden sands of the beach and the cows lie in the sun just like the people, I made up my mind to do three things: shave off my beard, go back home, and look for you. Your father told me you were still in London and taught me a word in Ladino, paciencia. So I took a deep breath and waited patiently. I knew you'd come back, and I knew that when we reunited we'd be together. I'm not leaving you again, Gabriela."

"And I thought I'd lost you forever," I whisper, "that my one chance had been taken from me. I thought I'd never love again. And here you are. You've come back."

I kiss him, melting into his arms. It's a miracle, I think to myself in awe. Here I am feeling love exactly where Becky told me I would: between my belly and my breasts.

Acknowledgments

My late father, Mordechai Yishai, waited a long time for me to finish writing this book so he could read it. I also awaited the moment when I would be able to hand him the manuscript with a dedication.

My father died a few months before the book was published. I do not have the words to thank him for the many hours he sat with me, telling me his Jerusalem stories and reliving an entire period with infinite love and patience. I treasure those moments. It was my father who chose the name Ermosa for my fictional family.

And when I think of my father, I always think about my mother, Levana Yishai, née Nachmias. They always come to me together. So it was in their lifetime and so it is after their death, and not a day goes by without me thinking of them both.

I owe a profound debt of gratitude to my beloved wise aunt, Miriam Nachum, my mother's sister, who gave me all the time I asked for, taught me Ladino words and expressions, and time traveled with me to the 1930s, '40s, and '50s. Thanks to what she related to me, those years took on shape, form, and life before my very eyes.

All my life my mother told me to observe her cousin Ben Zion—"Bentzi" as he was known in our family—to learn from him, broaden my knowledge. And I indeed learned and broadened my knowledge. My thanks to author Ben Zion Nachmias, from whose wonderful book *Hamsa* I learned about the customs of Jerusalem and the city's atmosphere at the beginning of the twentieth century.

Thanks to the various generations of the Nachmias and Yishai families for the inspiration and love they have heaped upon me since the day I was born, especially my two brothers Raffi and Alon.

Special thanks to my forever-young aunts Esther Mizrachi and Miriam Kadosh.

A huge thank-you to my dear friend Ronny Modan. I told Ronny that I dreamed about writing a novel, I showed her the first pages I'd written, and on the basis of what little she'd read, she'd decided to publish the book. It was an expression of faith I will never forget. And in the same breath I thank Shula and Oded Modan and the Modan family, especially Keren Uri, Naama Carmeli, Tali Tchelet, and Ada Vardi, for their unwavering support and the home they've given me since the day we met.

My heartfelt thanks to my superb Hebrew editors, Michal Heruti and Shimon Riklin, whose comments and clarifications were such a great help, and which constraints of space do not allow me to fully describe. Thank you, Michal, for your professionalism, meticulousness, direction, and support, and for the great interest you showed. Thank you, Shimon, for your patience, your accuracy, your attention to the smallest details, and your way of calming me. Without the two of you the book would not have been the sum of all its parts.

Thanks to my wonderful translator, Anthony Berris, my English editor, Melanie Fried, and to Staci Burt, Karen Masnica, Brant Janeway, Nancy Inglis, and all those who worked behind the scenes at Thomas Dunne Books/St. Martin's Press. Thank you also to Vick Giasov, Tal Shoham, Aviad Ivri, and all those at the Israeli consulate who supported this book's publication.

Thanks to a wonderful woman, the miracle worker, my beloved friend Raya Strauss Ben Dror. Thank you, Raya, for believing in me from day one, and for entrusting me with writing my first book, *Strauss: The Story of a Family and an Industry,* the story of your family. You believed in me when I did not yet believe that I could write an entire book. You gave me my first opportunity. I will be forever grateful.

Thanks to Chava Levi, Rocheleh Kerstein, Kami Wahaba, and Ariella Aflallo. Each of you is unique in her own way for me, and I deeply appreciate the fact that you're always there for me, enveloping me with unconditional love.

My thanks to my colleagues at *Olam Ha'isha,* Avi Dassa, Haggai Malamud, and Michal Hamri, and especially editor in chief Mary York, for the years of working together and for the many things I've learned from you.

And to my beloved children, Maya, Dan, and Uri—thank you.

Made in United States
North Haven, CT
02 June 2022

19762157R10231